OUTCAST

BY KIRKMAN & AZACETA

VOLUME 3: THIS LITTLE LIGHT

OUTCAST BY KIRKMAN & AZACETA
VOL. 3: THIS LITTLE LIGHT
June 2016
First printing

ISBN: 978-1-63215-693-8

Published by Image Comics, Inc.

Office of publication: 2001 Center Street, 6th Floor,
Berkeley, CA 94704.

For information regarding the CPSIA on this printed
material call: 203-595-3636 and provide reference #
RICH - 682151.

Robert Kirkman
Creator, Writer

Paul Azaceta
Artist

Elizabeth Breitweiser
Colorist

Rus Wooton
Letterer

Paul Azaceta
Elizabeth Breitweiser
Cover

Arielle Basich
Assistant Editor

Sean Mackiewicz
Editor

Rian Hughes
Logo Design

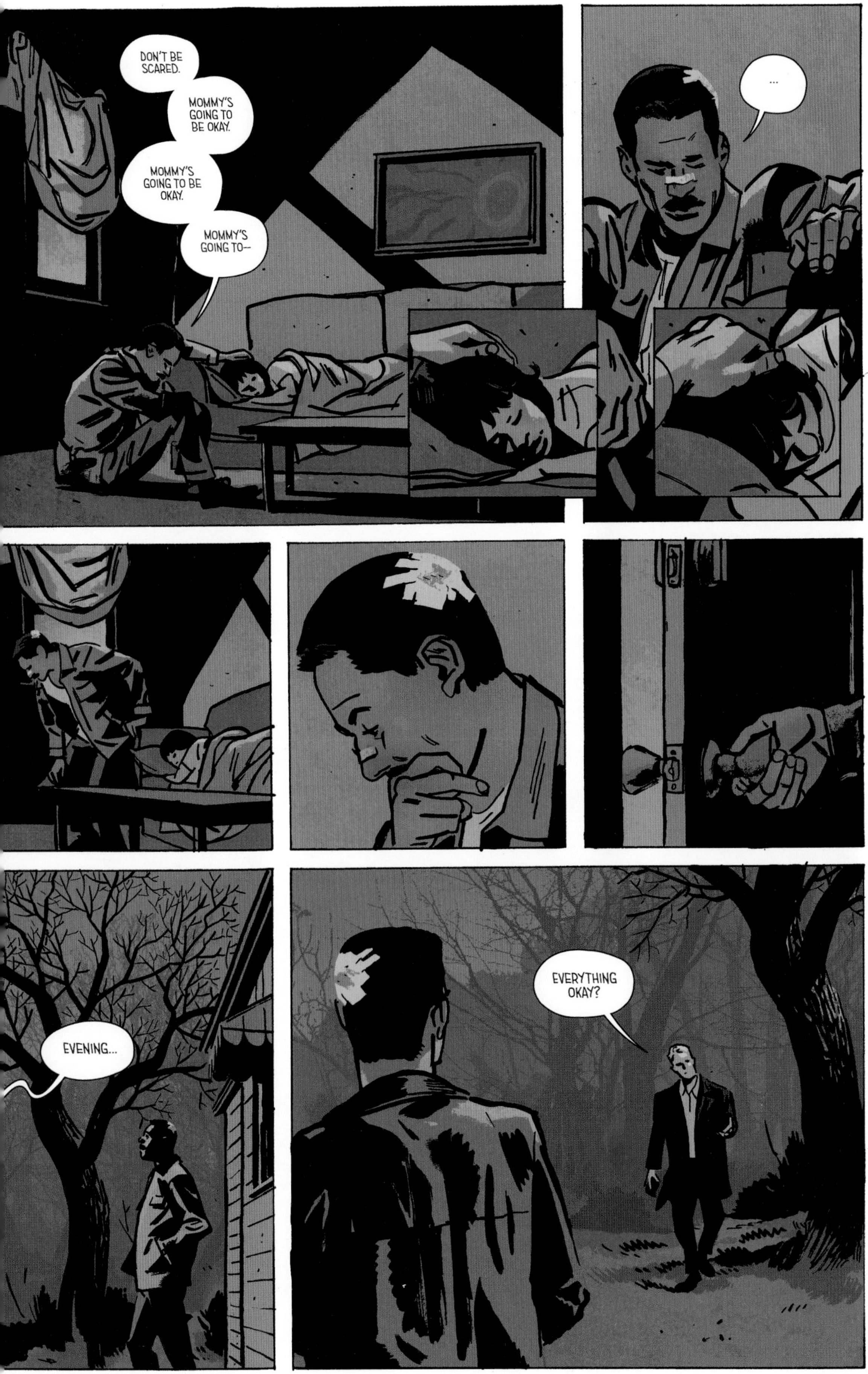
DON'T BE SCARED.
MOMMY'S GOING TO BE OKAY.
MOMMY'S GOING TO BE OKAY.
MOMMY'S GOING TO--
...
EVENING...
EVERYTHING OKAY?

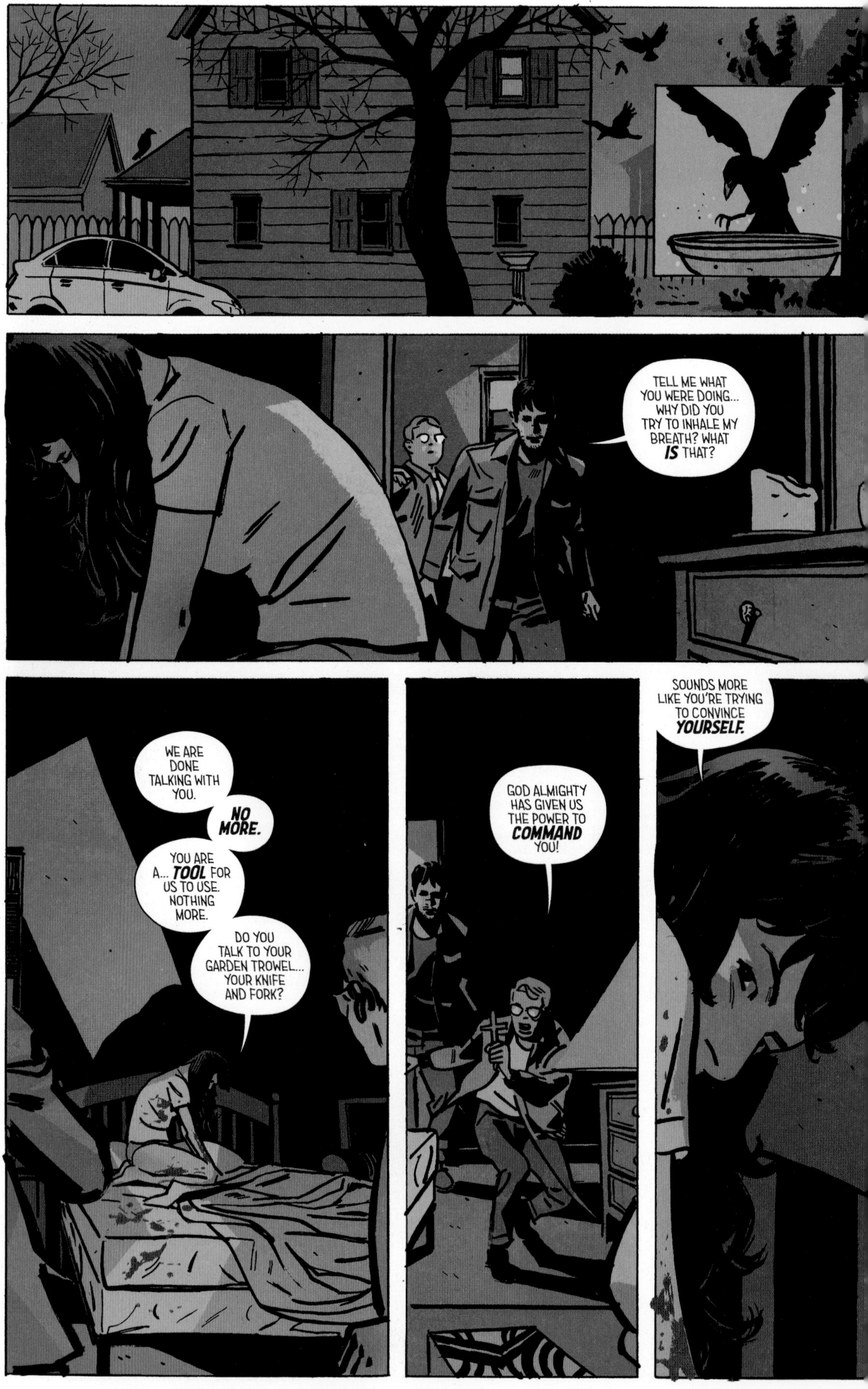
TELL ME WHAT YOU WERE DOING... WHY DID YOU TRY TO INHALE MY BREATH? WHAT **IS** THAT?
WE ARE DONE TALKING WITH YOU.
NO MORE.
YOU ARE A... **TOOL** FOR US TO USE. NOTHING MORE.
DO YOU TALK TO YOUR GARDEN TROWEL... YOUR KNIFE AND FORK?
GOD ALMIGHTY HAS GIVEN US THE POWER TO **COMMAND** YOU!
SOUNDS MORE LIKE YOU'RE TRYING TO CONVINCE **YOURSELF.**

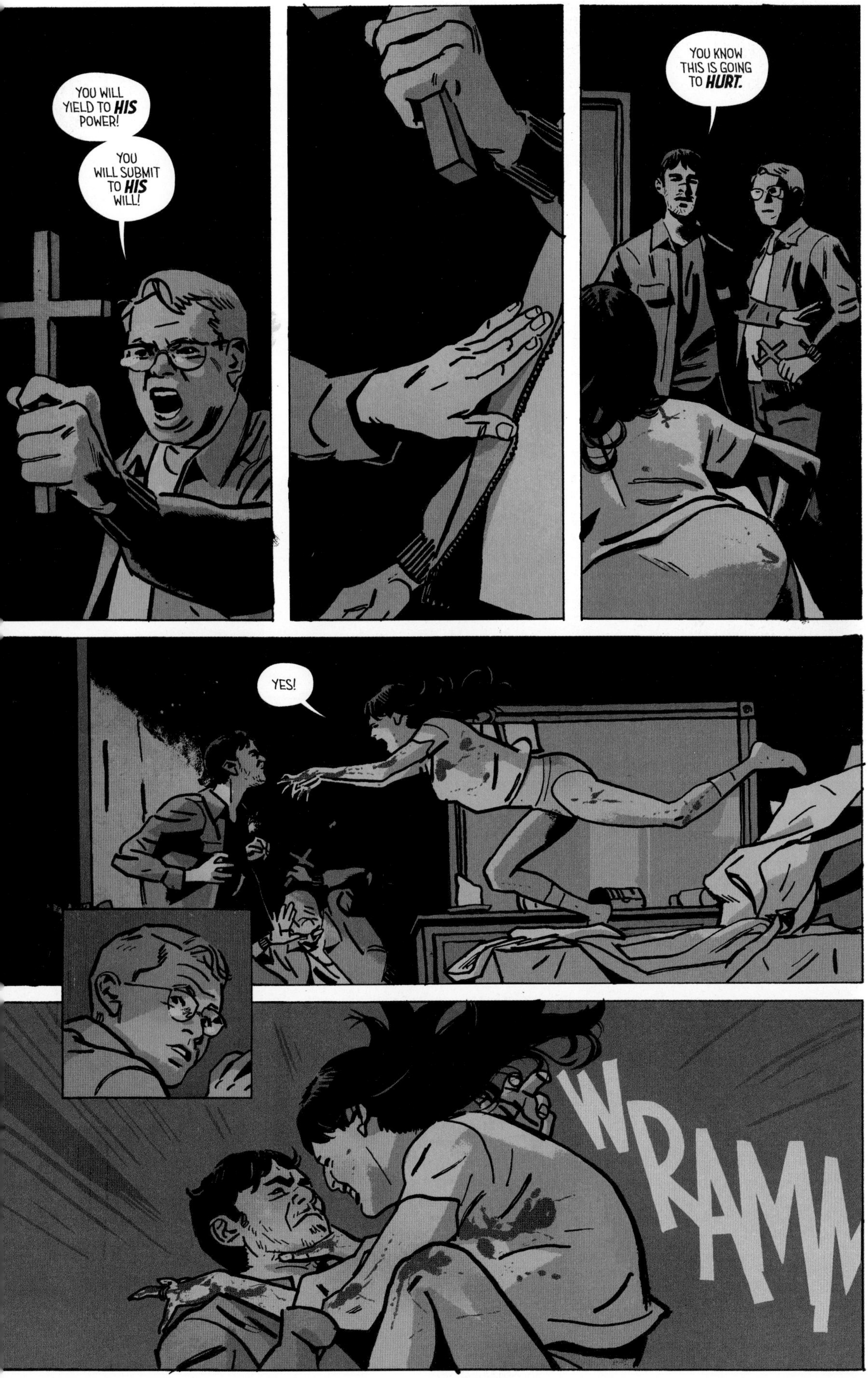
YOU WILL YIELD TO **HIS** POWER!
YOU WILL SUBMIT TO **HIS** WILL!
YOU KNOW THIS IS GOING TO **HURT.**
YES!
WRAMM

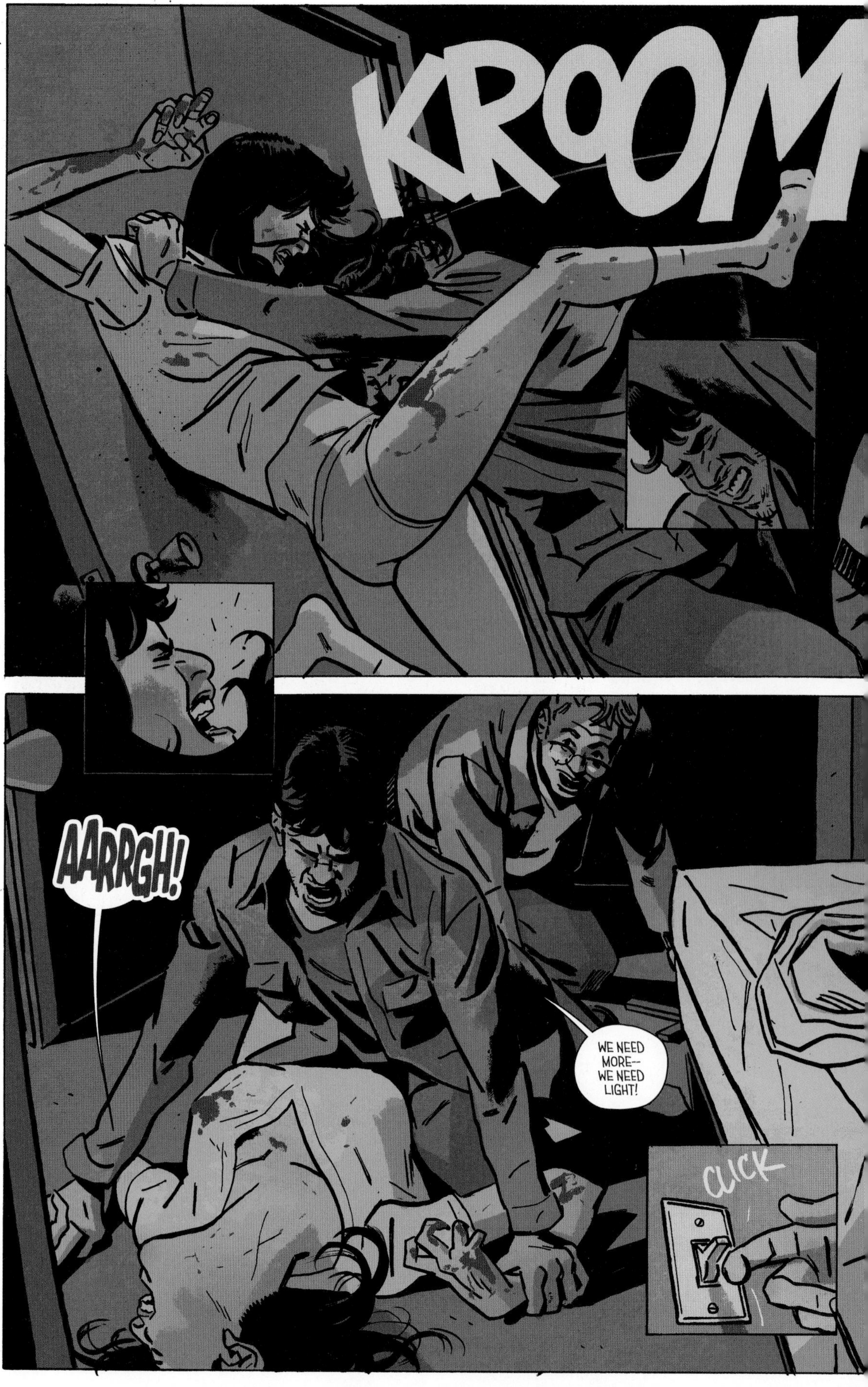
KROOM
AARRGH!
WE NEED MORE-- WE NEED LIGHT!
CLICK

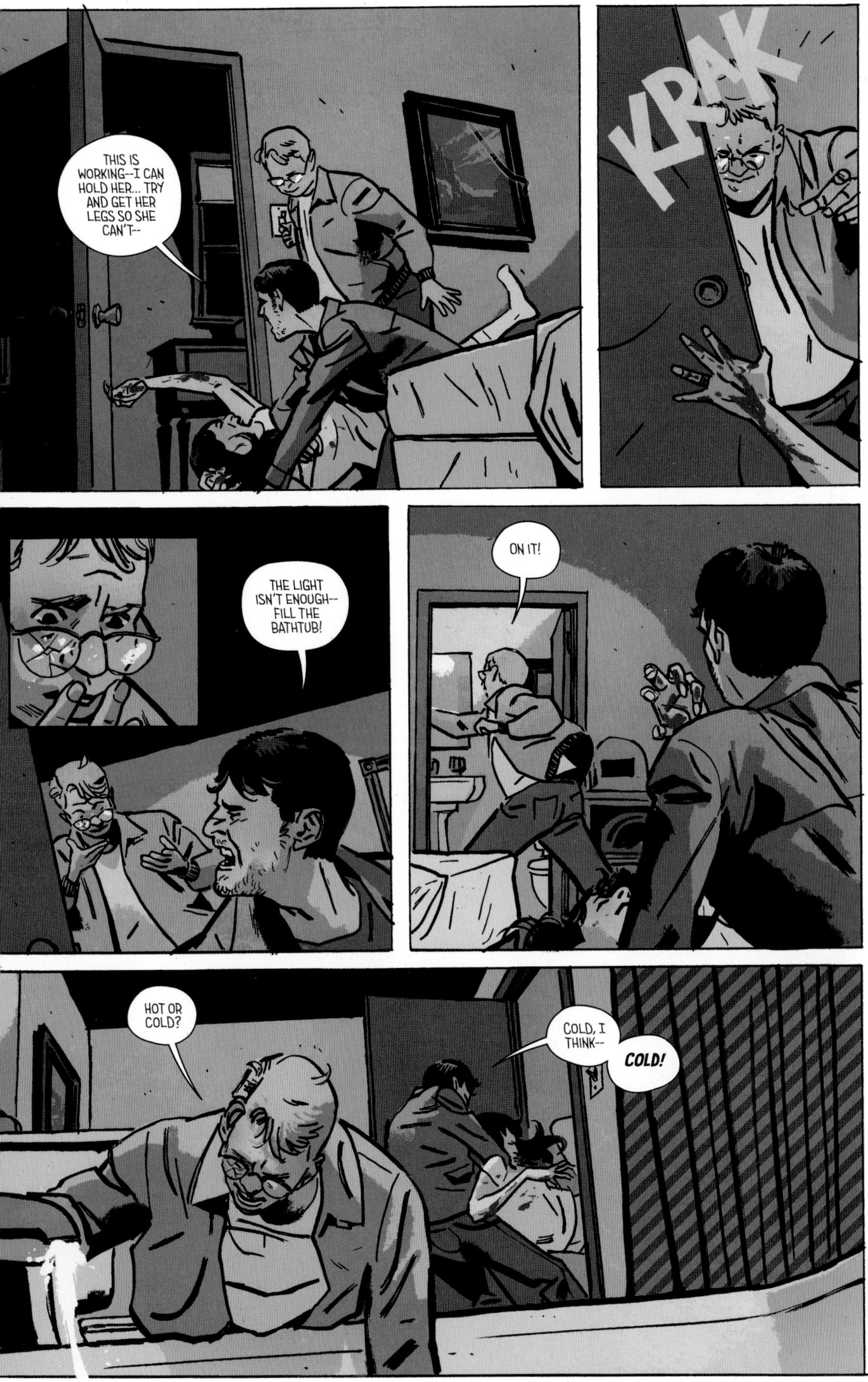

THIS IS WORKING--I CAN HOLD HER... TRY AND GET HER LEGS SO SHE CAN'T--
KRAK
THE LIGHT ISN'T ENOUGH--FILL THE BATHTUB!
ON IT!
HOT OR COLD?
COLD, I THINK--
COLD!

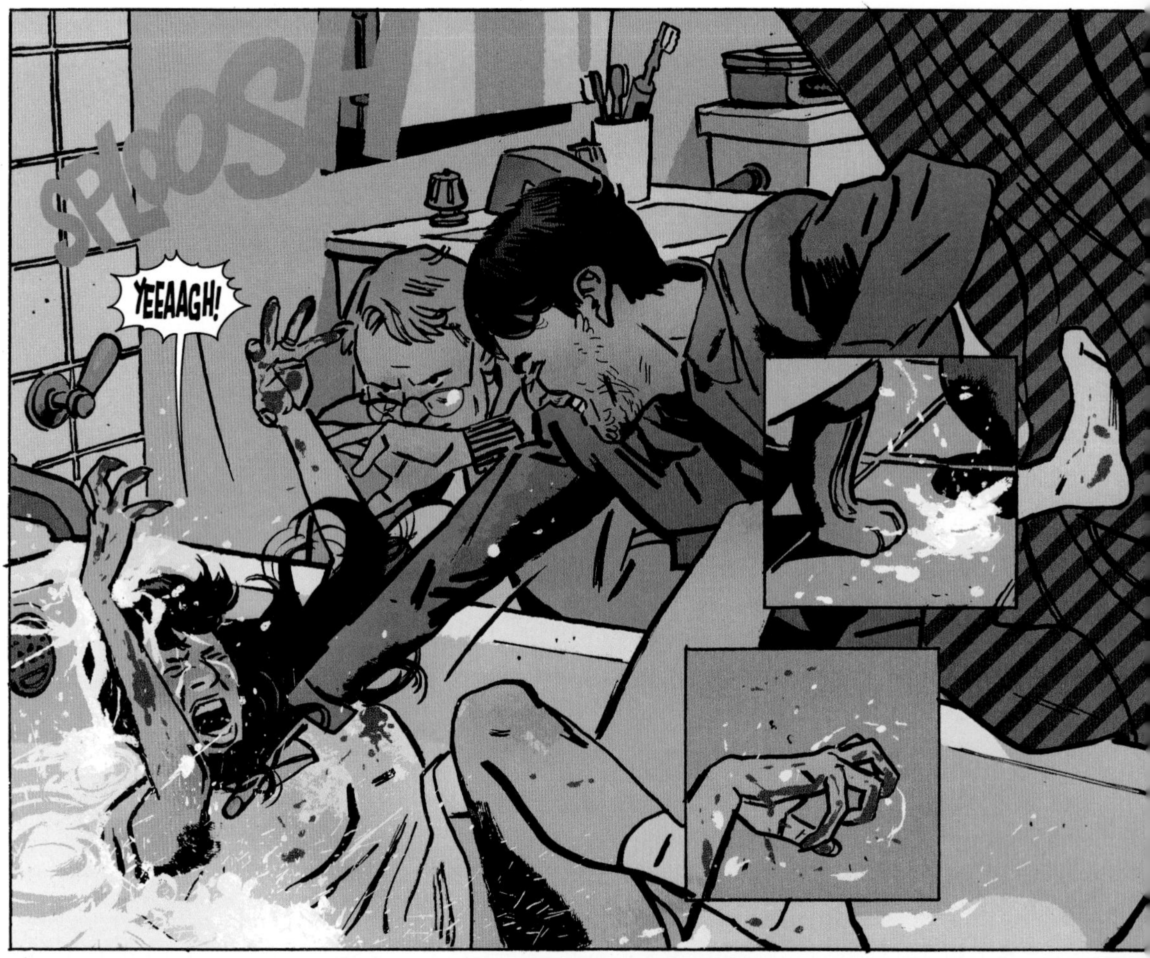
SPLOOSH
YEEAAGH!

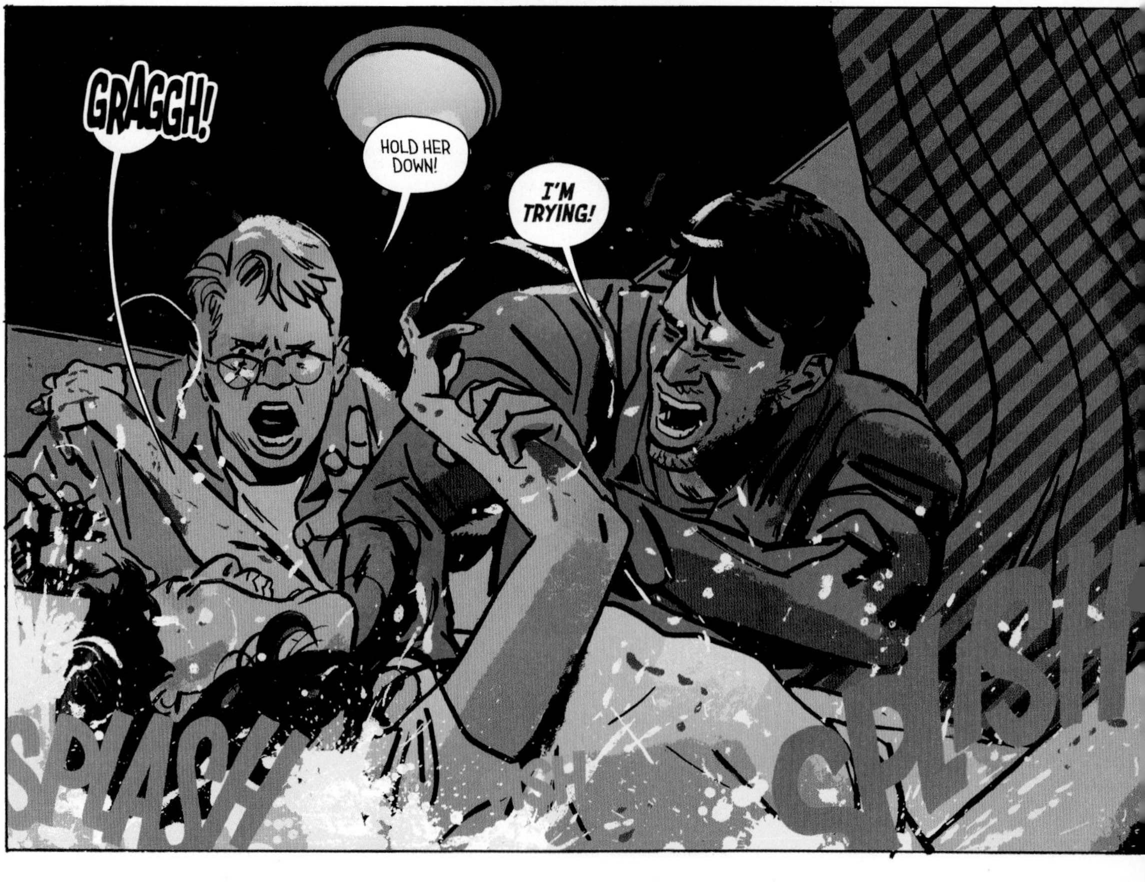
GRAGGH!
HOLD HER DOWN!
I'M TRYING!
SPLASH

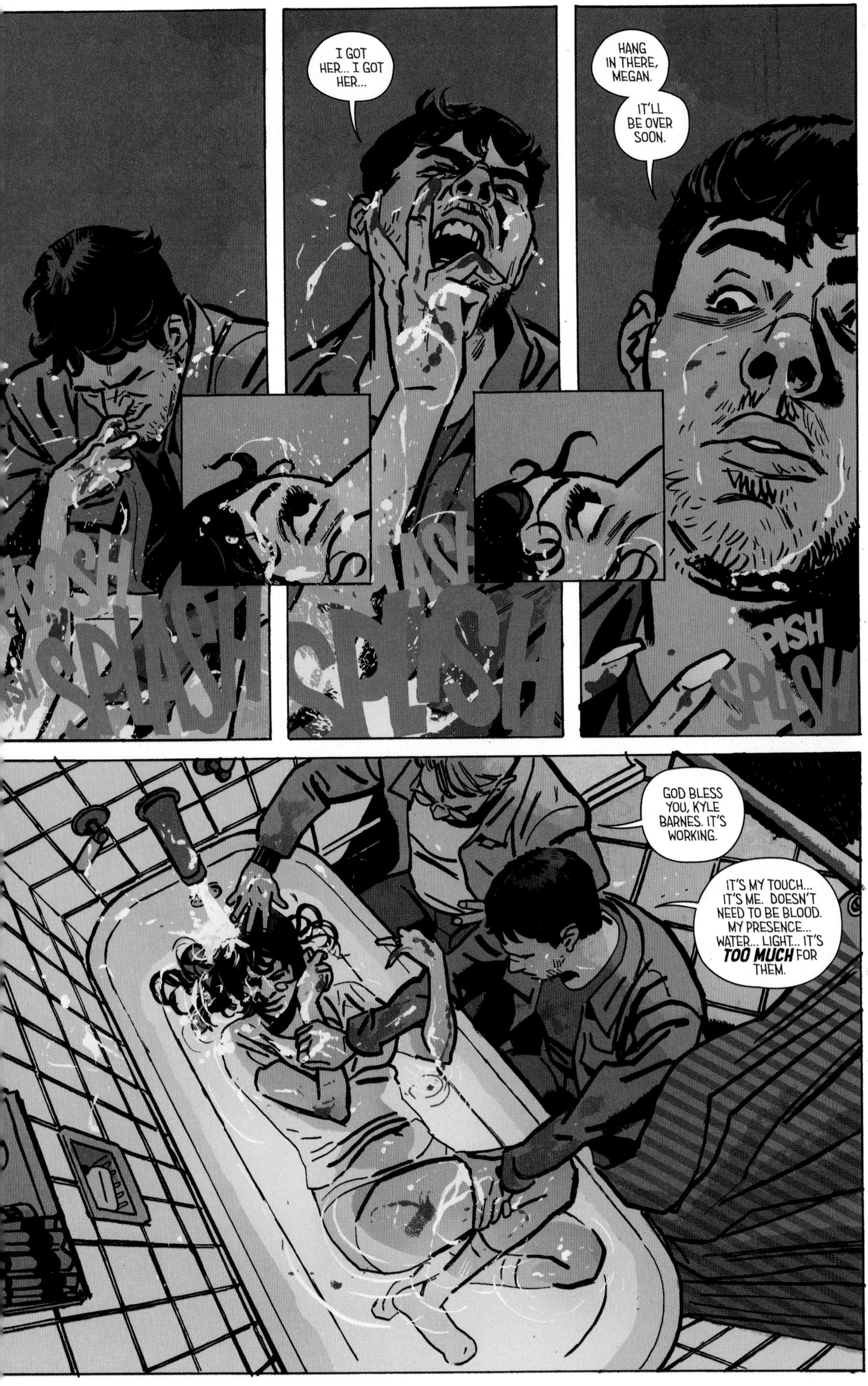
SPLOOSH
SPLASH
I GOT HER... I GOT HER...
SPLASH
HANG IN THERE, MEGAN.
IT'LL BE OVER SOON.
PISH
SPLASH
GOD BLESS YOU, KYLE BARNES. IT'S WORKING.
IT'S MY TOUCH... IT'S ME. DOESN'T NEED TO BE BLOOD. MY PRESENCE... WATER... LIGHT... IT'S **TOO MUCH** FOR THEM.

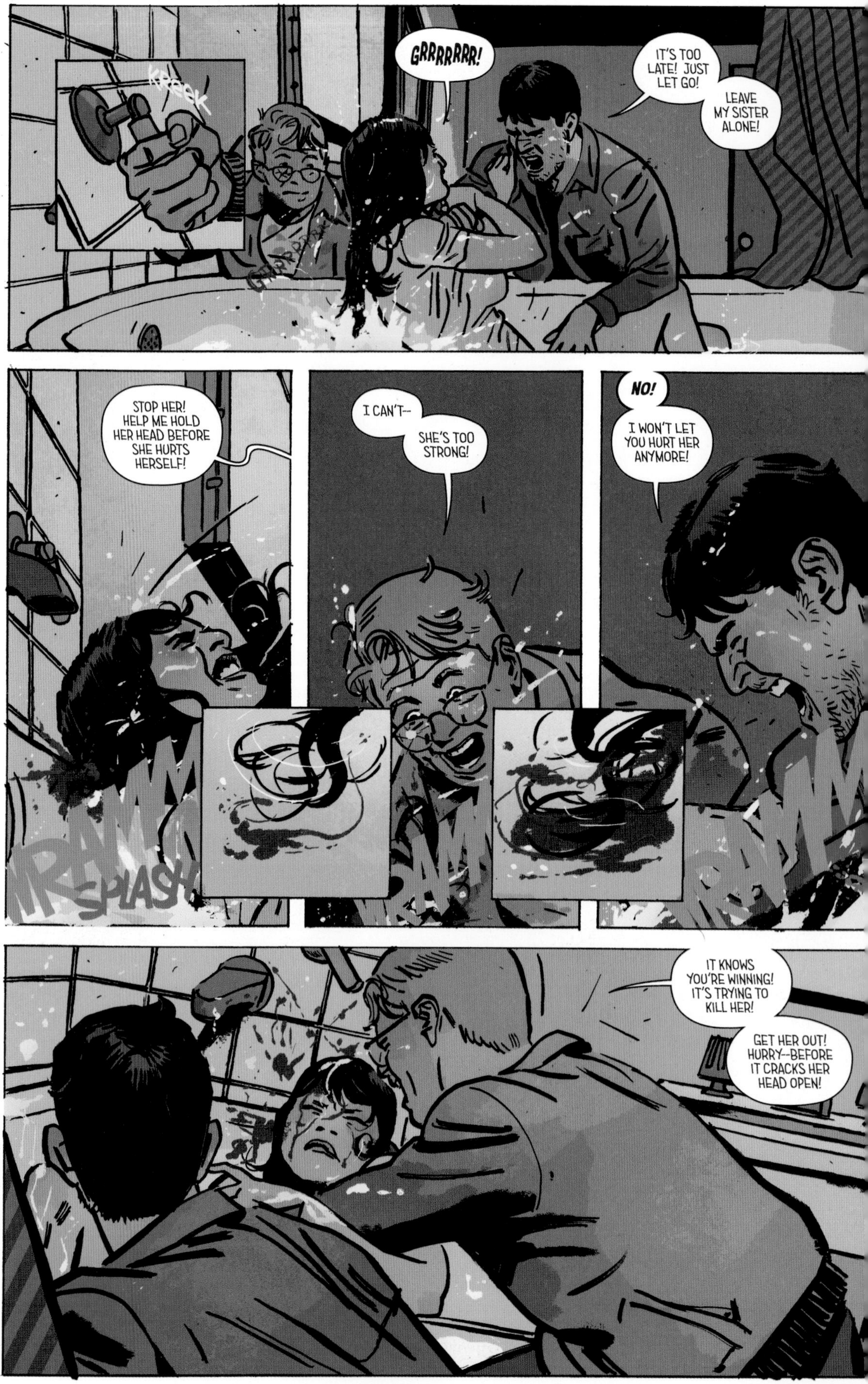
KREEK
GRRRRRRR!
IT'S TOO LATE! JUST LET GO!
LEAVE MY SISTER ALONE!
STOP HER! HELP ME HOLD HER HEAD BEFORE SHE HURTS HERSELF!
SPLASH
I CAN'T--
SHE'S TOO STRONG!
NO!
I WON'T LET YOU HURT HER ANYMORE!
IT KNOWS YOU'RE WINNING! IT'S TRYING TO KILL HER!
GET HER OUT! HURRY--BEFORE IT CRACKS HER HEAD OPEN!

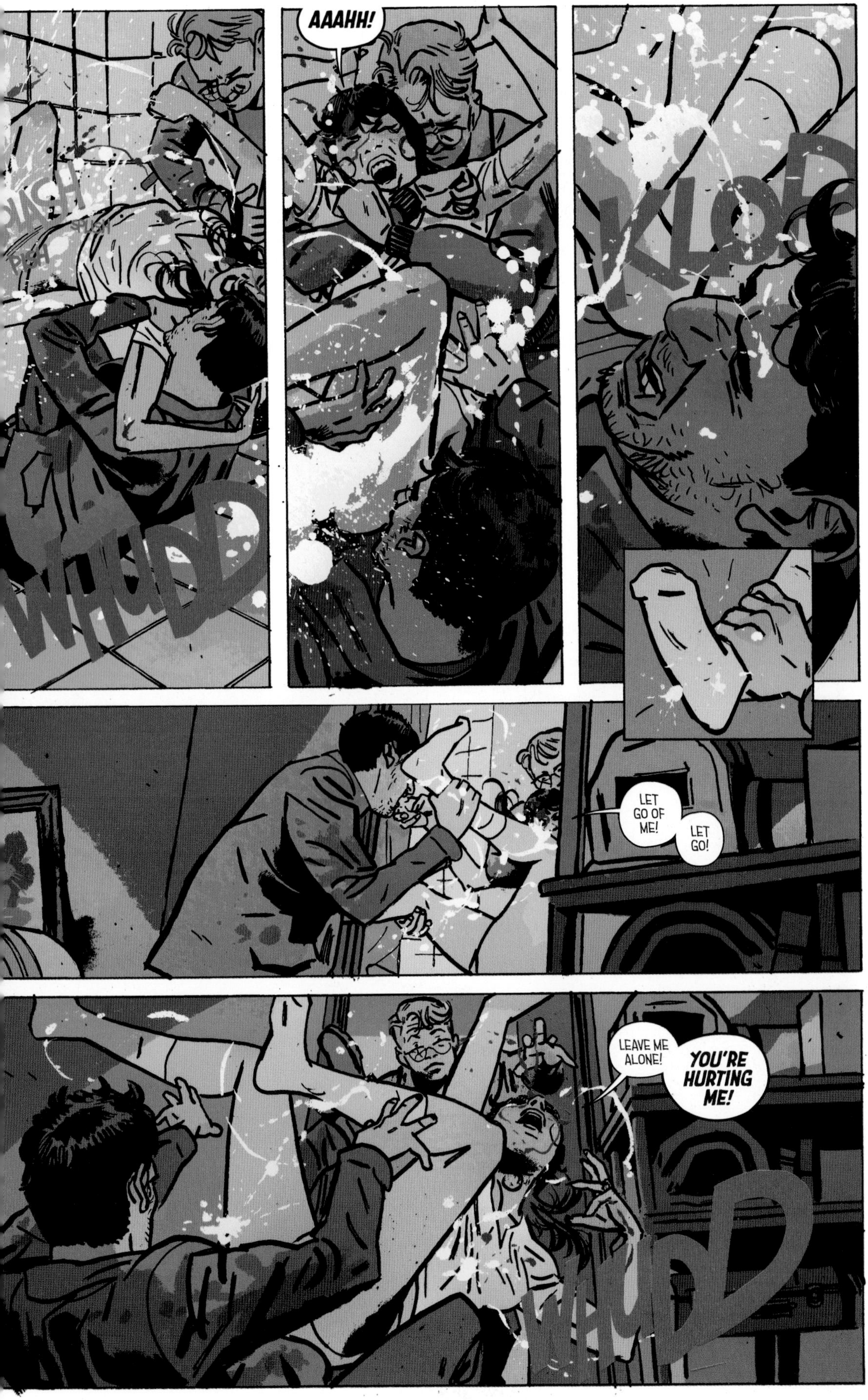
SPLISH
WHUDD
AAAHH!
KLOP
LET GO OF ME!
LET GO!
LEAVE ME ALONE!
YOU'RE HURTING ME!
WHUDD

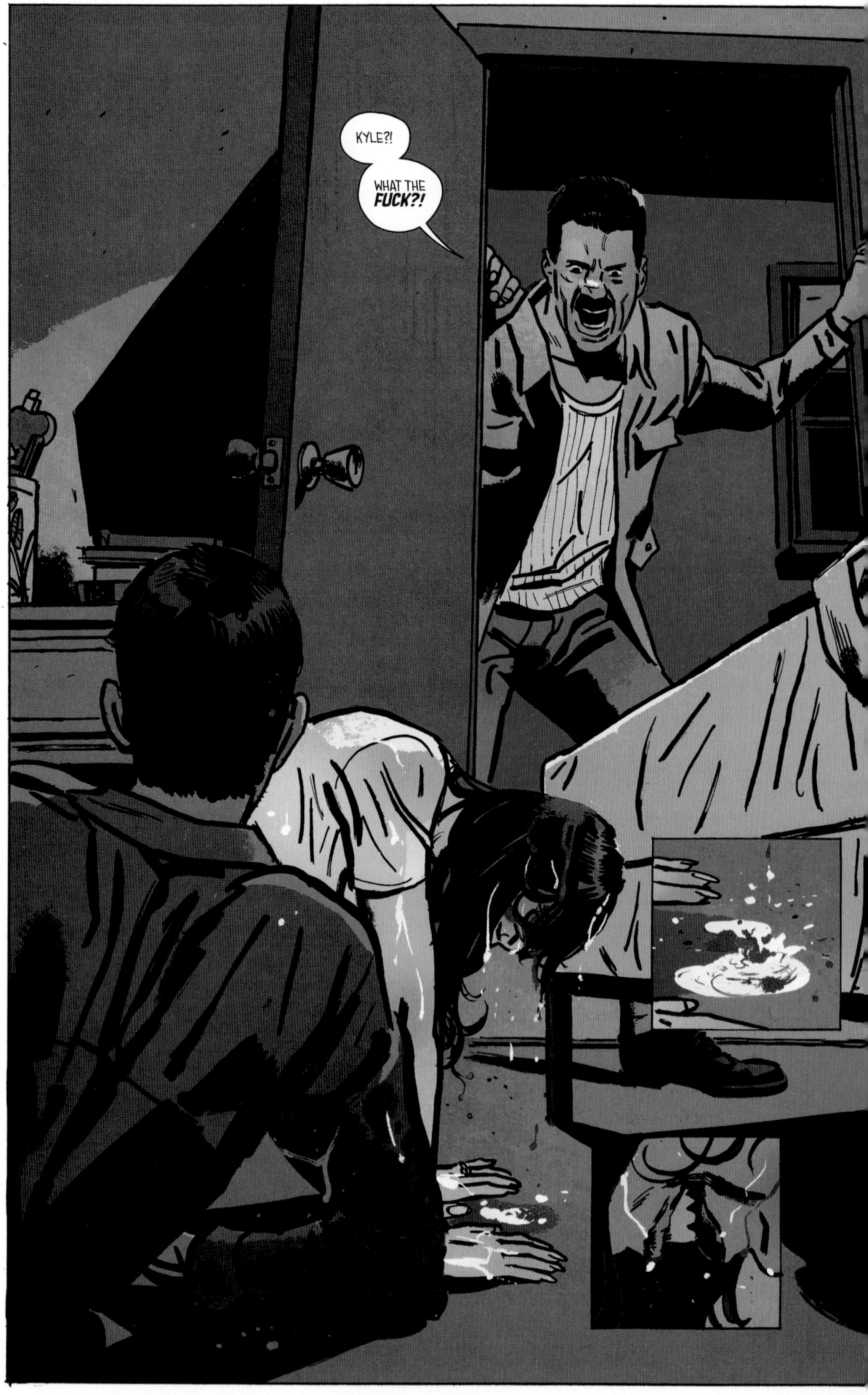
KYLE?!
WHAT THE FUCK?!

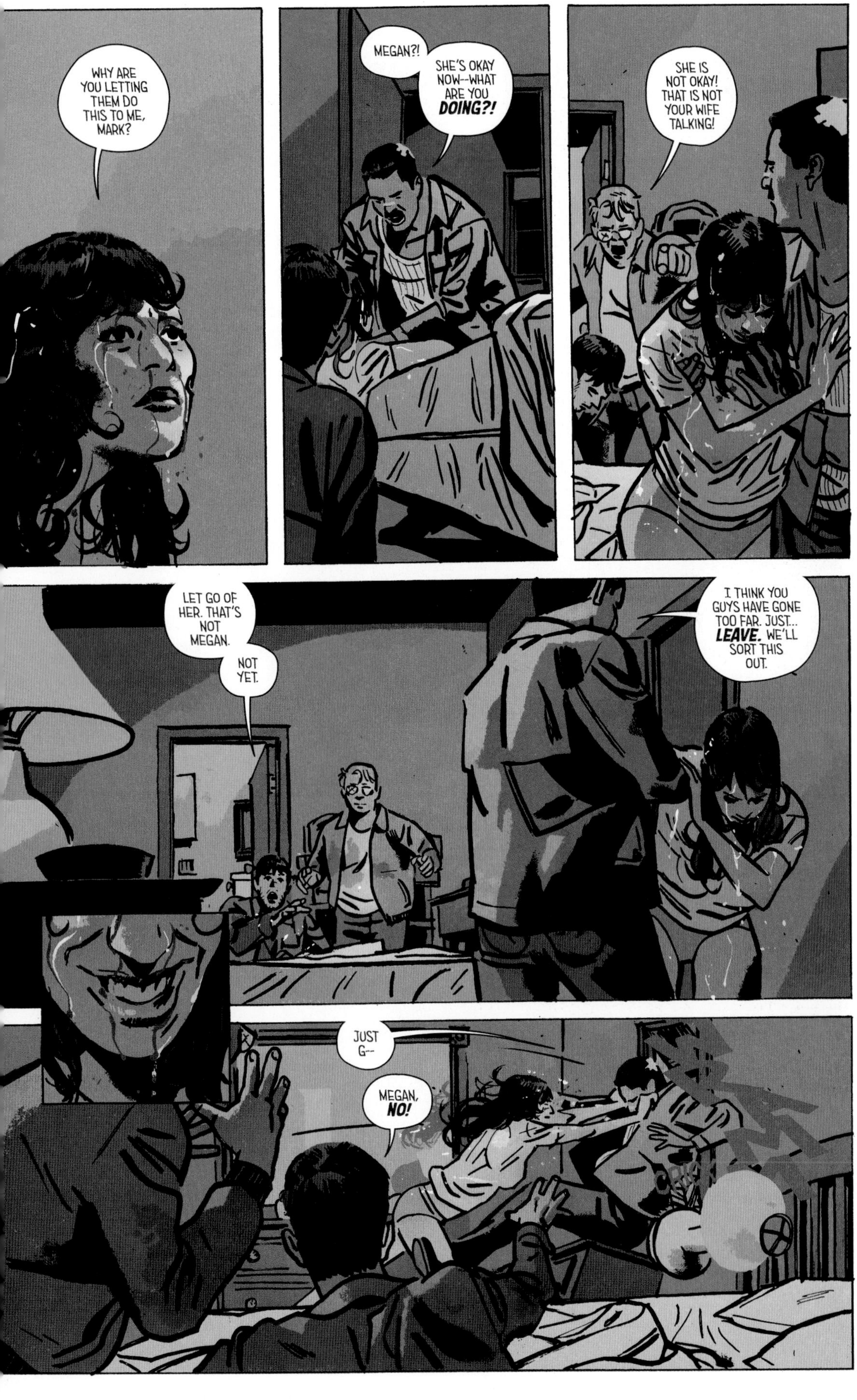

WHY ARE YOU LETTING THEM DO THIS TO ME, MARK?
MEGAN?!
SHE'S OKAY NOW--WHAT ARE YOU **DOING?!**
SHE IS NOT OKAY! THAT IS NOT YOUR WIFE TALKING!
LET GO OF HER. THAT'S NOT MEGAN.
NOT YET.
I THINK YOU GUYS HAVE GONE TOO FAR. JUST... **LEAVE.** WE'LL SORT THIS OUT.
JUST G--
MEGAN, **NO!**

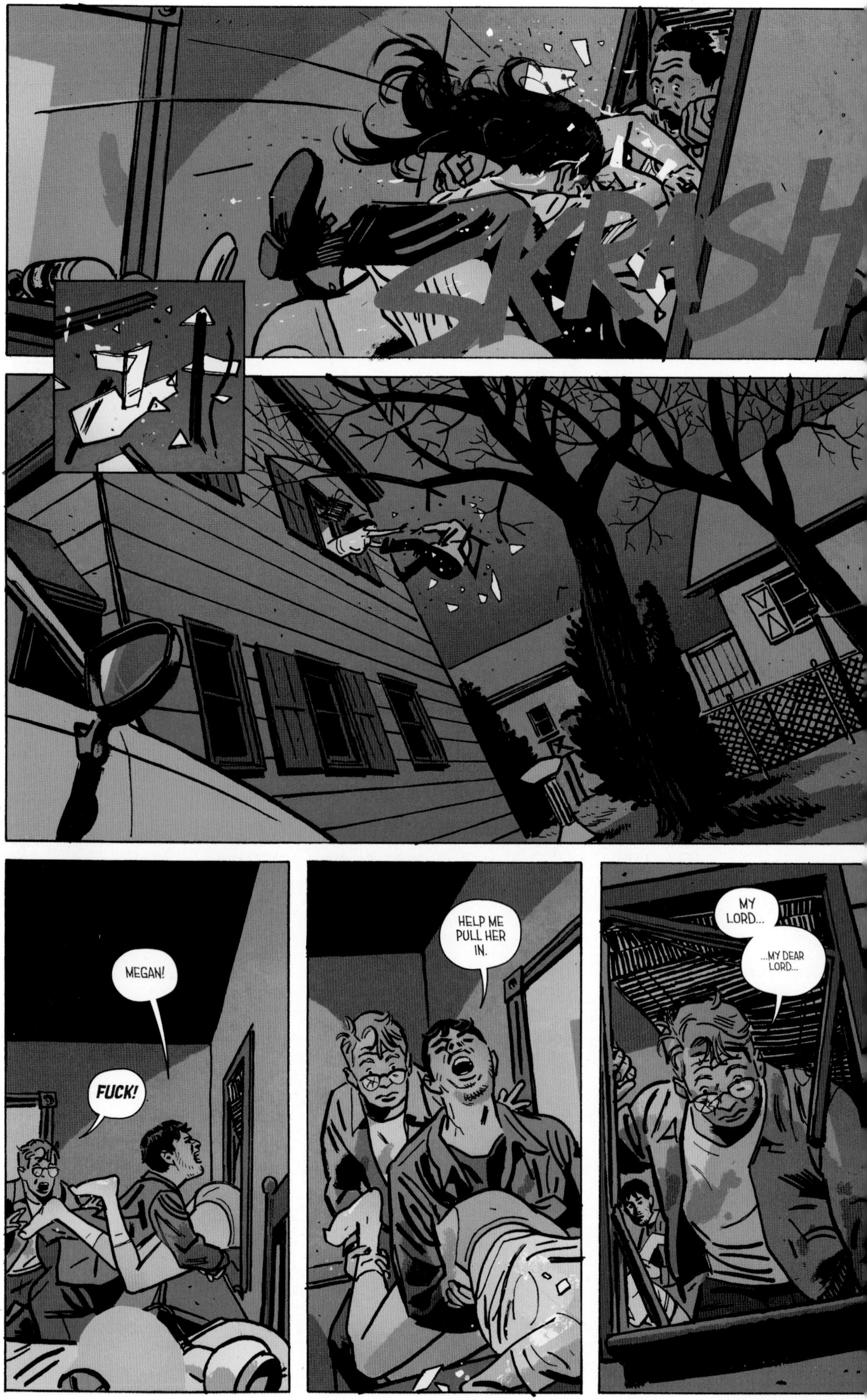
SKRASH
MEGAN!
FUCK!
HELP ME PULL HER IN.
MY LORD...
...MY DEAR LORD...

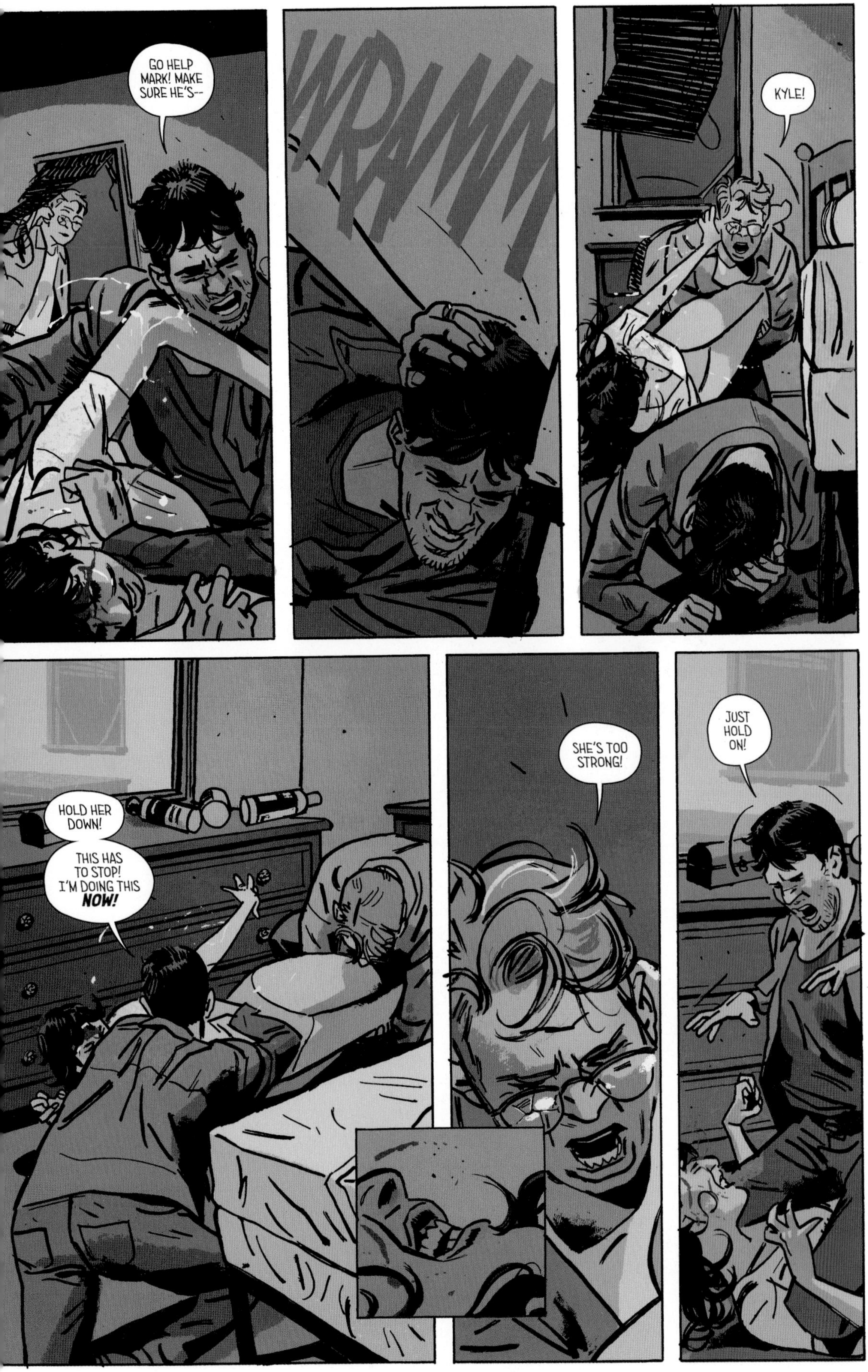
GO HELP MARK! MAKE SURE HE'S--
WRAMM
KYLE!
HOLD HER DOWN!
THIS HAS TO STOP! I'M DOING THIS NOW!
SHE'S TOO STRONG!
JUST HOLD ON!

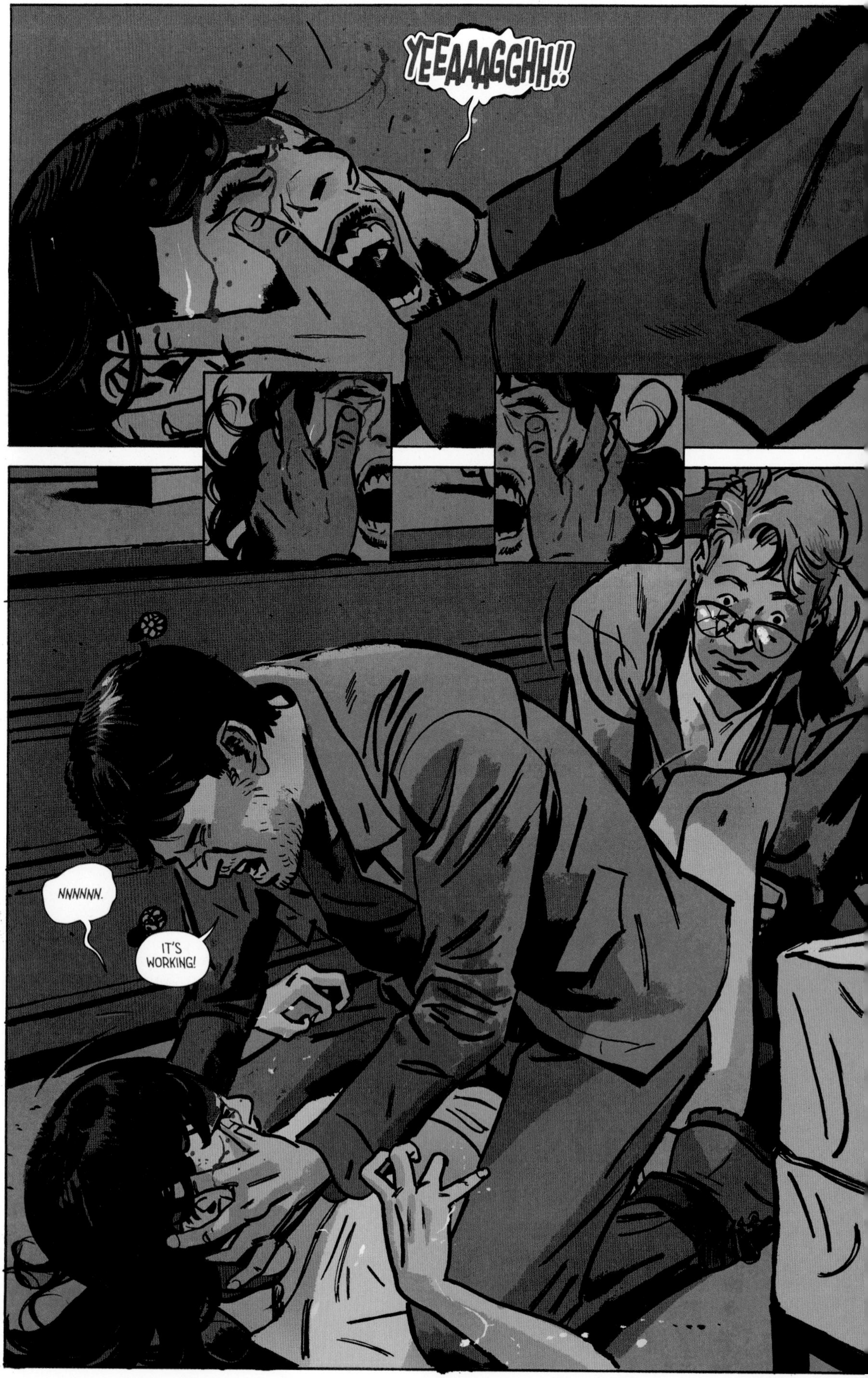
YEEAAAGGHH!!
NNNNNN.
IT'S WORKING!

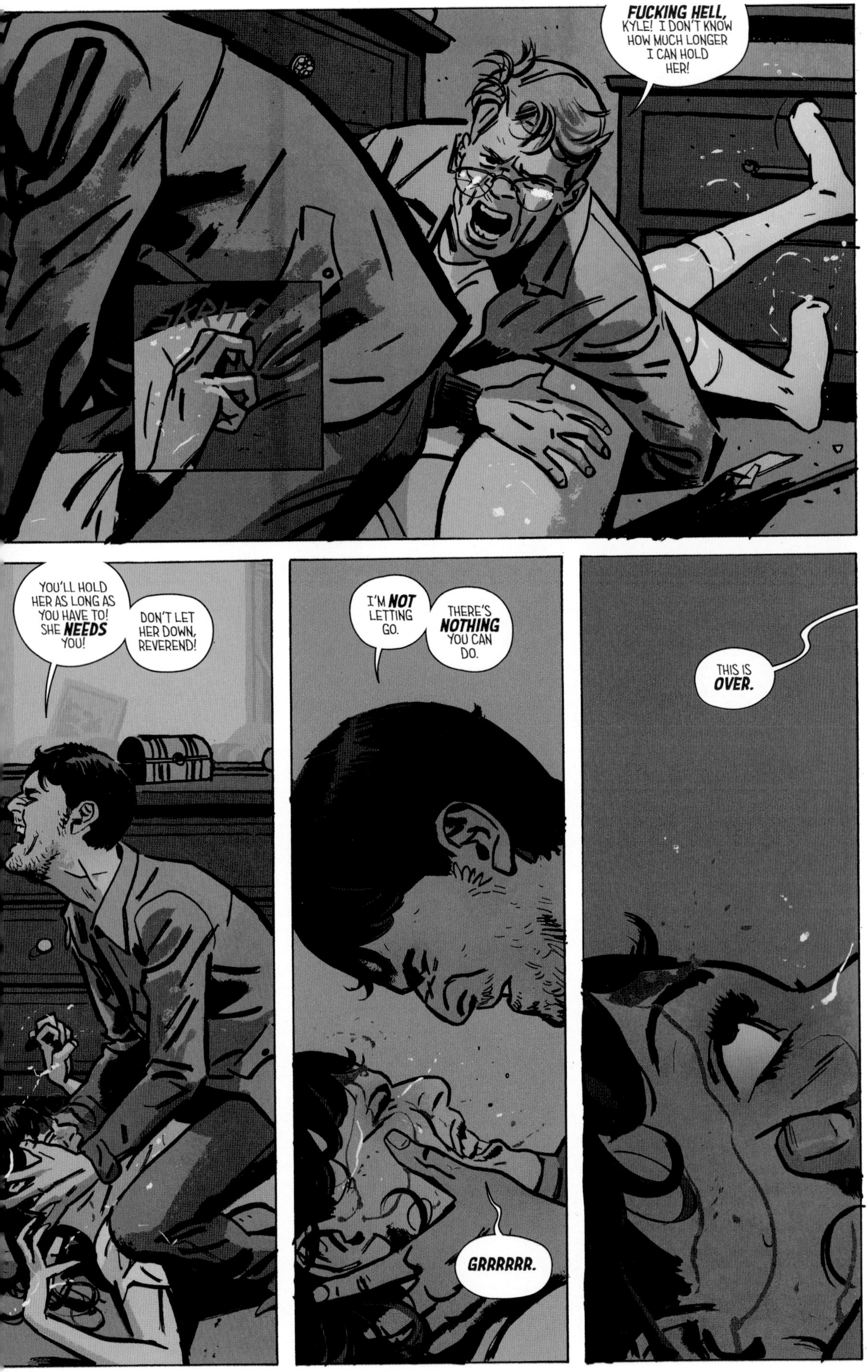
FUCKING HELL, KYLE! I DON'T KNOW HOW MUCH LONGER I CAN HOLD HER!
SKRITC
YOU'LL HOLD HER AS LONG AS YOU HAVE TO! SHE NEEDS YOU!
DON'T LET HER DOWN, REVEREND!
I'M NOT LETTING GO.
THERE'S NOTHING YOU CAN DO.
GRRRRRR.
THIS IS OVER.

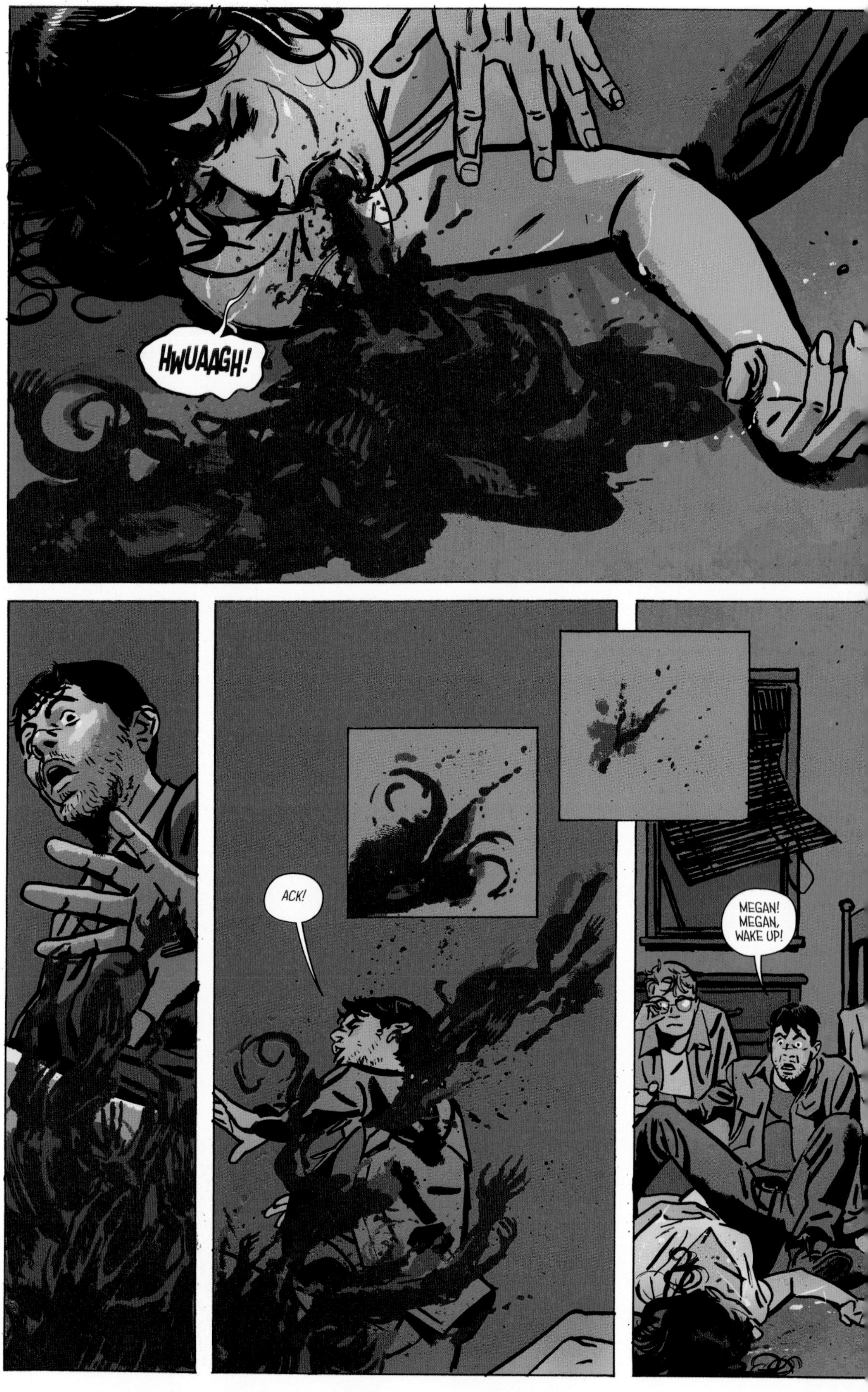
HWUAAGH!
ACK!
MEGAN! MEGAN, WAKE UP!

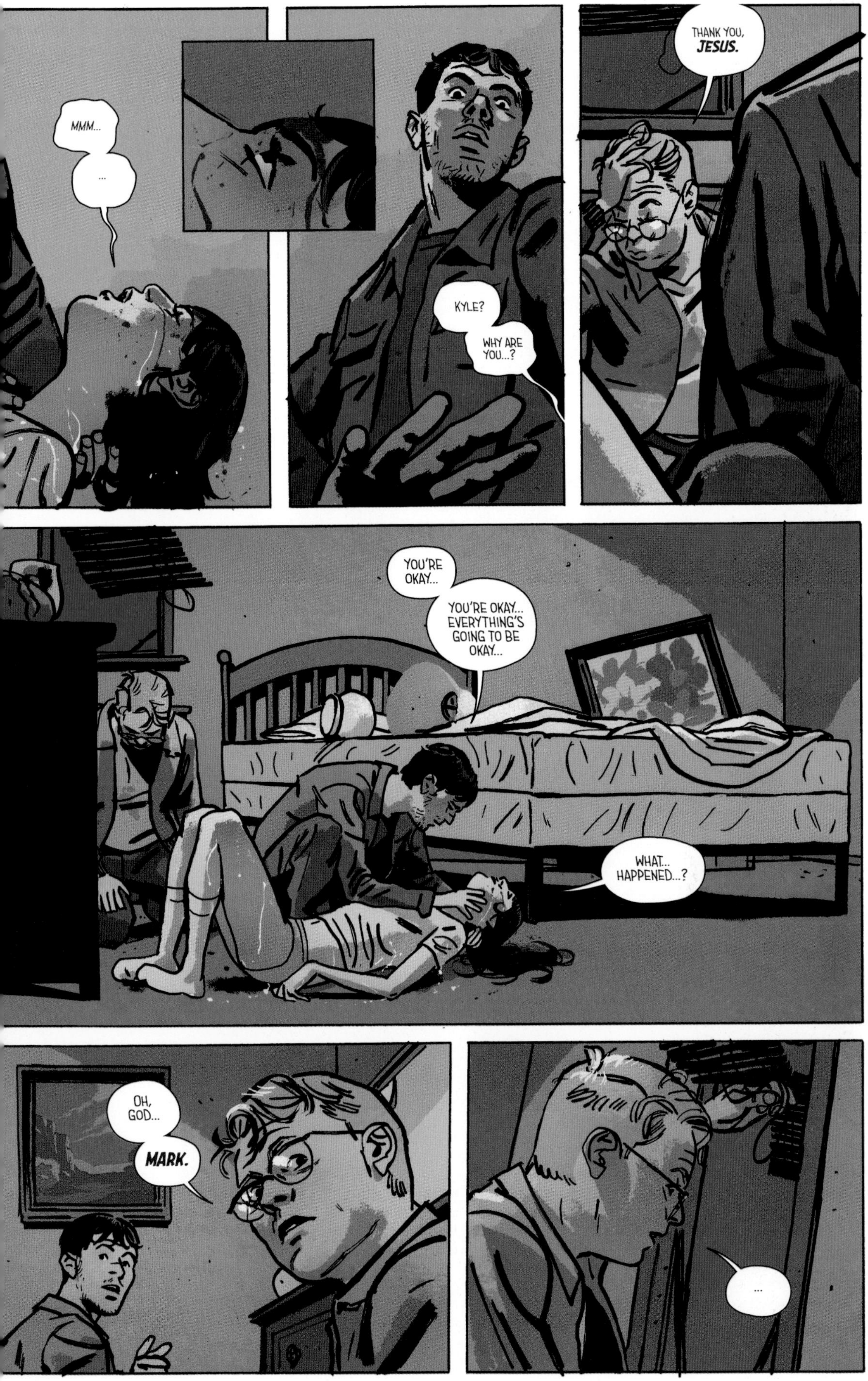
MMM...
...
KYLE?
WHY ARE YOU...?
THANK YOU, JESUS.
YOU'RE OKAY...
YOU'RE OKAY... EVERYTHING'S GOING TO BE OKAY...
WHAT... HAPPENED...?
OH, GOD...
MARK.
...

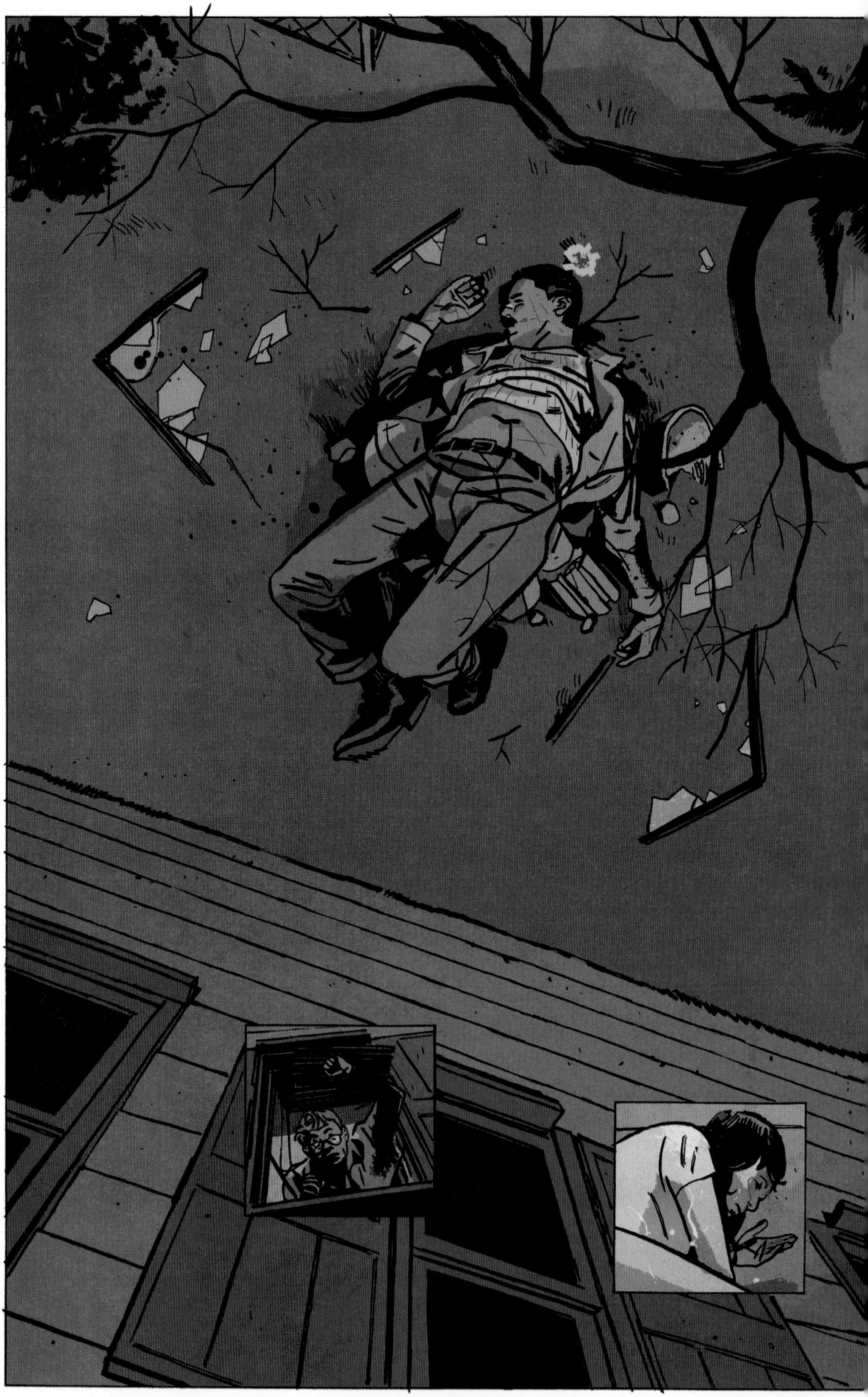

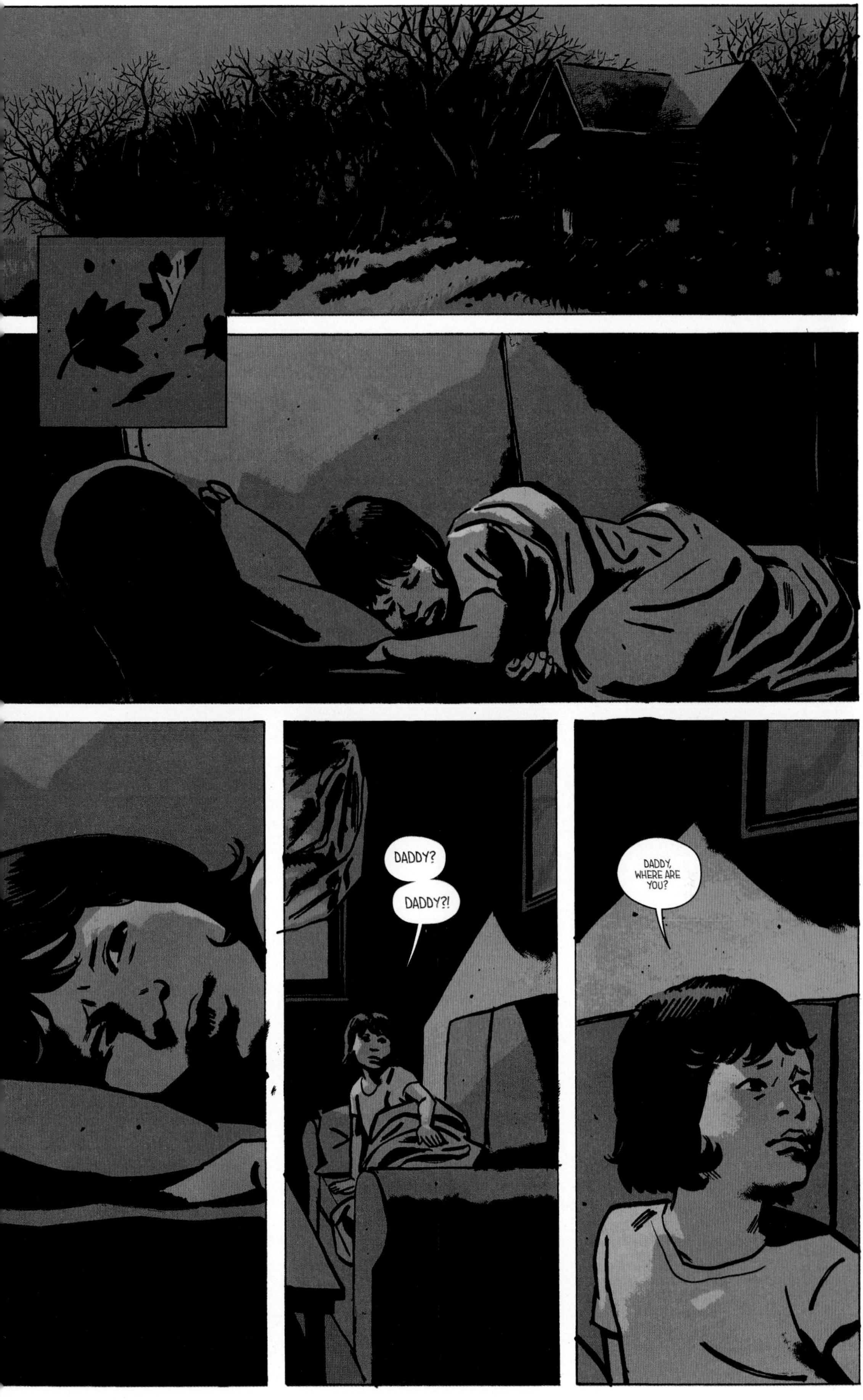
DADDY?
DADDY?!
DADDY, WHERE ARE YOU?

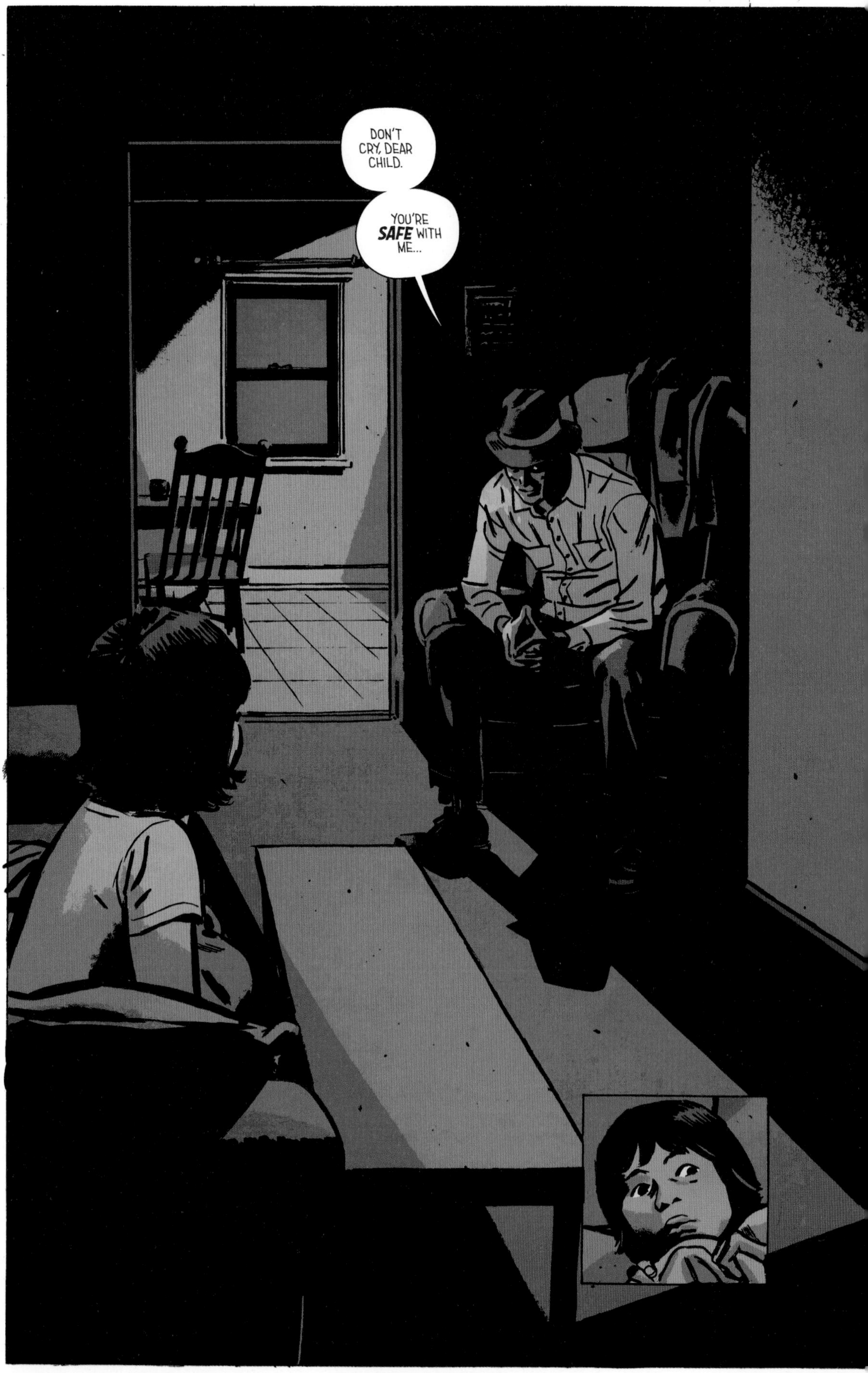
DON'T CRY, DEAR CHILD.
YOU'RE **SAFE** WITH ME...

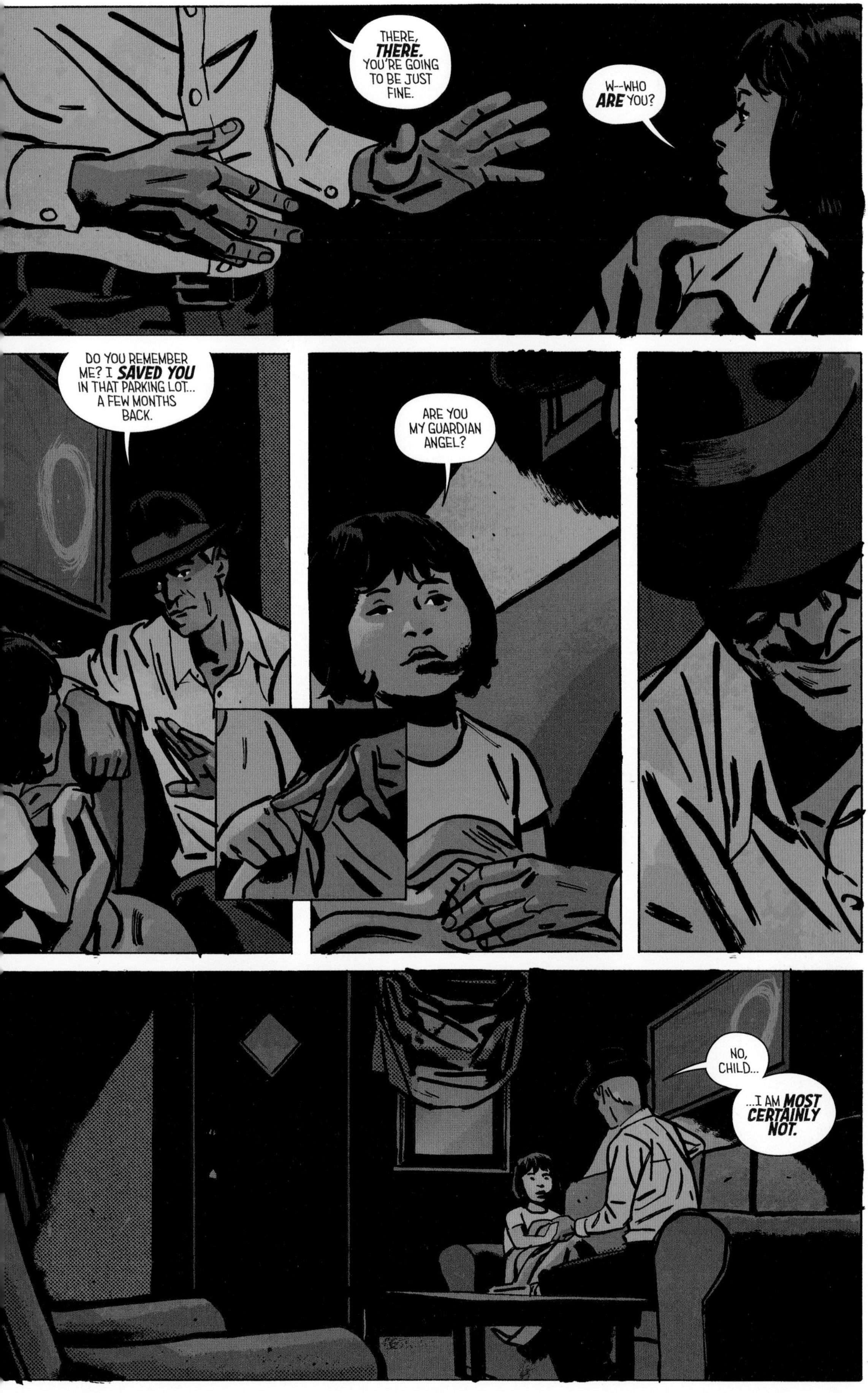
THERE, THERE. YOU'RE GOING TO BE JUST FINE.
W--WHO ARE YOU?
DO YOU REMEMBER ME? I SAVED YOU IN THAT PARKING LOT... A FEW MONTHS BACK.
ARE YOU MY GUARDIAN ANGEL?
NO, CHILD...
...I AM MOST CERTAINLY NOT.

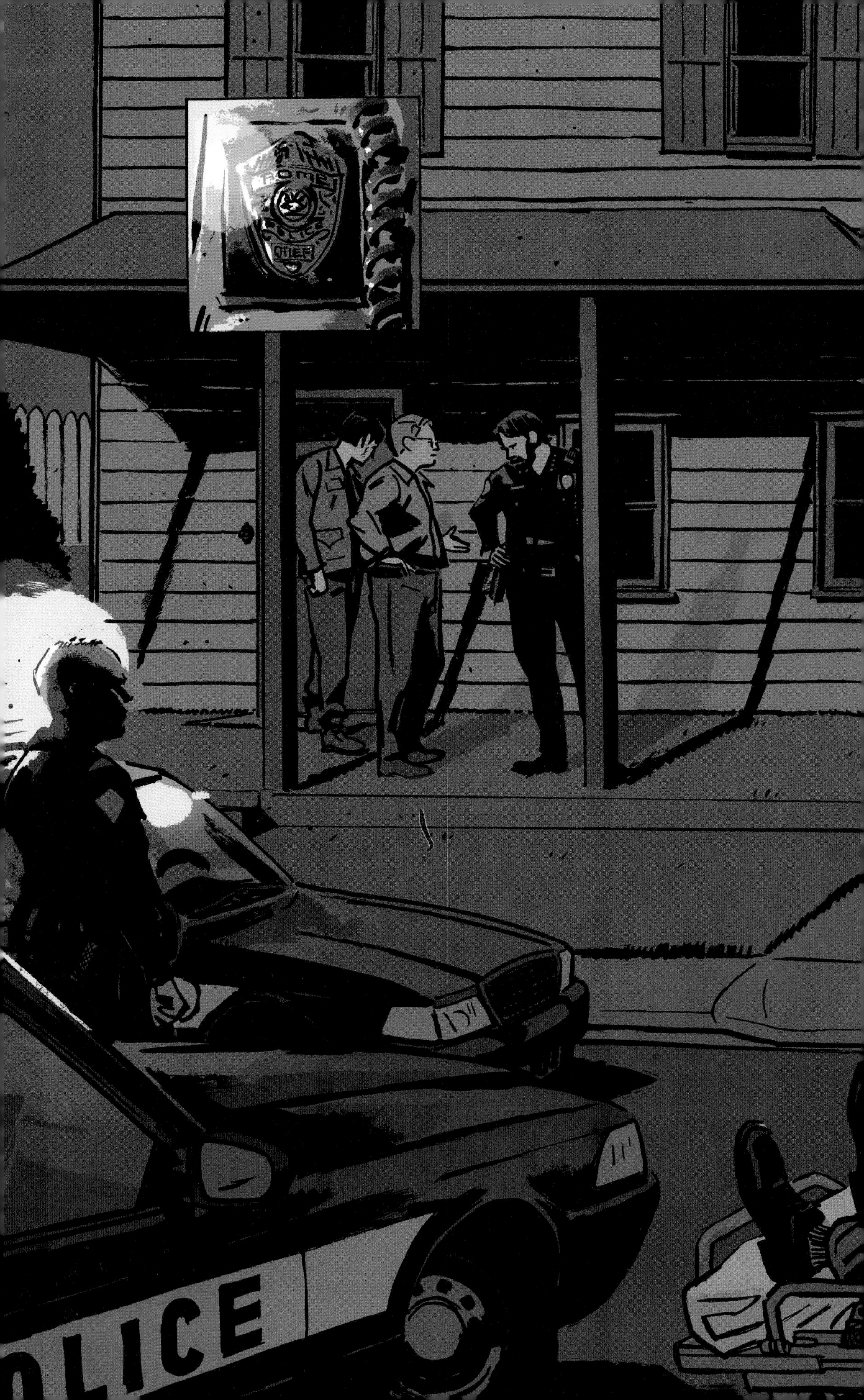
ROME
CHIEF
OLICE

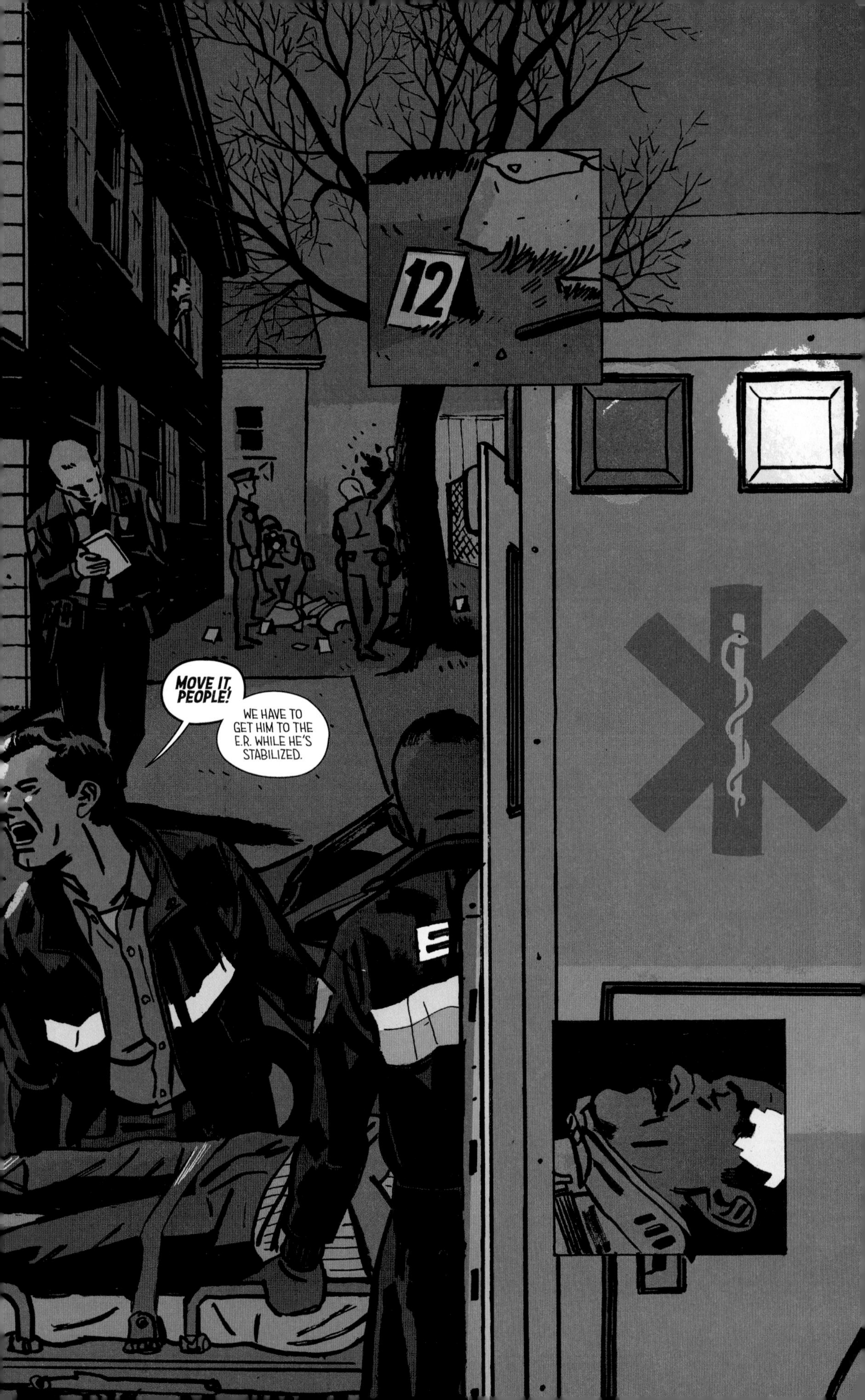
12
MOVE IT, PEOPLE!
WE HAVE TO GET HIM TO THE E.R. WHILE HE'S STABILIZED.

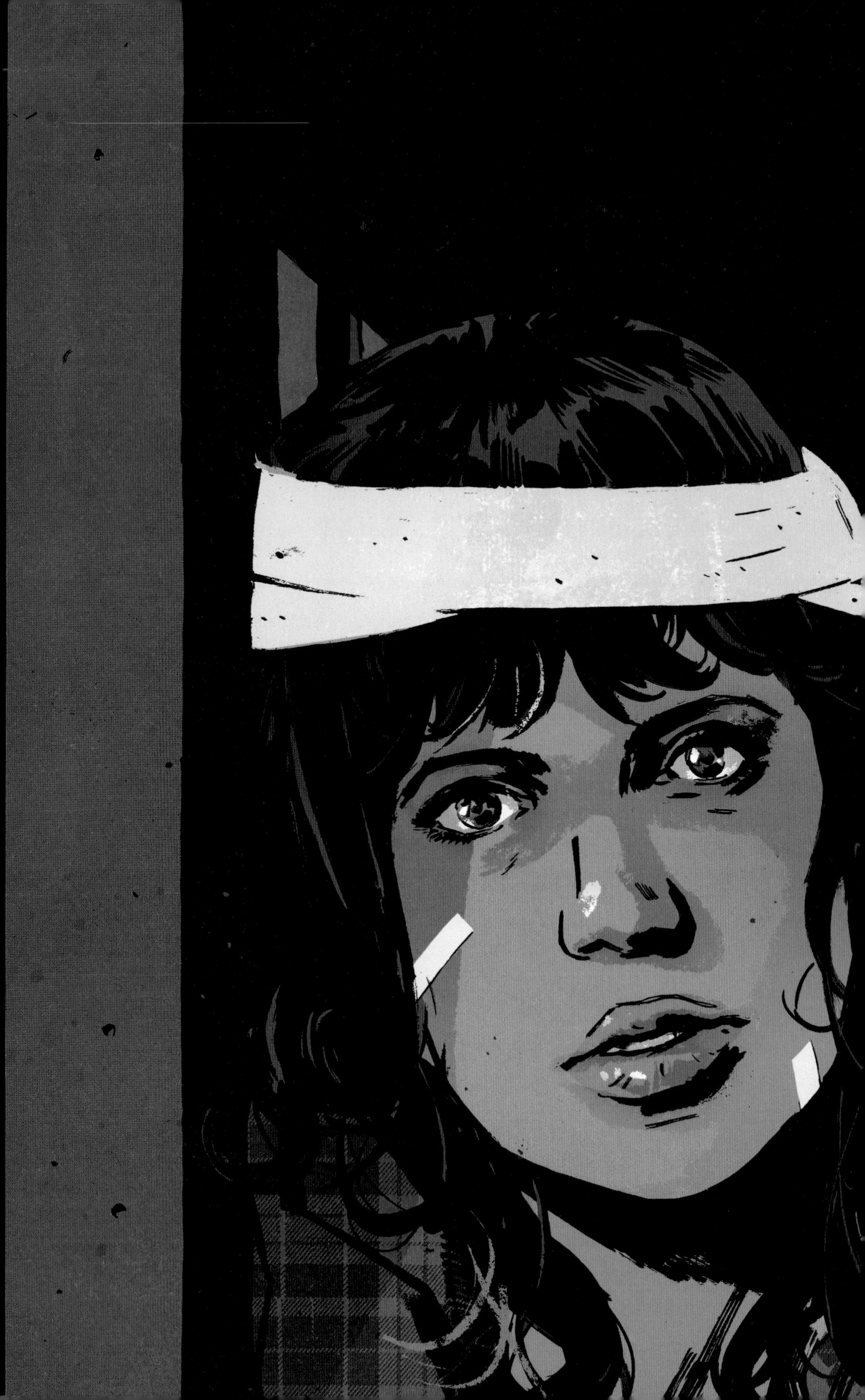

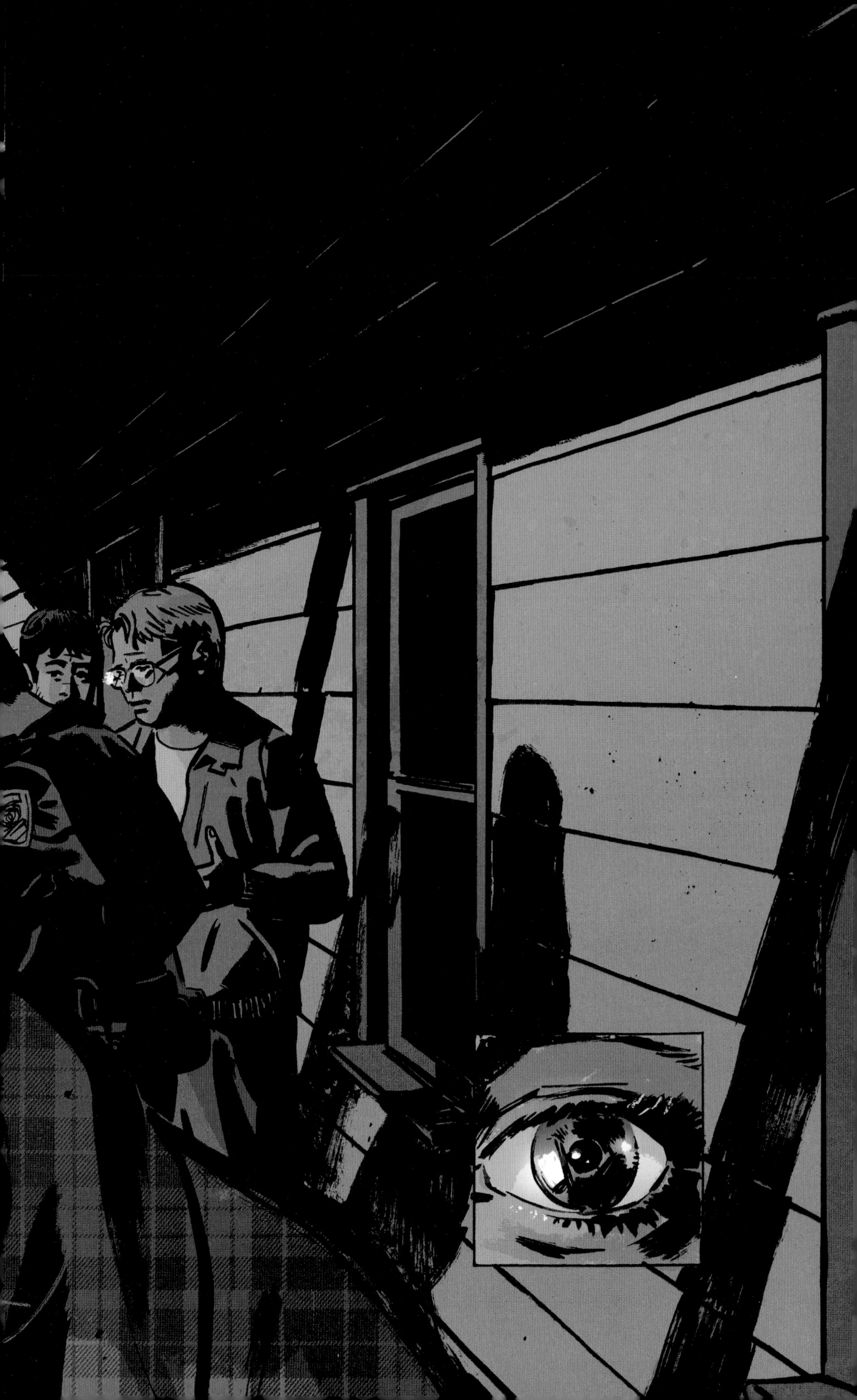

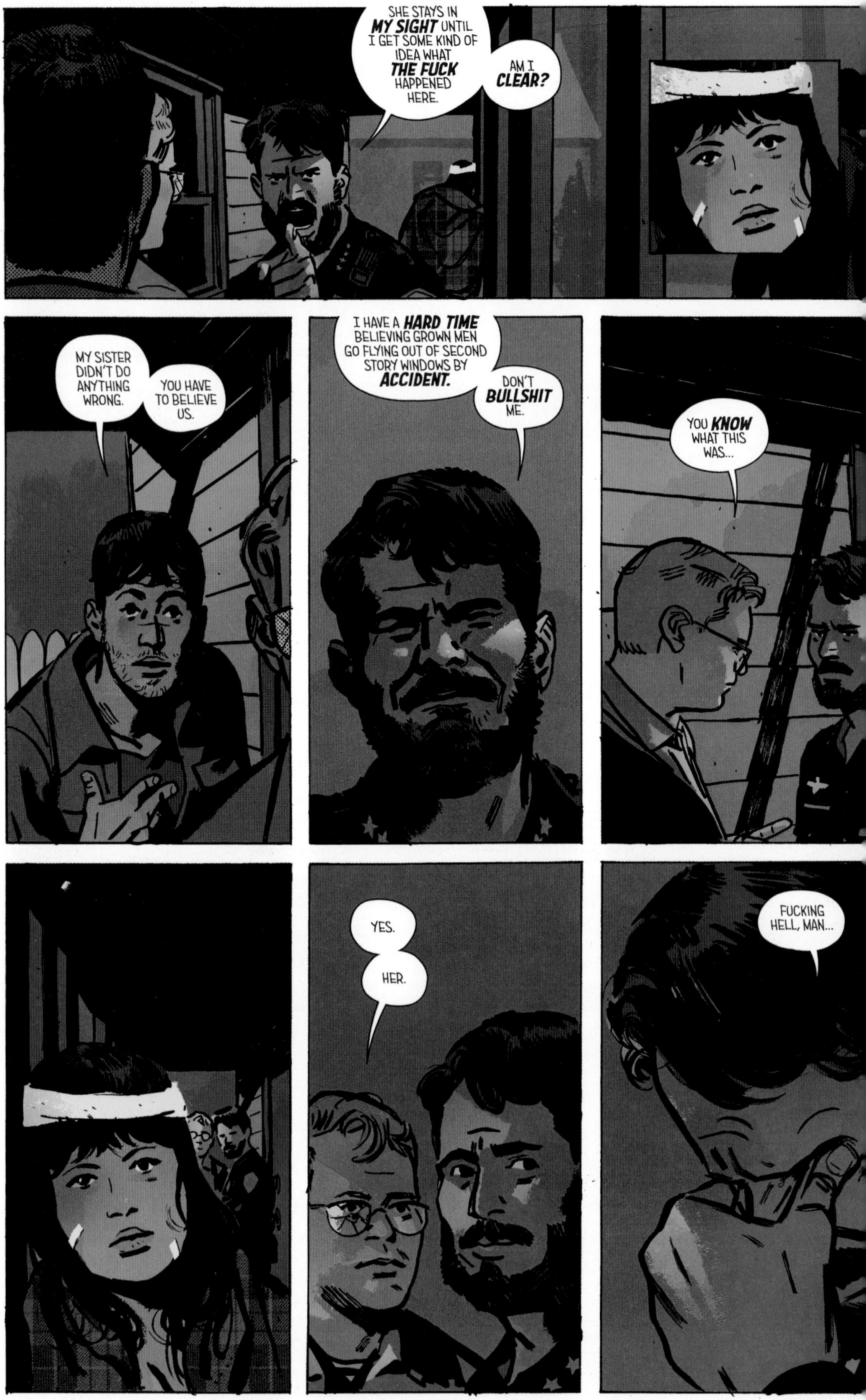
SHE STAYS IN MY SIGHT UNTIL I GET SOME KIND OF IDEA WHAT THE FUCK HAPPENED HERE.
AM I CLEAR?
MY SISTER DIDN'T DO ANYTHING WRONG.
YOU HAVE TO BELIEVE US.
I HAVE A HARD TIME BELIEVING GROWN MEN GO FLYING OUT OF SECOND STORY WINDOWS BY ACCIDENT.
DON'T BULLSHIT ME.
YOU KNOW WHAT THIS WAS...
YES.
HER.
FUCKING HELL, MAN...

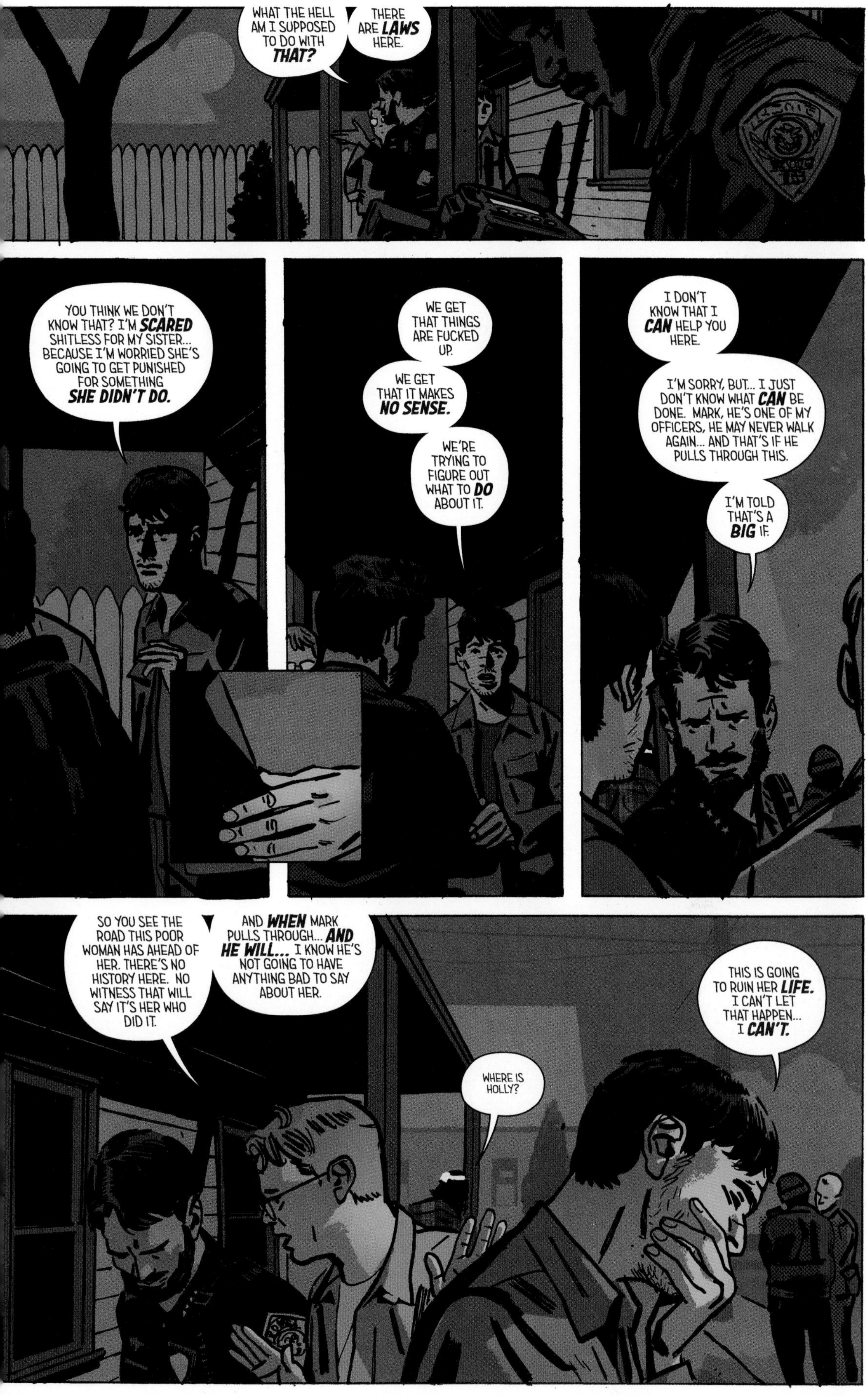
WHAT THE HELL AM I SUPPOSED TO DO WITH THAT?
THERE ARE LAWS HERE.
YOU THINK WE DON'T KNOW THAT? I'M SCARED SHITLESS FOR MY SISTER... BECAUSE I'M WORRIED SHE'S GOING TO GET PUNISHED FOR SOMETHING SHE DIDN'T DO.
WE GET THAT THINGS ARE FUCKED UP.
WE GET THAT IT MAKES NO SENSE.
WE'RE TRYING TO FIGURE OUT WHAT TO DO ABOUT IT.
I DON'T KNOW THAT I CAN HELP YOU HERE.
I'M SORRY, BUT... I JUST DON'T KNOW WHAT CAN BE DONE. MARK, HE'S ONE OF MY OFFICERS, HE MAY NEVER WALK AGAIN... AND THAT'S IF HE PULLS THROUGH THIS.
I'M TOLD THAT'S A BIG IF.
SO YOU SEE THE ROAD THIS POOR WOMAN HAS AHEAD OF HER. THERE'S NO HISTORY HERE. NO WITNESS THAT WILL SAY IT'S HER WHO DID IT.
AND WHEN MARK PULLS THROUGH... AND HE WILL... I KNOW HE'S NOT GOING TO HAVE ANYTHING BAD TO SAY ABOUT HER.
WHERE IS HOLLY?
THIS IS GOING TO RUIN HER LIFE. I CAN'T LET THAT HAPPEN... I CAN'T.

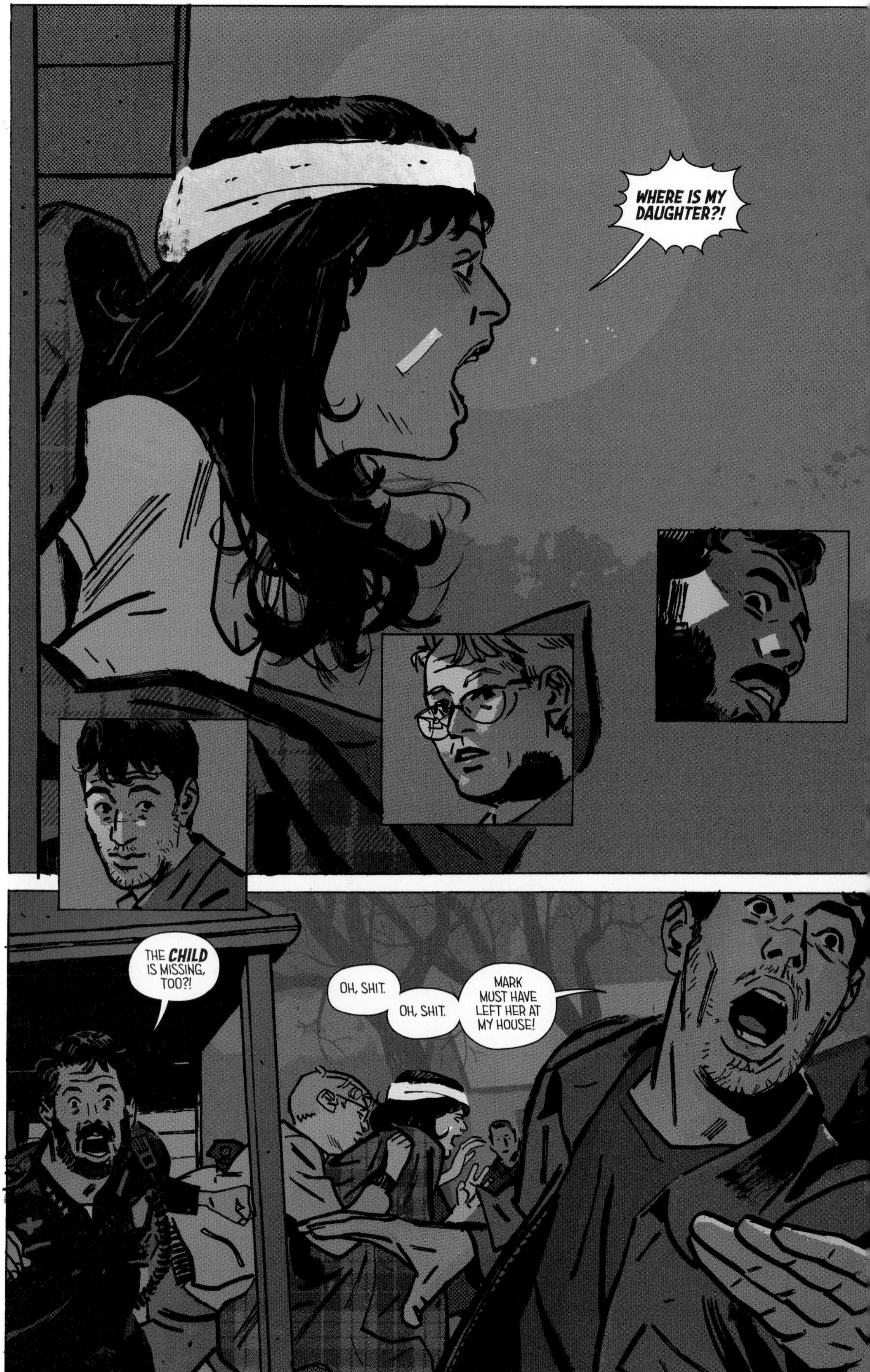
WHERE IS MY DAUGHTER?!
THE CHILD IS MISSING, TOO?!
OH, SHIT.
OH, SHIT.
MARK MUST HAVE LEFT HER AT MY HOUSE!

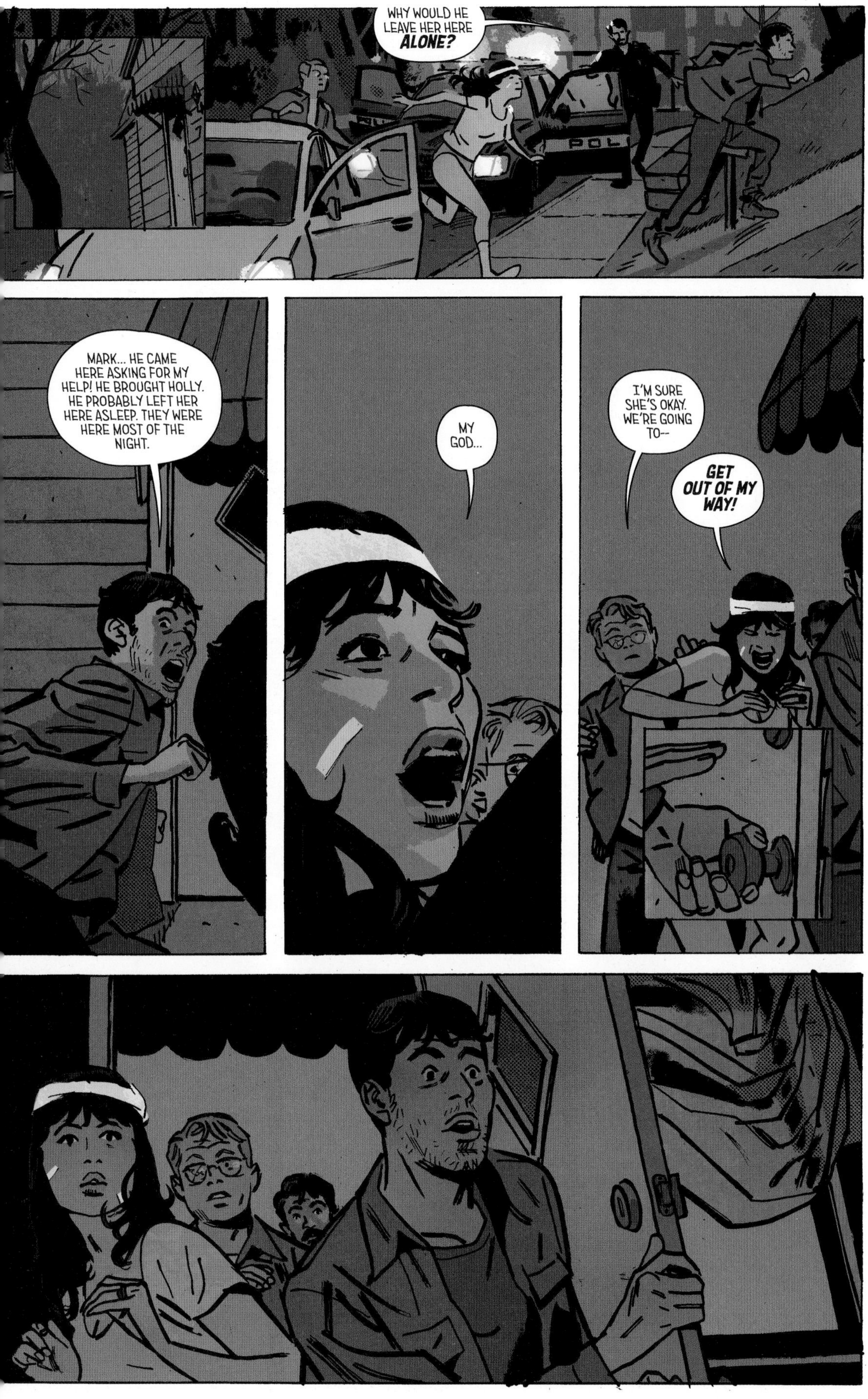
WHY WOULD HE LEAVE HER HERE ALONE?
MARK... HE CAME HERE ASKING FOR MY HELP! HE BROUGHT HOLLY. HE PROBABLY LEFT HER HERE ASLEEP. THEY WERE HERE MOST OF THE NIGHT.
MY GOD...
I'M SURE SHE'S OKAY. WE'RE GOING TO--
GET OUT OF MY WAY!

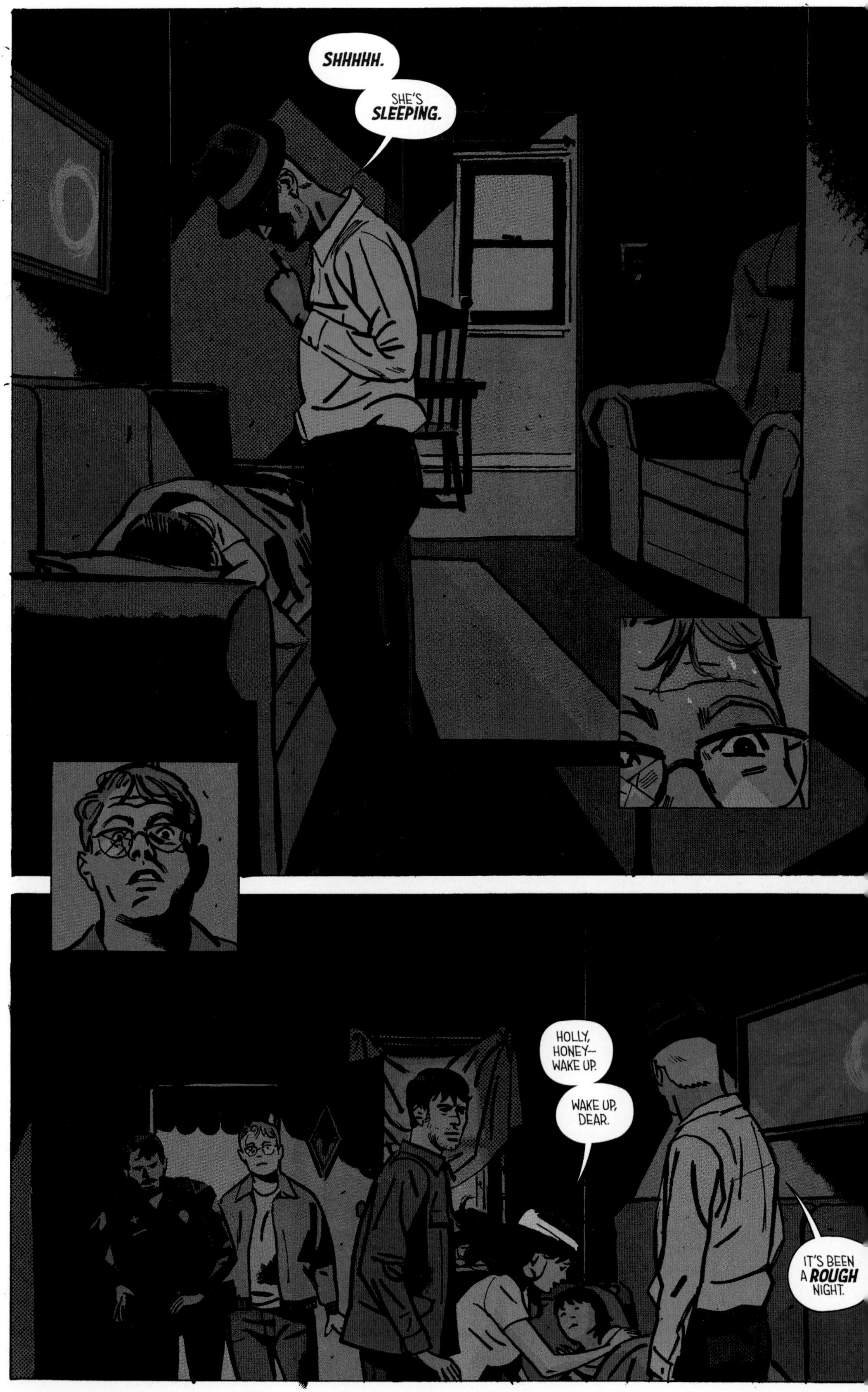
SHHHHH.
SHE'S SLEEPING.
HOLLY, HONEY-- WAKE UP.
WAKE UP, DEAR.
IT'S BEEN A ROUGH NIGHT.

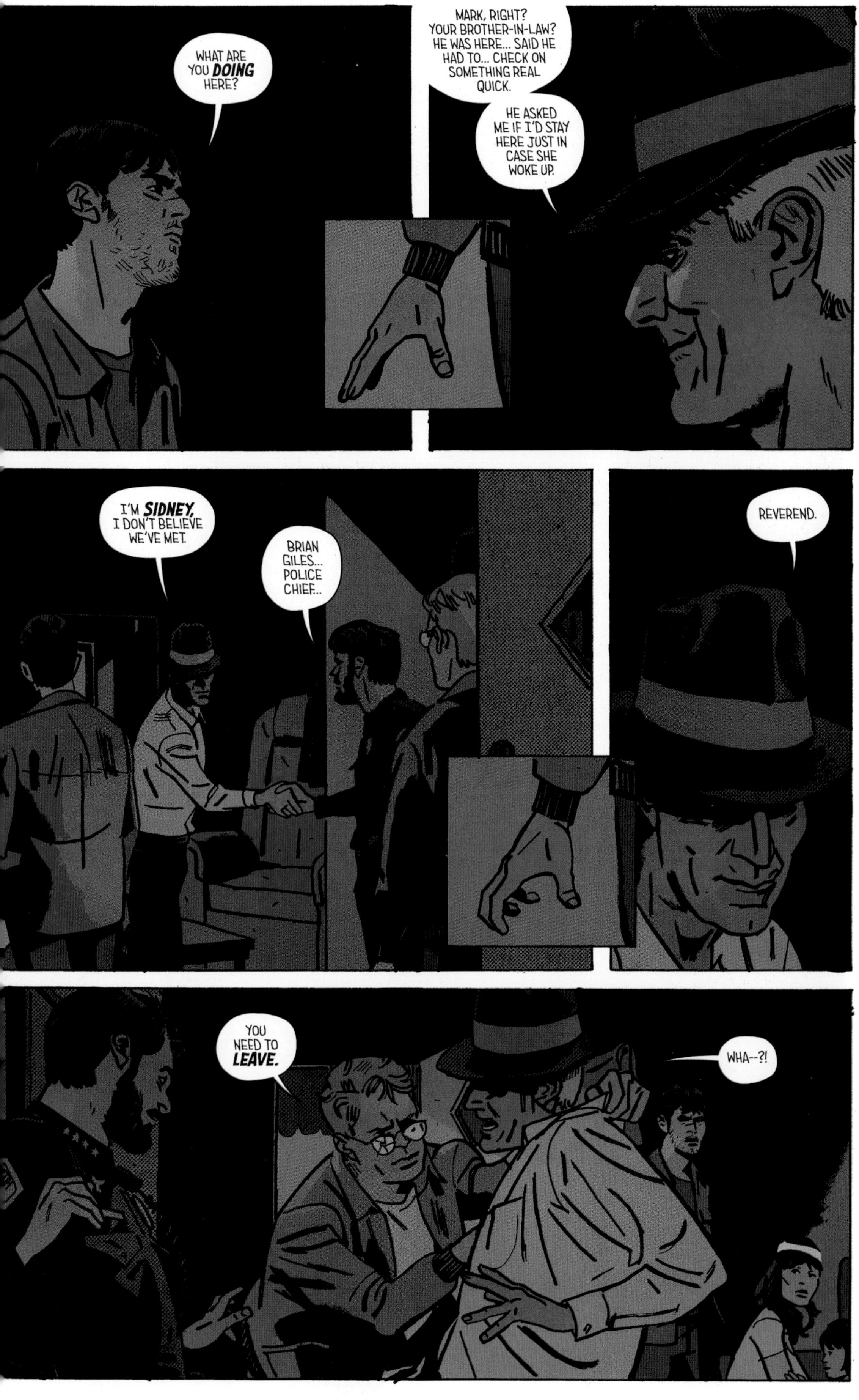
WHAT ARE YOU DOING HERE?
MARK, RIGHT? YOUR BROTHER-IN-LAW? HE WAS HERE... SAID HE HAD TO... CHECK ON SOMETHING REAL QUICK.
HE ASKED ME IF I'D STAY HERE JUST IN CASE SHE WOKE UP.
I'M SIDNEY, I DON'T BELIEVE WE'VE MET.
BRIAN GILES... POLICE CHIEF...
REVEREND.
YOU NEED TO LEAVE.
WHA--?!

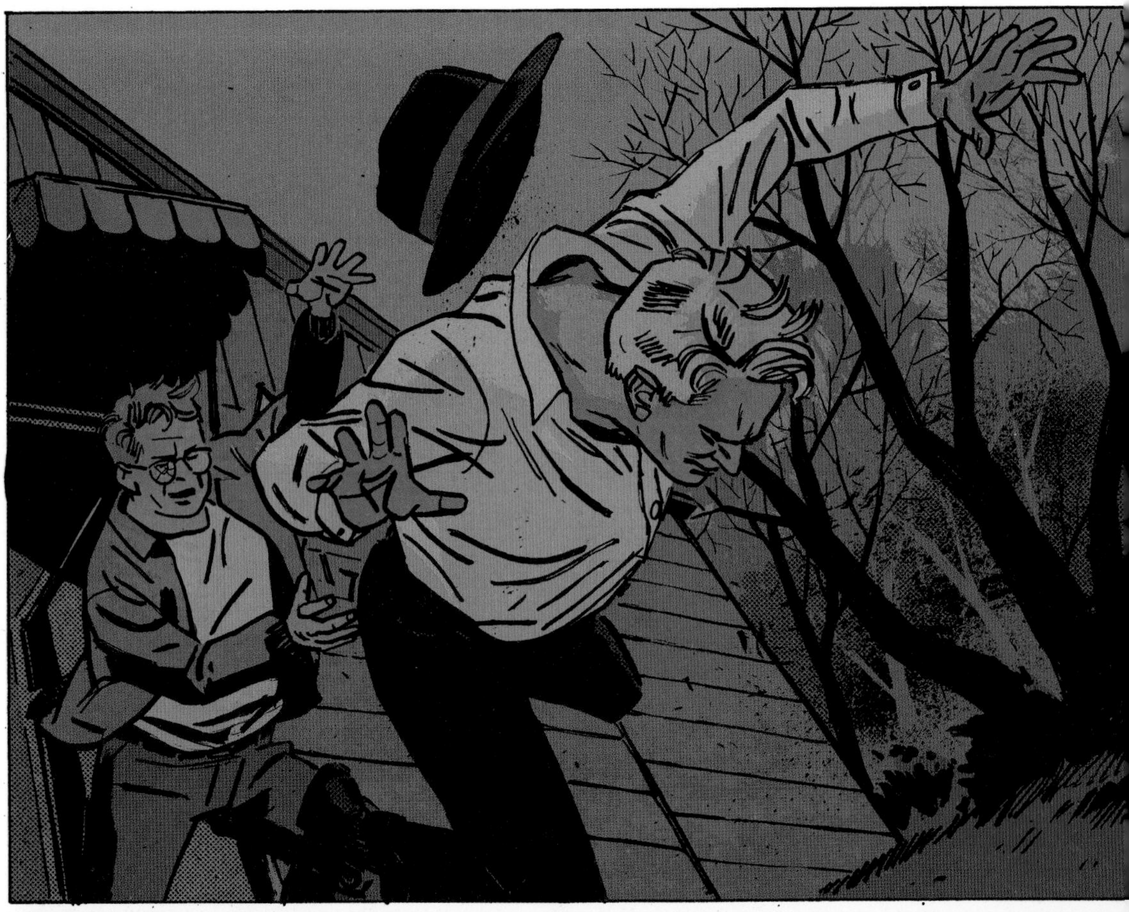

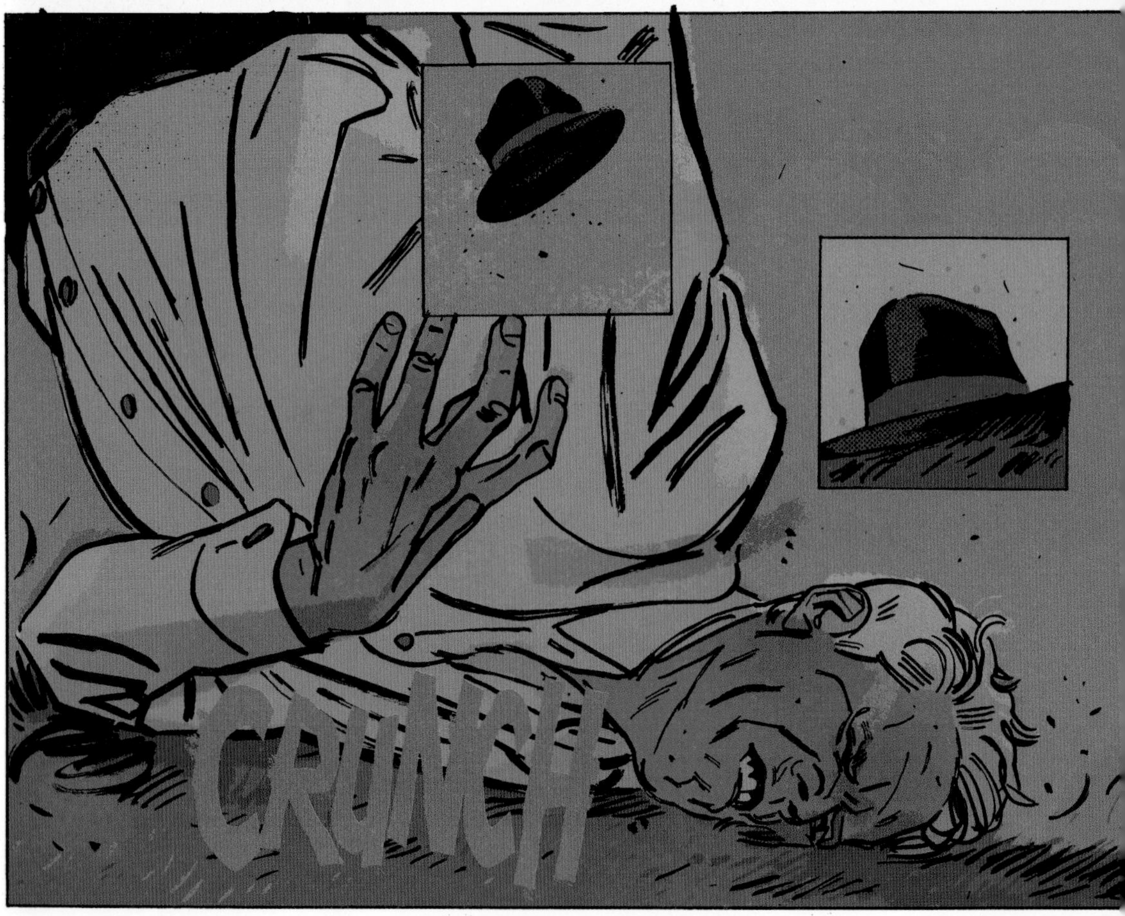
CRUNCH

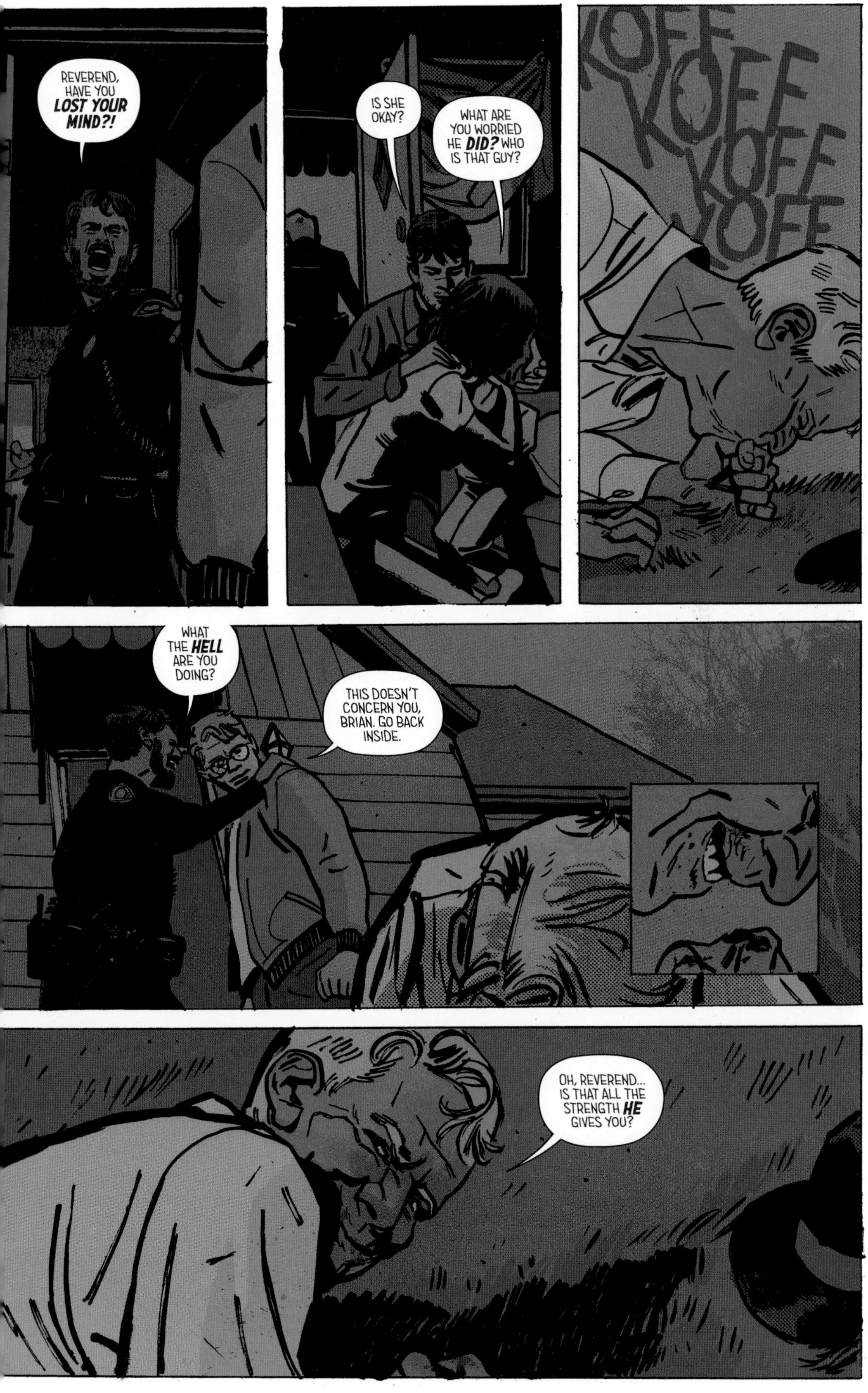
REVEREND, HAVE YOU LOST YOUR MIND?!
IS SHE OKAY?
WHAT ARE YOU WORRIED HE DID? WHO IS THAT GUY?
KOFF KOFF KOFF KOFF
WHAT THE HELL ARE YOU DOING?
THIS DOESN'T CONCERN YOU, BRIAN. GO BACK INSIDE.
OH, REVEREND... IS THAT ALL THE STRENGTH HE GIVES YOU?

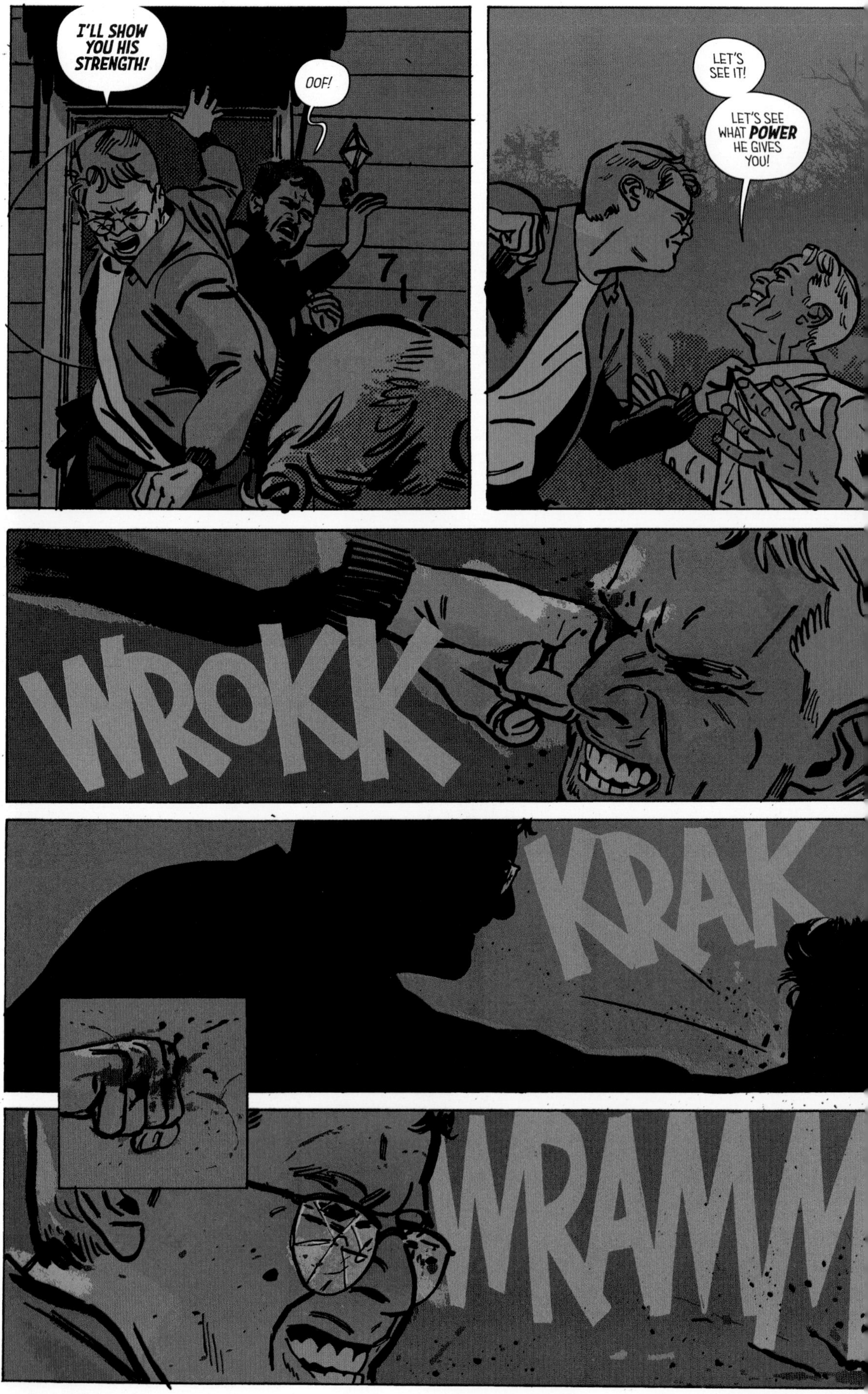
I'LL SHOW YOU HIS STRENGTH!
OOF!
717
LET'S SEE IT!
LET'S SEE WHAT **POWER** HE GIVES YOU!
WROKK
KRAK
WRAMM

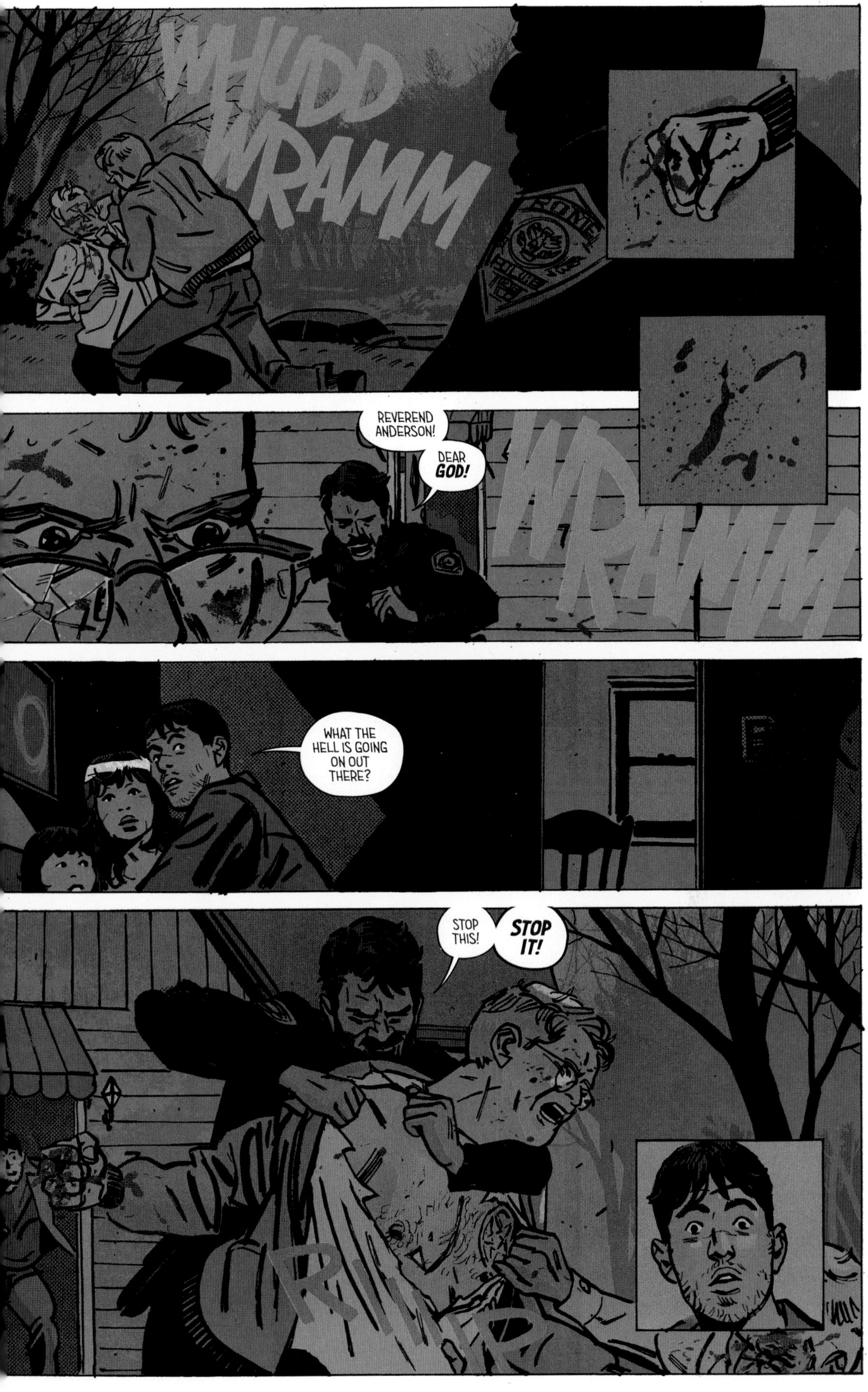
WHUDD
WRAMM
REVEREND ANDERSON!
DEAR GOD!
WRAMM
WHAT THE HELL IS GOING ON OUT THERE?
STOP THIS!
STOP IT!

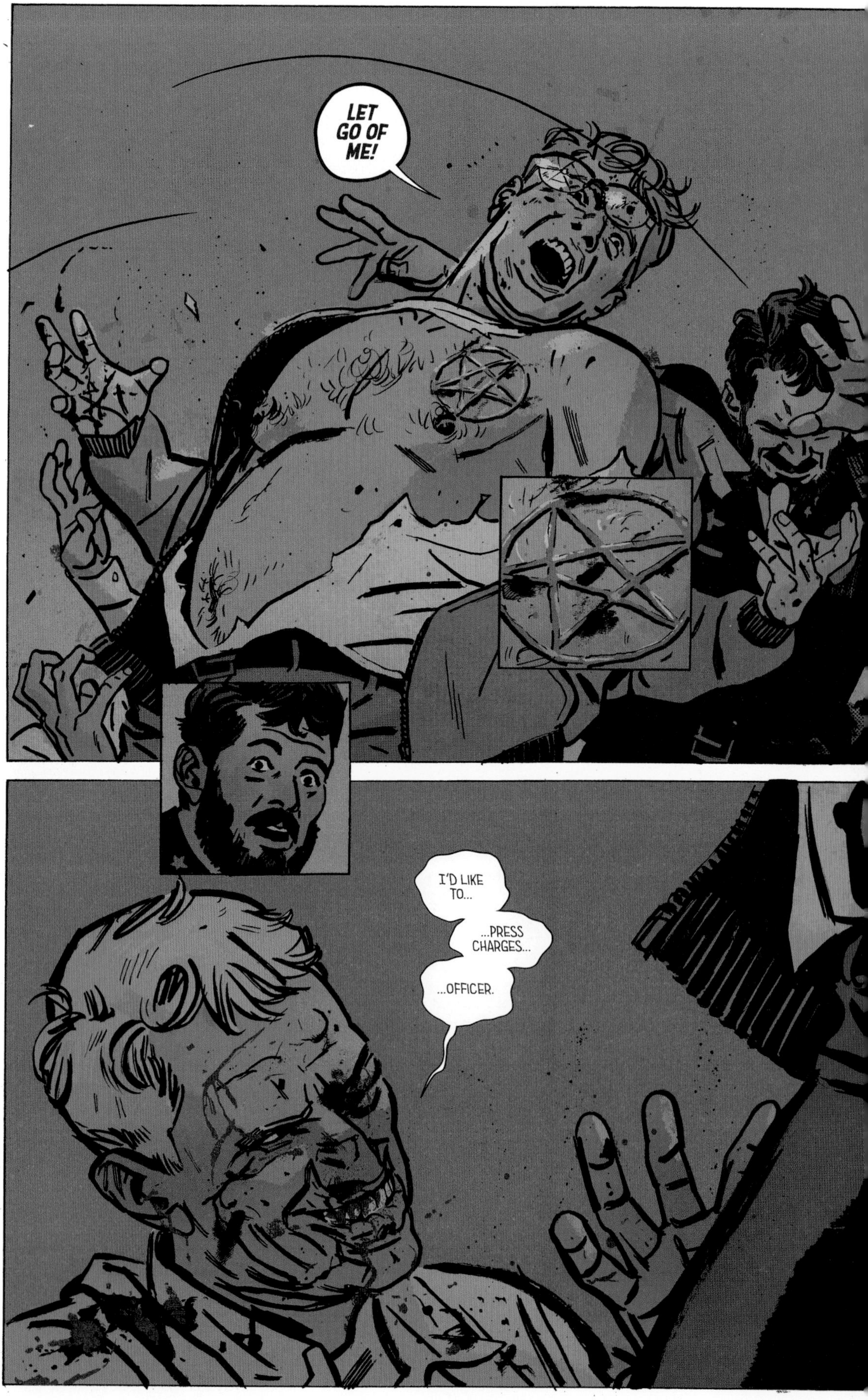
LET GO OF ME!
I'D LIKE TO...
...PRESS CHARGES...
...OFFICER.

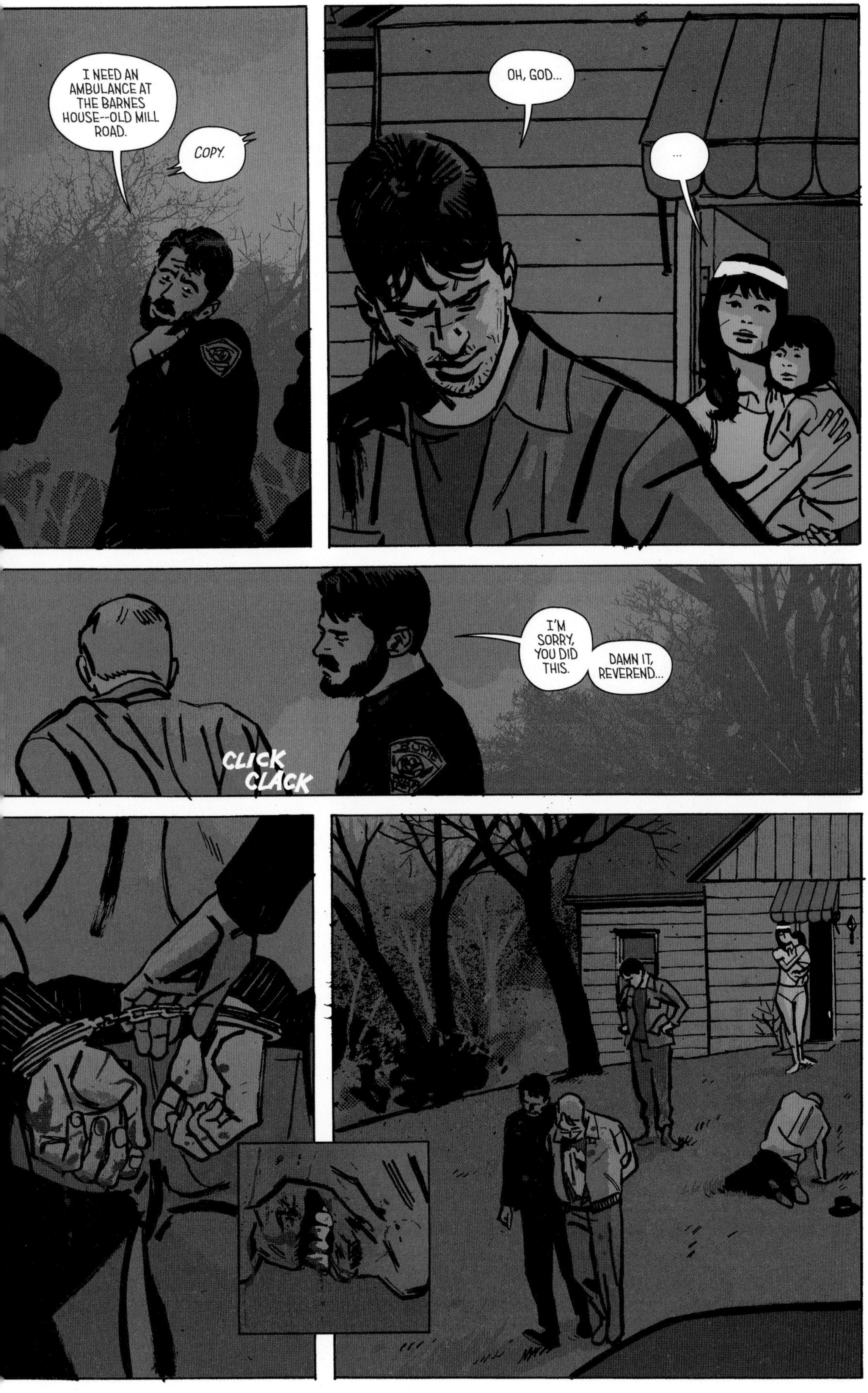
I NEED AN AMBULANCE AT THE BARNES HOUSE--OLD MILL ROAD.
COPY.
OH, GOD...
...
I'M SORRY, YOU DID THIS.
DAMN IT, REVEREND...
CLICK
CLACK

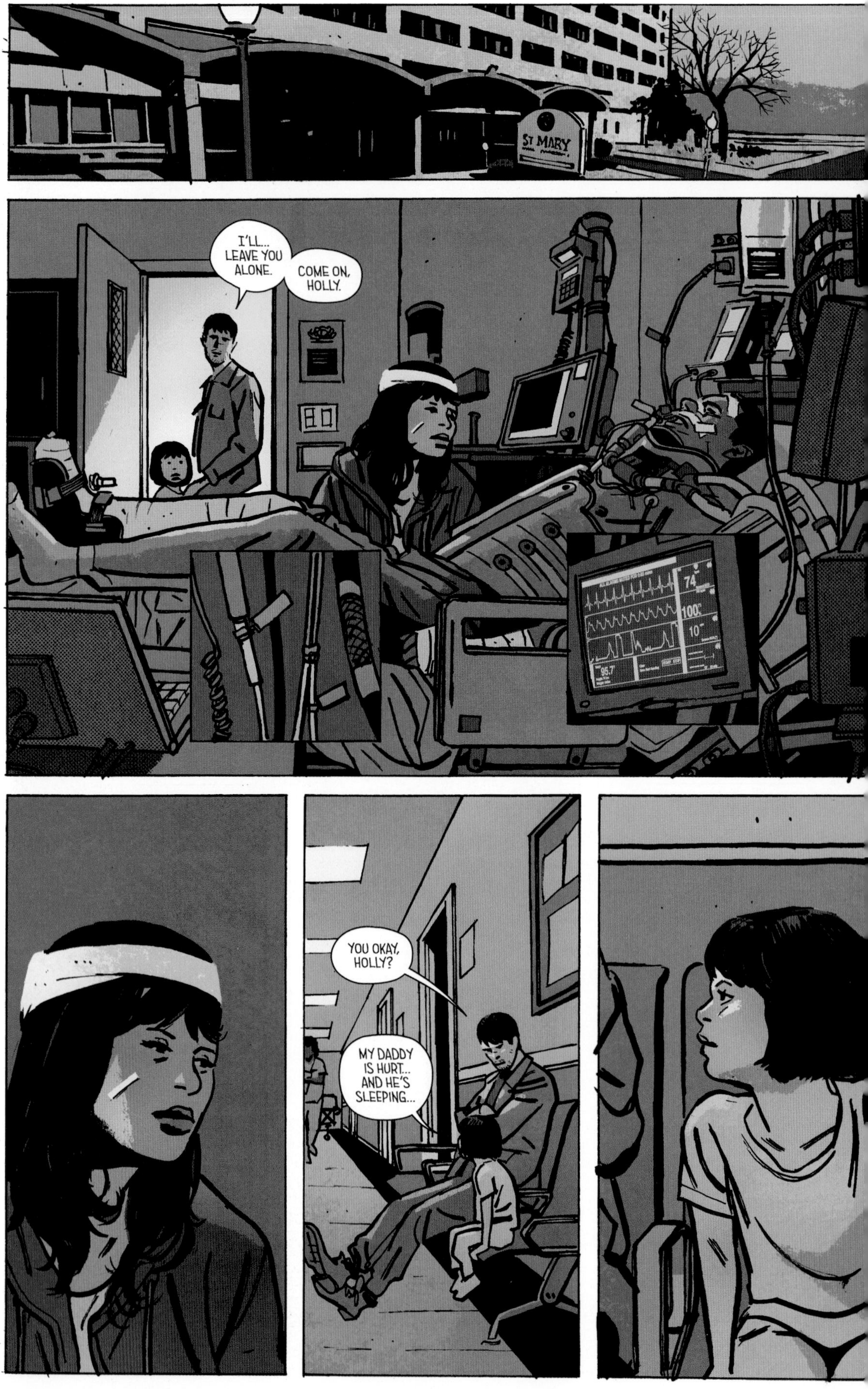
ST MARY
I'LL... LEAVE YOU ALONE.
COME ON, HOLLY.
YOU OKAY, HOLLY?
MY DADDY IS HURT... AND HE'S SLEEPING...

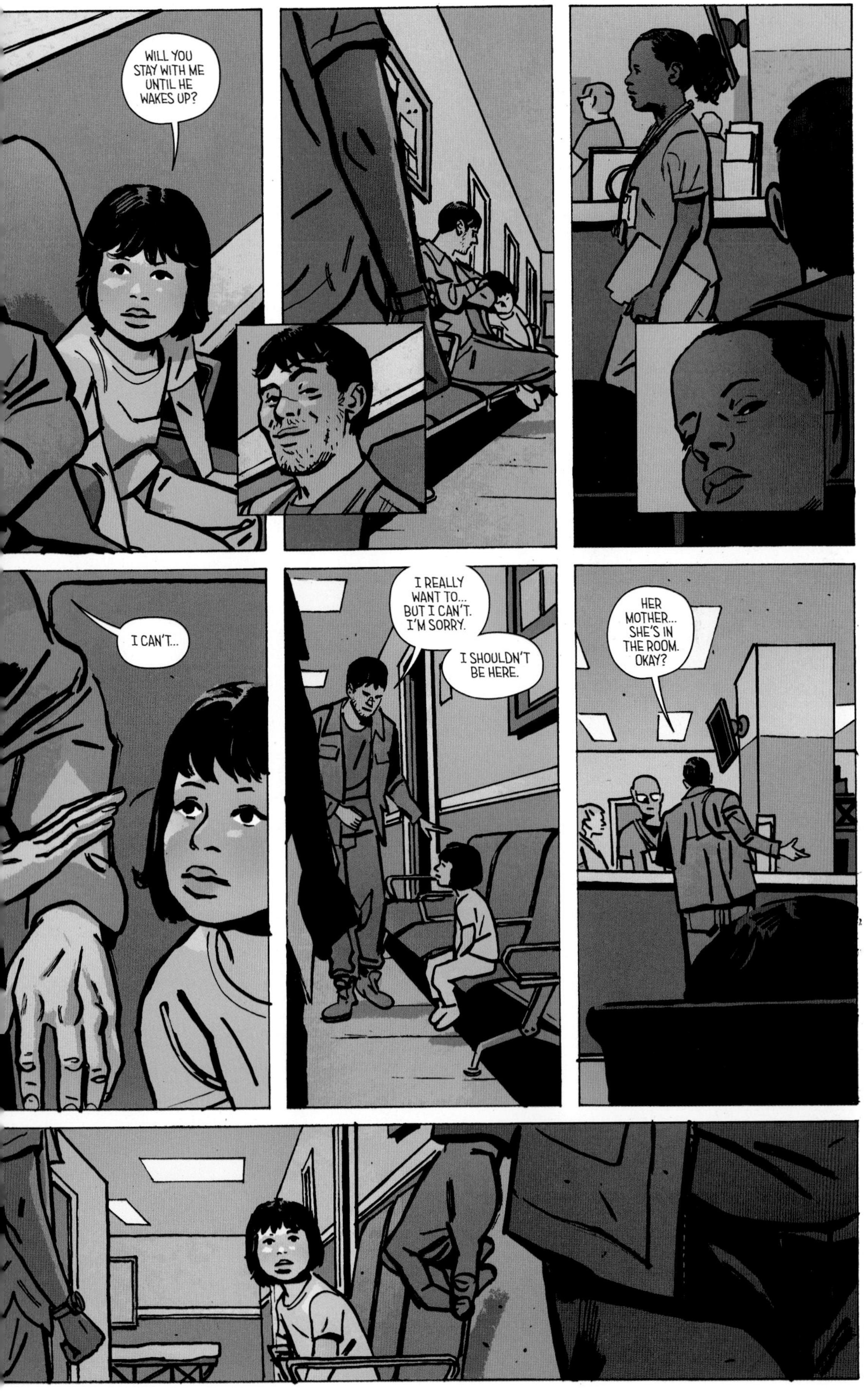
WILL YOU STAY WITH ME UNTIL HE WAKES UP?
I CAN'T...
I REALLY WANT TO... BUT I CAN'T. I'M SORRY.
I SHOULDN'T BE HERE.
HER MOTHER... SHE'S IN THE ROOM. OKAY?

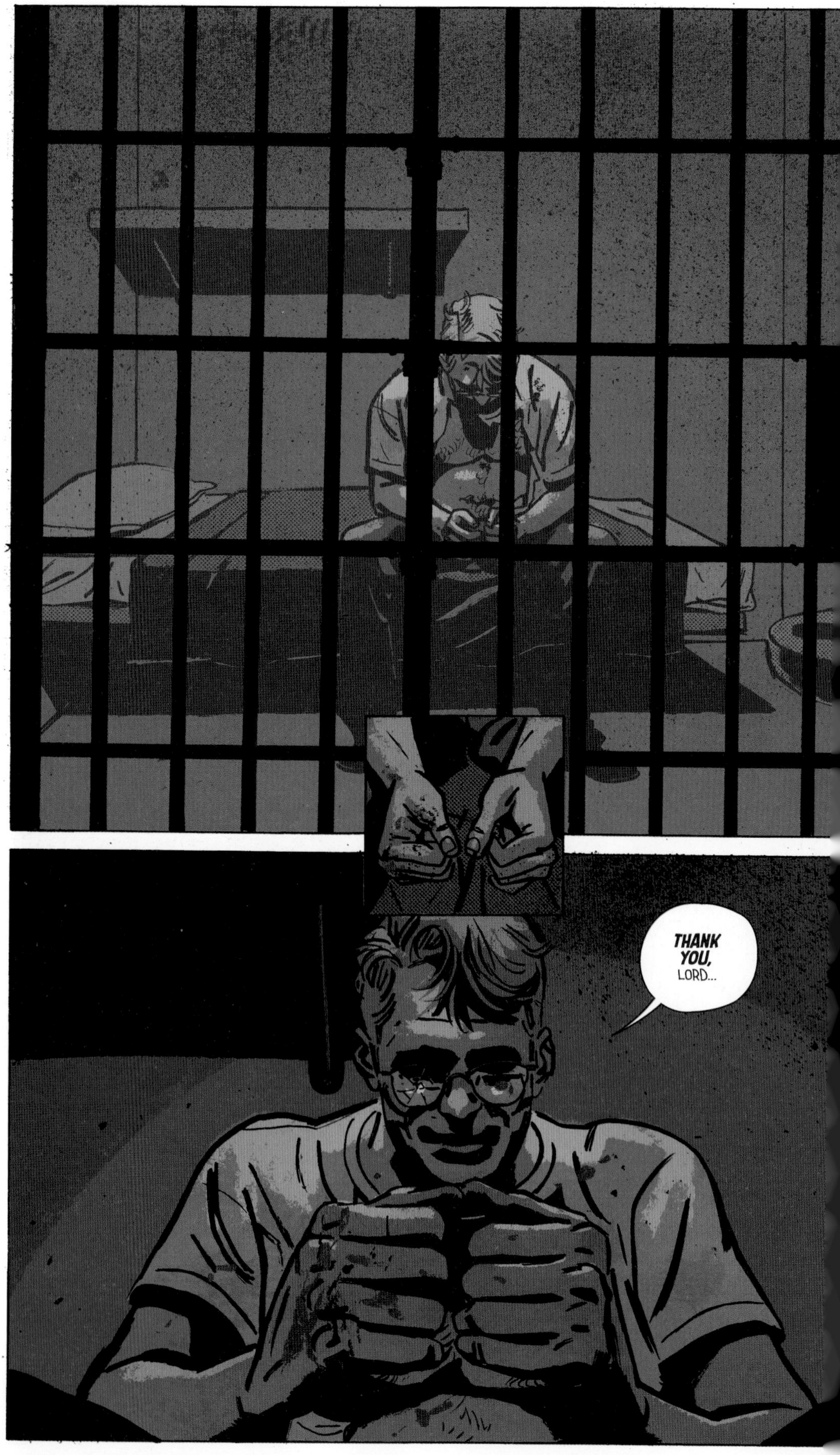
THANK YOU, LORD...

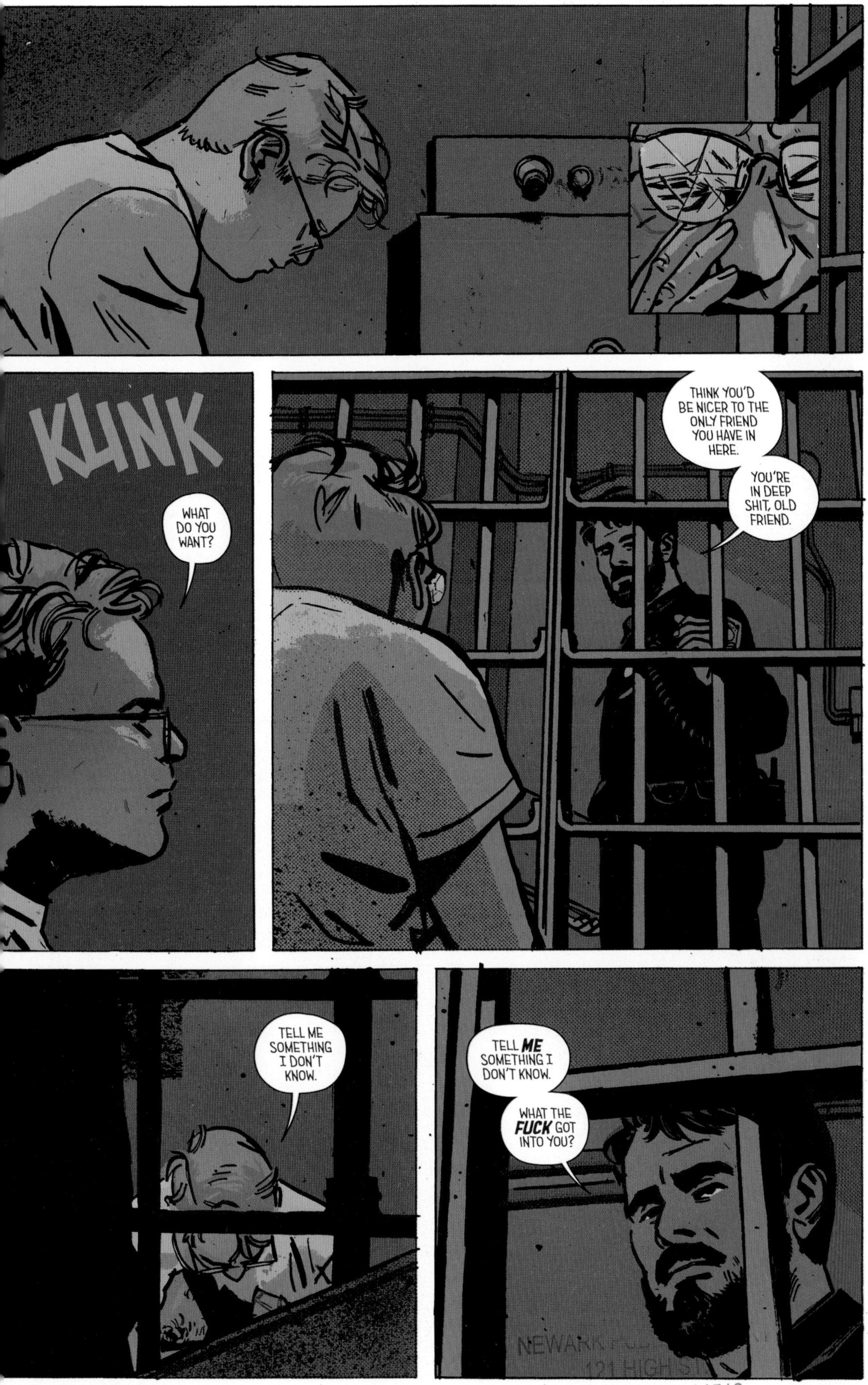
KLUNK
WHAT DO YOU WANT?
THINK YOU'D BE NICER TO THE ONLY FRIEND YOU HAVE IN HERE.
YOU'RE IN DEEP SHIT, OLD FRIEND.
TELL ME SOMETHING I DON'T KNOW.
TELL ***ME*** SOMETHING I DON'T KNOW.
WHAT THE ***FUCK*** GOT INTO YOU?

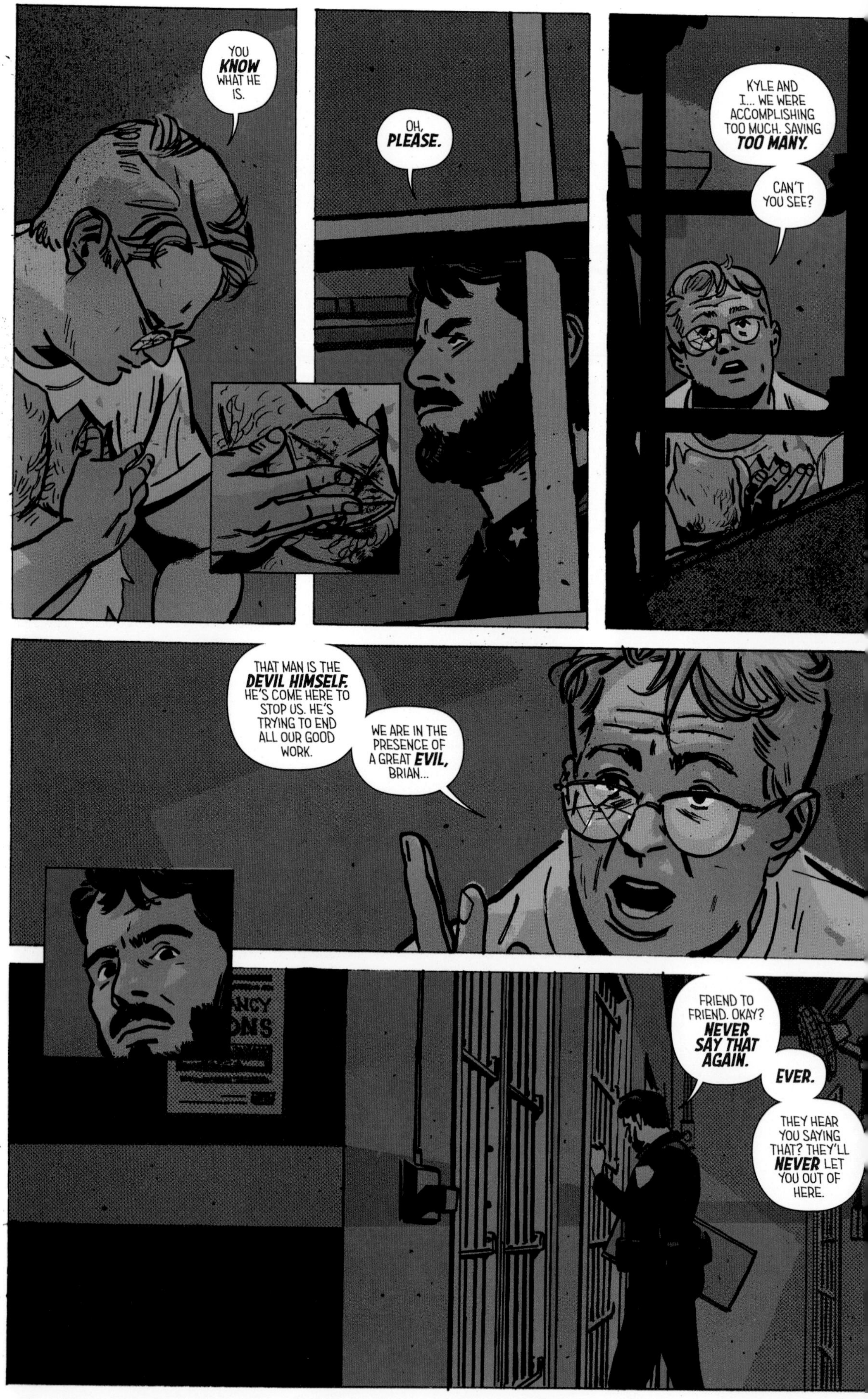

YOU **KNOW** WHAT HE IS.
OH, **PLEASE.**
KYLE AND I... WE WERE ACCOMPLISHING TOO MUCH. SAVING **TOO MANY.**
CAN'T YOU SEE?
THAT MAN IS THE **DEVIL HIMSELF.** HE'S COME HERE TO STOP US. HE'S TRYING TO END ALL OUR GOOD WORK.
WE ARE IN THE PRESENCE OF A GREAT **EVIL,** BRIAN...
FRIEND TO FRIEND. OKAY? **NEVER SAY THAT AGAIN.**
EVER.
THEY HEAR YOU SAYING THAT? THEY'LL **NEVER** LET YOU OUT OF HERE.

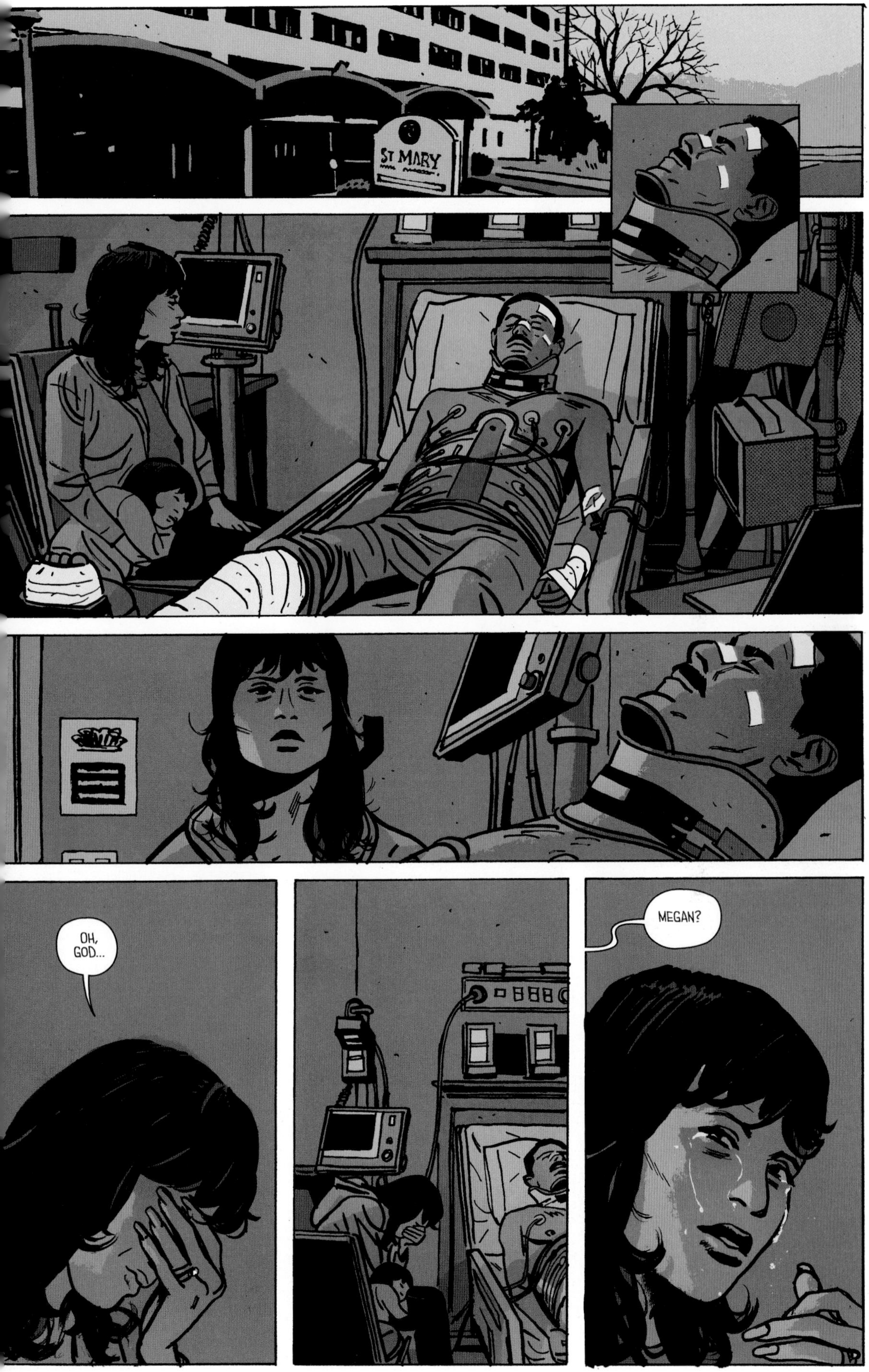
ST MARY
OH, GOD...
MEGAN?

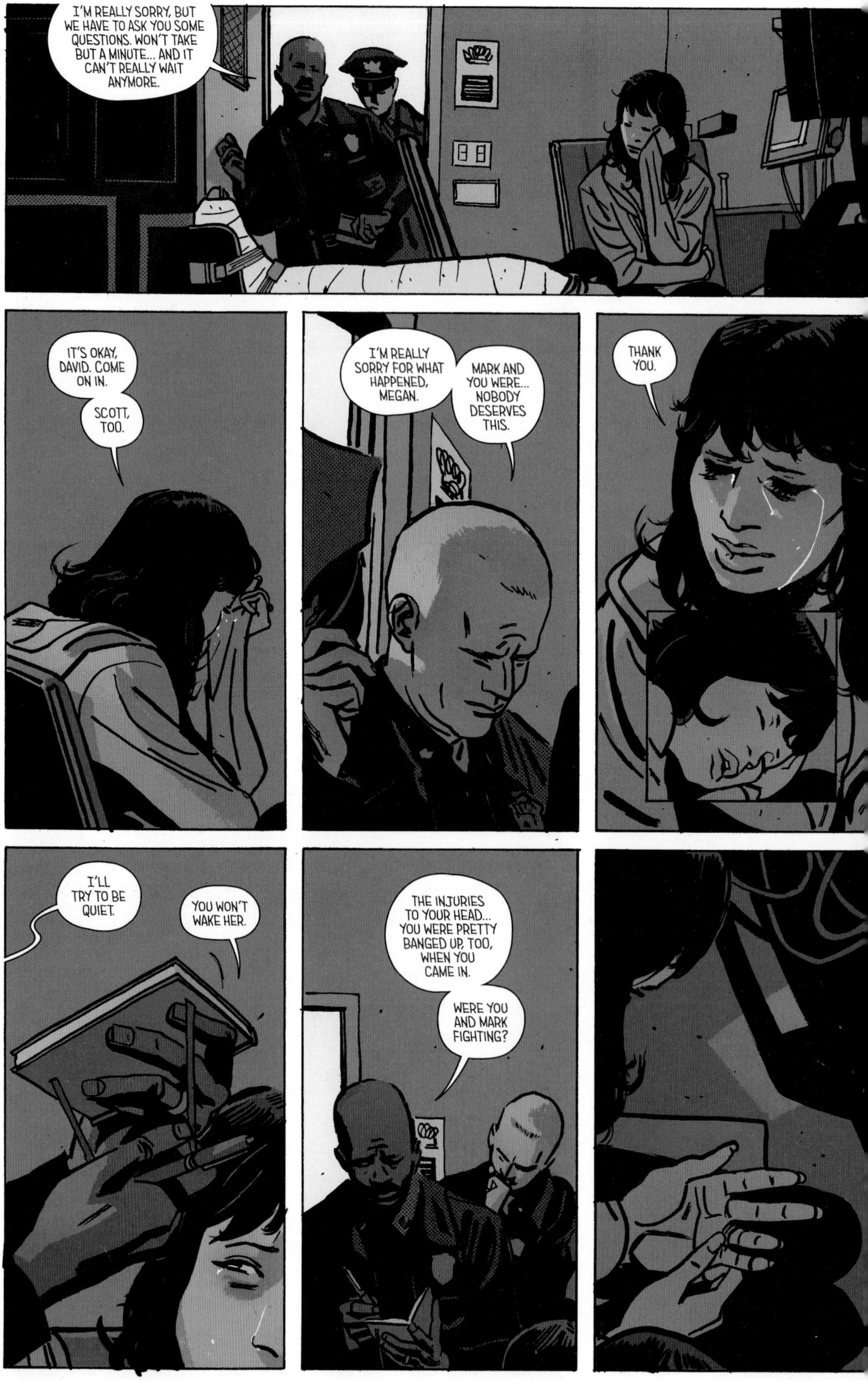
I'M REALLY SORRY, BUT WE HAVE TO ASK YOU SOME QUESTIONS. WON'T TAKE BUT A MINUTE... AND IT CAN'T REALLY WAIT ANYMORE.
IT'S OKAY, DAVID. COME ON IN.
SCOTT, TOO.
I'M REALLY SORRY FOR WHAT HAPPENED, MEGAN.
MARK AND YOU WERE... NOBODY DESERVES THIS.
THANK YOU.
I'LL TRY TO BE QUIET.
YOU WON'T WAKE HER.
THE INJURIES TO YOUR HEAD... YOU WERE PRETTY BANGED UP, TOO, WHEN YOU CAME IN.
WERE YOU AND MARK FIGHTING?

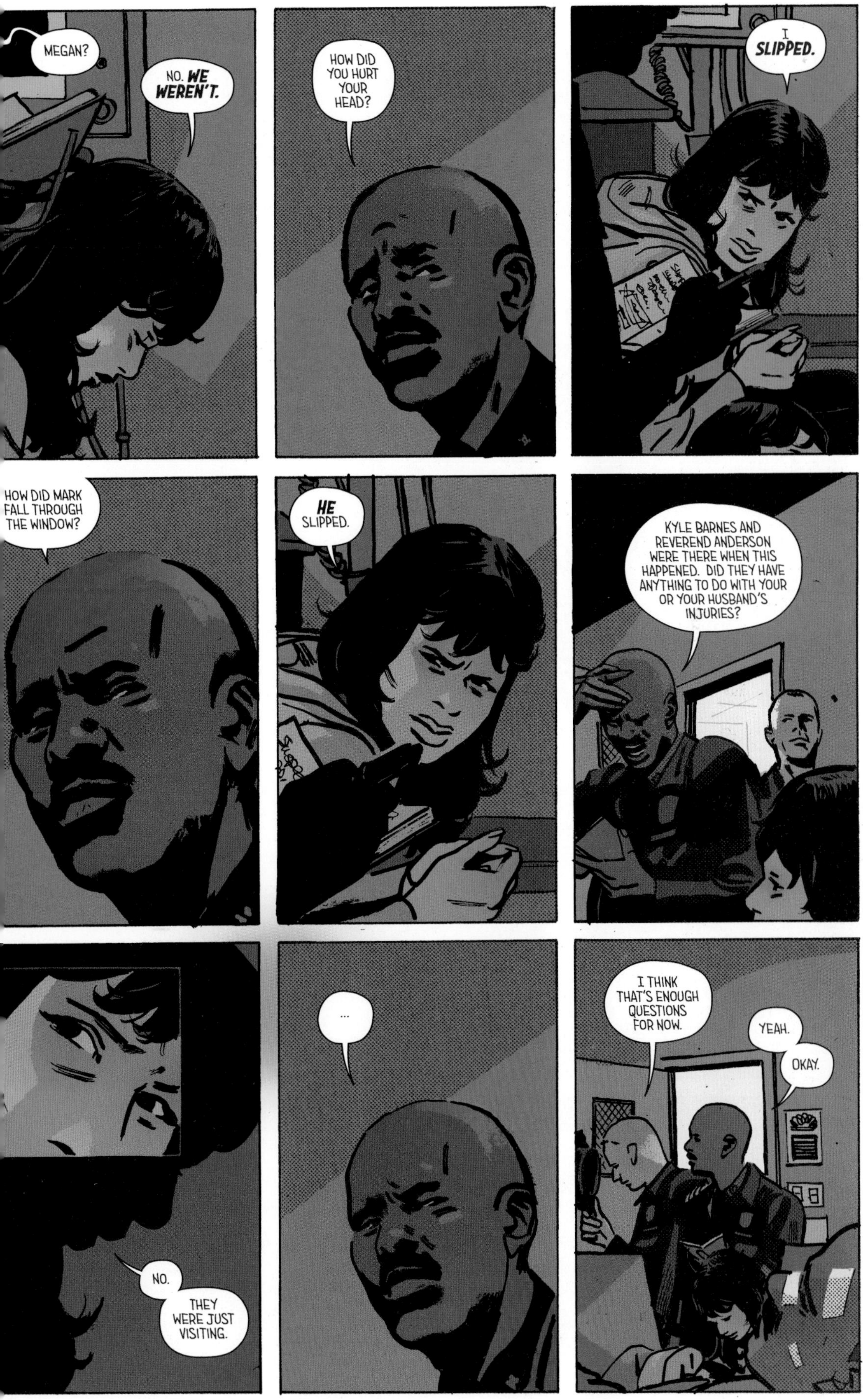
MEGAN?
NO. **WE WEREN'T.**
HOW DID YOU HURT YOUR HEAD?
I **SLIPPED.**
HOW DID MARK FALL THROUGH THE WINDOW?
HE SLIPPED.
KYLE BARNES AND REVEREND ANDERSON WERE THERE WHEN THIS HAPPENED. DID THEY HAVE ANYTHING TO DO WITH YOUR OR YOUR HUSBAND'S INJURIES?
NO.
THEY WERE JUST VISITING.
...
I THINK THAT'S ENOUGH QUESTIONS FOR NOW.
YEAH.
OKAY.

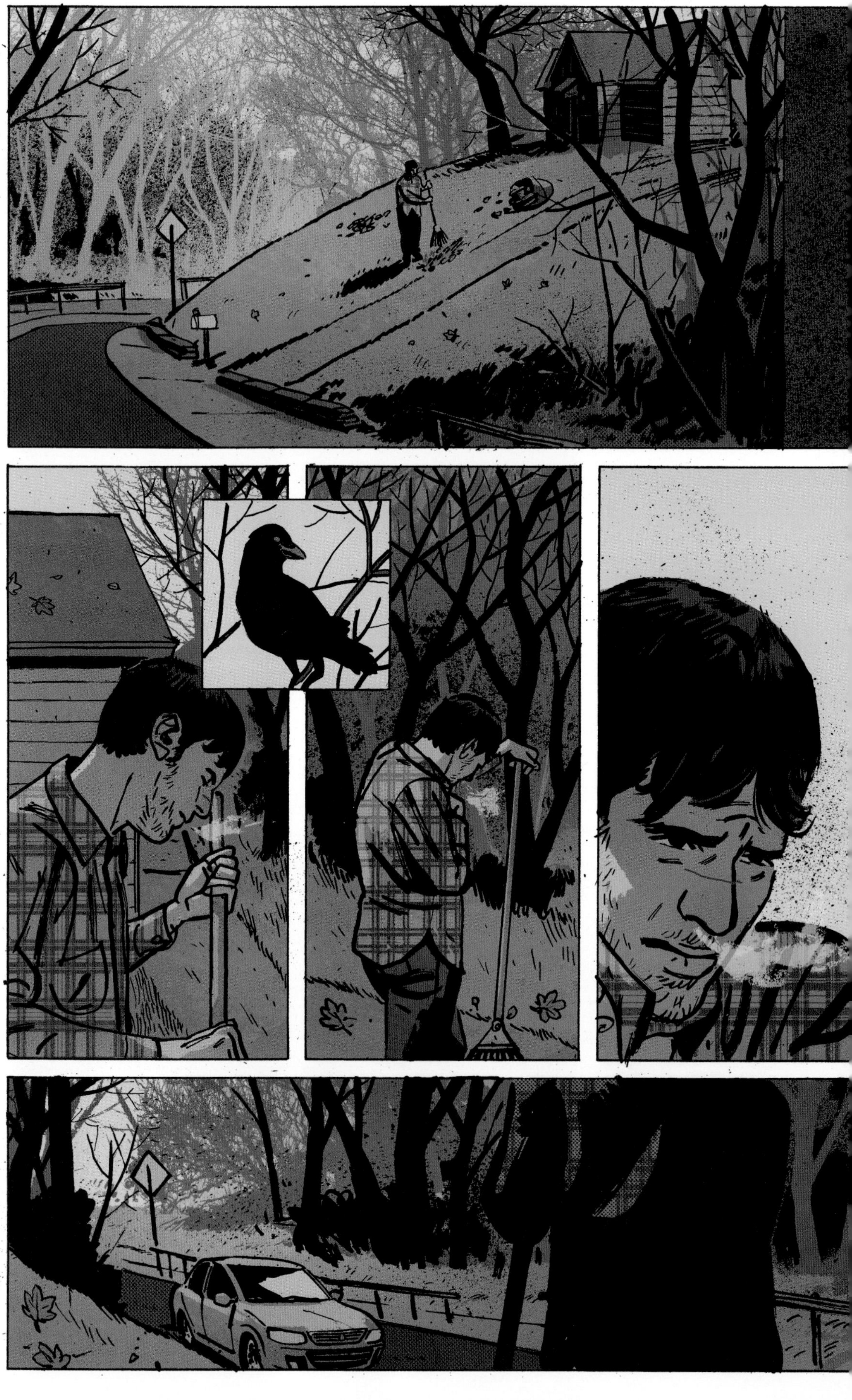

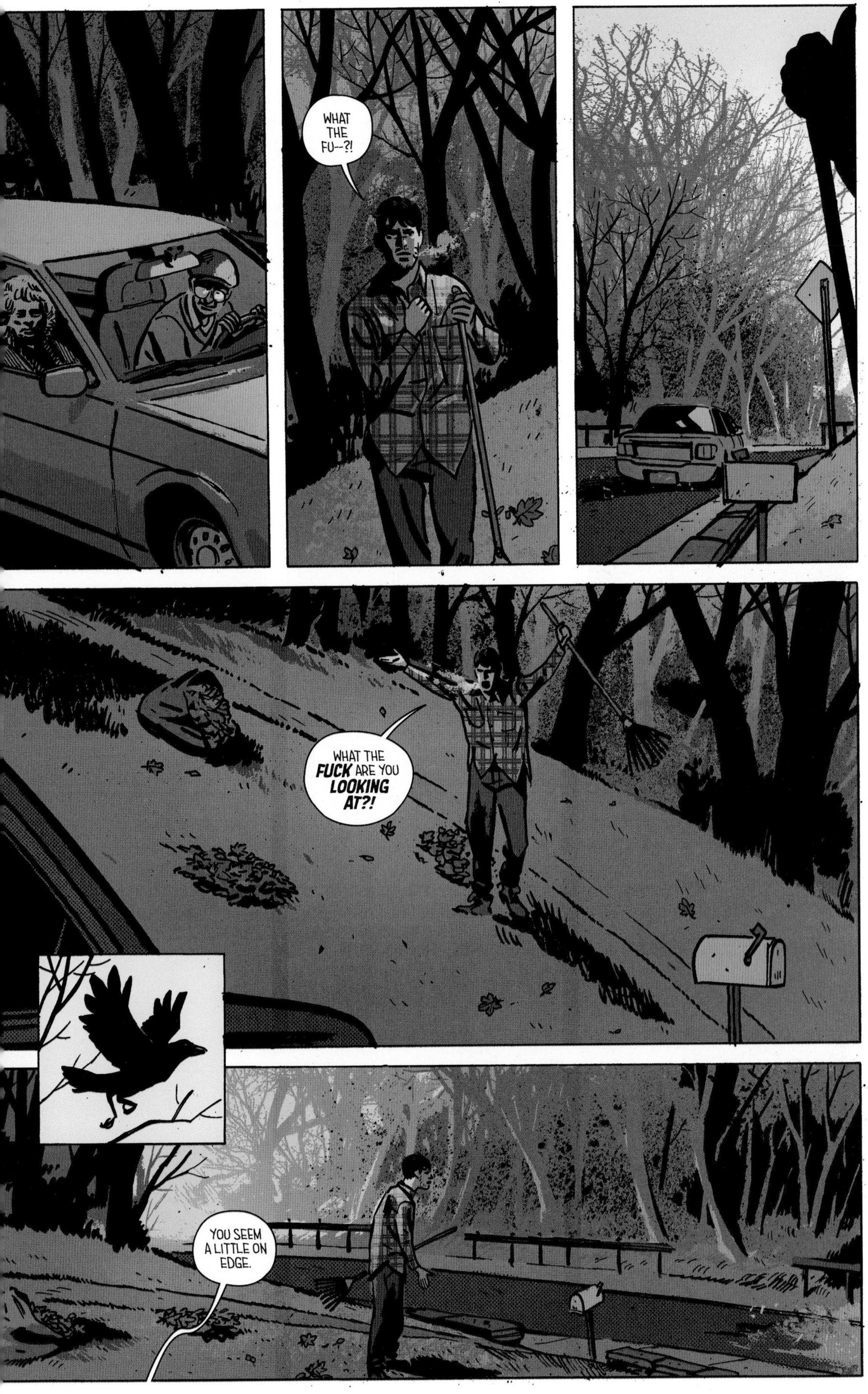
WHAT THE FU--?!
WHAT THE FUCK ARE YOU LOOKING AT?!
YOU SEEM A LITTLE ON EDGE.

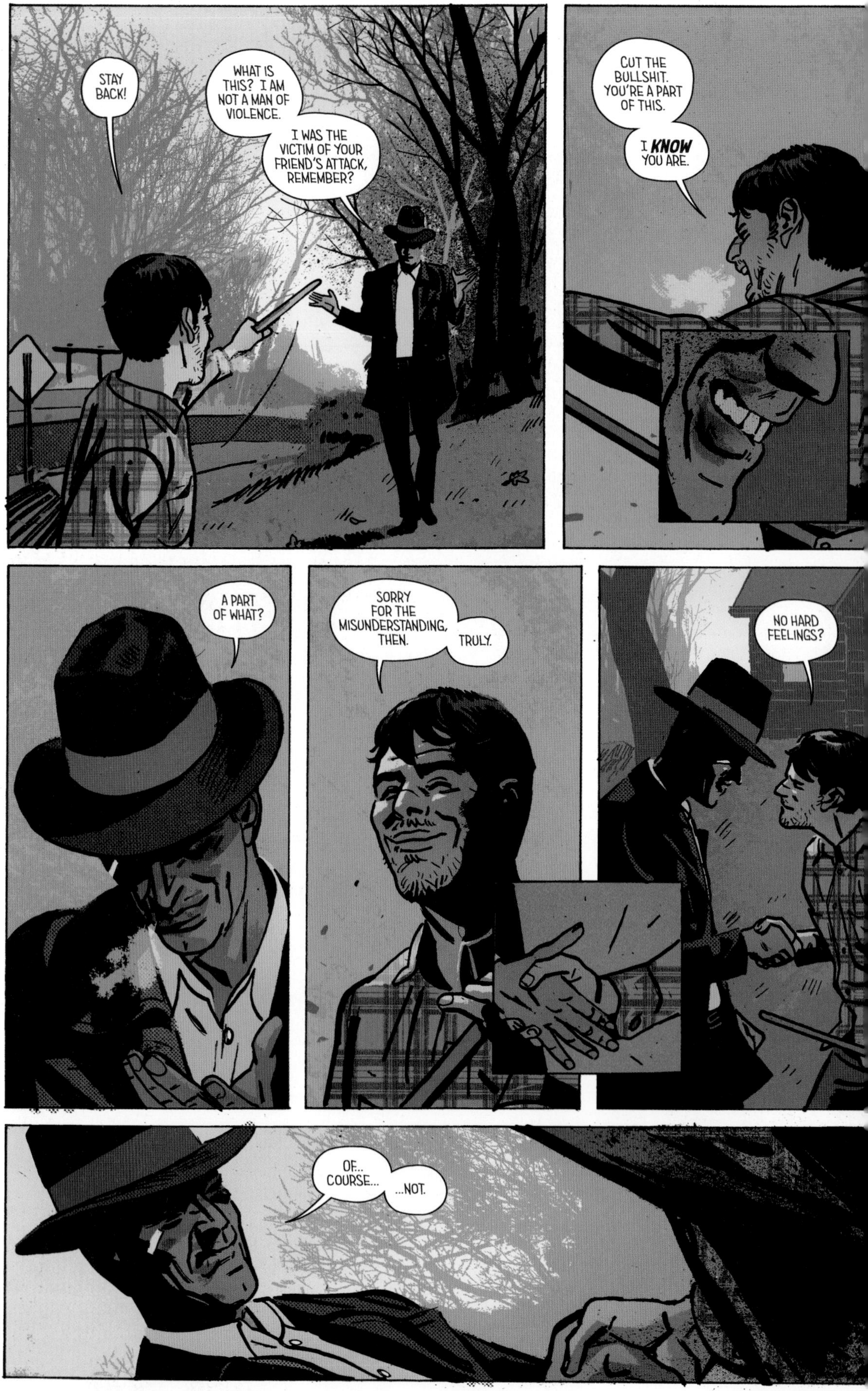
STAY BACK!
WHAT IS THIS? I AM NOT A MAN OF VIOLENCE.
I WAS THE VICTIM OF YOUR FRIEND'S ATTACK, REMEMBER?
CUT THE BULLSHIT. YOU'RE A PART OF THIS.
I **KNOW** YOU ARE.
A PART OF WHAT?
SORRY FOR THE MISUNDERSTANDING, THEN.
TRULY.
NO HARD FEELINGS?
OF.. COURSE...
...NOT.

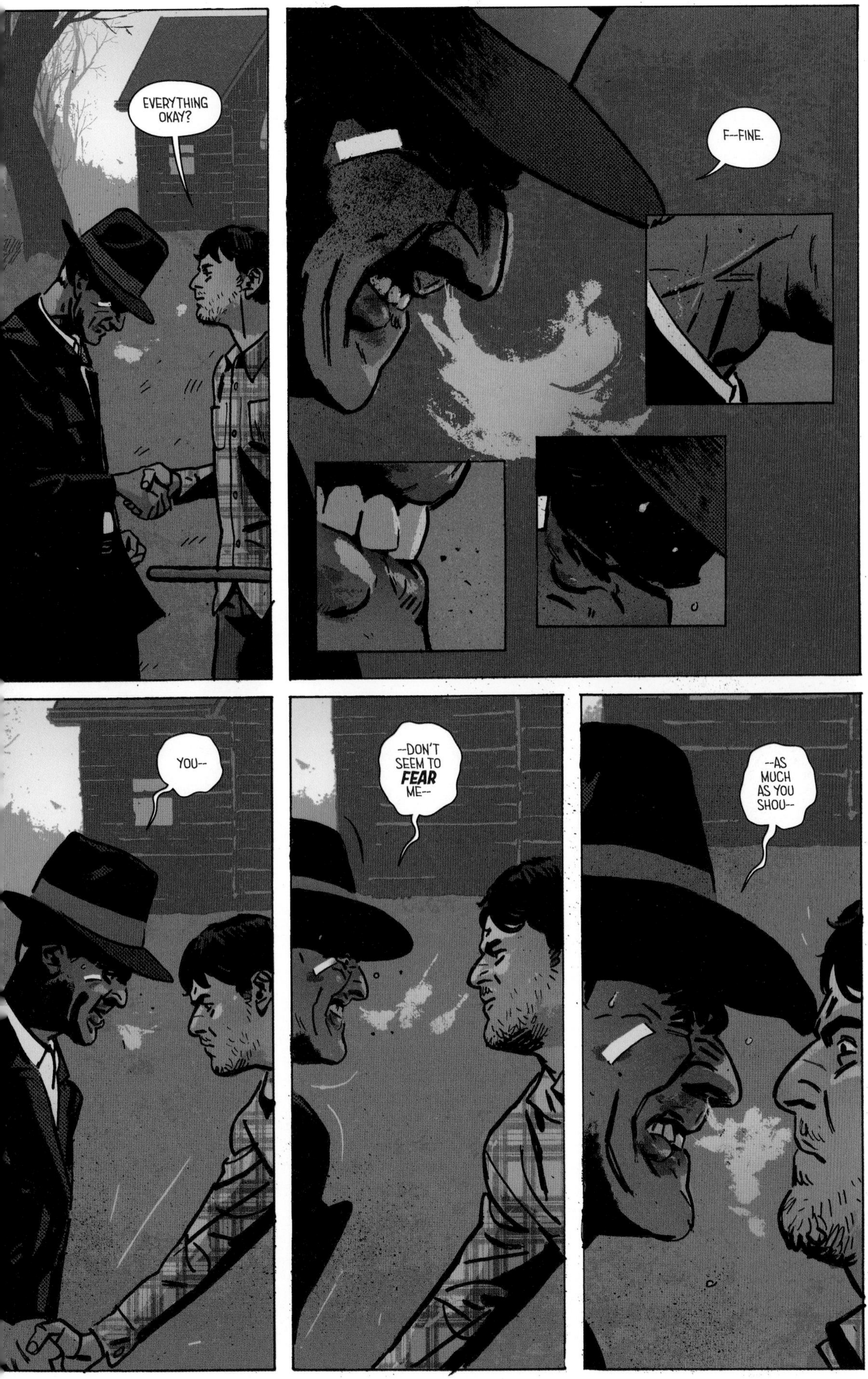
EVERYTHING OKAY?
F--FINE.
YOU--
--DON'T SEEM TO FEAR ME--
--AS MUCH AS YOU SHOU--

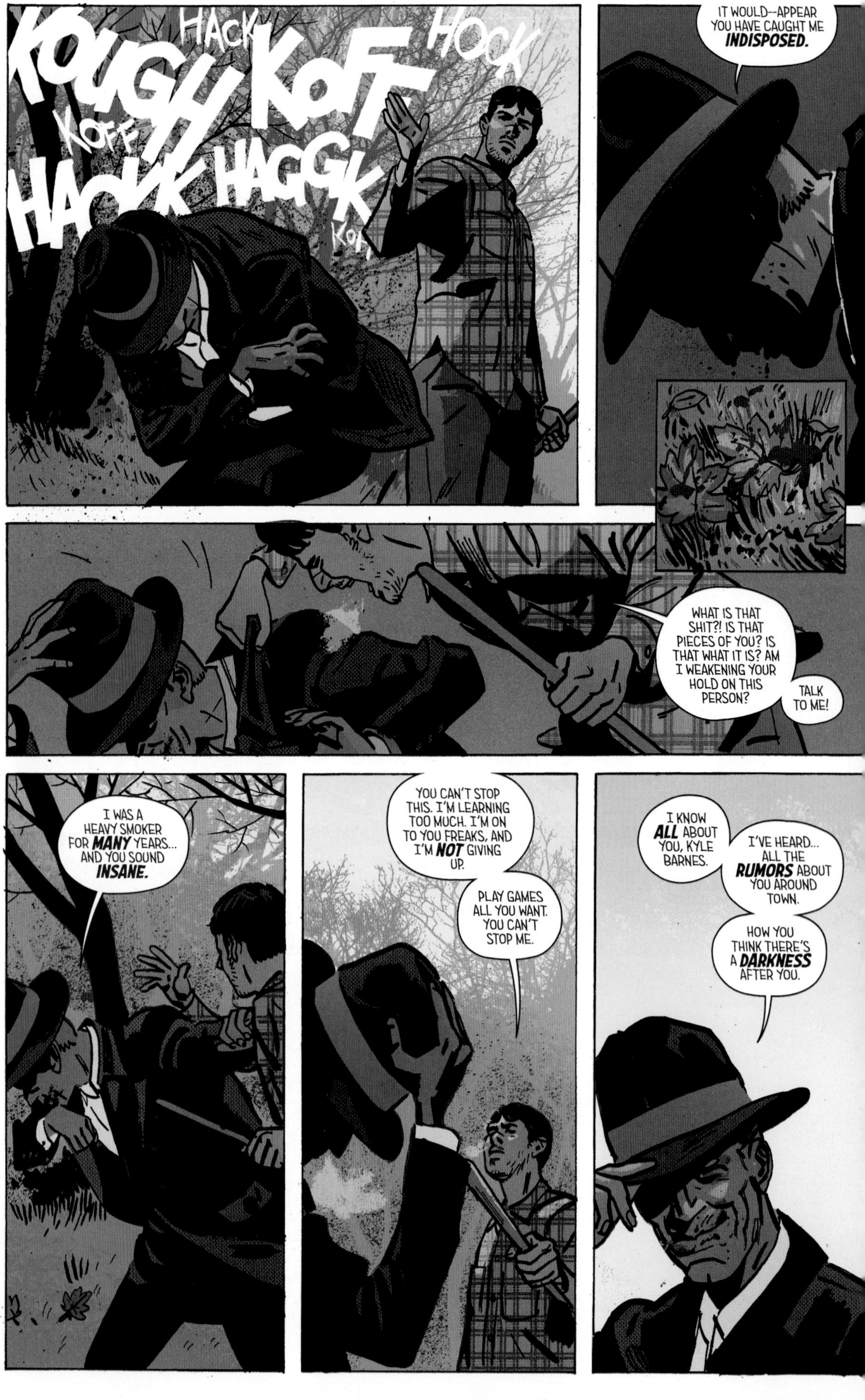
KOUGH KOFF HACK HOCK
KOFF
HACKK HAGGK
KOH
IT WOULD--APPEAR YOU HAVE CAUGHT ME INDISPOSED.
WHAT IS THAT SHIT?! IS THAT PIECES OF YOU? IS THAT WHAT IT IS? AM I WEAKENING YOUR HOLD ON THIS PERSON?
TALK TO ME!
I WAS A HEAVY SMOKER FOR MANY YEARS... AND YOU SOUND INSANE.
YOU CAN'T STOP THIS. I'M LEARNING TOO MUCH. I'M ON TO YOU FREAKS, AND I'M NOT GIVING UP.
PLAY GAMES ALL YOU WANT. YOU CAN'T STOP ME.
I KNOW ALL ABOUT YOU, KYLE BARNES.
I'VE HEARD... ALL THE RUMORS ABOUT YOU AROUND TOWN.
HOW YOU THINK THERE'S A DARKNESS AFTER YOU.

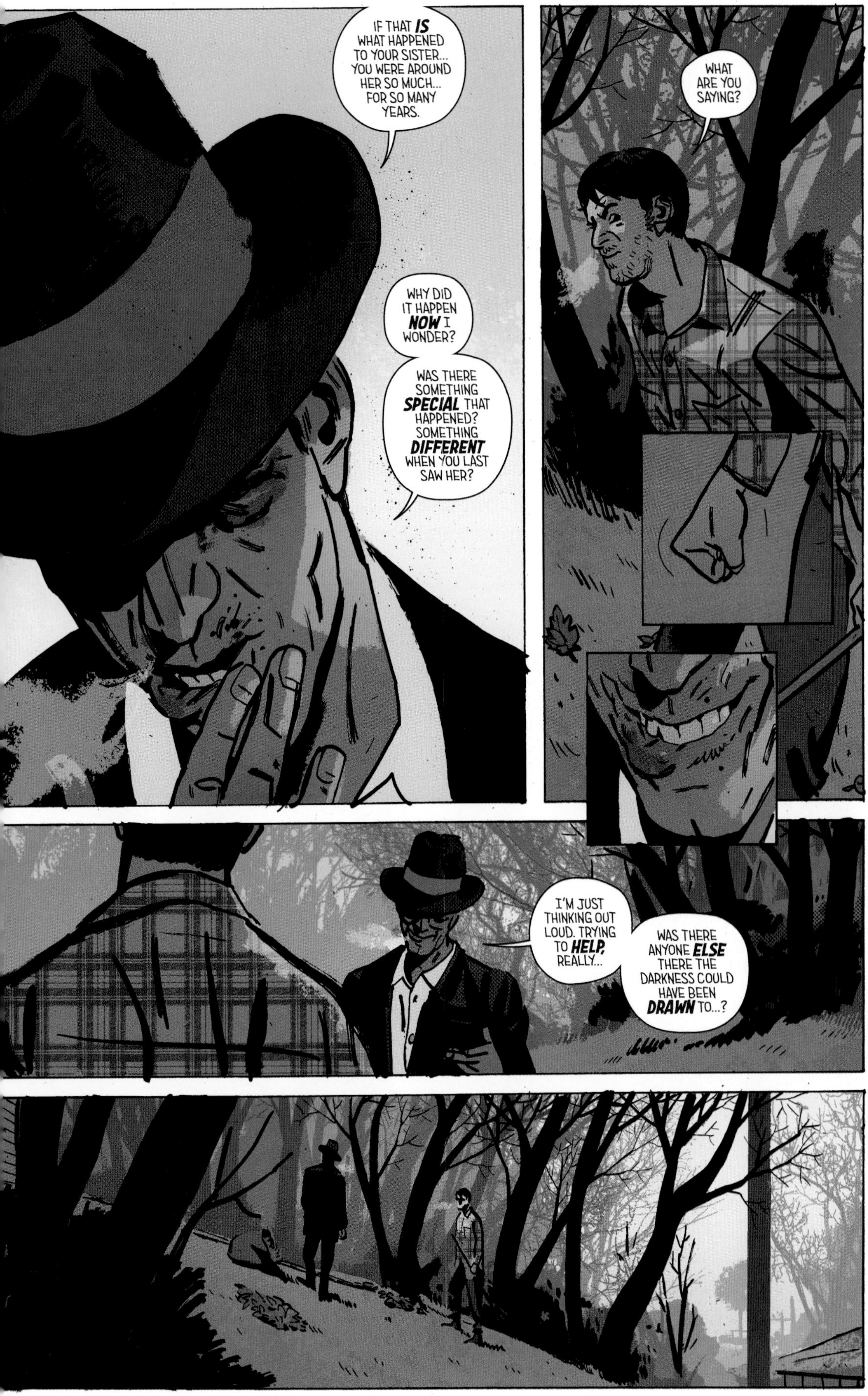

IF THAT IS WHAT HAPPENED TO YOUR SISTER... YOU WERE AROUND HER SO MUCH... FOR SO MANY YEARS.
WHY DID IT HAPPEN NOW I WONDER?
WAS THERE SOMETHING SPECIAL THAT HAPPENED? SOMETHING DIFFERENT WHEN YOU LAST SAW HER?
WHAT ARE YOU SAYING?
I'M JUST THINKING OUT LOUD. TRYING TO HELP, REALLY...
WAS THERE ANYONE ELSE THERE THE DARKNESS COULD HAVE BEEN DRAWN TO...?

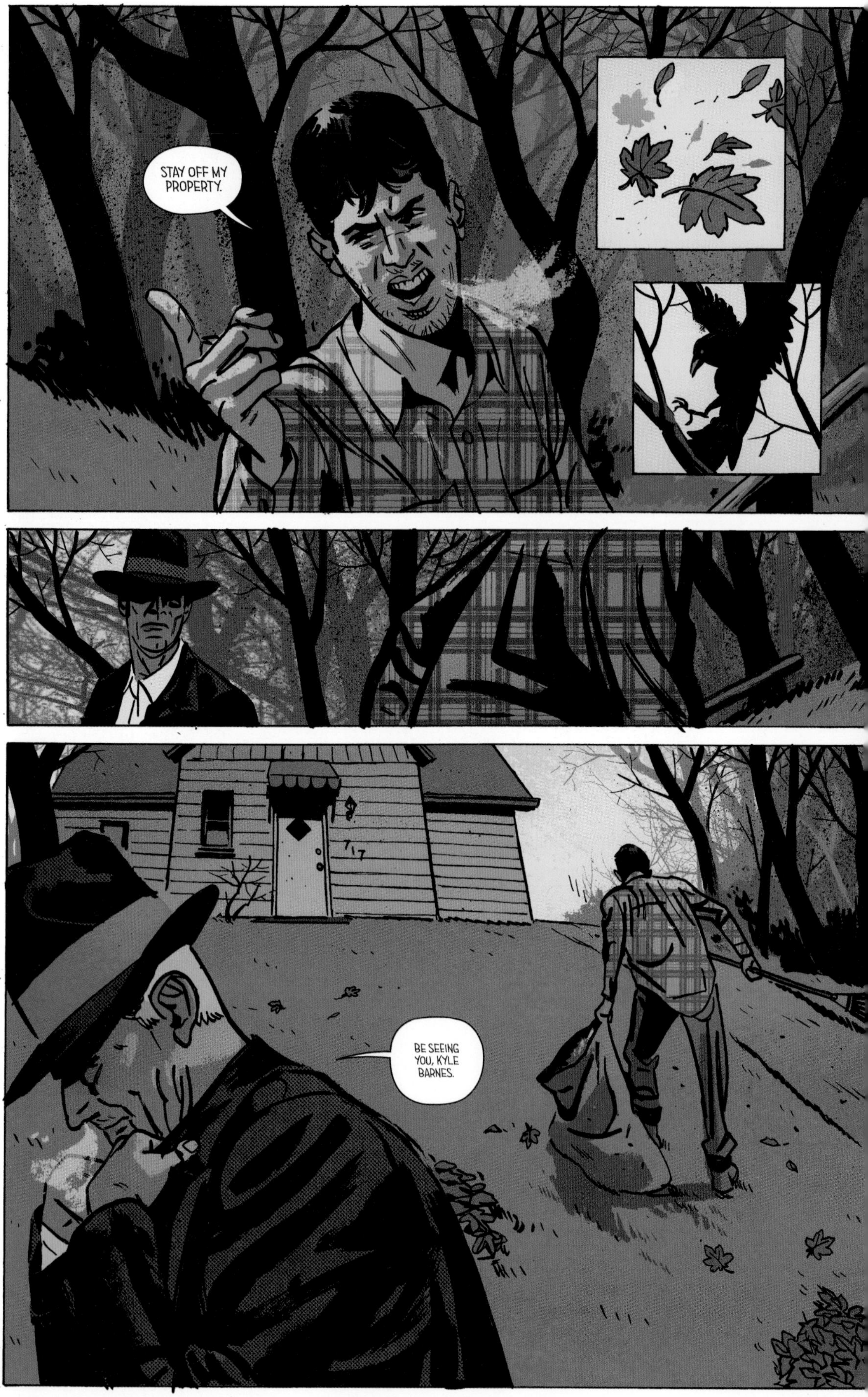
STAY OFF MY PROPERTY.
BE SEEING YOU, KYLE BARNES.

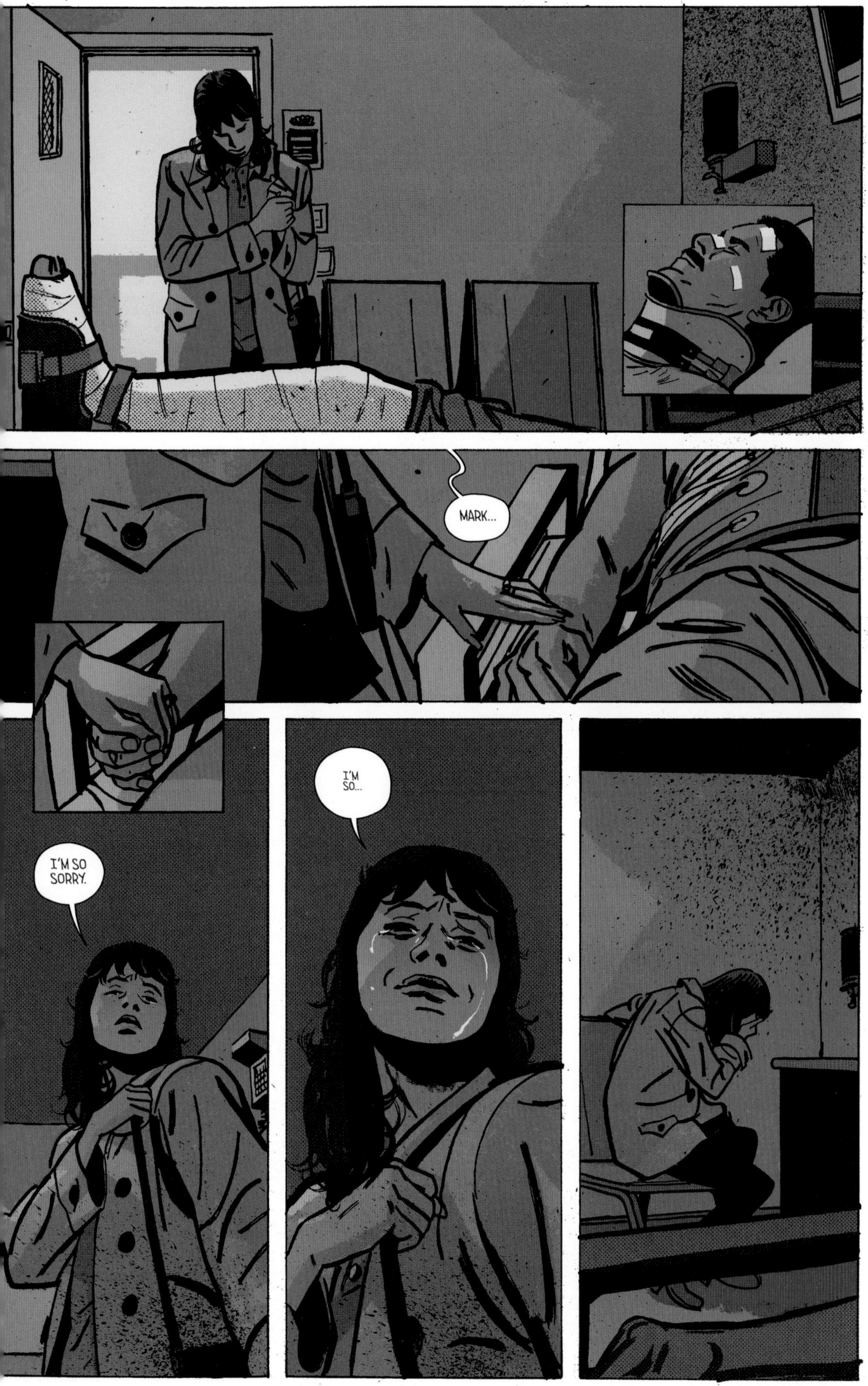
MARK...
I'M SO SORRY.
I'M SO...

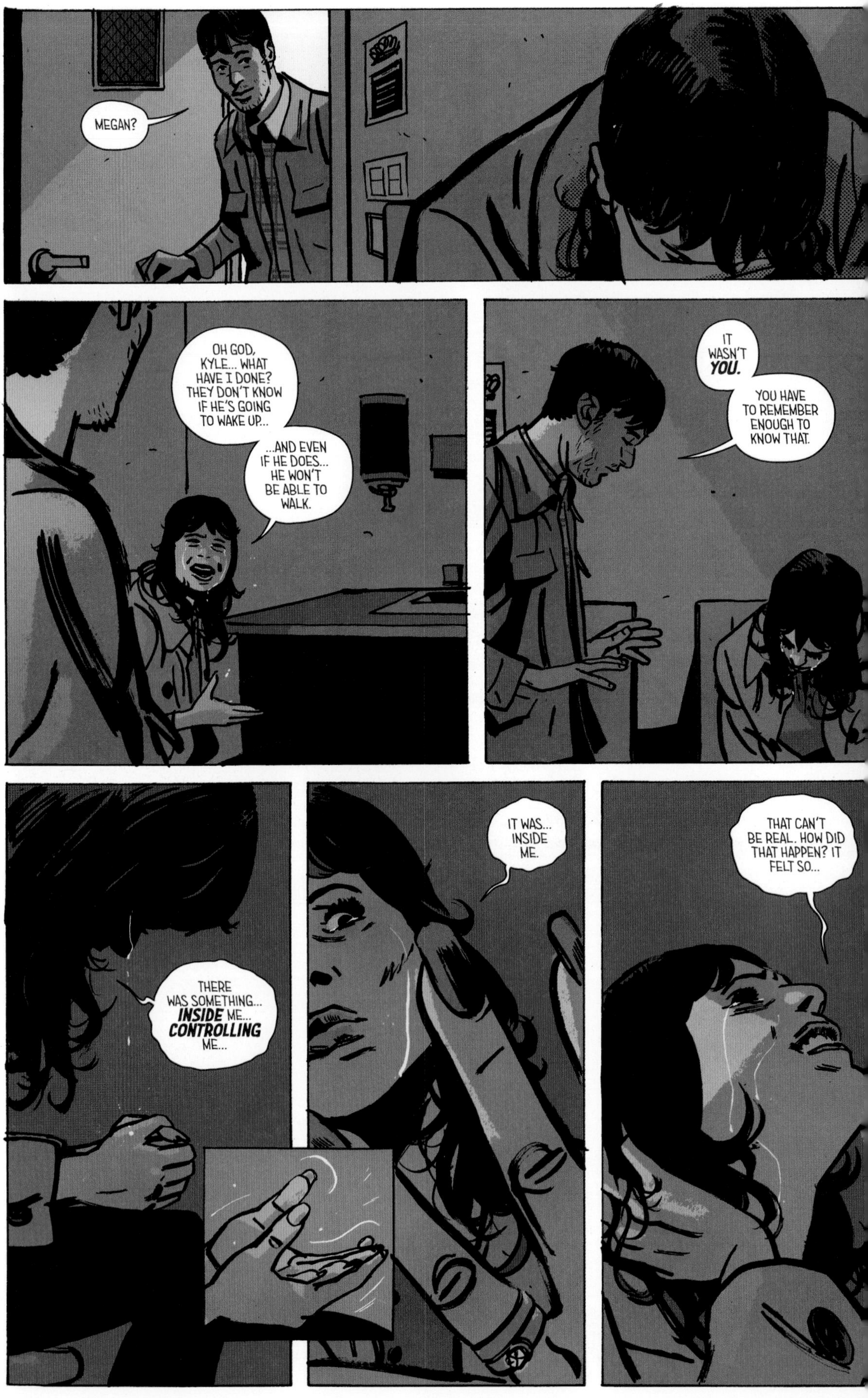
MEGAN?
OH GOD, KYLE... WHAT HAVE I DONE? THEY DON'T KNOW IF HE'S GOING TO WAKE UP...
...AND EVEN IF HE DOES... HE WON'T BE ABLE TO WALK.
IT WASN'T **YOU.**
YOU HAVE TO REMEMBER ENOUGH TO KNOW THAT.
THERE WAS SOMETHING... **INSIDE** ME... **CONTROLLING** ME...
IT WAS... INSIDE ME.
THAT CAN'T BE REAL. HOW DID THAT HAPPEN? IT FELT SO...

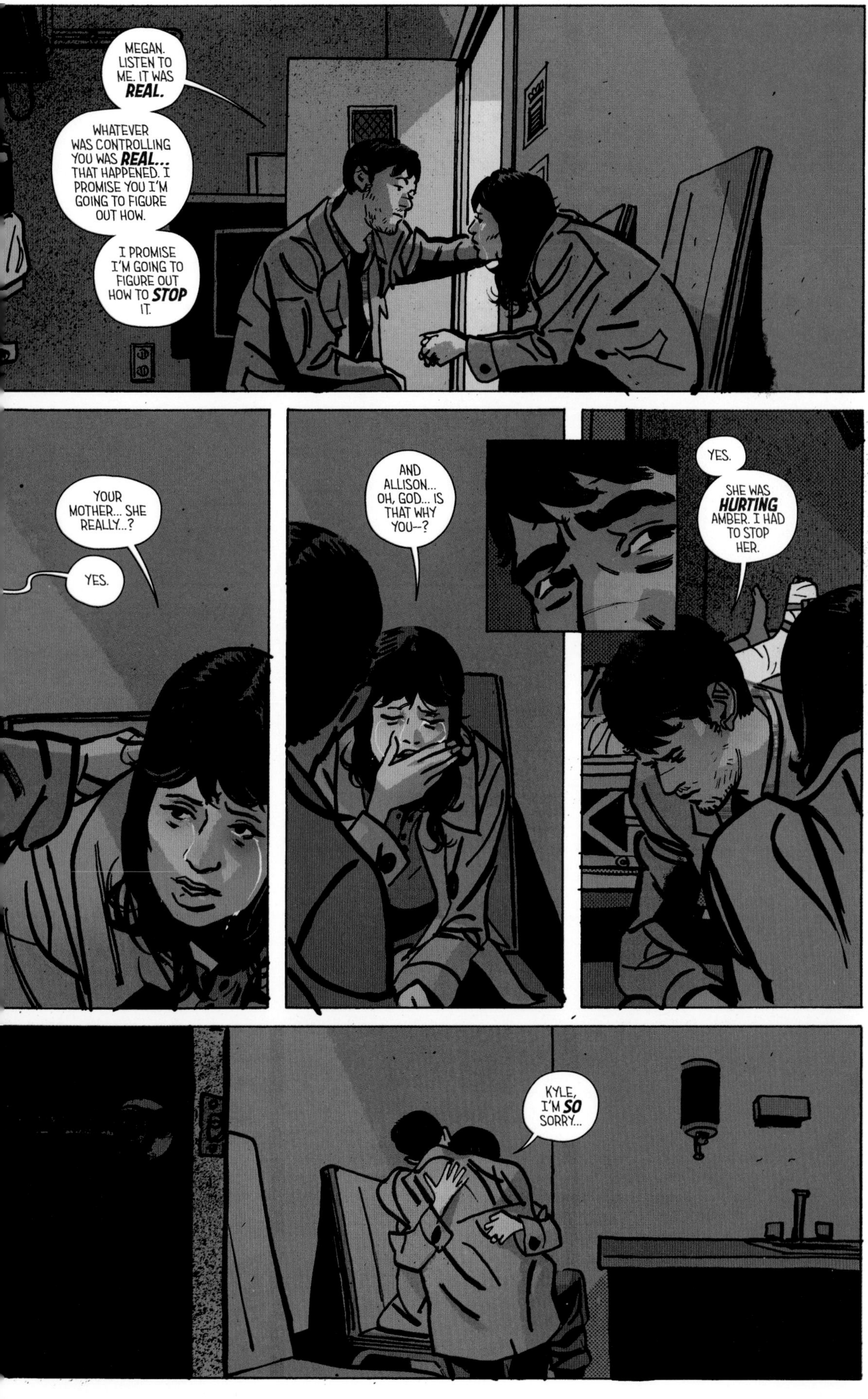
MEGAN. LISTEN TO ME. IT WAS REAL.
WHATEVER WAS CONTROLLING YOU WAS REAL... THAT HAPPENED. I PROMISE YOU I'M GOING TO FIGURE OUT HOW.
I PROMISE I'M GOING TO FIGURE OUT HOW TO STOP IT.
YOUR MOTHER... SHE REALLY...?
YES.
AND ALLISON... OH, GOD... IS THAT WHY YOU--?
YES.
SHE WAS HURTING AMBER. I HAD TO STOP HER.
KYLE, I'M SO SORRY...

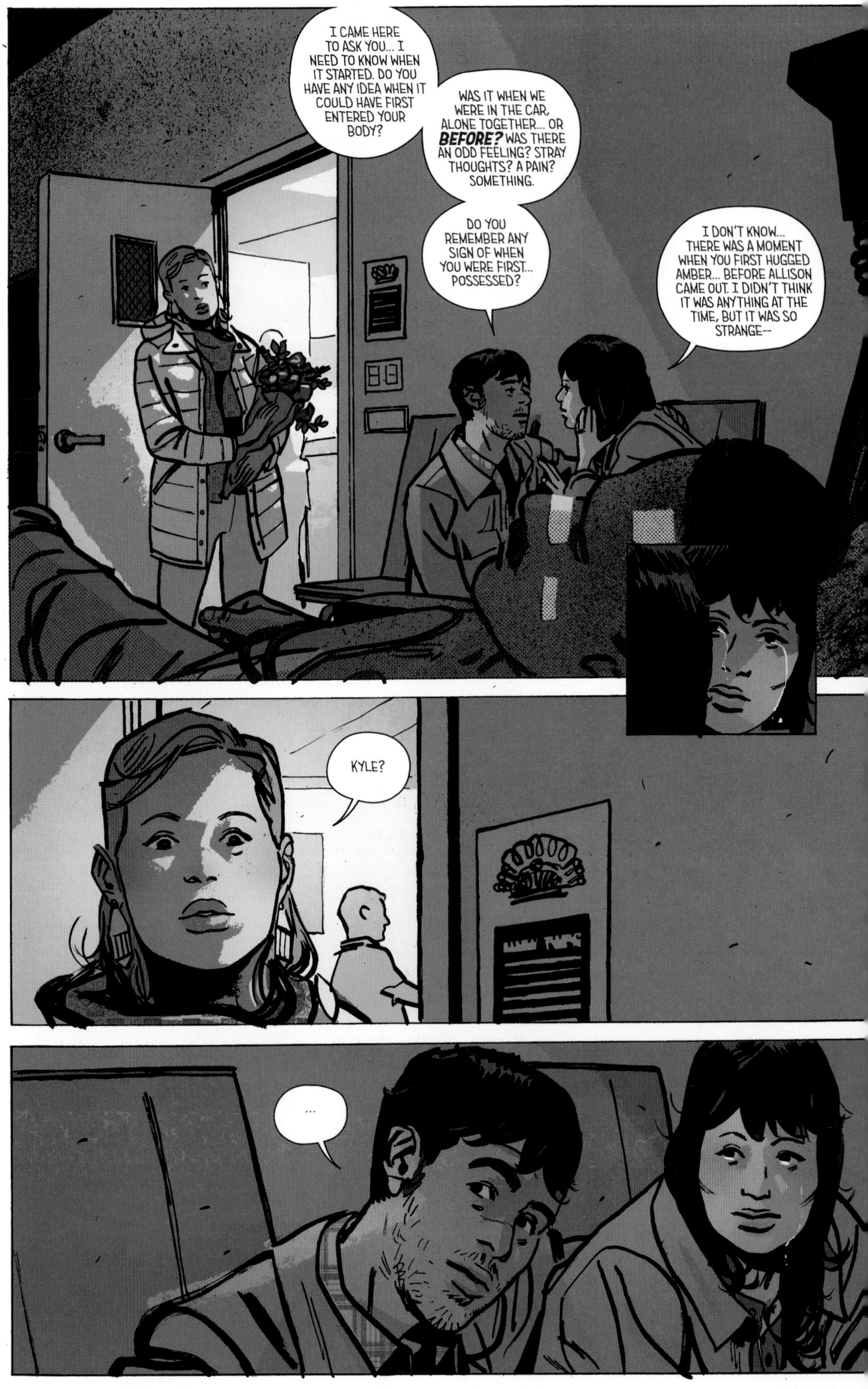
I CAME HERE TO ASK YOU... I NEED TO KNOW WHEN IT STARTED. DO YOU HAVE ANY IDEA WHEN IT COULD HAVE FIRST ENTERED YOUR BODY?
WAS IT WHEN WE WERE IN THE CAR, ALONE TOGETHER... OR **BEFORE?** WAS THERE AN ODD FEELING? STRAY THOUGHTS? A PAIN? SOMETHING.
DO YOU REMEMBER ANY SIGN OF WHEN YOU WERE FIRST... POSSESSED?
I DON'T KNOW... THERE WAS A MOMENT WHEN YOU FIRST HUGGED AMBER... BEFORE ALLISON CAME OUT. I DIDN'T THINK IT WAS ANYTHING AT THE TIME, BUT IT WAS SO STRANGE--
KYLE?
...

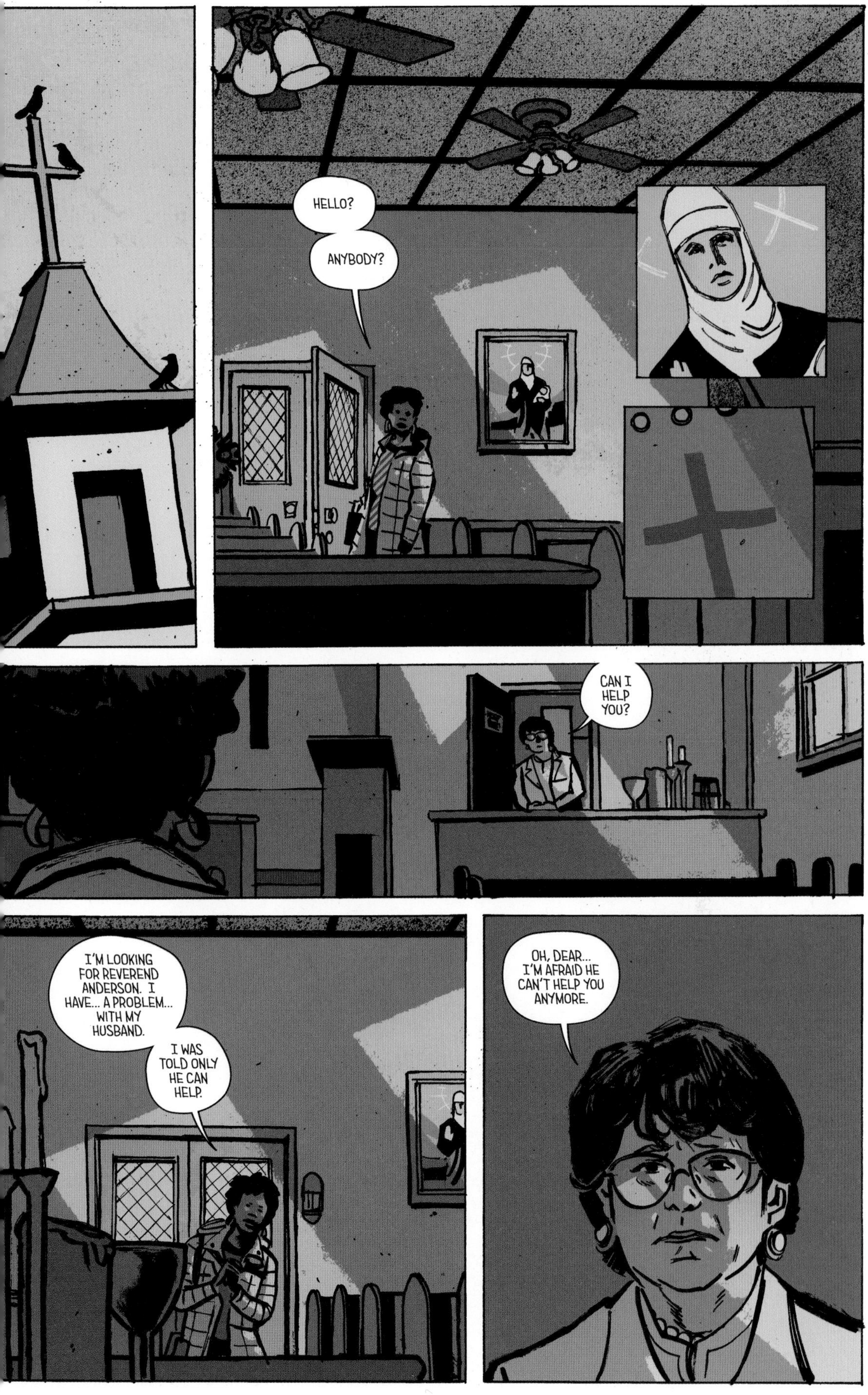
HELLO?
ANYBODY?
CAN I HELP YOU?
I'M LOOKING FOR REVEREND ANDERSON. I HAVE... A PROBLEM... WITH MY HUSBAND.
I WAS TOLD ONLY HE CAN HELP.
OH, DEAR... I'M AFRAID HE CAN'T HELP YOU ANYMORE.

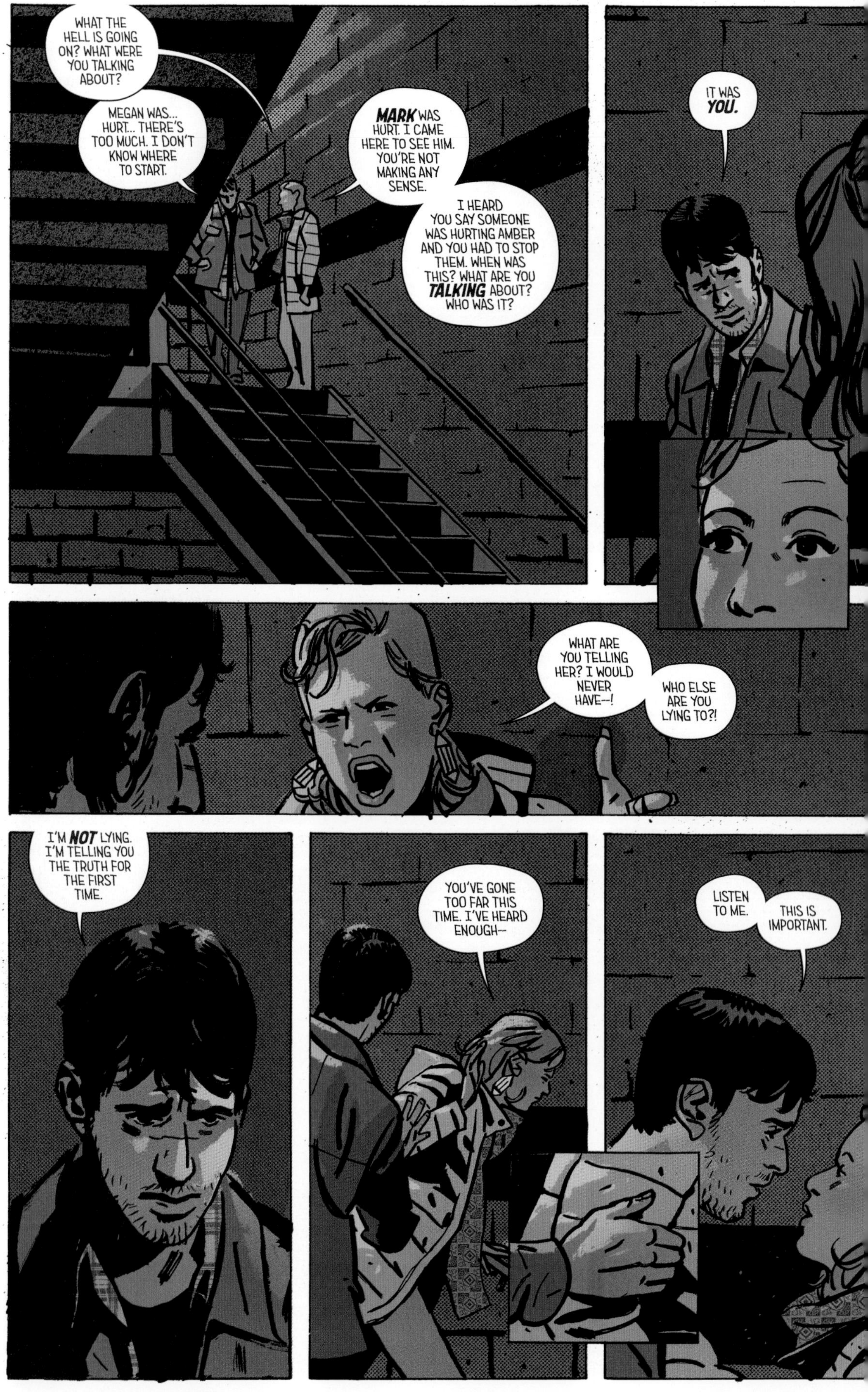
WHAT THE HELL IS GOING ON? WHAT WERE YOU TALKING ABOUT?
MEGAN WAS... HURT... THERE'S TOO MUCH. I DON'T KNOW WHERE TO START.
MARK WAS HURT. I CAME HERE TO SEE HIM. YOU'RE NOT MAKING ANY SENSE.
I HEARD YOU SAY SOMEONE WAS HURTING AMBER AND YOU HAD TO STOP THEM. WHEN WAS THIS? WHAT ARE YOU TALKING ABOUT? WHO WAS IT?
IT WAS YOU.
WHAT ARE YOU TELLING HER? I WOULD NEVER HAVE--!
WHO ELSE ARE YOU LYING TO?!
I'M NOT LYING. I'M TELLING YOU THE TRUTH FOR THE FIRST TIME.
YOU'VE GONE TOO FAR THIS TIME. I'VE HEARD ENOUGH--
LISTEN TO ME.
THIS IS IMPORTANT.

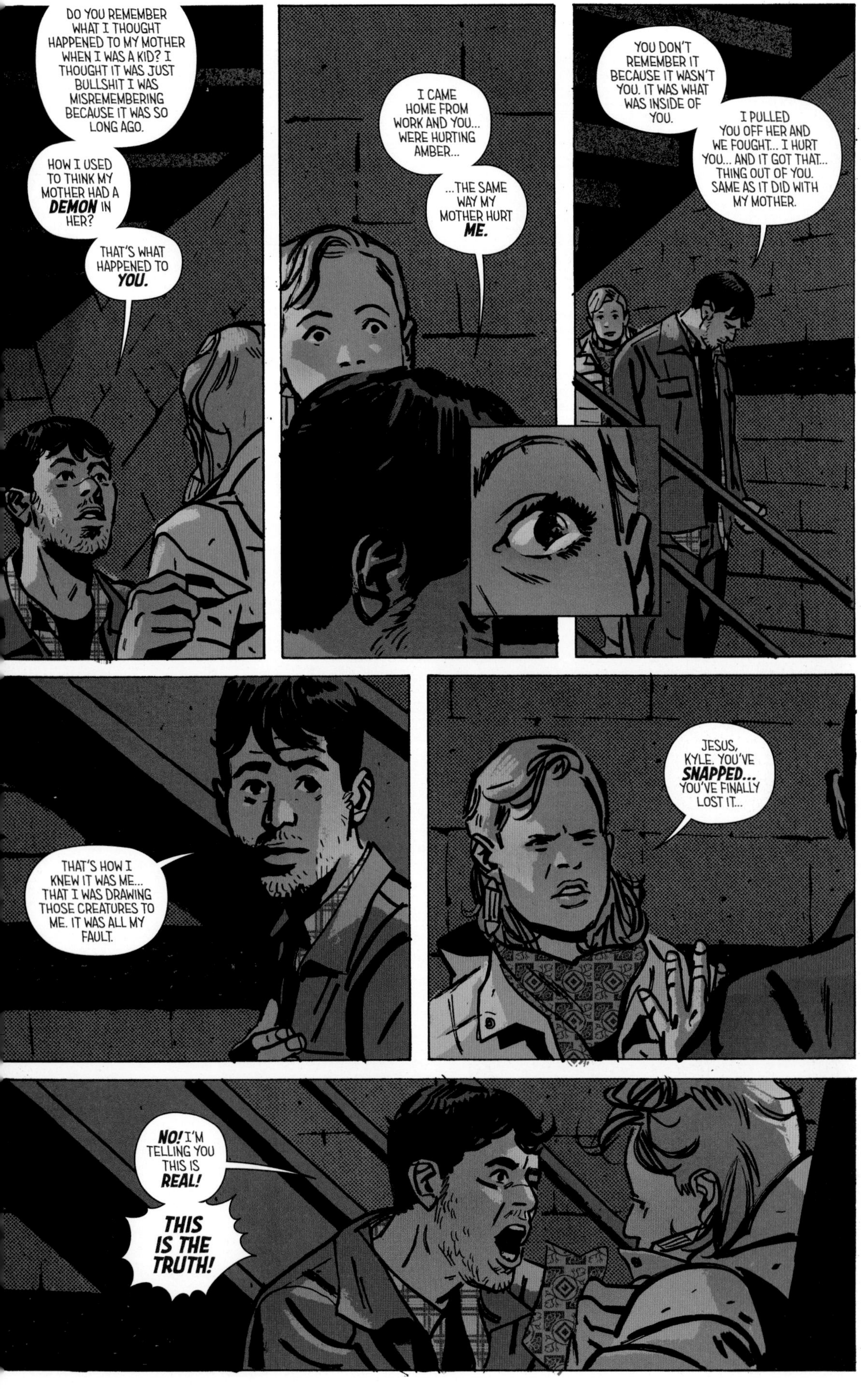
DO YOU REMEMBER WHAT I THOUGHT HAPPENED TO MY MOTHER WHEN I WAS A KID? I THOUGHT IT WAS JUST BULLSHIT I WAS MISREMEMBERING BECAUSE IT WAS SO LONG AGO.
HOW I USED TO THINK MY MOTHER HAD A DEMON IN HER?
THAT'S WHAT HAPPENED TO YOU.
I CAME HOME FROM WORK AND YOU... WERE HURTING AMBER...
...THE SAME WAY MY MOTHER HURT ME.
YOU DON'T REMEMBER IT BECAUSE IT WASN'T YOU. IT WAS WHAT WAS INSIDE OF YOU.
I PULLED YOU OFF HER AND WE FOUGHT... I HURT YOU... AND IT GOT THAT... THING OUT OF YOU. SAME AS IT DID WITH MY MOTHER.
THAT'S HOW I KNEW IT WAS ME... THAT I WAS DRAWING THOSE CREATURES TO ME. IT WAS ALL MY FAULT.
JESUS, KYLE. YOU'VE SNAPPED... YOU'VE FINALLY LOST IT...
NO! I'M TELLING YOU THIS IS REAL!
THIS IS THE TRUTH!

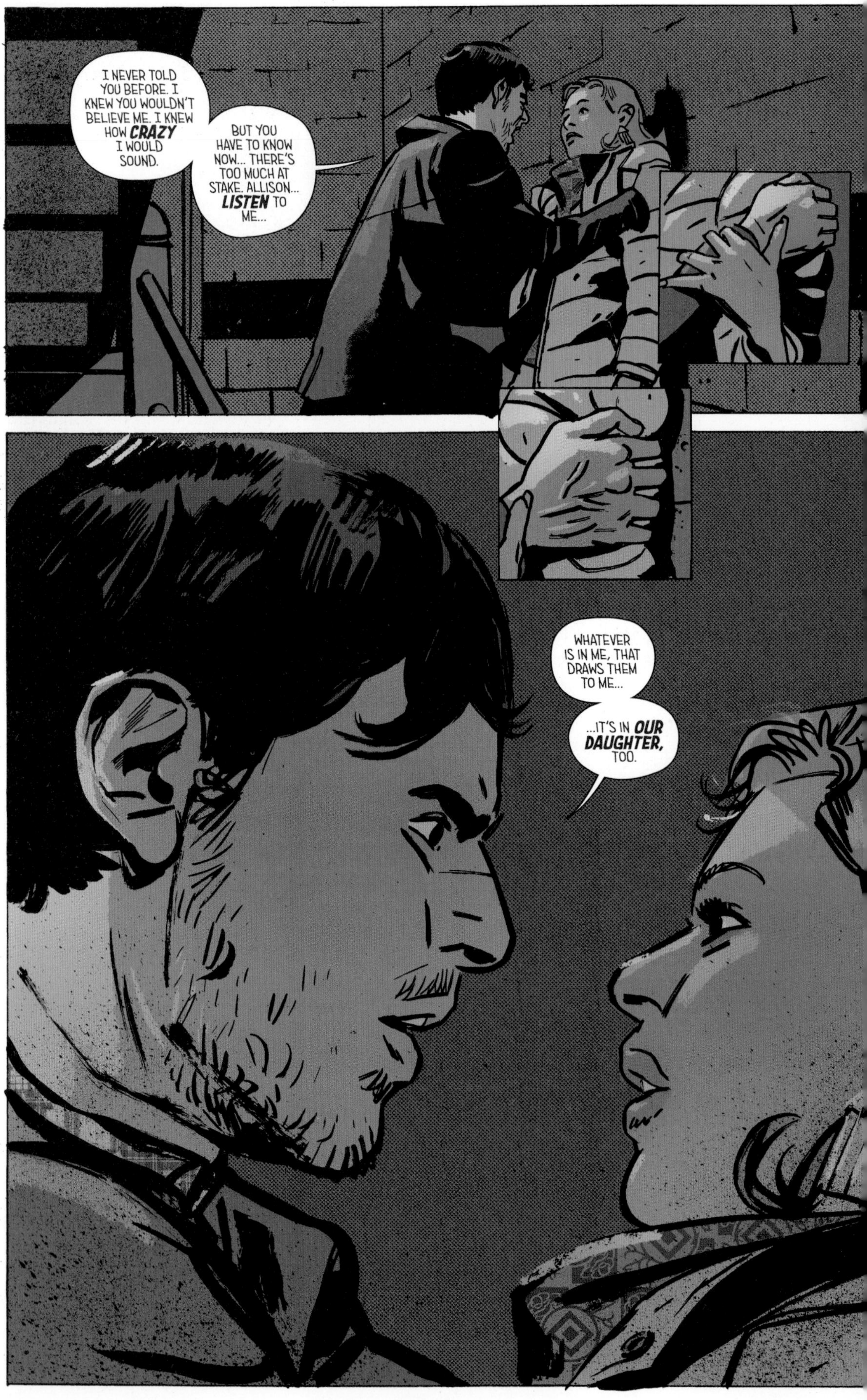
I NEVER TOLD YOU BEFORE. I KNEW YOU WOULDN'T BELIEVE ME. I KNEW HOW **CRAZY** I WOULD SOUND.
BUT YOU HAVE TO KNOW NOW... THERE'S TOO MUCH AT STAKE. ALLISON... **LISTEN** TO ME...
WHATEVER IS IN ME, THAT DRAWS THEM TO ME...
...IT'S IN **OUR DAUGHTER,** TOO.

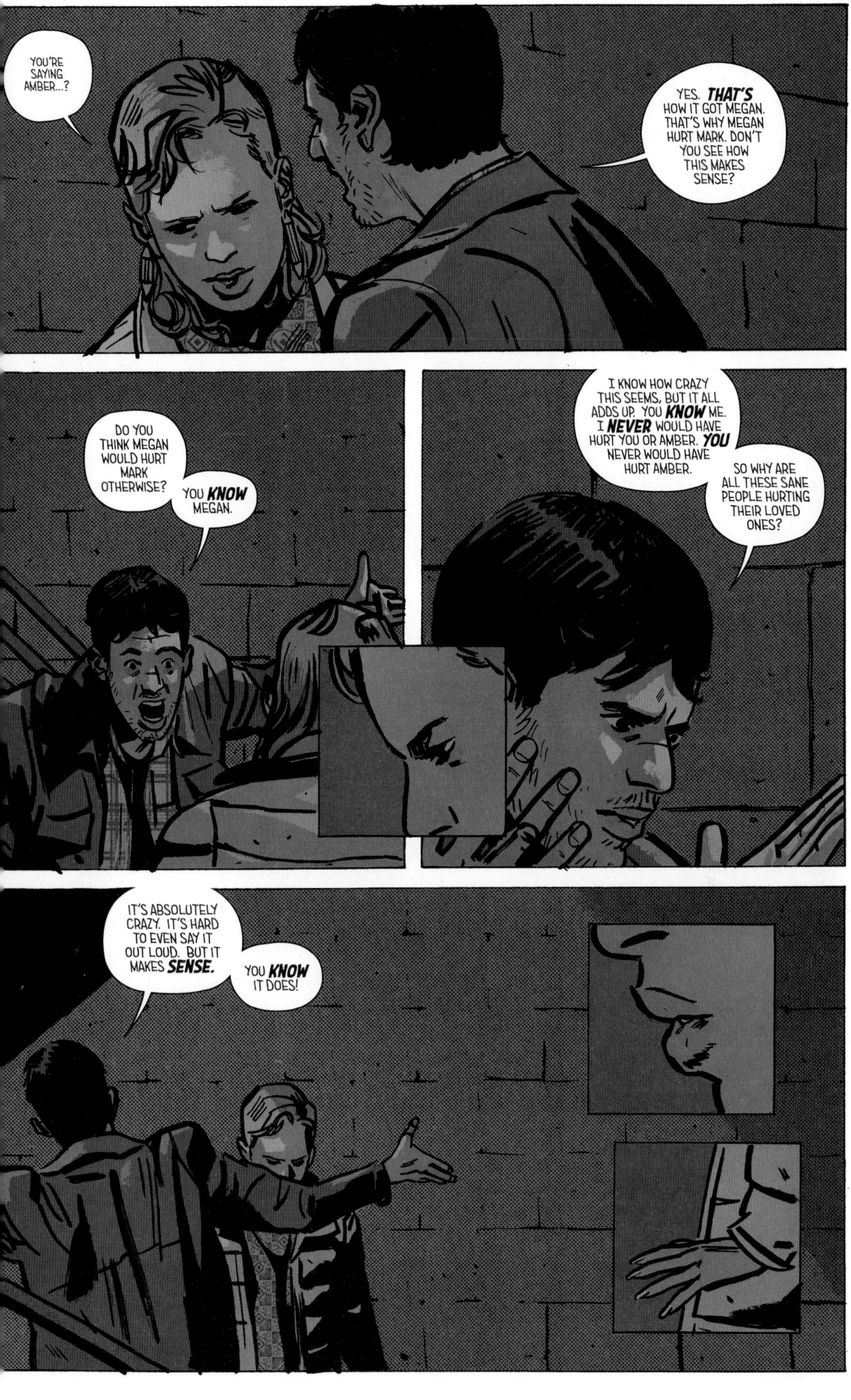
YOU'RE SAYING AMBER...?
YES. THAT'S HOW IT GOT MEGAN. THAT'S WHY MEGAN HURT MARK. DON'T YOU SEE HOW THIS MAKES SENSE?
DO YOU THINK MEGAN WOULD HURT MARK OTHERWISE?
YOU KNOW MEGAN.
I KNOW HOW CRAZY THIS SEEMS, BUT IT ALL ADDS UP. YOU KNOW ME. I NEVER WOULD HAVE HURT YOU OR AMBER. YOU NEVER WOULD HAVE HURT AMBER.
SO WHY ARE ALL THESE SANE PEOPLE HURTING THEIR LOVED ONES?
IT'S ABSOLUTELY CRAZY. IT'S HARD TO EVEN SAY IT OUT LOUD. BUT IT MAKES SENSE.
YOU KNOW IT DOES!

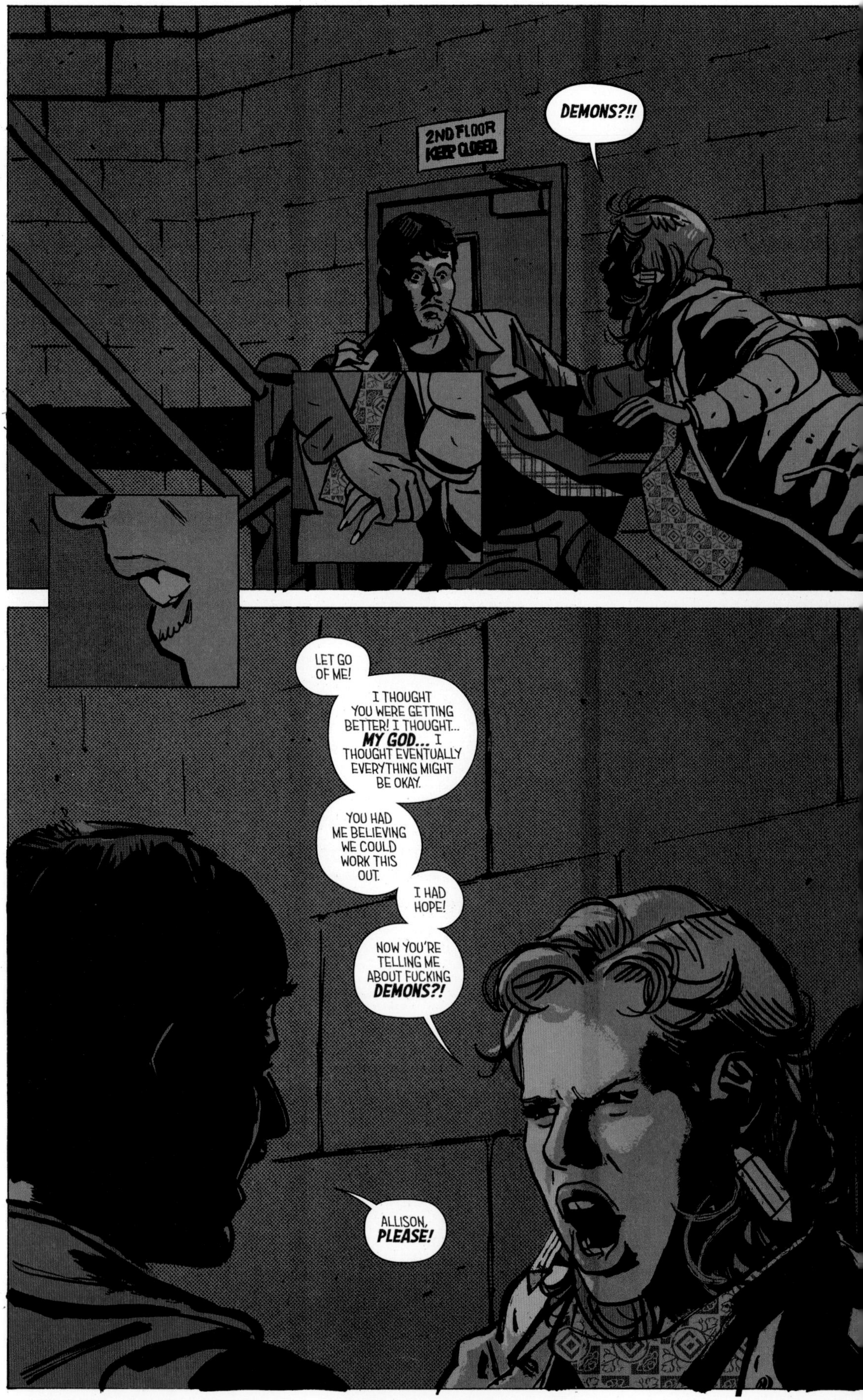
DEMONS?!!
2ND FLOOR KEEP CLOSED
LET GO OF ME!
I THOUGHT YOU WERE GETTING BETTER! I THOUGHT... MY GOD... I THOUGHT EVENTUALLY EVERYTHING MIGHT BE OKAY.
YOU HAD ME BELIEVING WE COULD WORK THIS OUT.
I HAD HOPE!
NOW YOU'RE TELLING ME ABOUT FUCKING DEMONS?!
ALLISON, PLEASE!

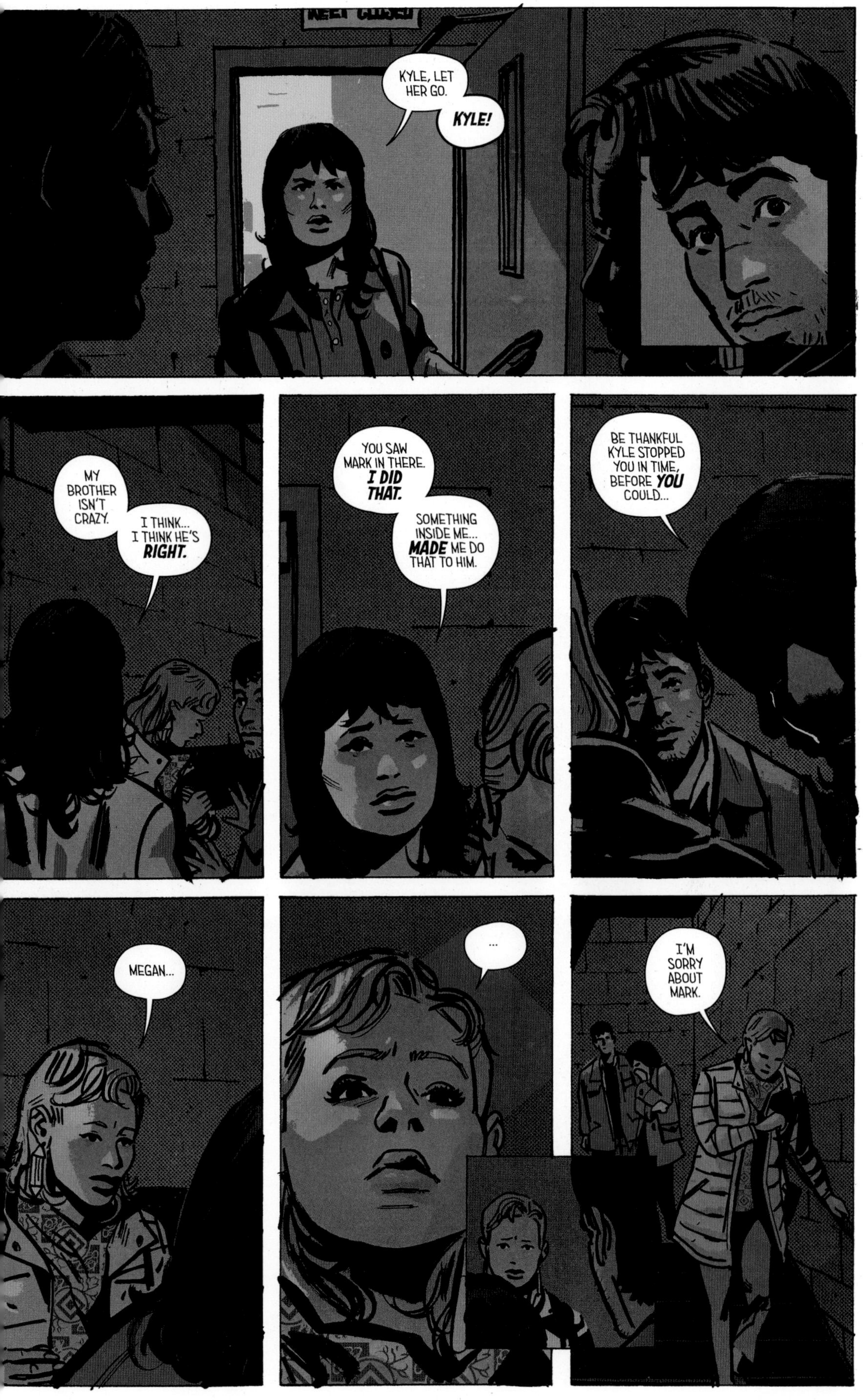
KYLE, LET HER GO.
KYLE!
MY BROTHER ISN'T CRAZY.
I THINK... I THINK HE'S RIGHT.
YOU SAW MARK IN THERE. I DID THAT.
SOMETHING INSIDE ME... MADE ME DO THAT TO HIM.
BE THANKFUL KYLE STOPPED YOU IN TIME, BEFORE YOU COULD...
MEGAN...
...
I'M SORRY ABOUT MARK.

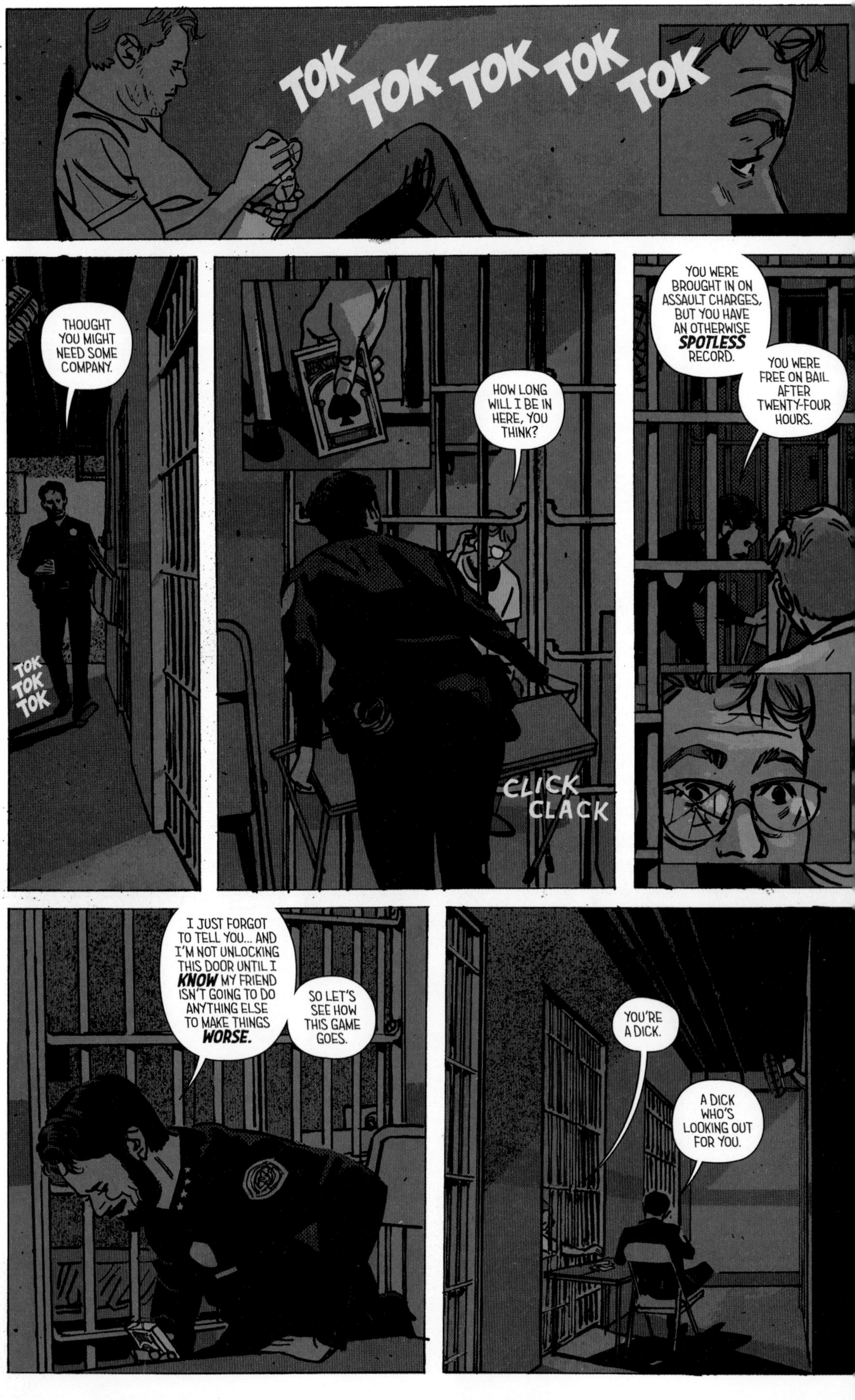
TOK TOK TOK TOK TOK
THOUGHT YOU MIGHT NEED SOME COMPANY.
TOK TOK TOK
HOW LONG WILL I BE IN HERE, YOU THINK?
CLICK CLACK
YOU WERE BROUGHT IN ON ASSAULT CHARGES, BUT YOU HAVE AN OTHERWISE SPOTLESS RECORD.
YOU WERE FREE ON BAIL AFTER TWENTY-FOUR HOURS.
I JUST FORGOT TO TELL YOU... AND I'M NOT UNLOCKING THIS DOOR UNTIL I KNOW MY FRIEND ISN'T GOING TO DO ANYTHING ELSE TO MAKE THINGS WORSE.
SO LET'S SEE HOW THIS GAME GOES.
YOU'RE A DICK.
A DICK WHO'S LOOKING OUT FOR YOU.

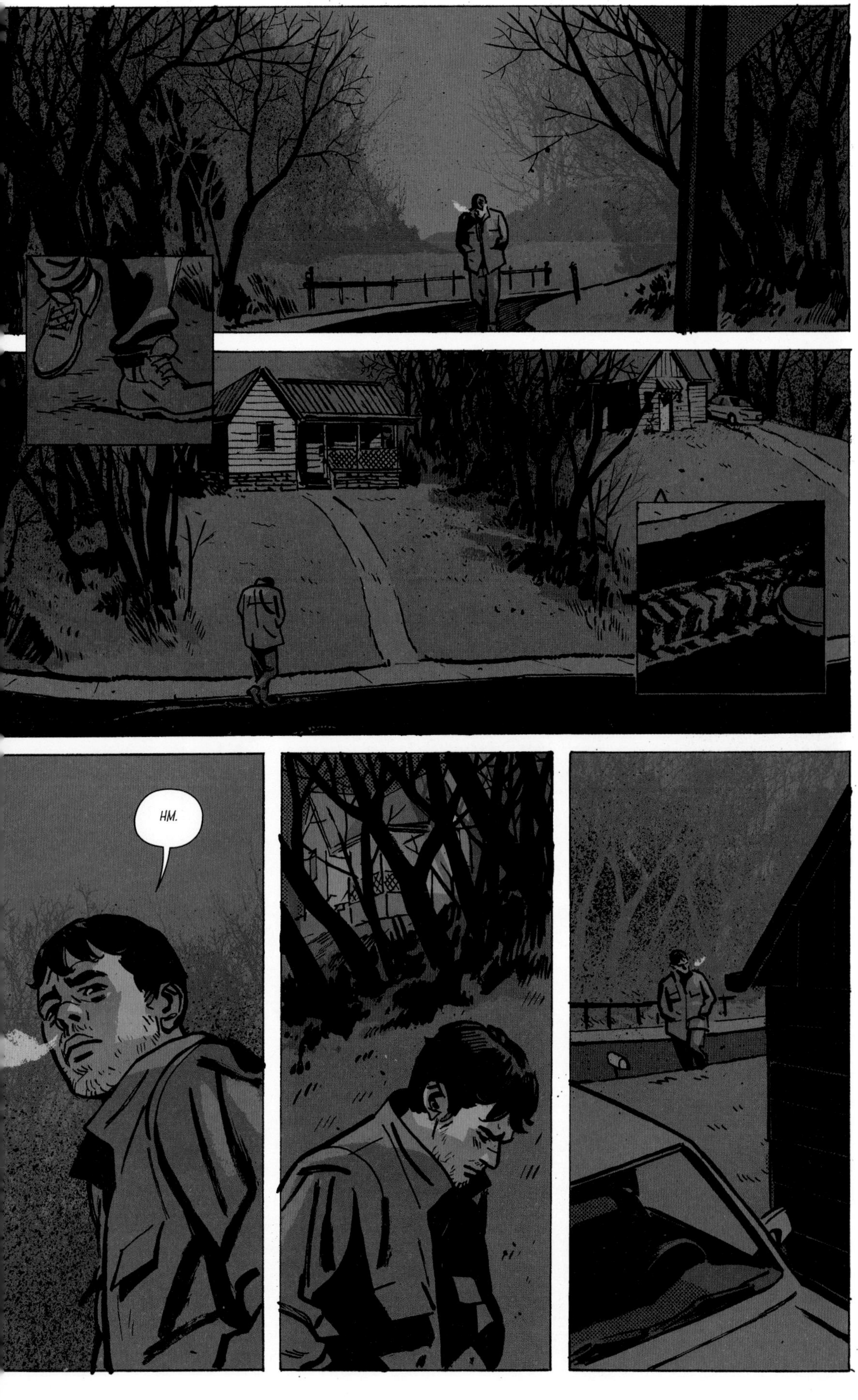
HM.

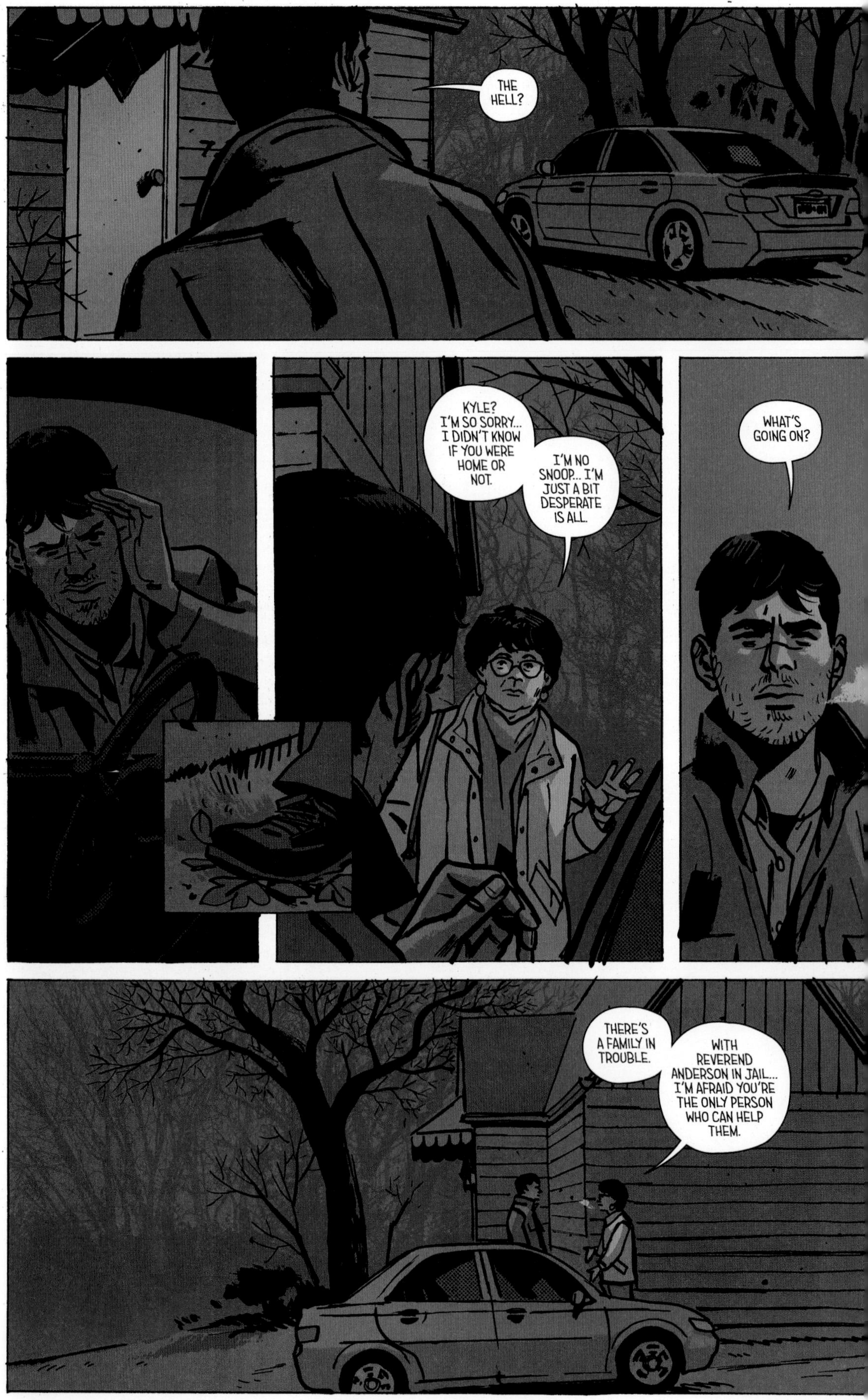
THE HELL?
KYLE? I'M SO SORRY... I DIDN'T KNOW IF YOU WERE HOME OR NOT.
I'M NO SNOOP... I'M JUST A BIT DESPERATE IS ALL.
WHAT'S GOING ON?
THERE'S A FAMILY IN TROUBLE.
WITH REVEREND ANDERSON IN JAIL... I'M AFRAID YOU'RE THE ONLY PERSON WHO CAN HELP THEM.

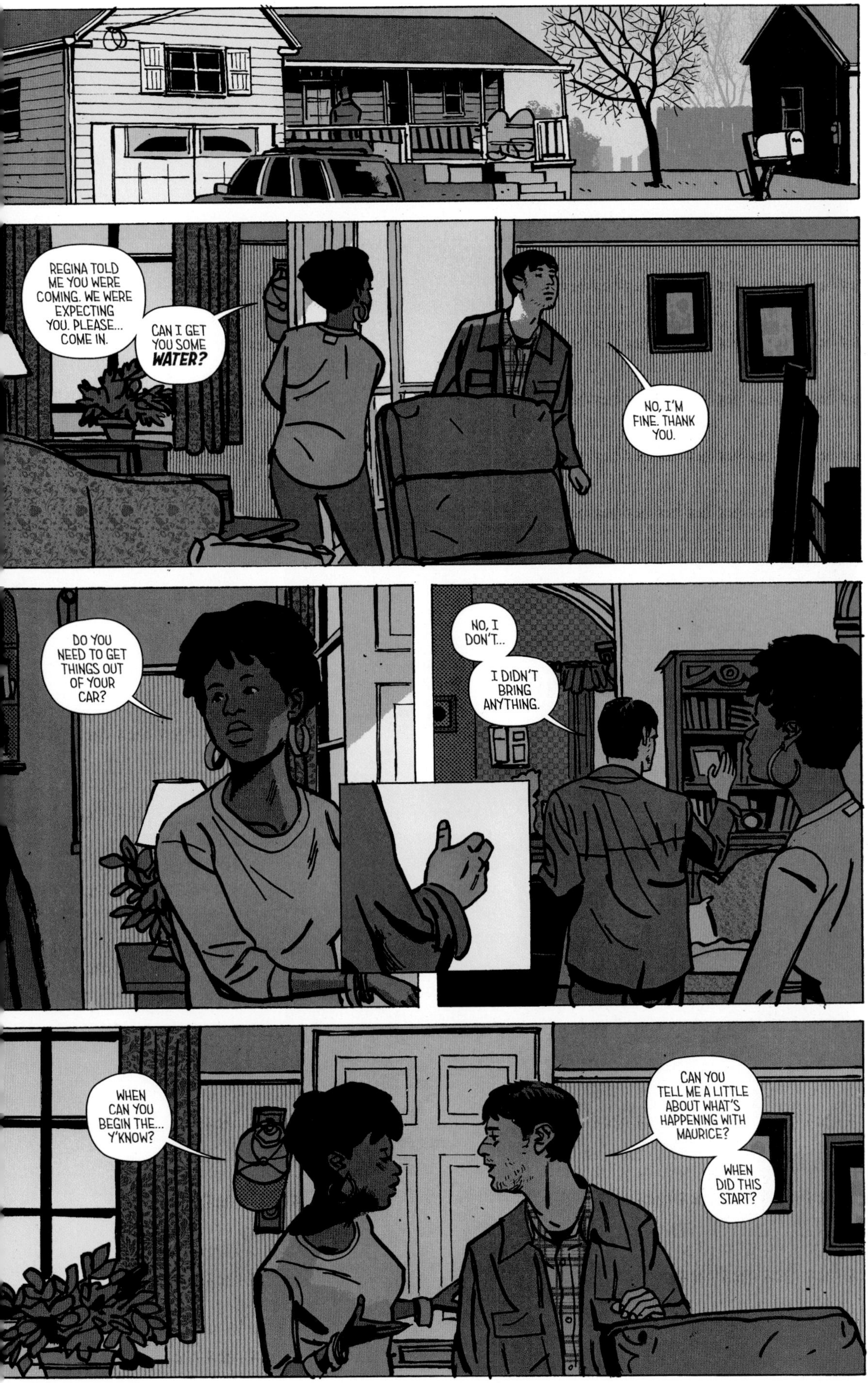
REGINA TOLD ME YOU WERE COMING. WE WERE EXPECTING YOU. PLEASE... COME IN.
CAN I GET YOU SOME *WATER?*
NO, I'M FINE. THANK YOU.
DO YOU NEED TO GET THINGS OUT OF YOUR CAR?
NO, I DON'T...
I DIDN'T BRING ANYTHING.
WHEN CAN YOU BEGIN THE... Y'KNOW?
CAN YOU TELL ME A LITTLE ABOUT WHAT'S HAPPENING WITH MAURICE?
WHEN DID THIS START?

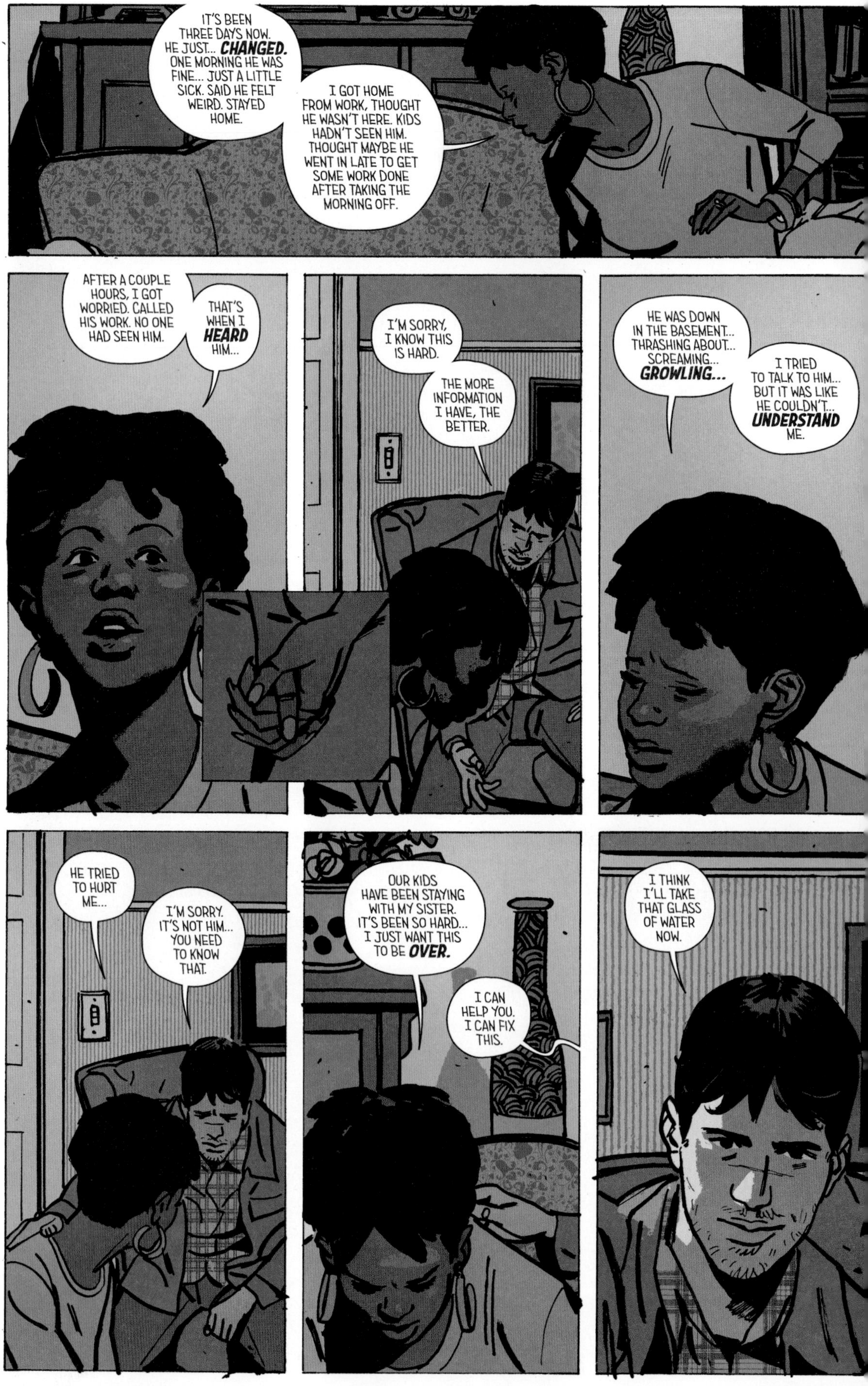
IT'S BEEN THREE DAYS NOW. HE JUST... CHANGED. ONE MORNING HE WAS FINE... JUST A LITTLE SICK. SAID HE FELT WEIRD. STAYED HOME.
I GOT HOME FROM WORK, THOUGHT HE WASN'T HERE. KIDS HADN'T SEEN HIM. THOUGHT MAYBE HE WENT IN LATE TO GET SOME WORK DONE AFTER TAKING THE MORNING OFF.
AFTER A COUPLE HOURS, I GOT WORRIED. CALLED HIS WORK. NO ONE HAD SEEN HIM.
THAT'S WHEN I HEARD HIM...
I'M SORRY, I KNOW THIS IS HARD.
THE MORE INFORMATION I HAVE, THE BETTER.
HE WAS DOWN IN THE BASEMENT... THRASHING ABOUT... SCREAMING... GROWLING...
I TRIED TO TALK TO HIM... BUT IT WAS LIKE HE COULDN'T... UNDERSTAND ME.
HE TRIED TO HURT ME...
I'M SORRY. IT'S NOT HIM... YOU NEED TO KNOW THAT.
OUR KIDS HAVE BEEN STAYING WITH MY SISTER. IT'S BEEN SO HARD... I JUST WANT THIS TO BE OVER.
I CAN HELP YOU. I CAN FIX THIS.
I THINK I'LL TAKE THAT GLASS OF WATER NOW.

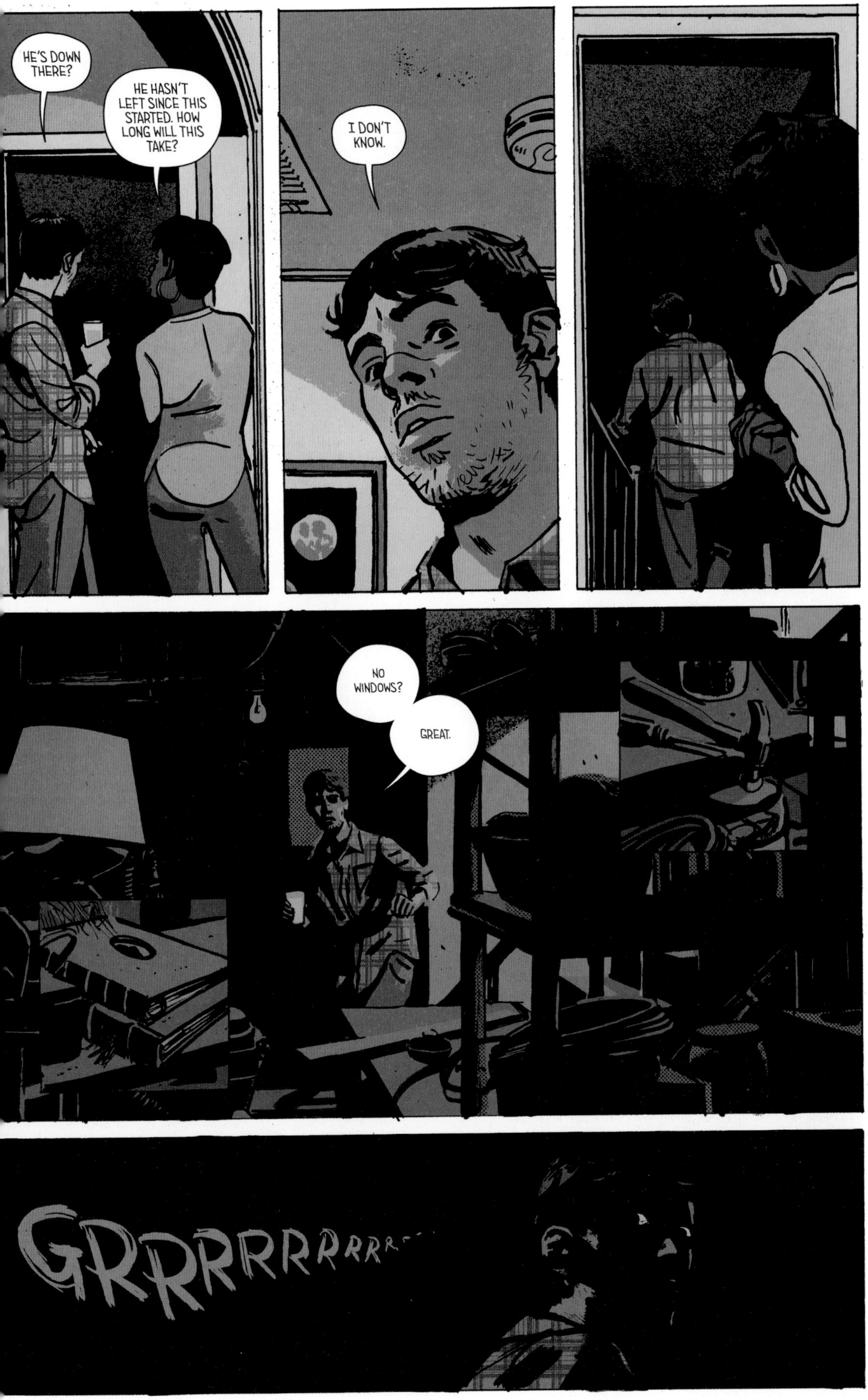
HE'S DOWN THERE?
HE HASN'T LEFT SINCE THIS STARTED. HOW LONG WILL THIS TAKE?
I DON'T KNOW.
NO WINDOWS?
GREAT.
GRRRRRRRRR

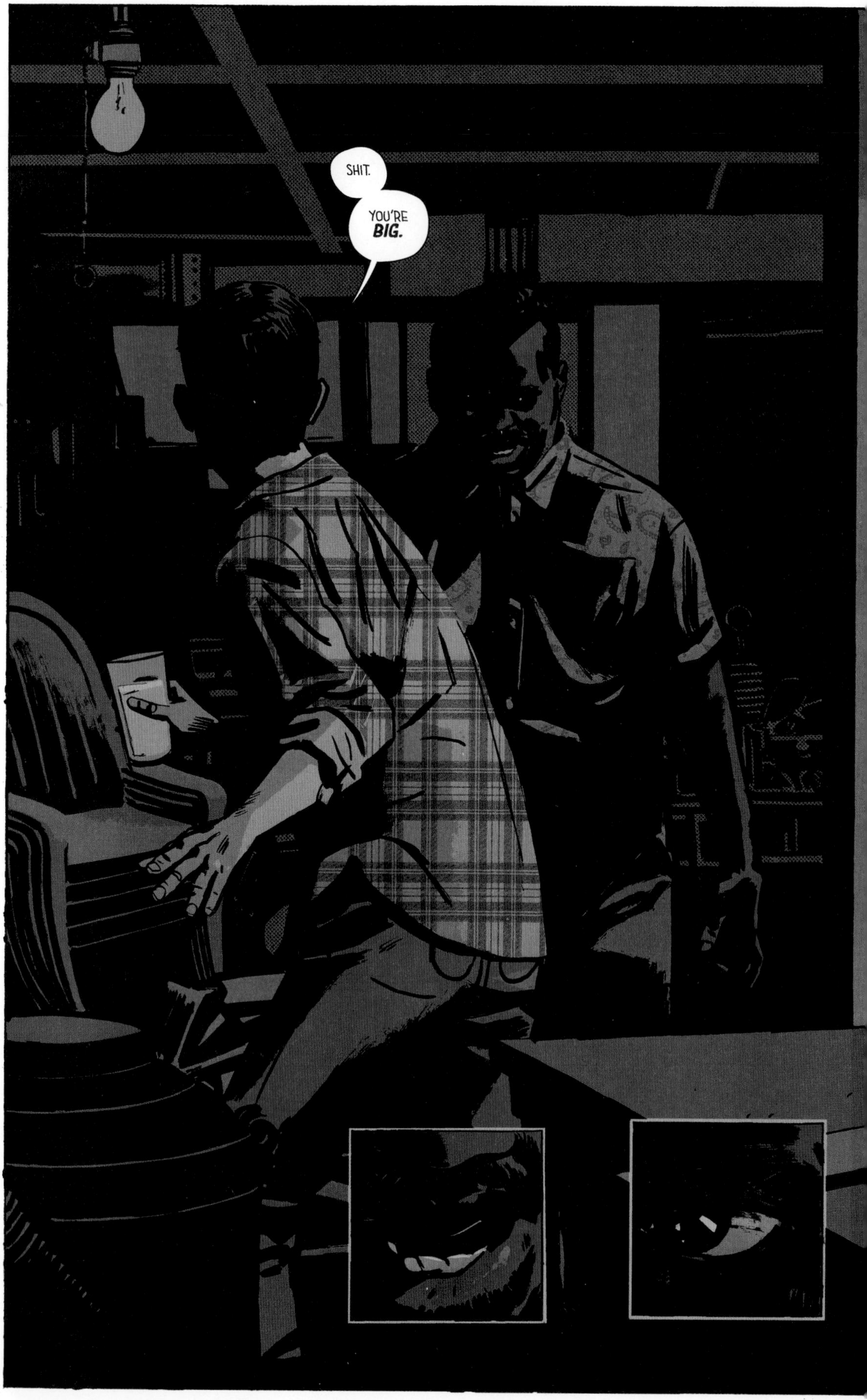
SHIT.
YOU'RE BIG.

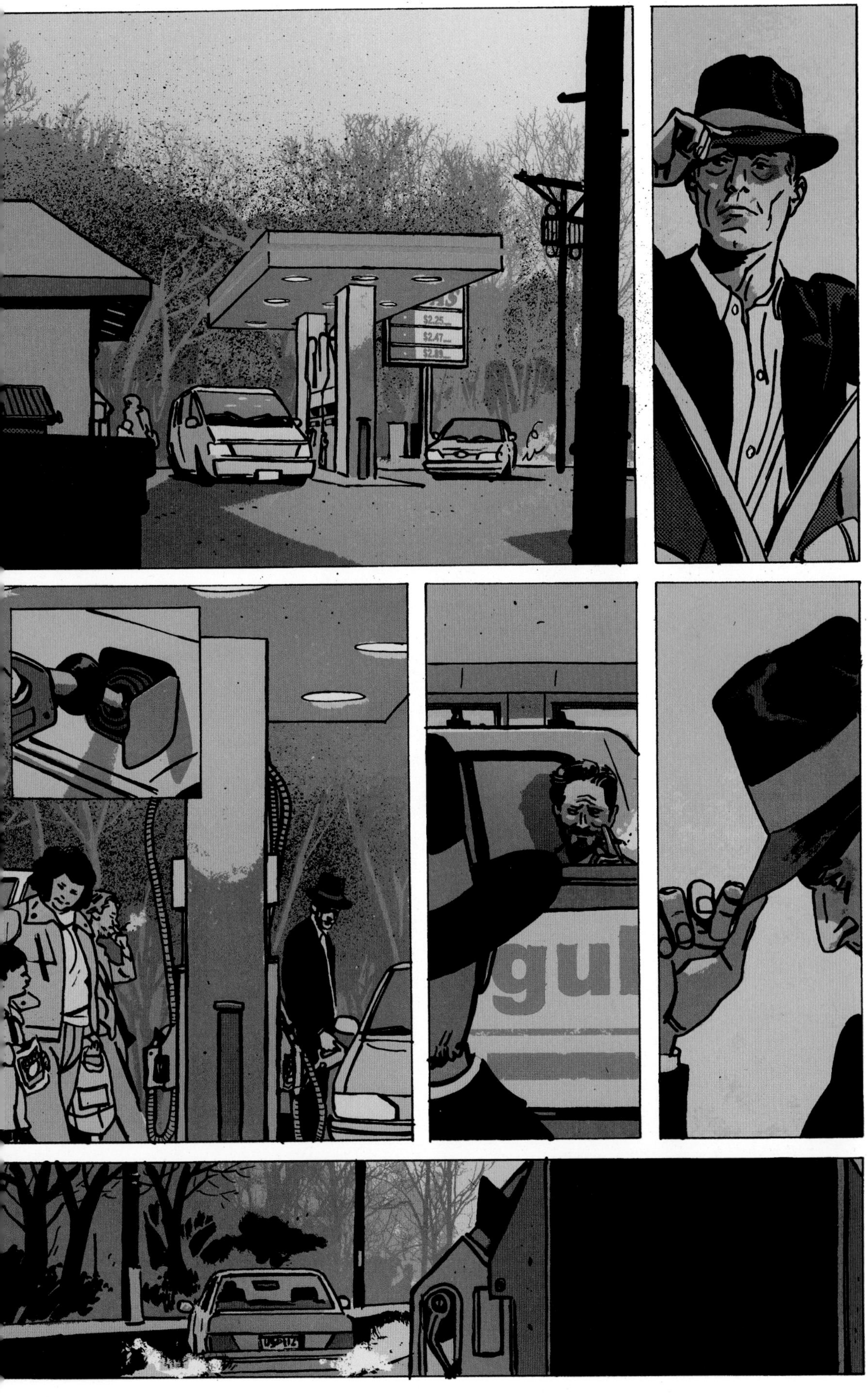
$2.25
$2.47
$2.89

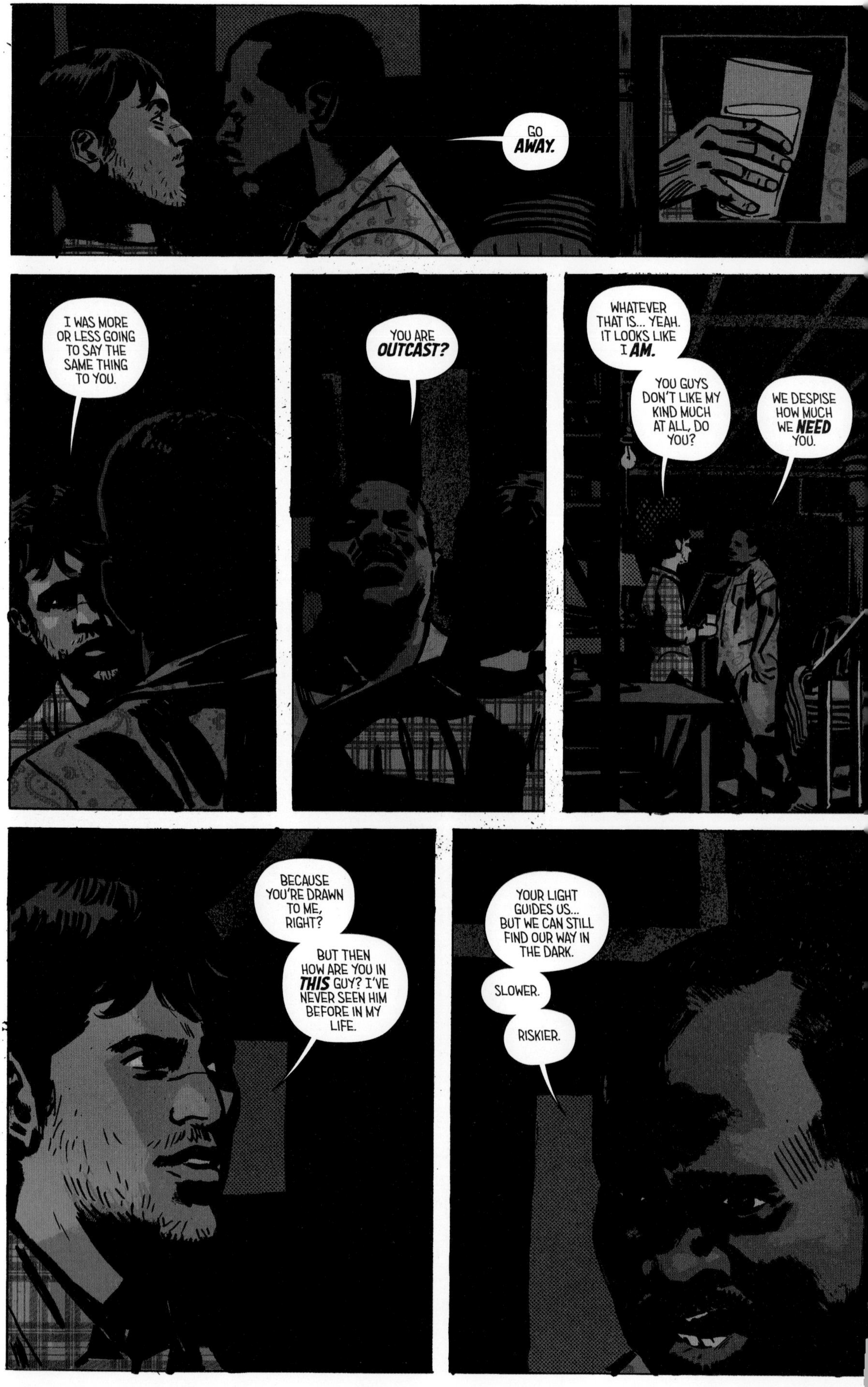
GO AWAY.
I WAS MORE OR LESS GOING TO SAY THE SAME THING TO YOU.
YOU ARE OUTCAST?
WHATEVER THAT IS... YEAH. IT LOOKS LIKE I AM.
YOU GUYS DON'T LIKE MY KIND MUCH AT ALL, DO YOU?
WE DESPISE HOW MUCH WE NEED YOU.
BECAUSE YOU'RE DRAWN TO ME, RIGHT?
BUT THEN HOW ARE YOU IN THIS GUY? I'VE NEVER SEEN HIM BEFORE IN MY LIFE.
YOUR LIGHT GUIDES US... BUT WE CAN STILL FIND OUR WAY IN THE DARK.
SLOWER.
RISKIER.

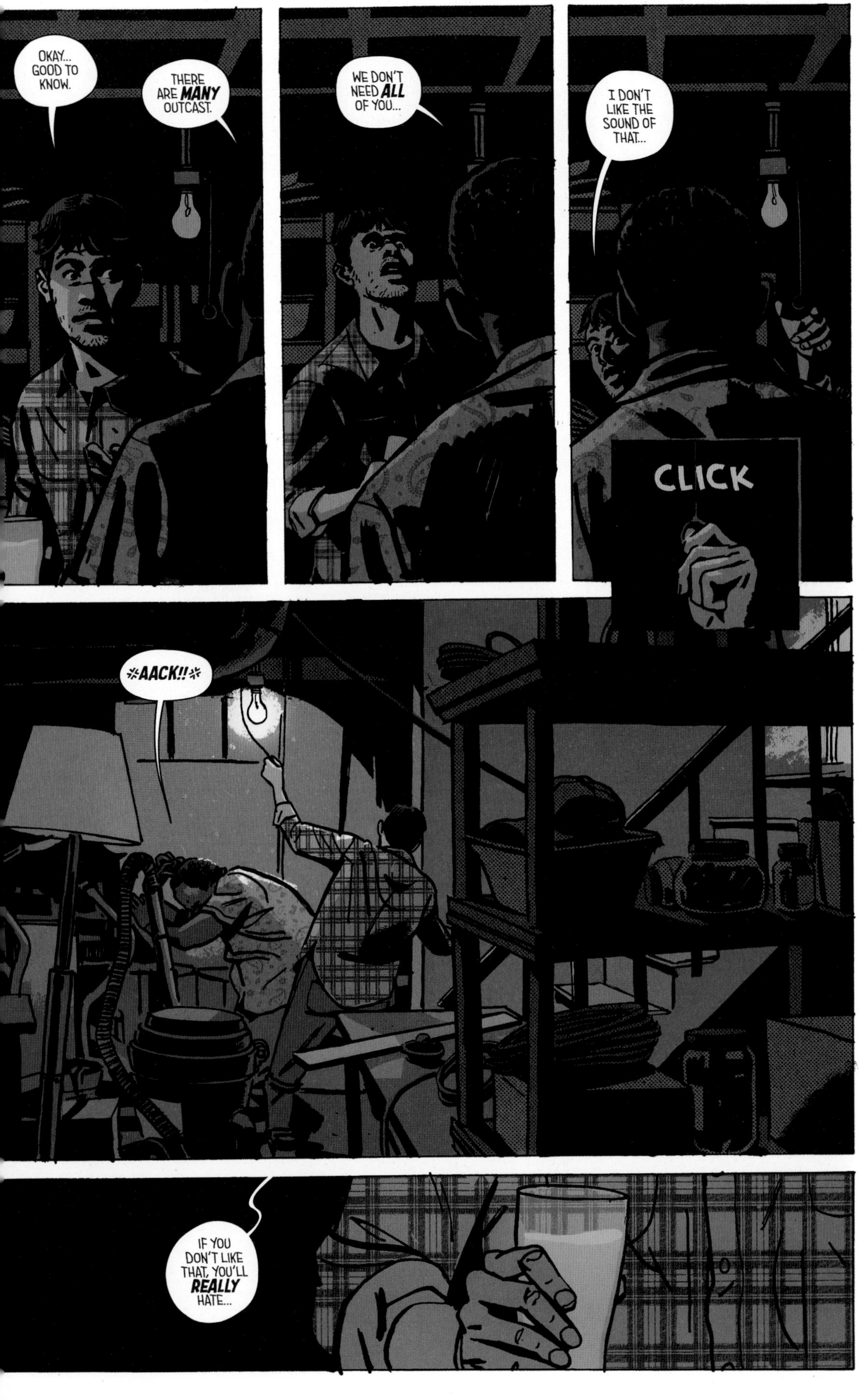
OKAY... GOOD TO KNOW.
THERE ARE MANY OUTCAST.
WE DON'T NEED ALL OF YOU...
I DON'T LIKE THE SOUND OF THAT...
CLICK
AACK!!
IF YOU DON'T LIKE THAT, YOU'LL REALLY HATE...

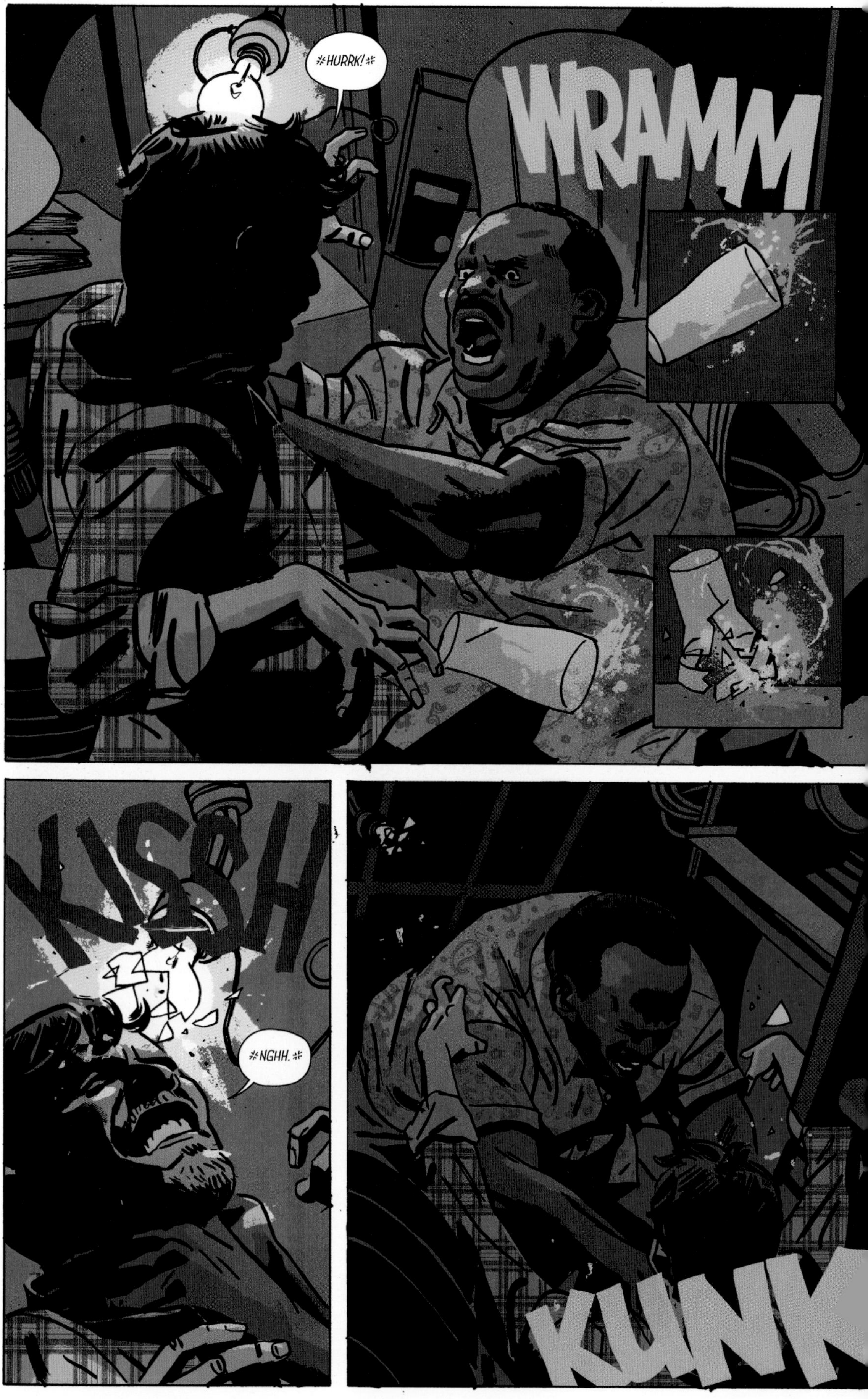

HURRK!
WRAMM
KISH
NGHH.
KUNK

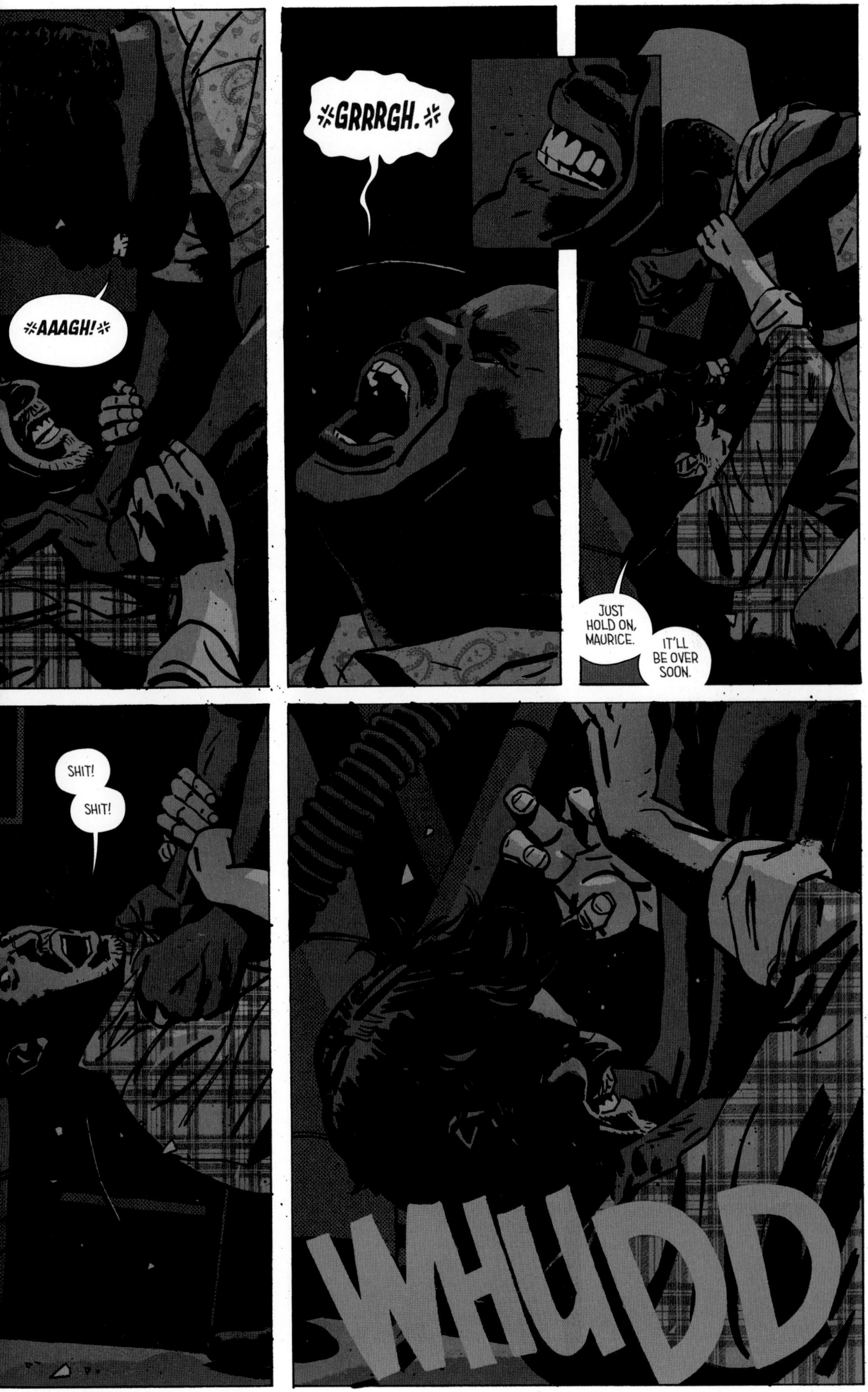

AAAGH!
GRRRGH.
JUST HOLD ON, MAURICE.
IT'LL BE OVER SOON.
SHIT!
SHIT!
WHUDD

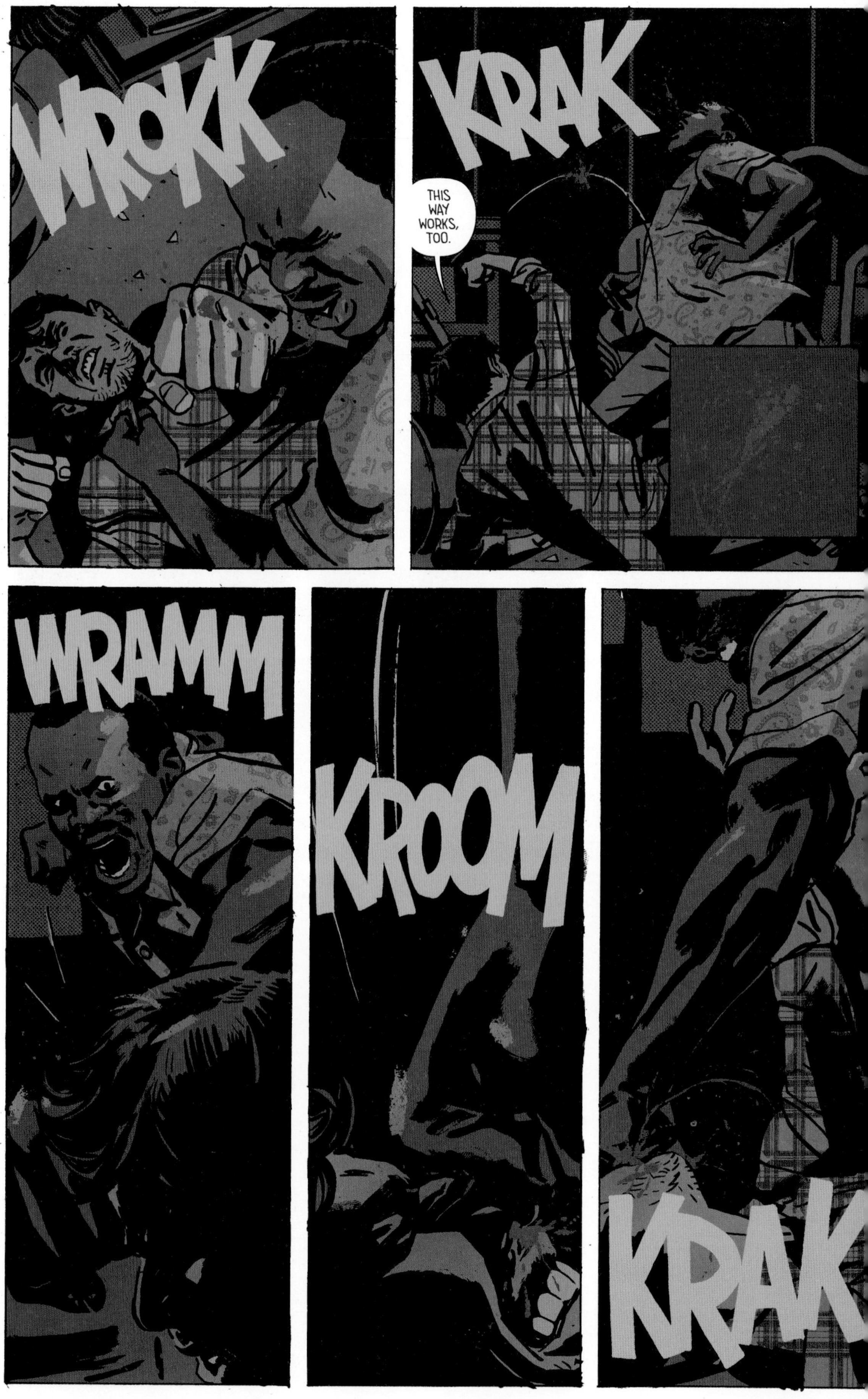
WROKK
KRAK
THIS WAY WORKS, TOO.
WRAMM
KROOM
KRAK

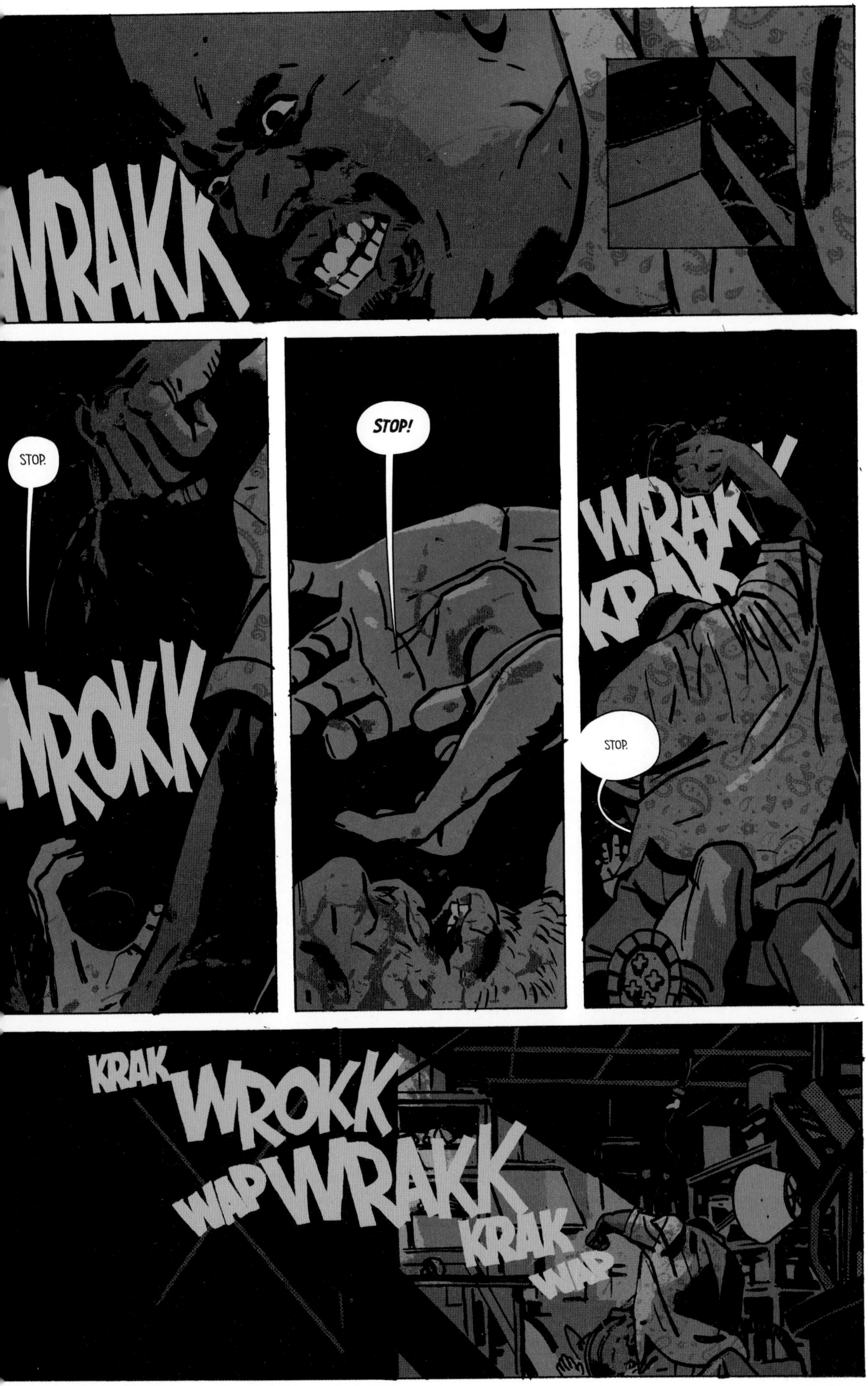
WRAKK
STOP.
WROKK
STOP!
WRAK
KRAK
STOP.
KRAK
WROKK
WAP
WRAKK
KRAK
WAP

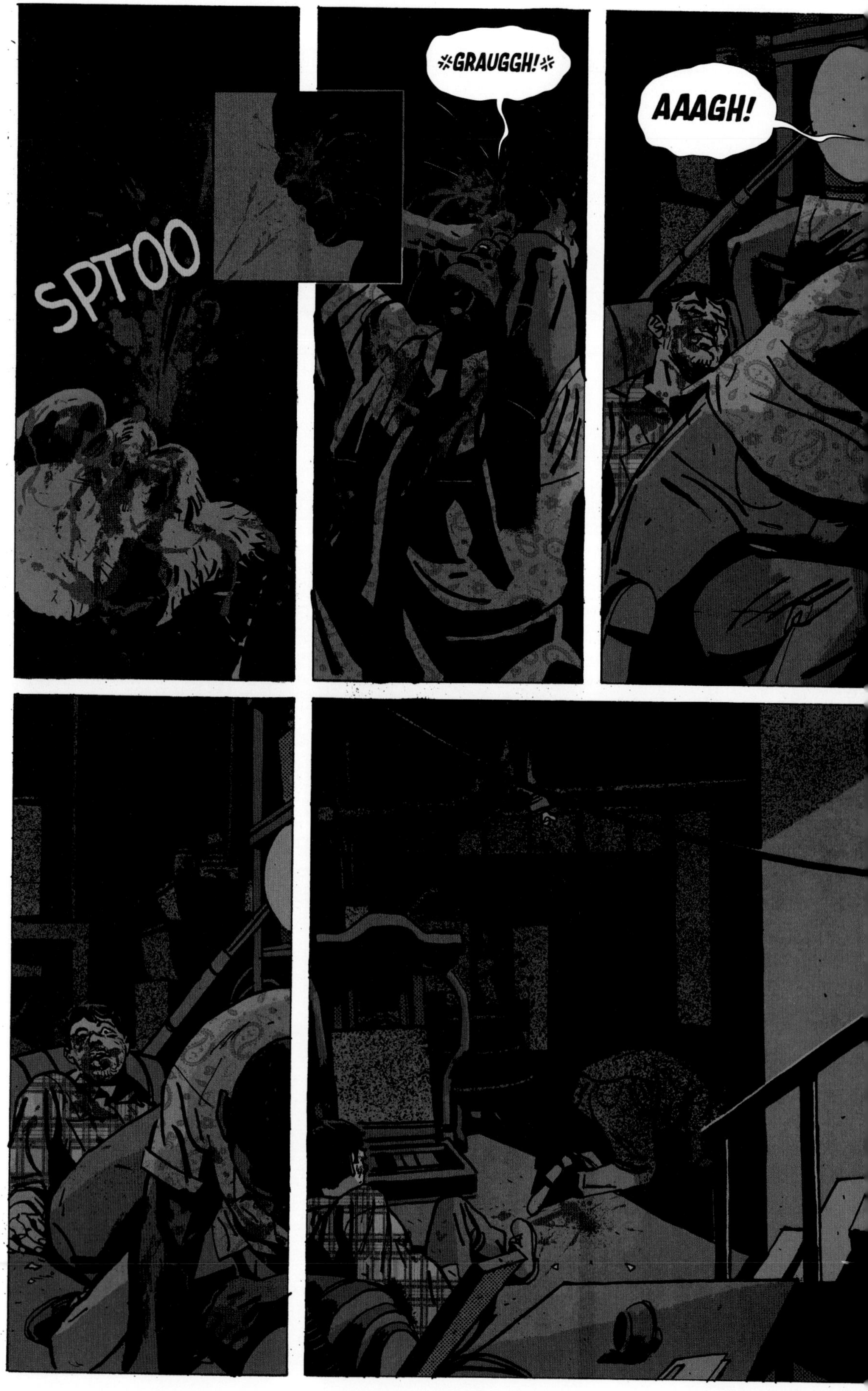
SPTOO
GRAUGGH!
AAAGH!

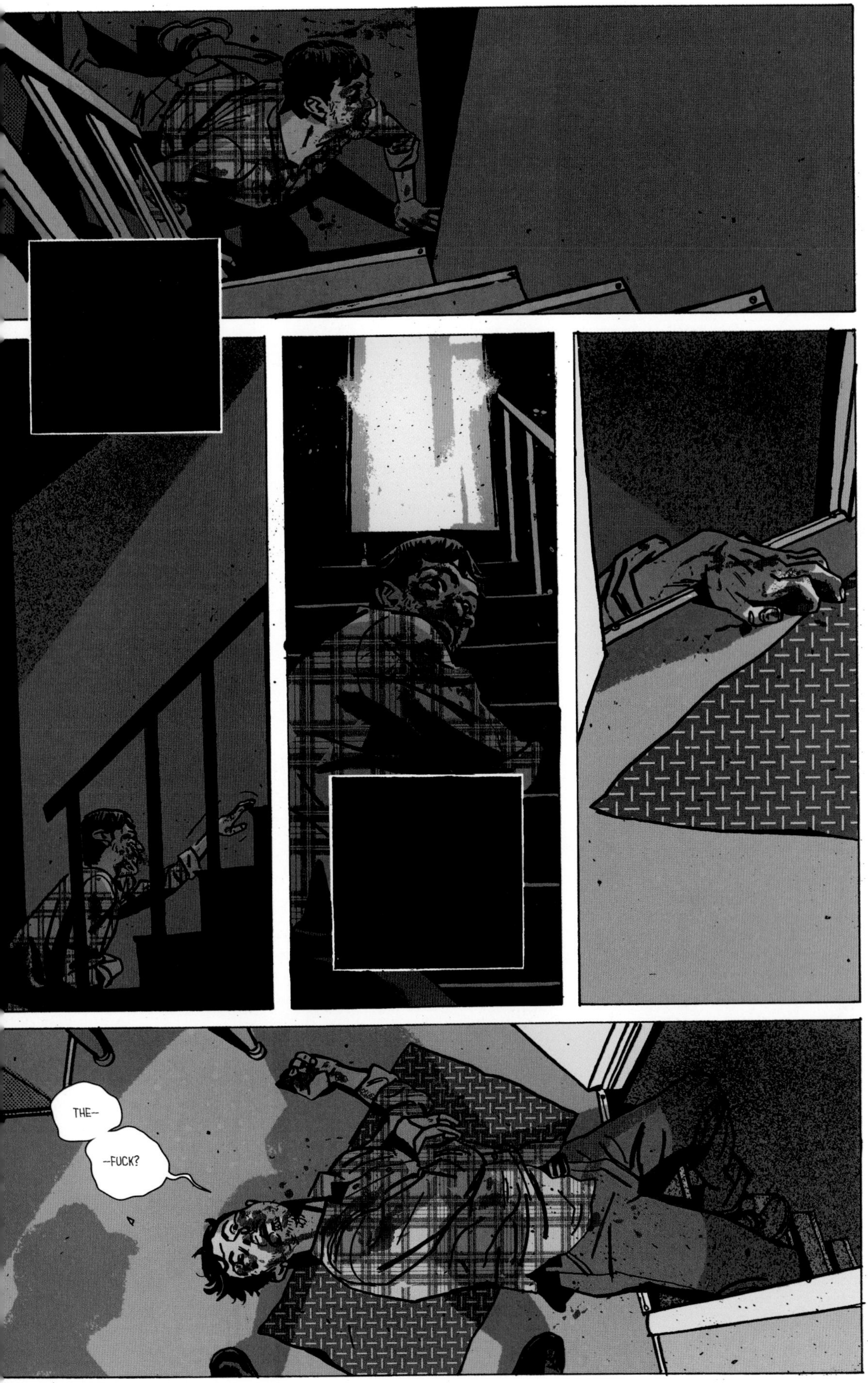
THE--
--FUCK?

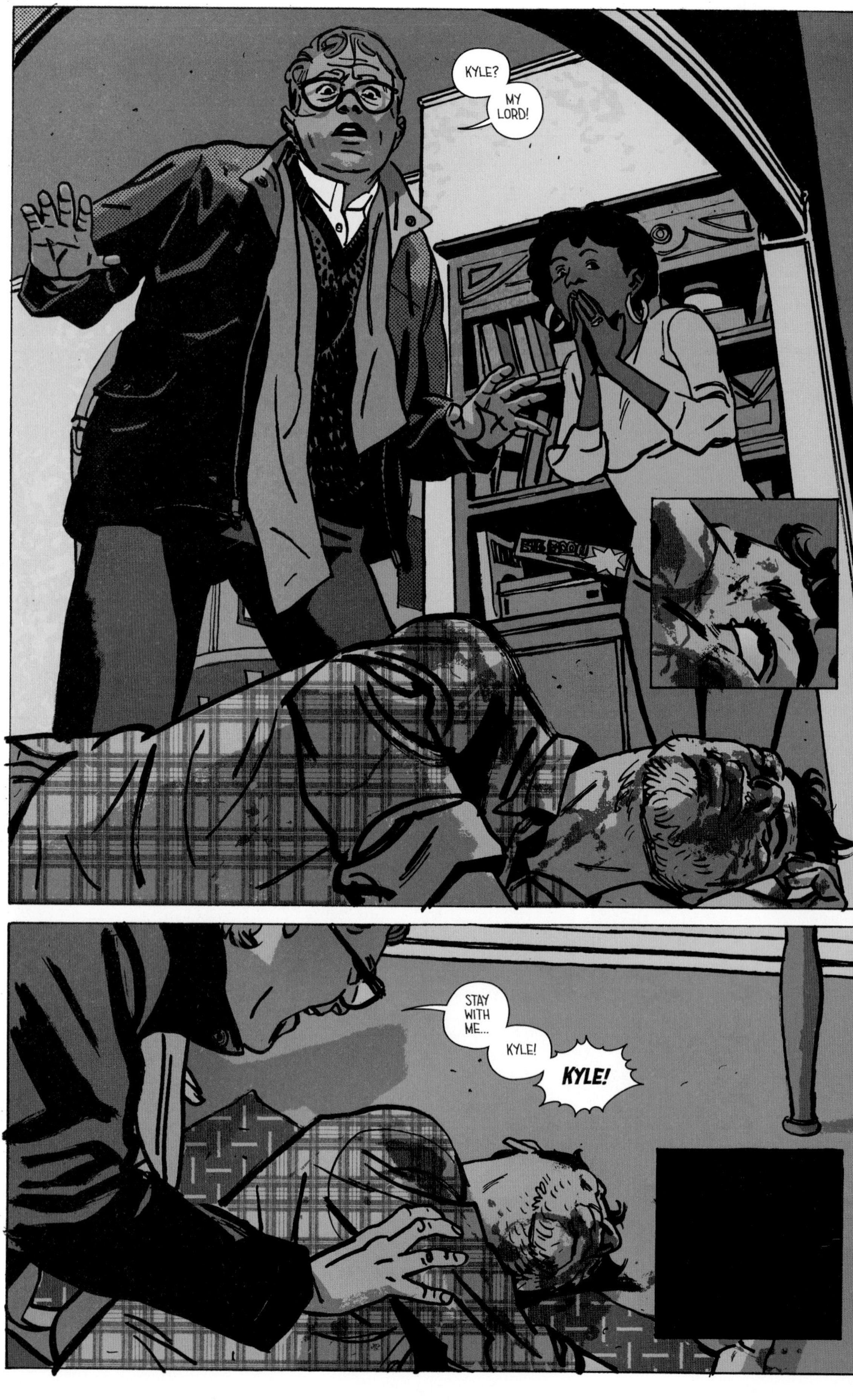
KYLE?
MY LORD!
STAY WITH ME...
KYLE!
KYLE!

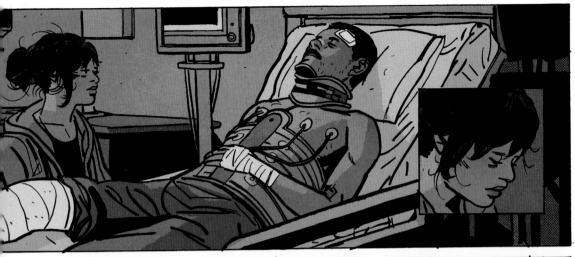

MEGAN?

ARE YOU OKAY?

AM I--?

AM I...

MEGAN?

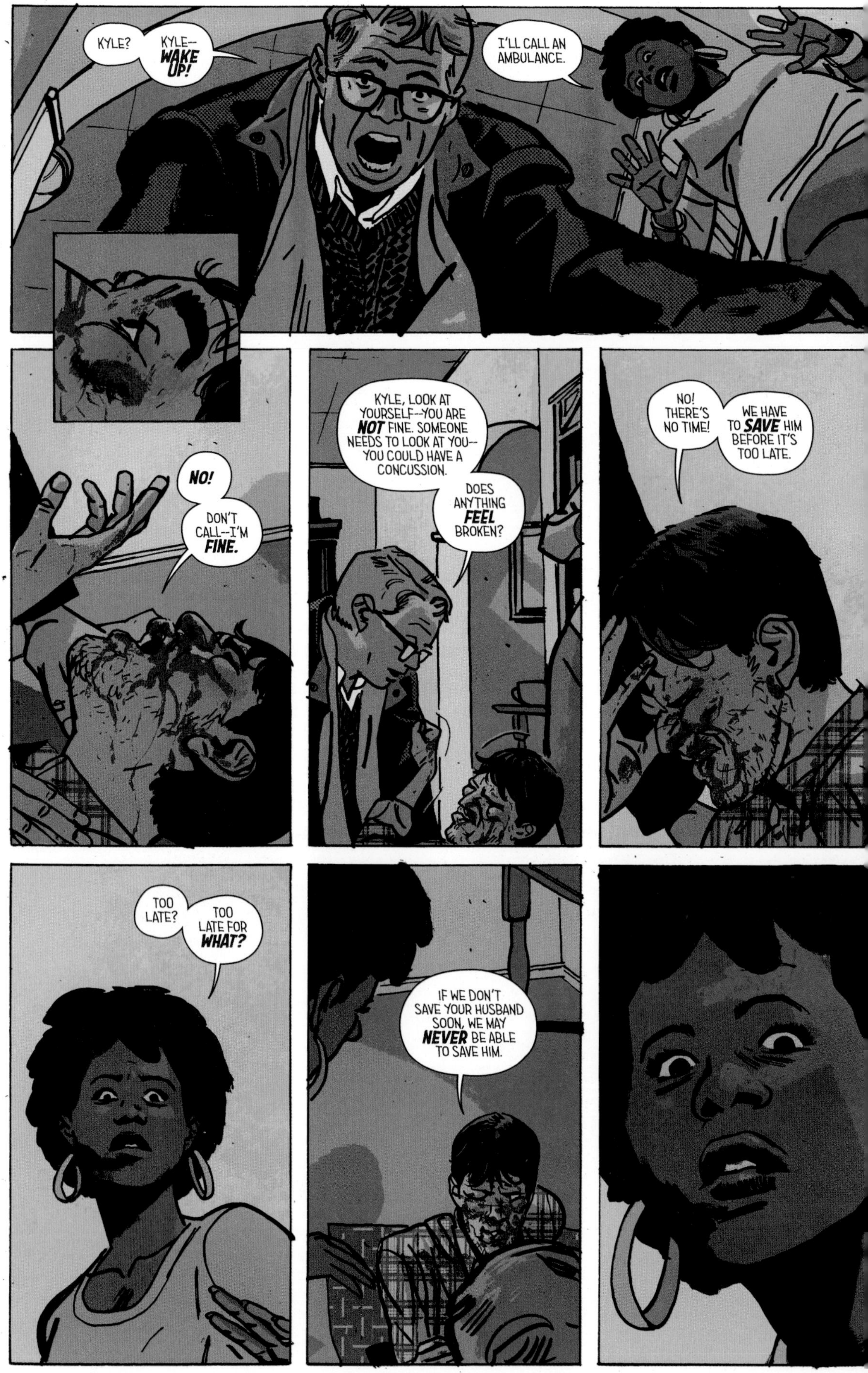
KYLE?
KYLE-- WAKE UP!
I'LL CALL AN AMBULANCE.
NO!
DON'T CALL--I'M FINE.
KYLE, LOOK AT YOURSELF--YOU ARE NOT FINE. SOMEONE NEEDS TO LOOK AT YOU--YOU COULD HAVE A CONCUSSION.
DOES ANYTHING FEEL BROKEN?
NO! THERE'S NO TIME!
WE HAVE TO SAVE HIM BEFORE IT'S TOO LATE.
TOO LATE?
TOO LATE FOR WHAT?
IF WE DON'T SAVE YOUR HUSBAND SOON, WE MAY NEVER BE ABLE TO SAVE HIM.

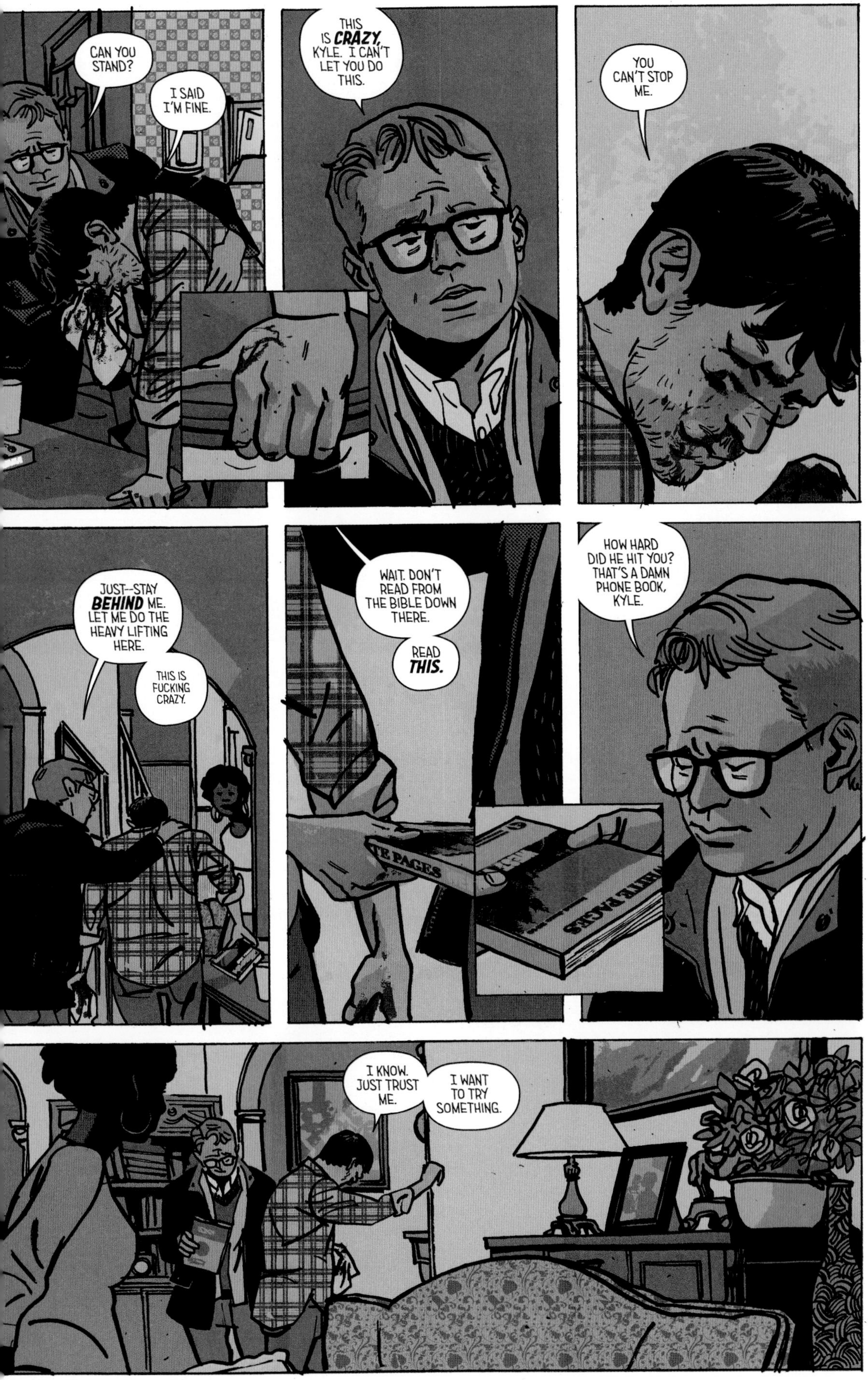
CAN YOU STAND?
I SAID I'M FINE.
THIS IS *CRAZY*, KYLE. I CAN'T LET YOU DO THIS.
YOU CAN'T STOP ME.
JUST--STAY **BEHIND** ME. LET ME DO THE HEAVY LIFTING HERE.
THIS IS FUCKING CRAZY.
WAIT. DON'T READ FROM THE BIBLE DOWN THERE.
READ **THIS.**
HOW HARD DID HE HIT YOU? THAT'S A DAMN PHONE BOOK, KYLE.
I KNOW. JUST TRUST ME.
I WANT TO TRY SOMETHING.

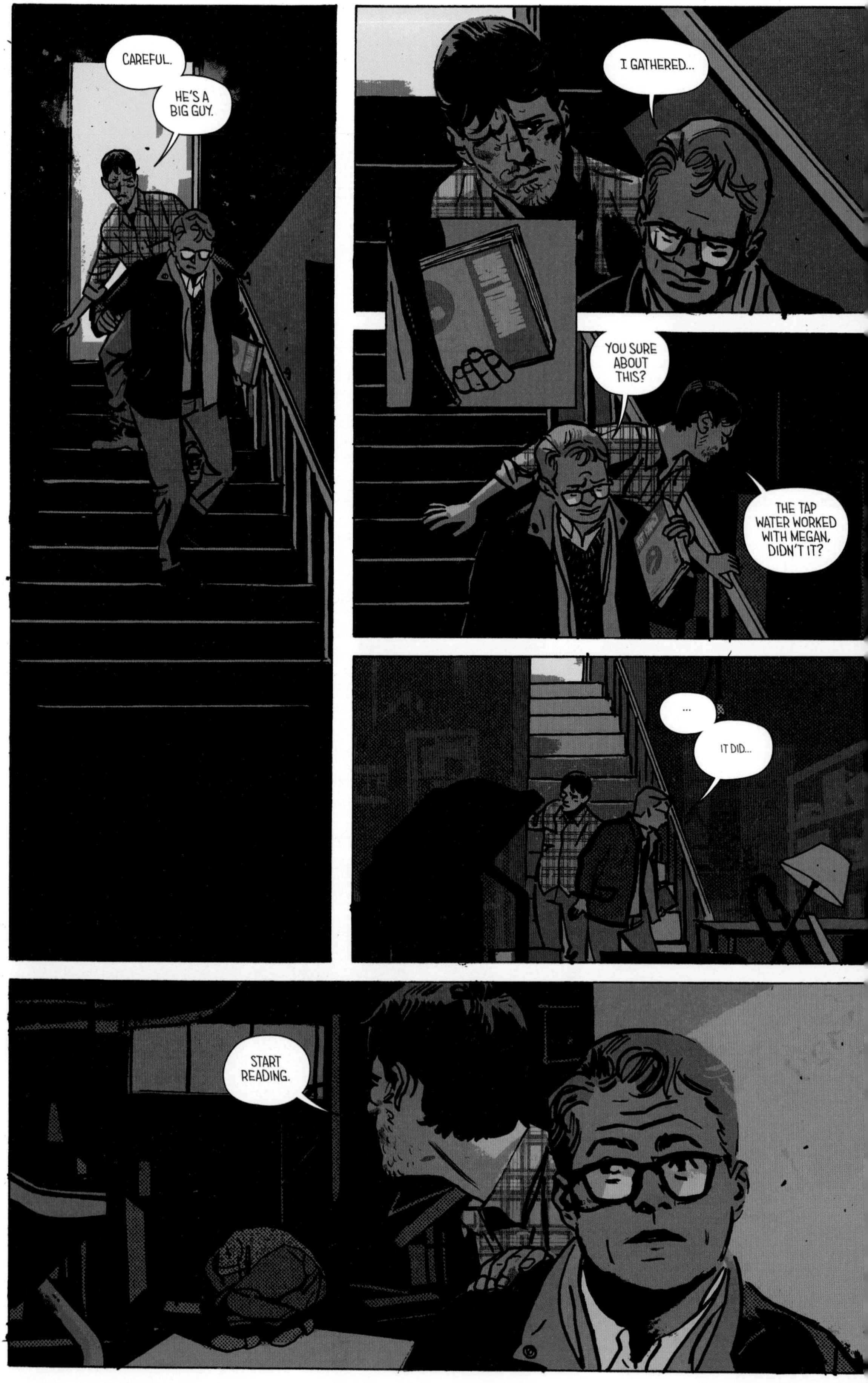
CAREFUL.
HE'S A BIG GUY.
I GATHERED...
YOU SURE ABOUT THIS?
THE TAP WATER WORKED WITH MEGAN, DIDN'T IT?
...
IT DID...
START READING.

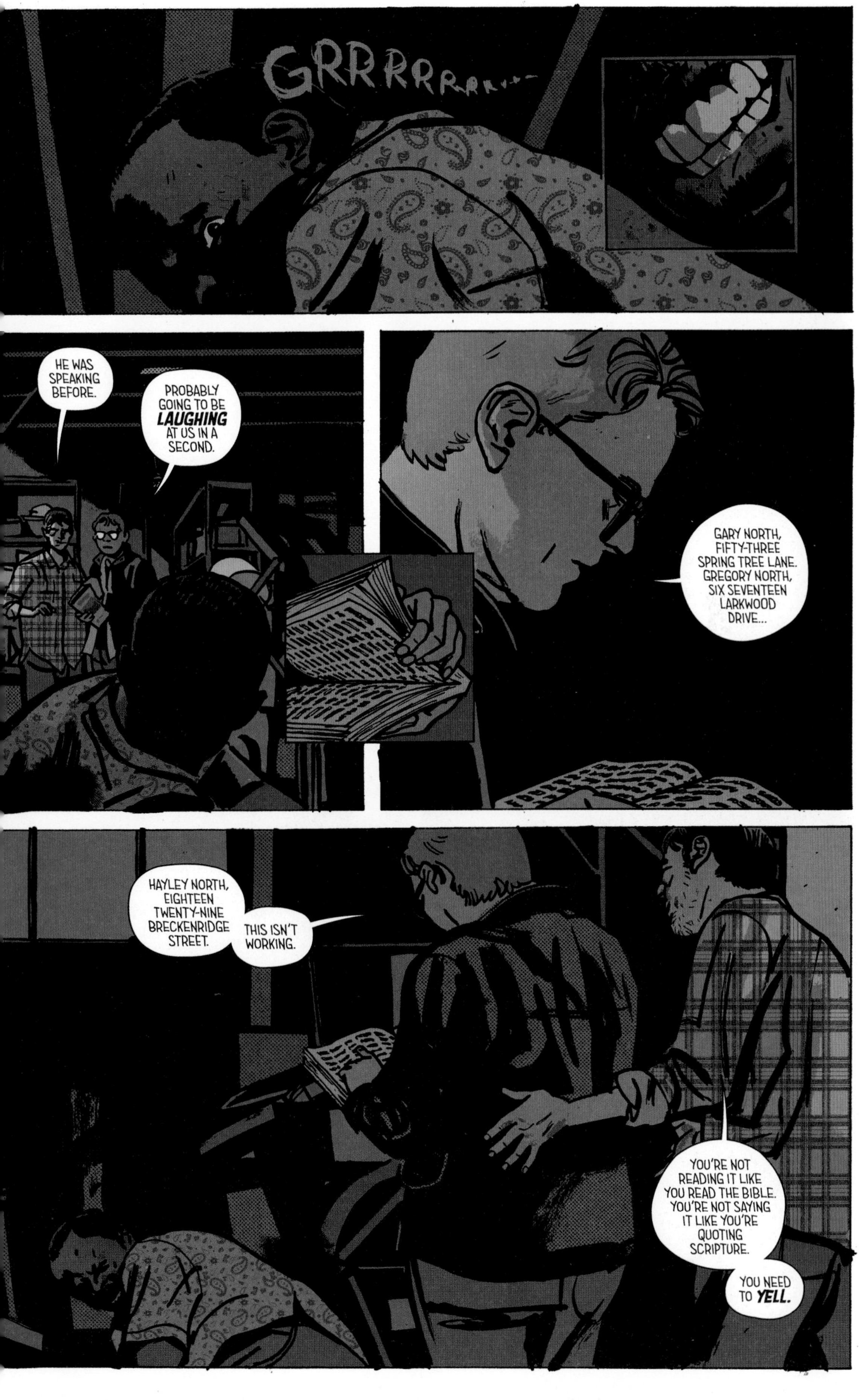
GRRRRRRRR...
HE WAS SPEAKING BEFORE.
PROBABLY GOING TO BE *LAUGHING* AT US IN A SECOND.
GARY NORTH, FIFTY-THREE SPRING TREE LANE. GREGORY NORTH, SIX SEVENTEEN LARKWOOD DRIVE...
HAYLEY NORTH, EIGHTEEN TWENTY-NINE BRECKENRIDGE STREET.
THIS ISN'T WORKING.
YOU'RE NOT READING IT LIKE YOU READ THE BIBLE. YOU'RE NOT SAYING IT LIKE YOU'RE QUOTING SCRIPTURE.
YOU NEED TO *YELL.*

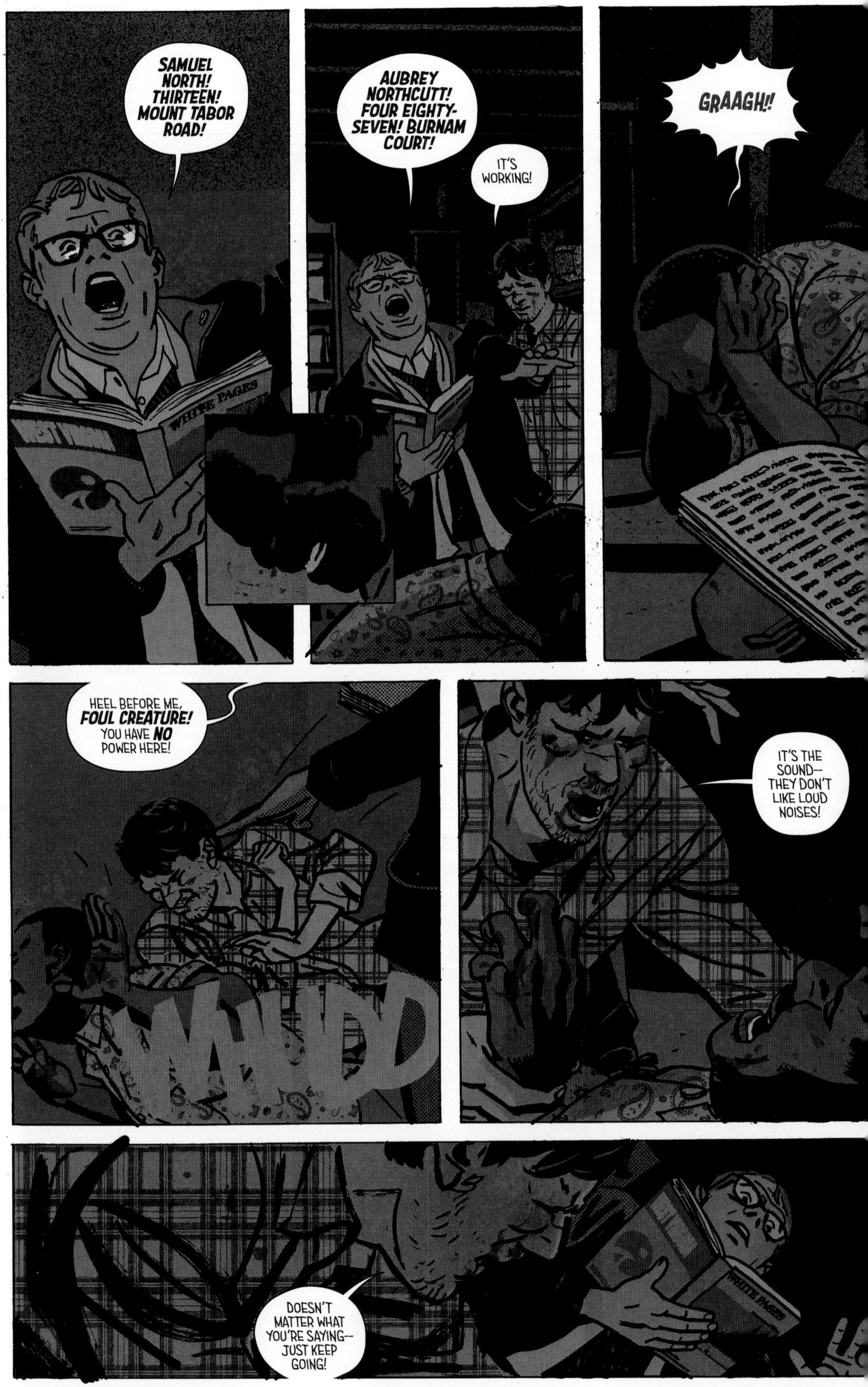
SAMUEL NORTH! THIRTEEN! MOUNT TABOR ROAD!
AUBREY NORTHCUTT! FOUR EIGHTY-SEVEN! BURNAM COURT!
IT'S WORKING!
GRAAGH!!
HEEL BEFORE ME, FOUL CREATURE! YOU HAVE NO POWER HERE!
WHUDD
IT'S THE SOUND-- THEY DON'T LIKE LOUD NOISES!
DOESN'T MATTER WHAT YOU'RE SAYING-- JUST KEEP GOING!

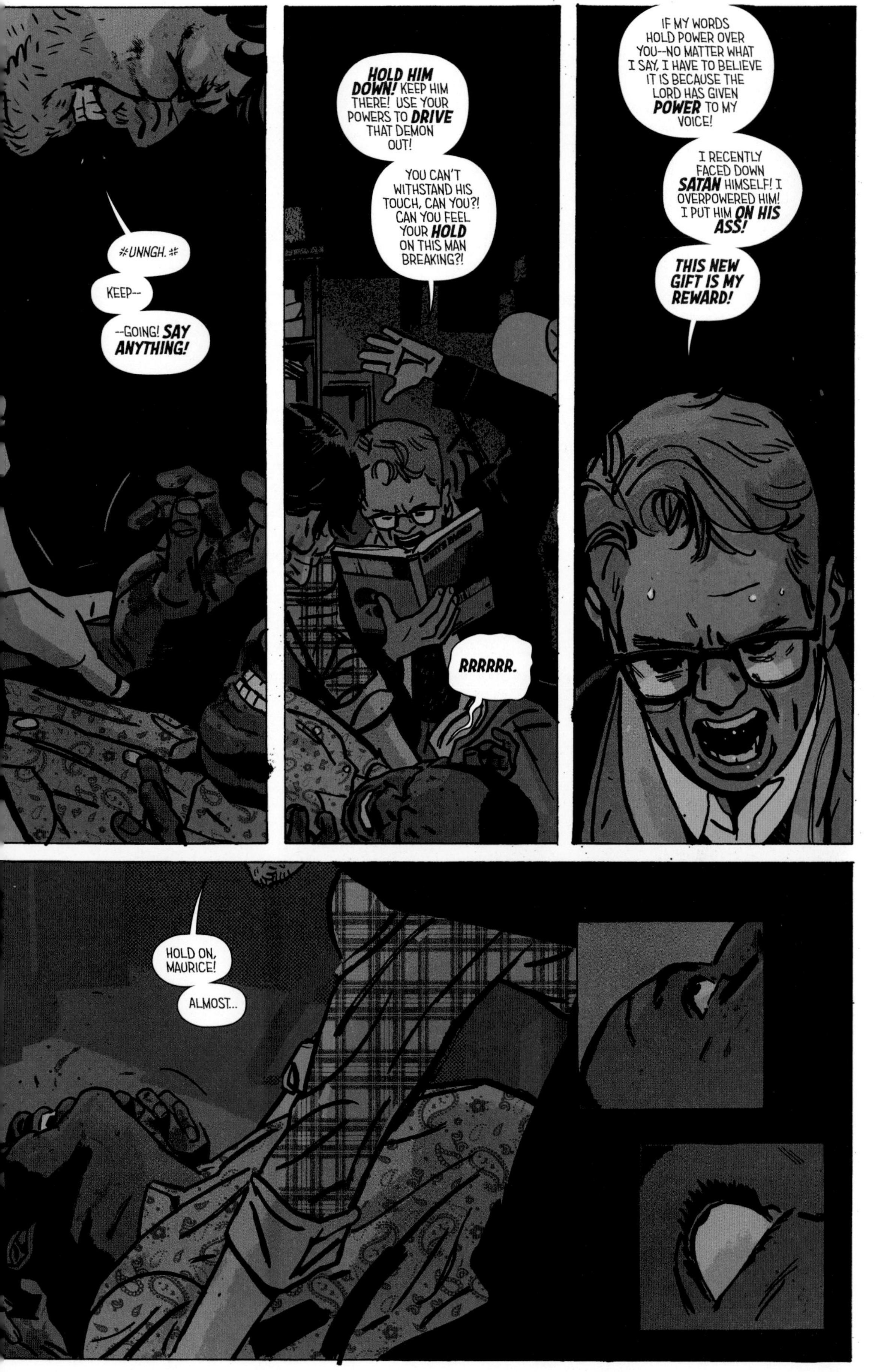

#UNNGH.#
KEEP--
--GOING! SAY ANYTHING!
HOLD HIM DOWN! KEEP HIM THERE! USE YOUR POWERS TO DRIVE THAT DEMON OUT!
YOU CAN'T WITHSTAND HIS TOUCH, CAN YOU?! CAN YOU FEEL YOUR HOLD ON THIS MAN BREAKING?!
RRRRRR.
IF MY WORDS HOLD POWER OVER YOU--NO MATTER WHAT I SAY, I HAVE TO BELIEVE IT IS BECAUSE THE LORD HAS GIVEN POWER TO MY VOICE!
I RECENTLY FACED DOWN SATAN HIMSELF! I OVERPOWERED HIM! I PUT HIM ON HIS ASS!
THIS NEW GIFT IS MY REWARD!
HOLD ON, MAURICE!
ALMOST...

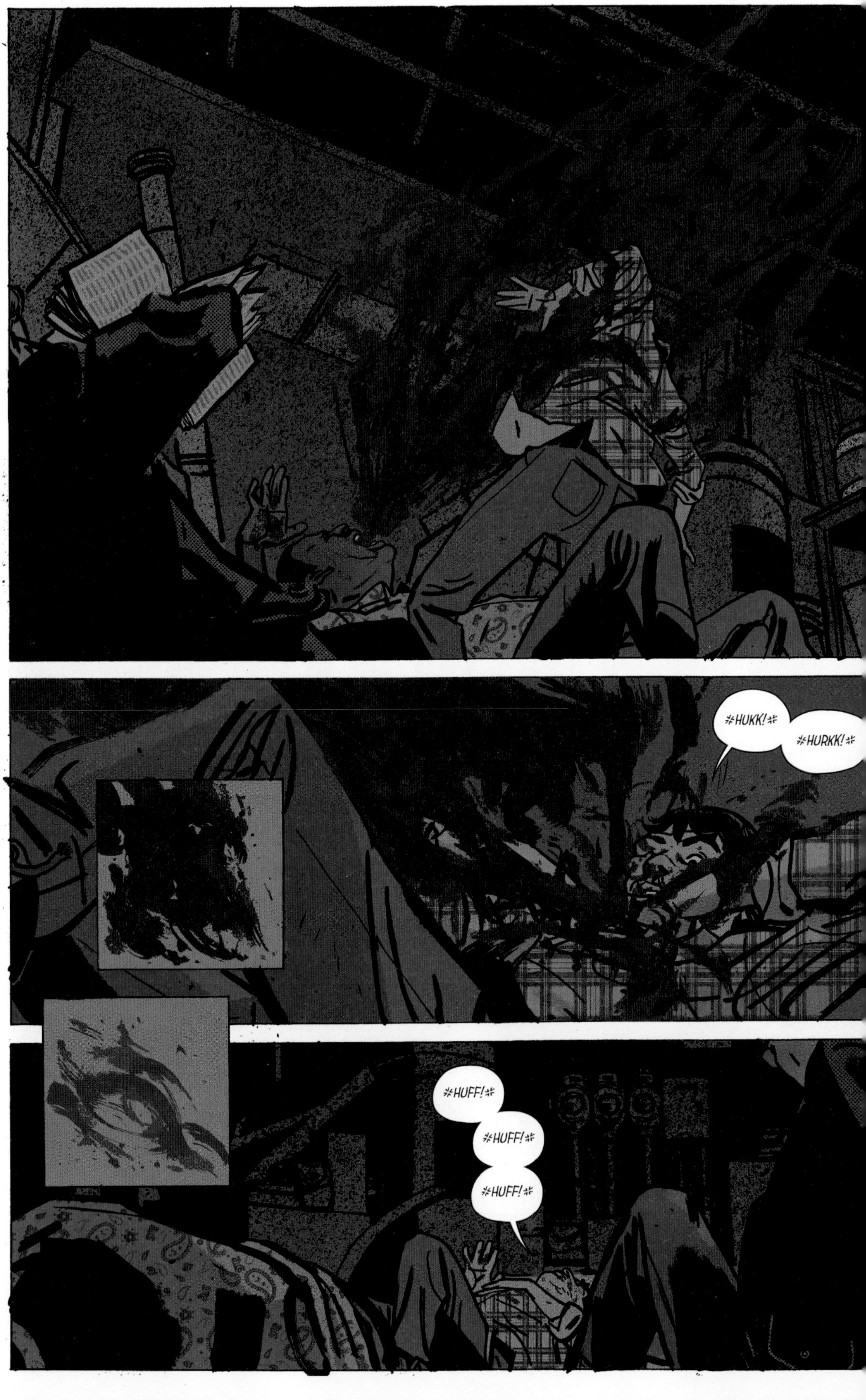

HUKK!
HURKK!
HUFF!
HUFF!
HUFF!

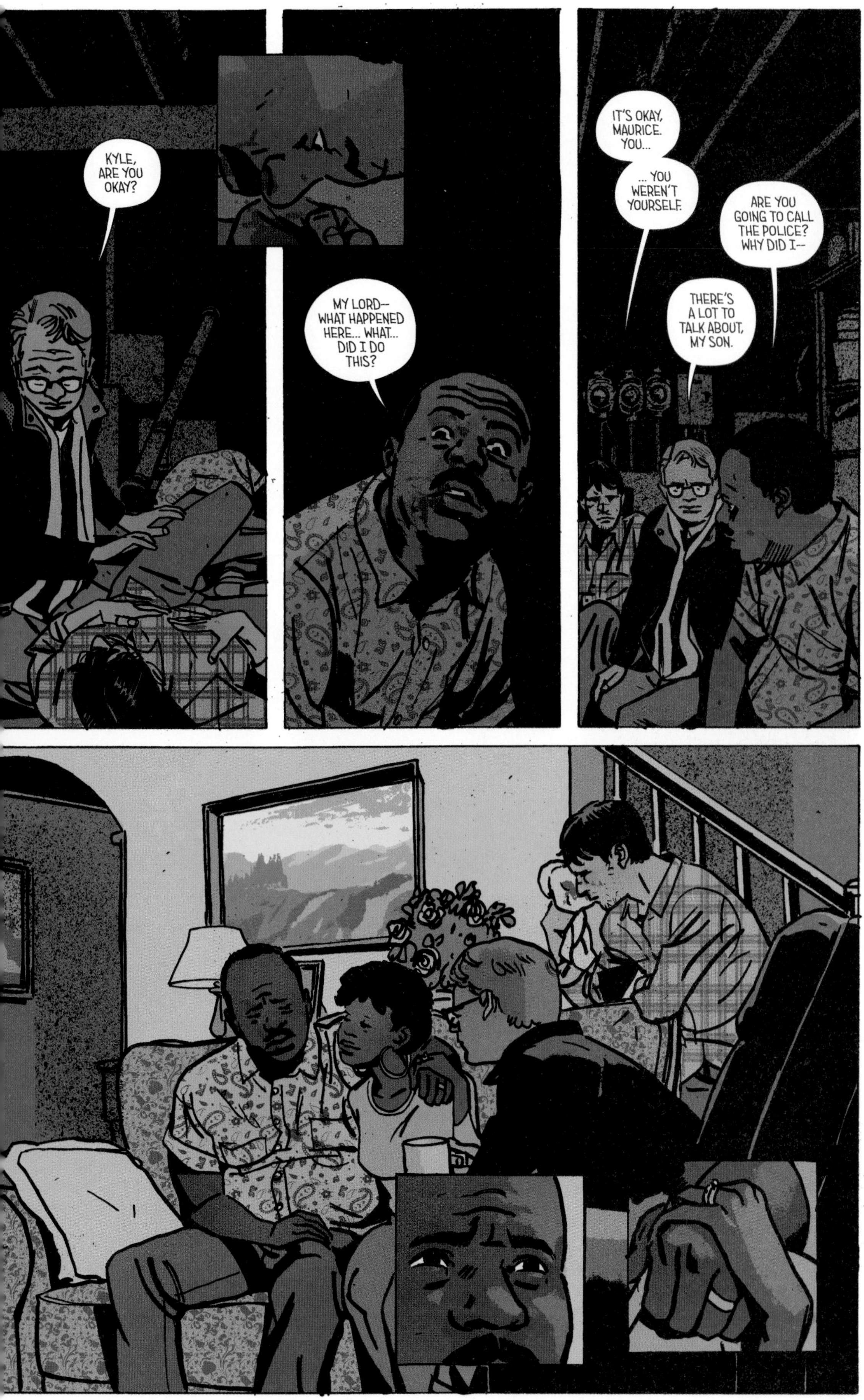

KYLE, ARE YOU OKAY?
MY LORD-- WHAT HAPPENED HERE... WHAT... DID I DO THIS?
IT'S OKAY, MAURICE. YOU...
... YOU WEREN'T YOURSELF.
ARE YOU GOING TO CALL THE POLICE? WHY DID I--
THERE'S A LOT TO TALK ABOUT, MY SON.

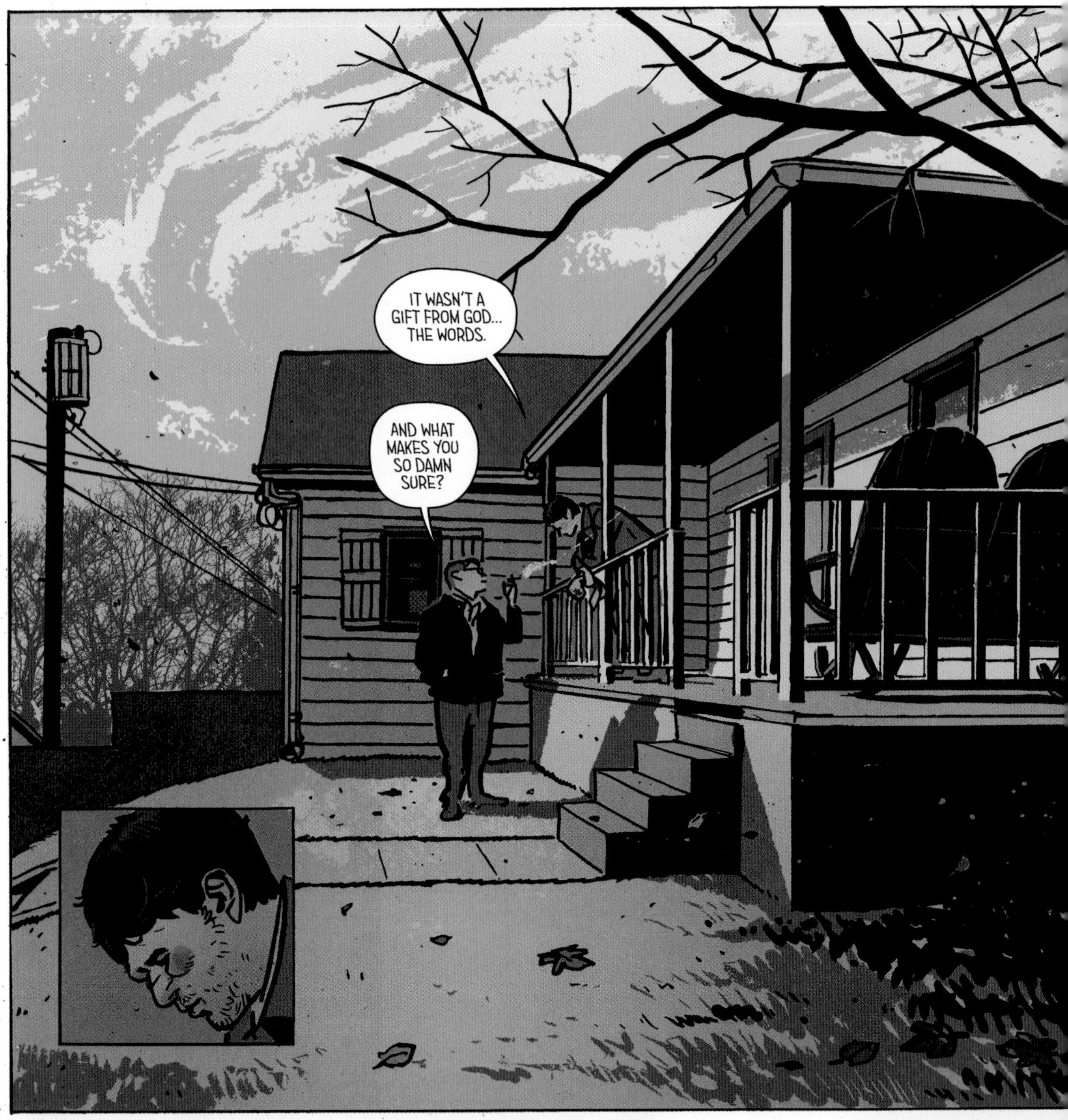
IT WASN'T A GIFT FROM GOD... THE WORDS.
AND WHAT MAKES YOU SO DAMN SURE?

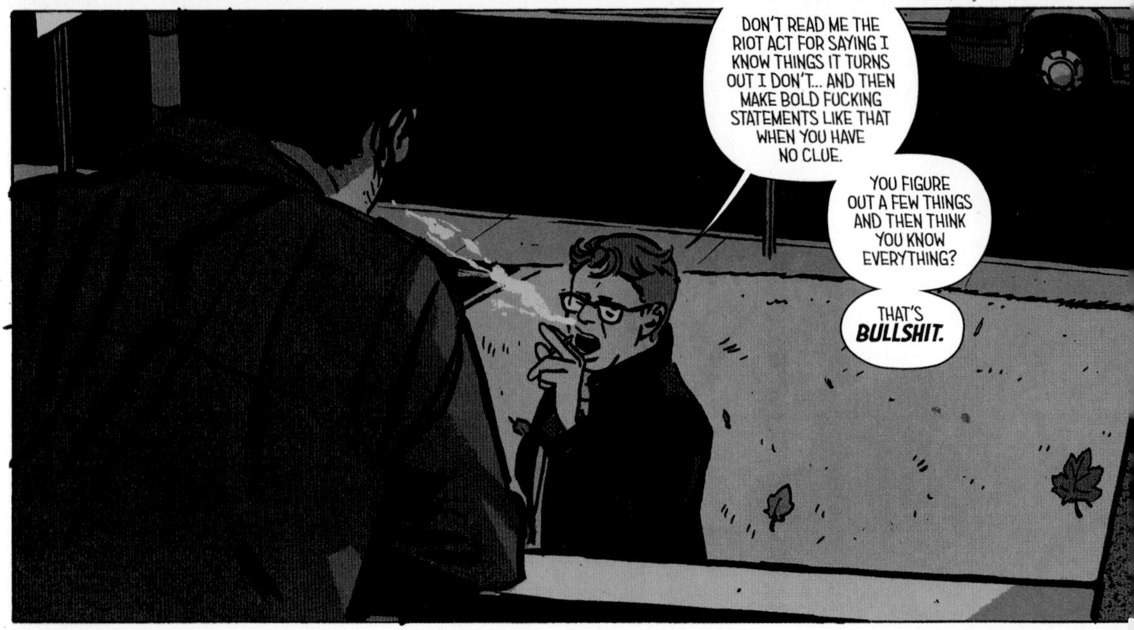
DON'T READ ME THE RIOT ACT FOR SAYING I KNOW THINGS IT TURNS OUT I DON'T... AND THEN MAKE BOLD FUCKING STATEMENTS LIKE THAT WHEN YOU HAVE NO CLUE.
YOU FIGURE OUT A FEW THINGS AND THEN THINK YOU KNOW EVERYTHING?
THAT'S **BULLSHIT.**

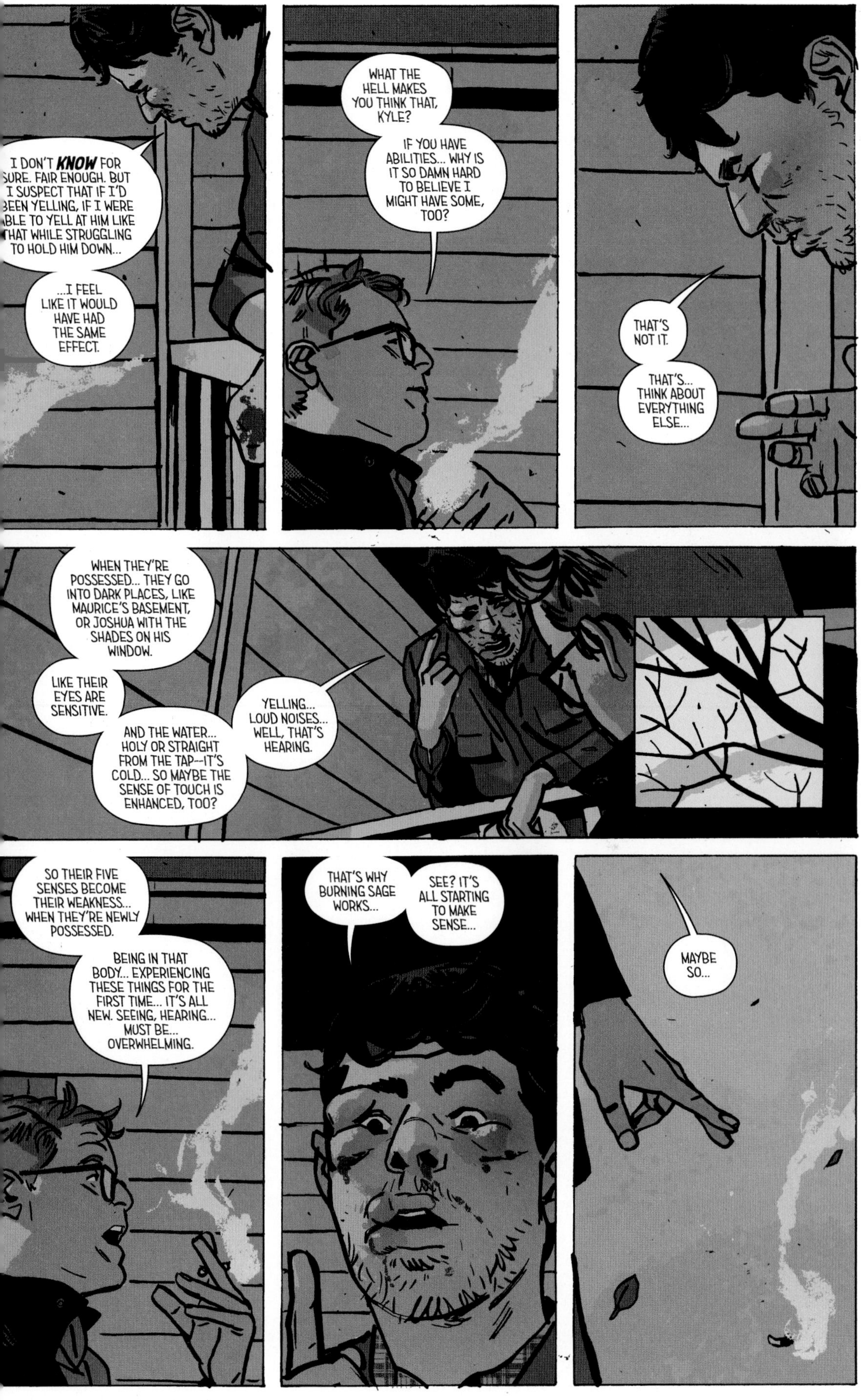
I DON'T **KNOW** FOR SURE. FAIR ENOUGH. BUT I SUSPECT THAT IF I'D BEEN YELLING, IF I WERE ABLE TO YELL AT HIM LIKE THAT WHILE STRUGGLING TO HOLD HIM DOWN...
...I FEEL LIKE IT WOULD HAVE HAD THE SAME EFFECT.
WHAT THE HELL MAKES YOU THINK THAT, KYLE?
IF YOU HAVE ABILITIES... WHY IS IT SO DAMN HARD TO BELIEVE I MIGHT HAVE SOME, TOO?
THAT'S NOT IT.
THAT'S... THINK ABOUT EVERYTHING ELSE...
WHEN THEY'RE POSSESSED... THEY GO INTO DARK PLACES, LIKE MAURICE'S BASEMENT, OR JOSHUA WITH THE SHADES ON HIS WINDOW.
LIKE THEIR EYES ARE SENSITIVE.
AND THE WATER... HOLY OR STRAIGHT FROM THE TAP--IT'S COLD... SO MAYBE THE SENSE OF TOUCH IS ENHANCED, TOO?
YELLING... LOUD NOISES... WELL, THAT'S HEARING.
SO THEIR FIVE SENSES BECOME THEIR WEAKNESS... WHEN THEY'RE NEWLY POSSESSED.
BEING IN THAT BODY... EXPERIENCING THESE THINGS FOR THE FIRST TIME... IT'S ALL NEW. SEEING, HEARING... MUST BE... OVERWHELMING.
THAT'S WHY BURNING SAGE WORKS...
SEE? IT'S ALL STARTING TO MAKE SENSE...
MAYBE SO...

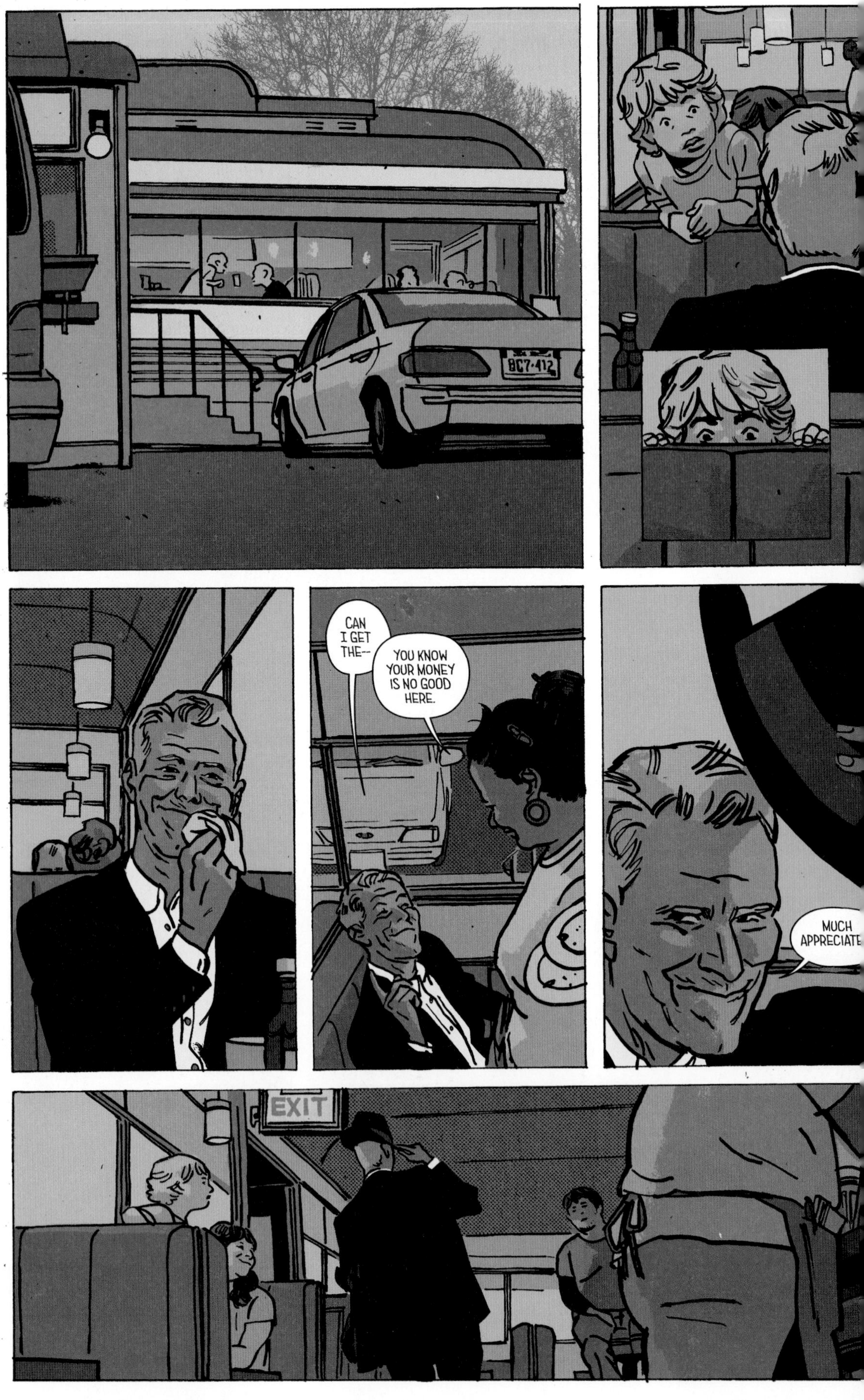
BC7·412
CAN I GET THE--
YOU KNOW YOUR MONEY IS NO GOOD HERE.
MUCH APPRECIATE
EXIT

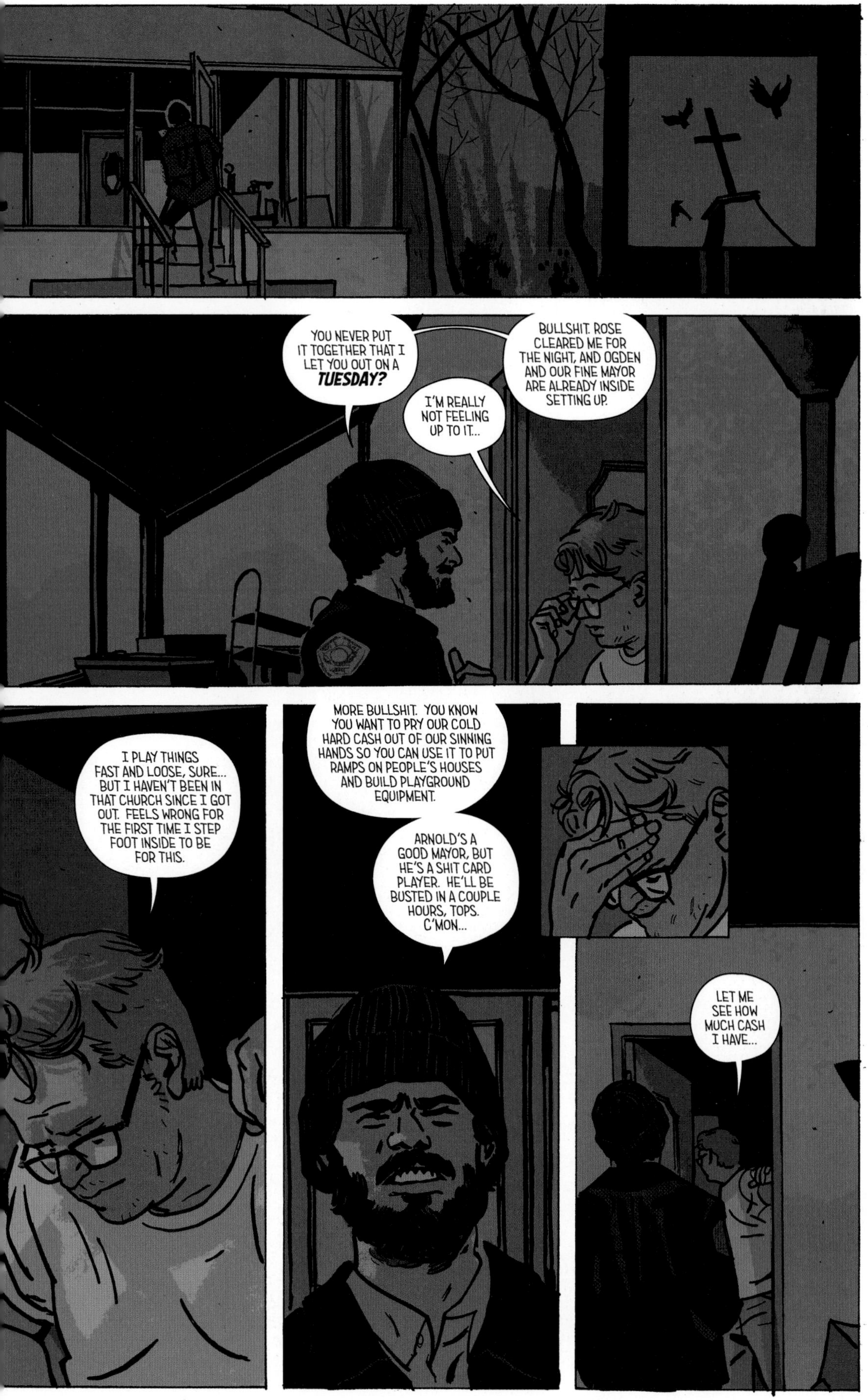

YOU NEVER PUT IT TOGETHER THAT I LET YOU OUT ON A *TUESDAY?*
BULLSHIT. ROSE CLEARED ME FOR THE NIGHT, AND OGDEN AND OUR FINE MAYOR ARE ALREADY INSIDE SETTING UP.
I'M REALLY NOT FEELING UP TO IT...
I PLAY THINGS FAST AND LOOSE, SURE... BUT I HAVEN'T BEEN IN THAT CHURCH SINCE I GOT OUT. FEELS WRONG FOR THE FIRST TIME I STEP FOOT INSIDE TO BE FOR THIS.
MORE BULLSHIT. YOU KNOW YOU WANT TO PRY OUR COLD HARD CASH OUT OF OUR SINNING HANDS SO YOU CAN USE IT TO PUT RAMPS ON PEOPLE'S HOUSES AND BUILD PLAYGROUND EQUIPMENT.
ARNOLD'S A GOOD MAYOR, BUT HE'S A SHIT CARD PLAYER. HE'LL BE BUSTED IN A COUPLE HOURS, TOPS. C'MON...
LET ME SEE HOW MUCH CASH I HAVE...

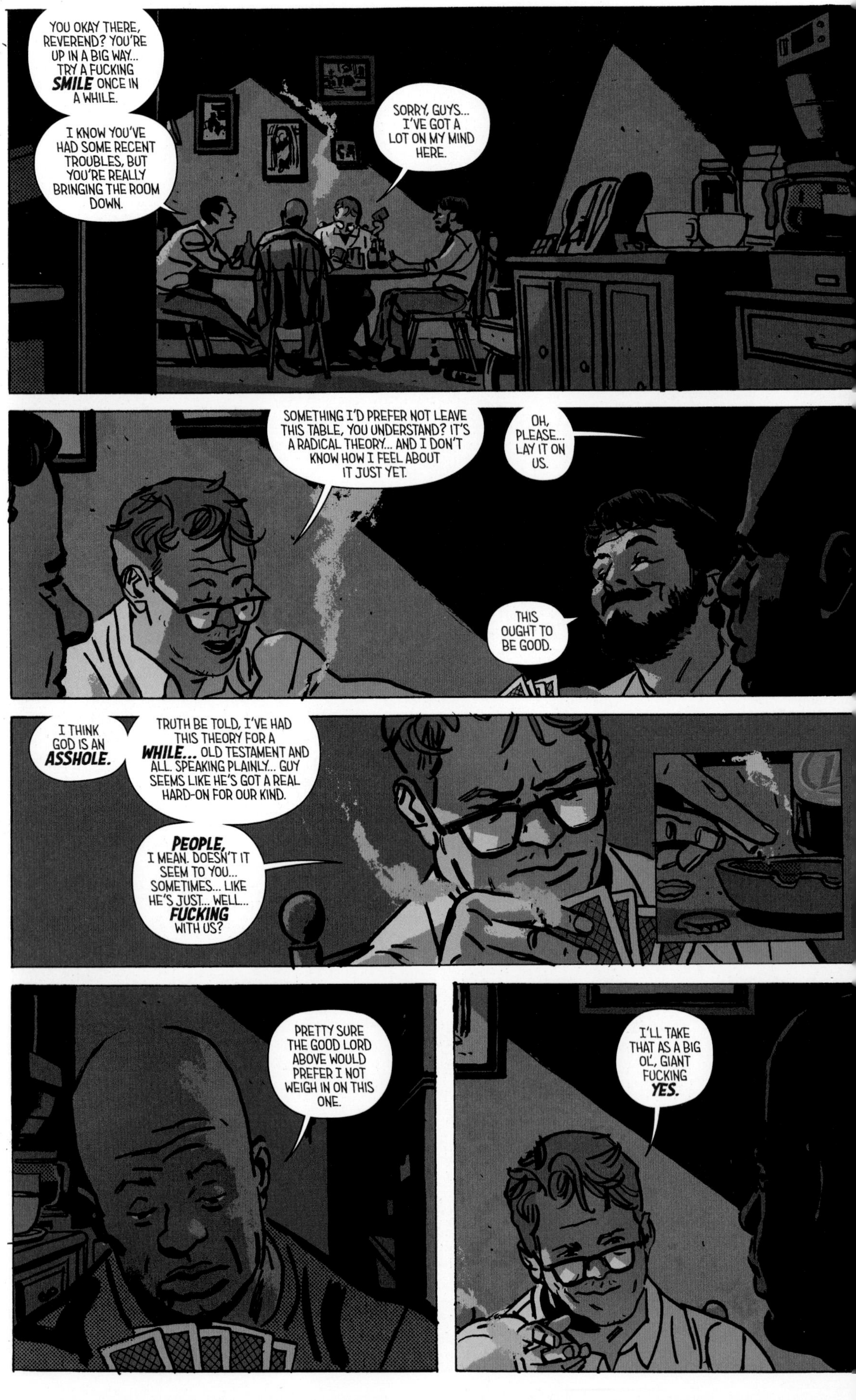

YOU OKAY THERE, REVEREND? YOU'RE UP IN A BIG WAY... TRY A FUCKING SMILE ONCE IN A WHILE.
I KNOW YOU'VE HAD SOME RECENT TROUBLES, BUT YOU'RE REALLY BRINGING THE ROOM DOWN.
SORRY, GUYS... I'VE GOT A LOT ON MY MIND HERE.
SOMETHING I'D PREFER NOT LEAVE THIS TABLE, YOU UNDERSTAND? IT'S A RADICAL THEORY... AND I DON'T KNOW HOW I FEEL ABOUT IT JUST YET.
OH, PLEASE... LAY IT ON US.
THIS OUGHT TO BE GOOD.
I THINK GOD IS AN ASSHOLE.
TRUTH BE TOLD, I'VE HAD THIS THEORY FOR A WHILE... OLD TESTAMENT AND ALL. SPEAKING PLAINLY... GUY SEEMS LIKE HE'S GOT A REAL HARD-ON FOR OUR KIND.
PEOPLE, I MEAN. DOESN'T IT SEEM TO YOU... SOMETIMES... LIKE HE'S JUST... WELL... FUCKING WITH US?
PRETTY SURE THE GOOD LORD ABOVE WOULD PREFER I NOT WEIGH IN ON THIS ONE.
I'LL TAKE THAT AS A BIG OL', GIANT FUCKING YES.

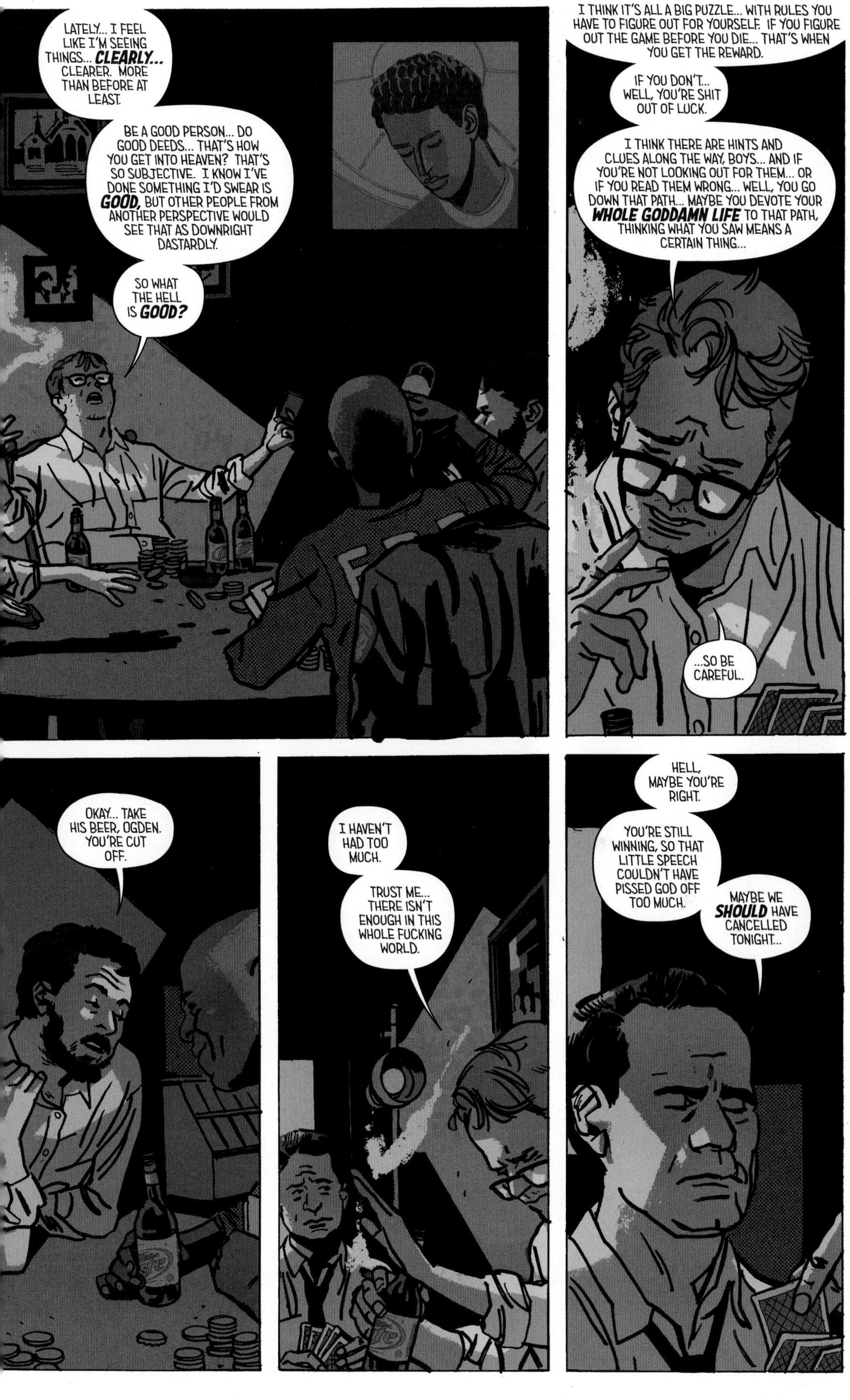
LATELY... I FEEL LIKE I'M SEEING THINGS... CLEARLY... CLEARER. MORE THAN BEFORE AT LEAST.
BE A GOOD PERSON... DO GOOD DEEDS... THAT'S HOW YOU GET INTO HEAVEN? THAT'S SO SUBJECTIVE. I KNOW I'VE DONE SOMETHING I'D SWEAR IS GOOD, BUT OTHER PEOPLE FROM ANOTHER PERSPECTIVE WOULD SEE THAT AS DOWNRIGHT DASTARDLY.
SO WHAT THE HELL IS GOOD?
I THINK IT'S ALL A BIG PUZZLE... WITH RULES YOU HAVE TO FIGURE OUT FOR YOURSELF. IF YOU FIGURE OUT THE GAME BEFORE YOU DIE... THAT'S WHEN YOU GET THE REWARD.
IF YOU DON'T... WELL, YOU'RE SHIT OUT OF LUCK.
I THINK THERE ARE HINTS AND CLUES ALONG THE WAY, BOYS... AND IF YOU'RE NOT LOOKING OUT FOR THEM... OR IF YOU READ THEM WRONG... WELL, YOU GO DOWN THAT PATH... MAYBE YOU DEVOTE YOUR WHOLE GODDAMN LIFE TO THAT PATH, THINKING WHAT YOU SAW MEANS A CERTAIN THING...
...SO BE CAREFUL.
OKAY... TAKE HIS BEER, OGDEN. YOU'RE CUT OFF.
I HAVEN'T HAD TOO MUCH.
TRUST ME... THERE ISN'T ENOUGH IN THIS WHOLE FUCKING WORLD.
HELL, MAYBE YOU'RE RIGHT.
YOU'RE STILL WINNING, SO THAT LITTLE SPEECH COULDN'T HAVE PISSED GOD OFF TOO MUCH.
MAYBE WE SHOULD HAVE CANCELLED TONIGHT...

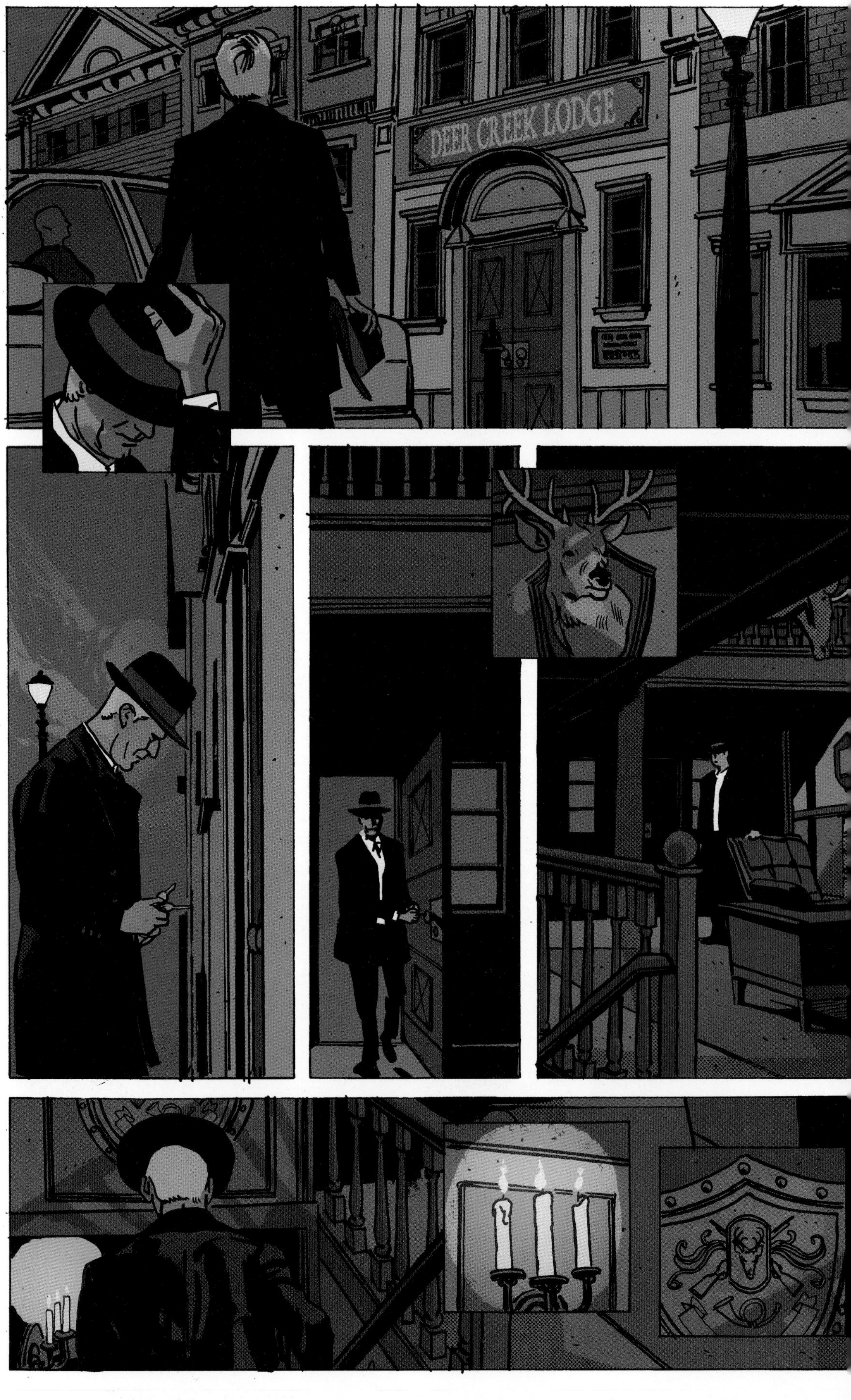
DEER CREEK LODGE

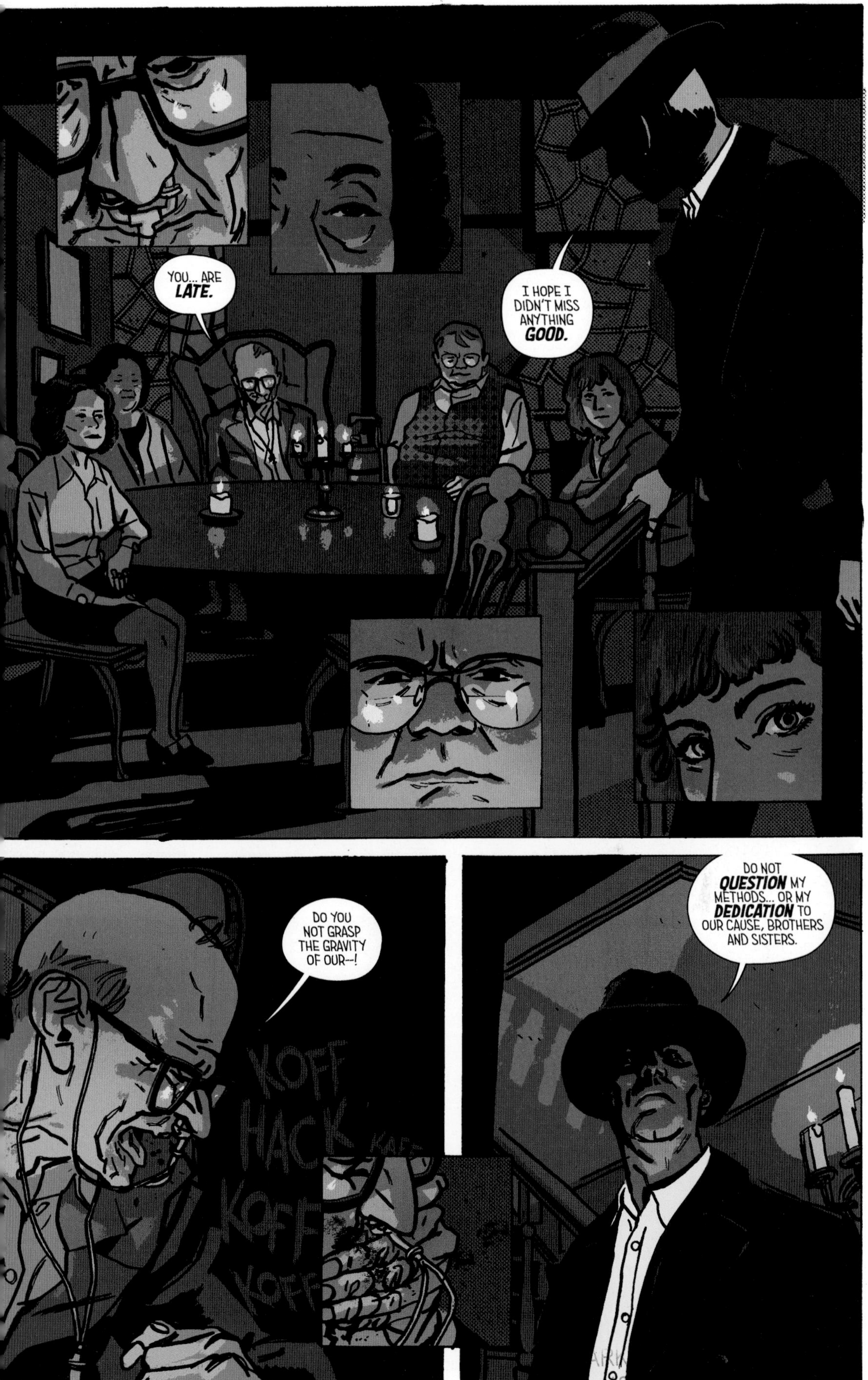
YOU... ARE **LATE.**
I HOPE I DIDN'T MISS ANYTHING **GOOD.**
DO YOU NOT GRASP THE GRAVITY OF OUR--!
KOFF
HACK
KAFF
KOFF
KOFF
DO NOT **QUESTION** MY METHODS... OR MY **DEDICATION** TO OUR CAUSE, BROTHERS AND SISTERS.

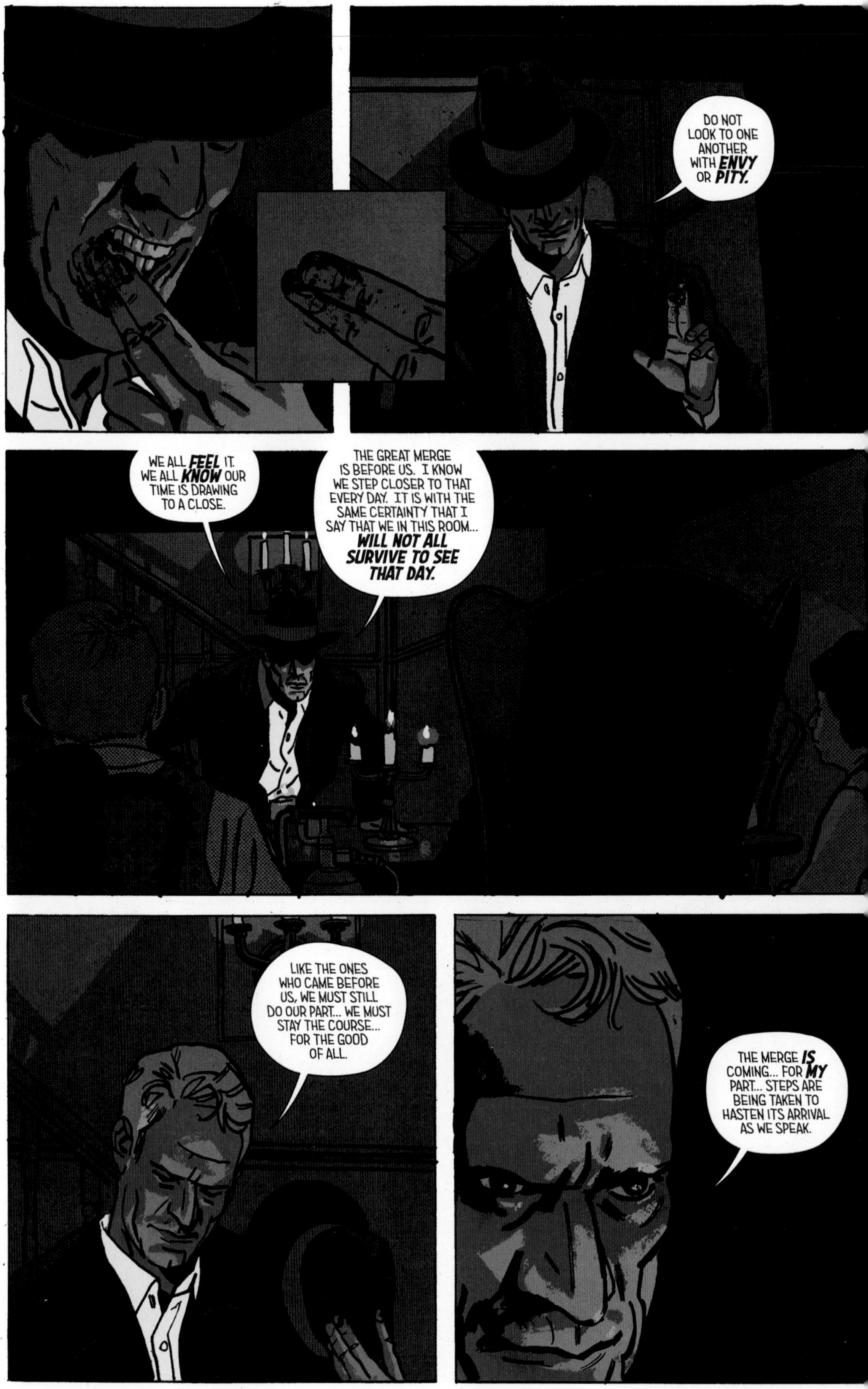
DO NOT LOOK TO ONE ANOTHER WITH ENVY OR PITY.
WE ALL FEEL IT. WE ALL KNOW OUR TIME IS DRAWING TO A CLOSE.
THE GREAT MERGE IS BEFORE US. I KNOW WE STEP CLOSER TO THAT EVERY DAY. IT IS WITH THE SAME CERTAINTY THAT I SAY THAT WE IN THIS ROOM... WILL NOT ALL SURVIVE TO SEE THAT DAY.
LIKE THE ONES WHO CAME BEFORE US, WE MUST STILL DO OUR PART... WE MUST STAY THE COURSE... FOR THE GOOD OF ALL.
THE MERGE IS COMING... FOR MY PART... STEPS ARE BEING TAKEN TO HASTEN ITS ARRIVAL AS WE SPEAK.

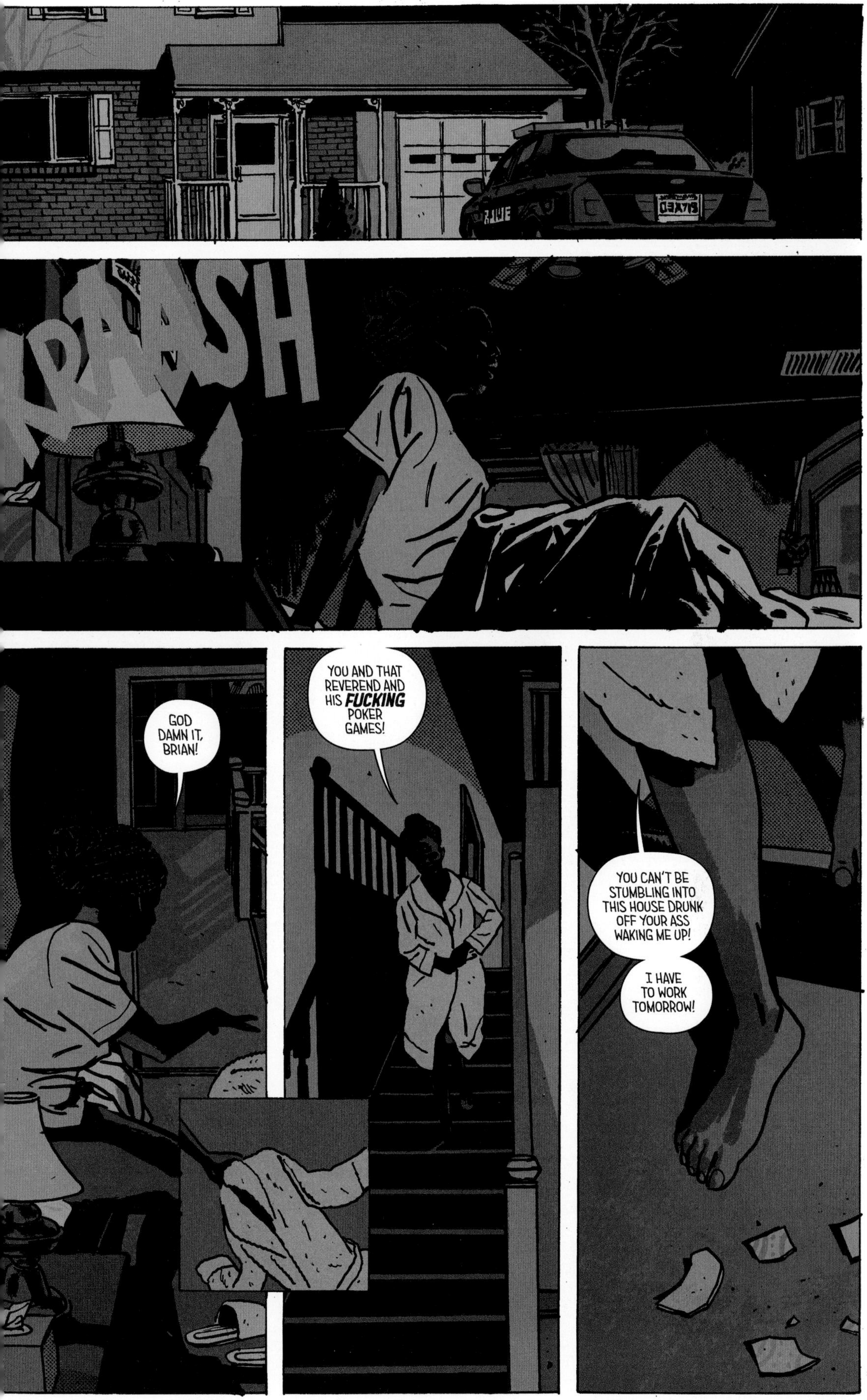
KRASH
GOD DAMN IT, BRIAN!
YOU AND THAT REVEREND AND HIS FUCKING POKER GAMES!
YOU CAN'T BE STUMBLING INTO THIS HOUSE DRUNK OFF YOUR ASS WAKING ME UP!
I HAVE TO WORK TOMORROW!

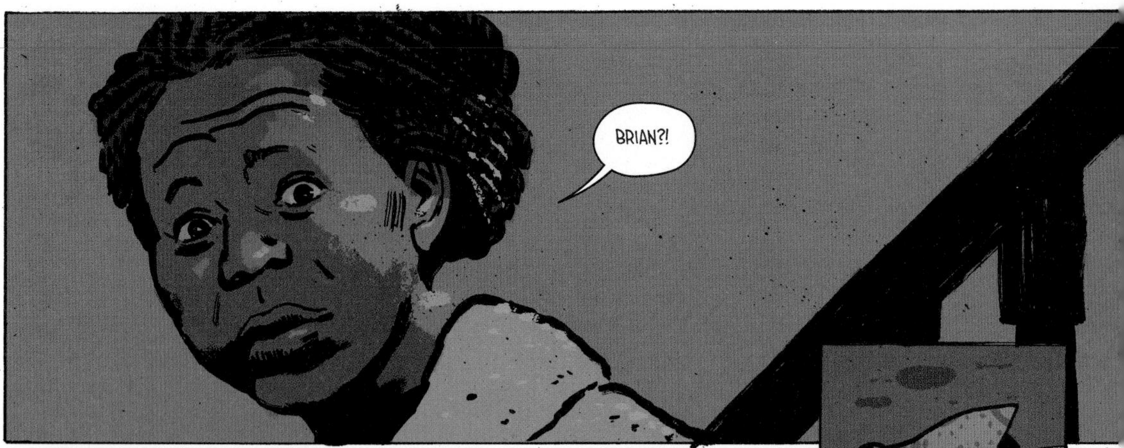
BRIAN?!

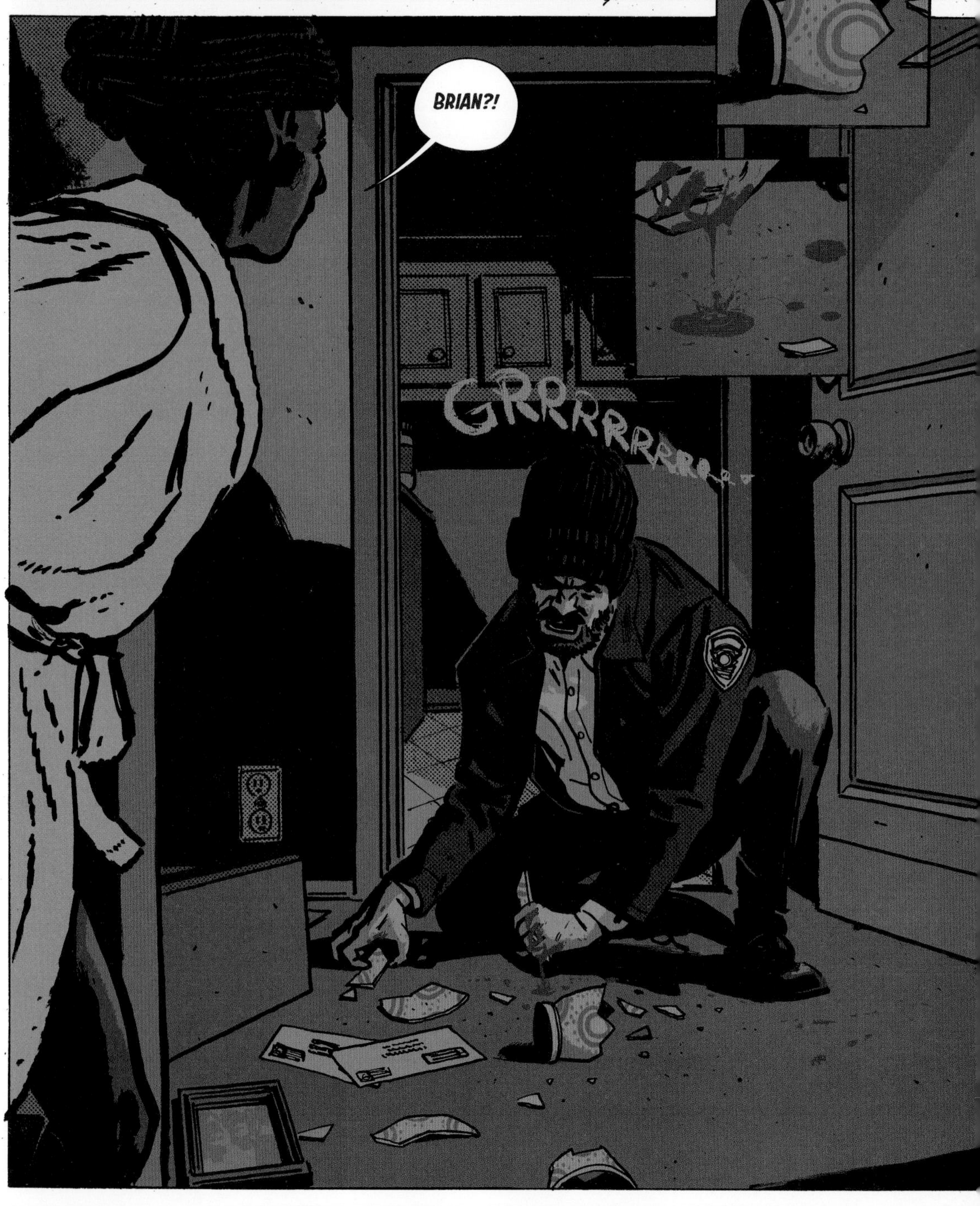
BRIAN?!
GRRRRRRRRR...

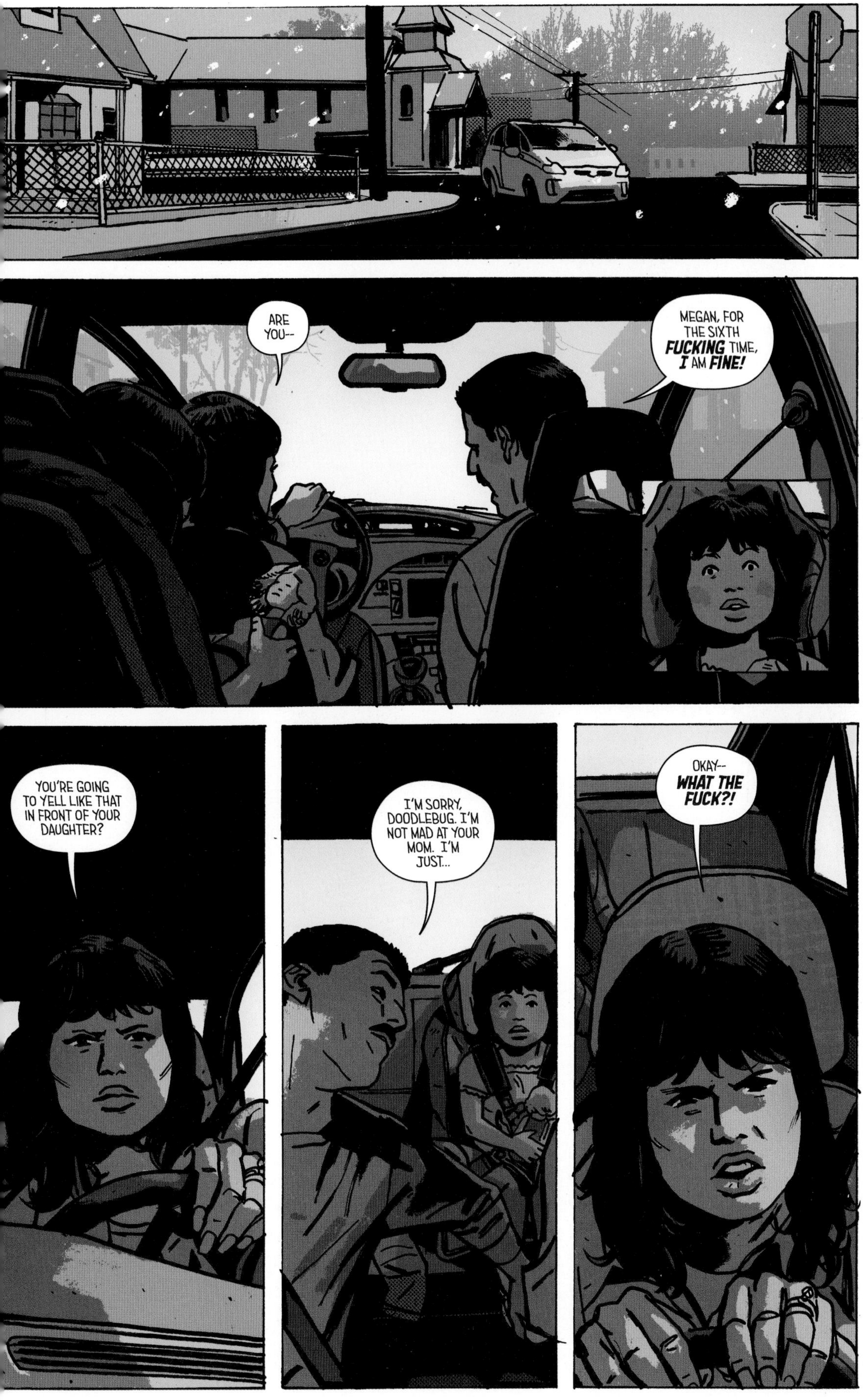
ARE YOU--
MEGAN, FOR THE SIXTH FUCKING TIME, I AM FINE!
YOU'RE GOING TO YELL LIKE THAT IN FRONT OF YOUR DAUGHTER?
I'M SORRY, DOODLEBUG. I'M NOT MAD AT YOUR MOM. I'M JUST...
OKAY-- WHAT THE FUCK?!

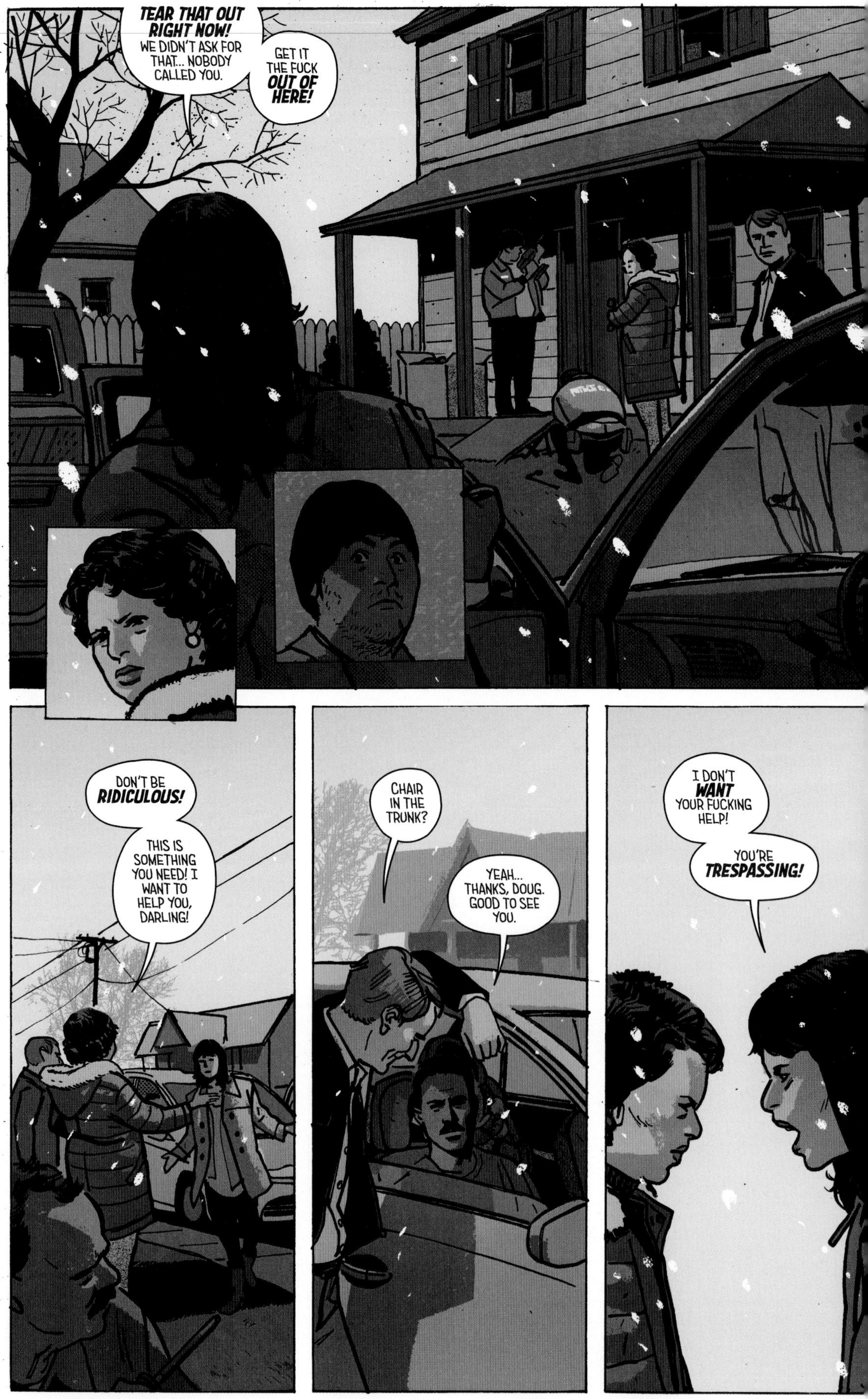
TEAR THAT OUT RIGHT NOW! WE DIDN'T ASK FOR THAT... NOBODY CALLED YOU.
GET IT THE FUCK OUT OF HERE!
DON'T BE RIDICULOUS!
THIS IS SOMETHING YOU NEED! I WANT TO HELP YOU, DARLING!
CHAIR IN THE TRUNK?
YEAH... THANKS, DOUG. GOOD TO SEE YOU.
I DON'T WANT YOUR FUCKING HELP!
YOU'RE TRESPASSING!

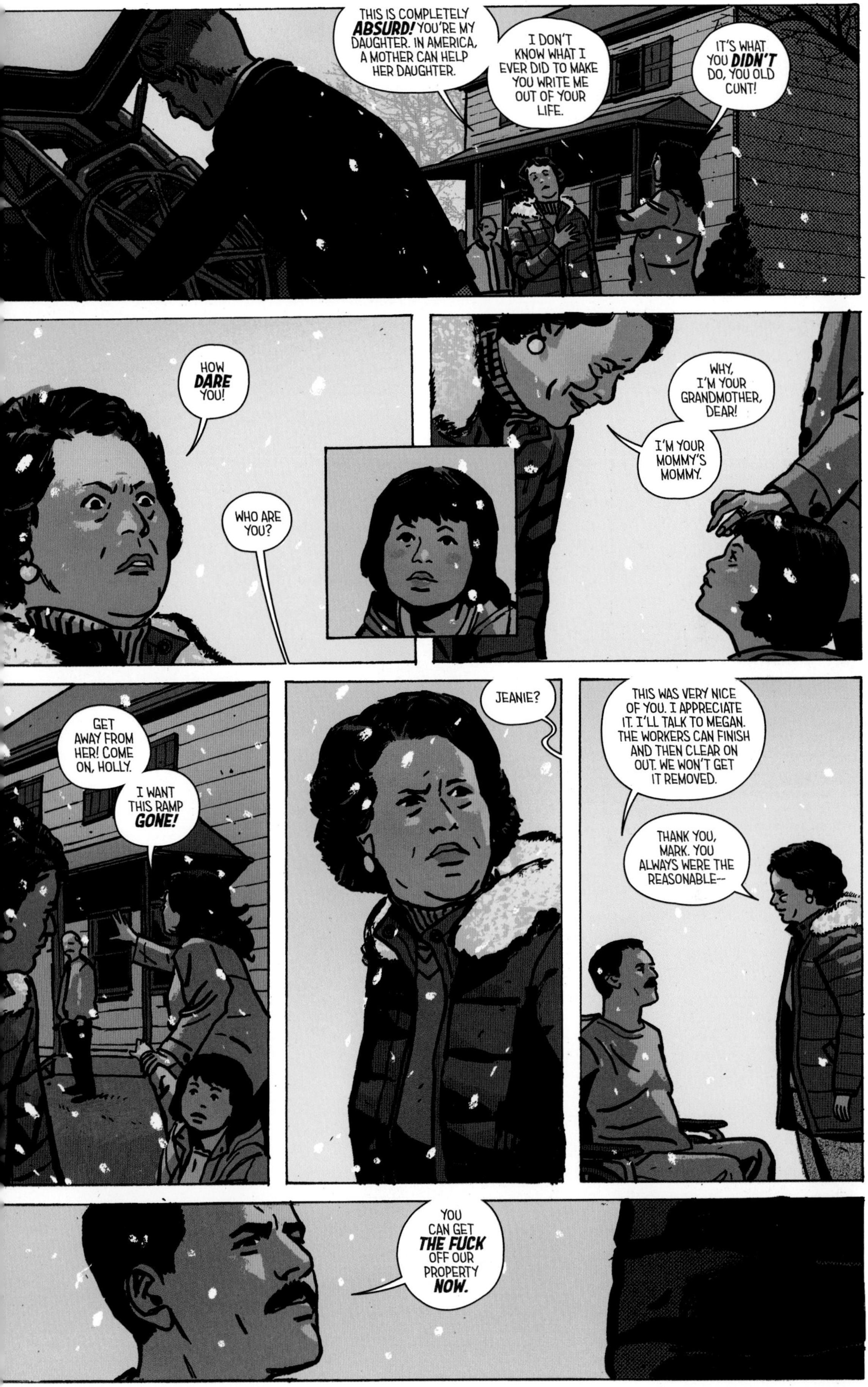
THIS IS COMPLETELY ABSURD! YOU'RE MY DAUGHTER. IN AMERICA, A MOTHER CAN HELP HER DAUGHTER.
I DON'T KNOW WHAT I EVER DID TO MAKE YOU WRITE ME OUT OF YOUR LIFE.
IT'S WHAT YOU DIDN'T DO, YOU OLD CUNT!
HOW DARE YOU!
WHO ARE YOU?
WHY, I'M YOUR GRANDMOTHER, DEAR!
I'M YOUR MOMMY'S MOMMY.
GET AWAY FROM HER! COME ON, HOLLY.
I WANT THIS RAMP GONE!
JEANIE?
THIS WAS VERY NICE OF YOU. I APPRECIATE IT. I'LL TALK TO MEGAN. THE WORKERS CAN FINISH AND THEN CLEAR ON OUT. WE WON'T GET IT REMOVED.
THANK YOU, MARK. YOU ALWAYS WERE THE REASONABLE--
YOU CAN GET THE FUCK OFF OUR PROPERTY NOW.

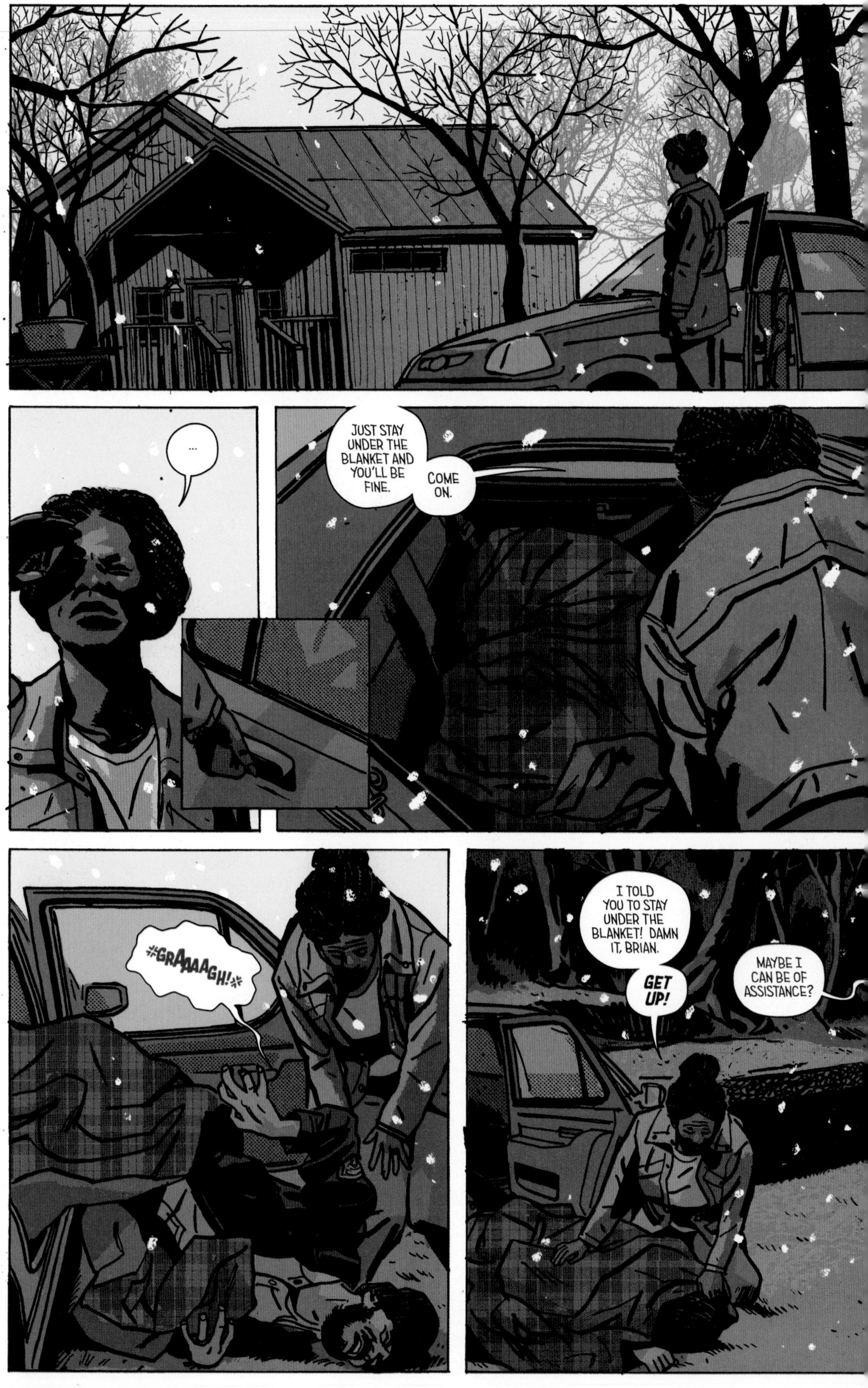
...
JUST STAY UNDER THE BLANKET AND YOU'LL BE FINE.
COME ON.
GRAAAAGH!
I TOLD YOU TO STAY UNDER THE BLANKET! DAMN IT, BRIAN.
GET UP!
MAYBE I CAN BE OF ASSISTANCE?

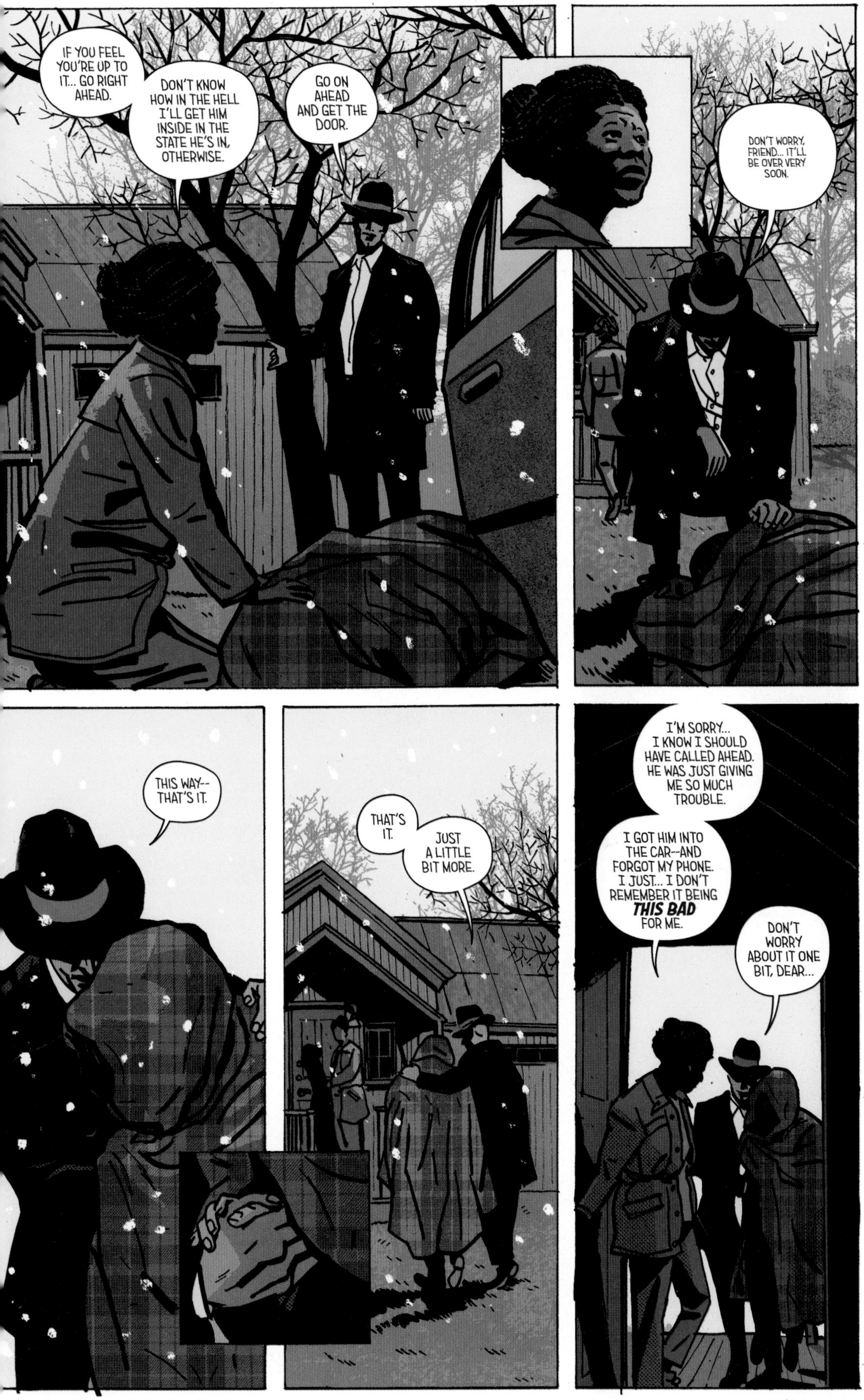
IF YOU FEEL YOU'RE UP TO IT... GO RIGHT AHEAD.
DON'T KNOW HOW IN THE HELL I'LL GET HIM INSIDE IN THE STATE HE'S IN, OTHERWISE.
GO ON AHEAD AND GET THE DOOR.
DON'T WORRY, FRIEND... IT'LL BE OVER VERY SOON.
THIS WAY-- THAT'S IT.
THAT'S IT.
JUST A LITTLE BIT MORE.
I'M SORRY... I KNOW I SHOULD HAVE CALLED AHEAD. HE WAS JUST GIVING ME SO MUCH TROUBLE.
I GOT HIM INTO THE CAR--AND FORGOT MY PHONE. I JUST... I DON'T REMEMBER IT BEING THIS BAD FOR ME.
DON'T WORRY ABOUT IT ONE BIT, DEAR...

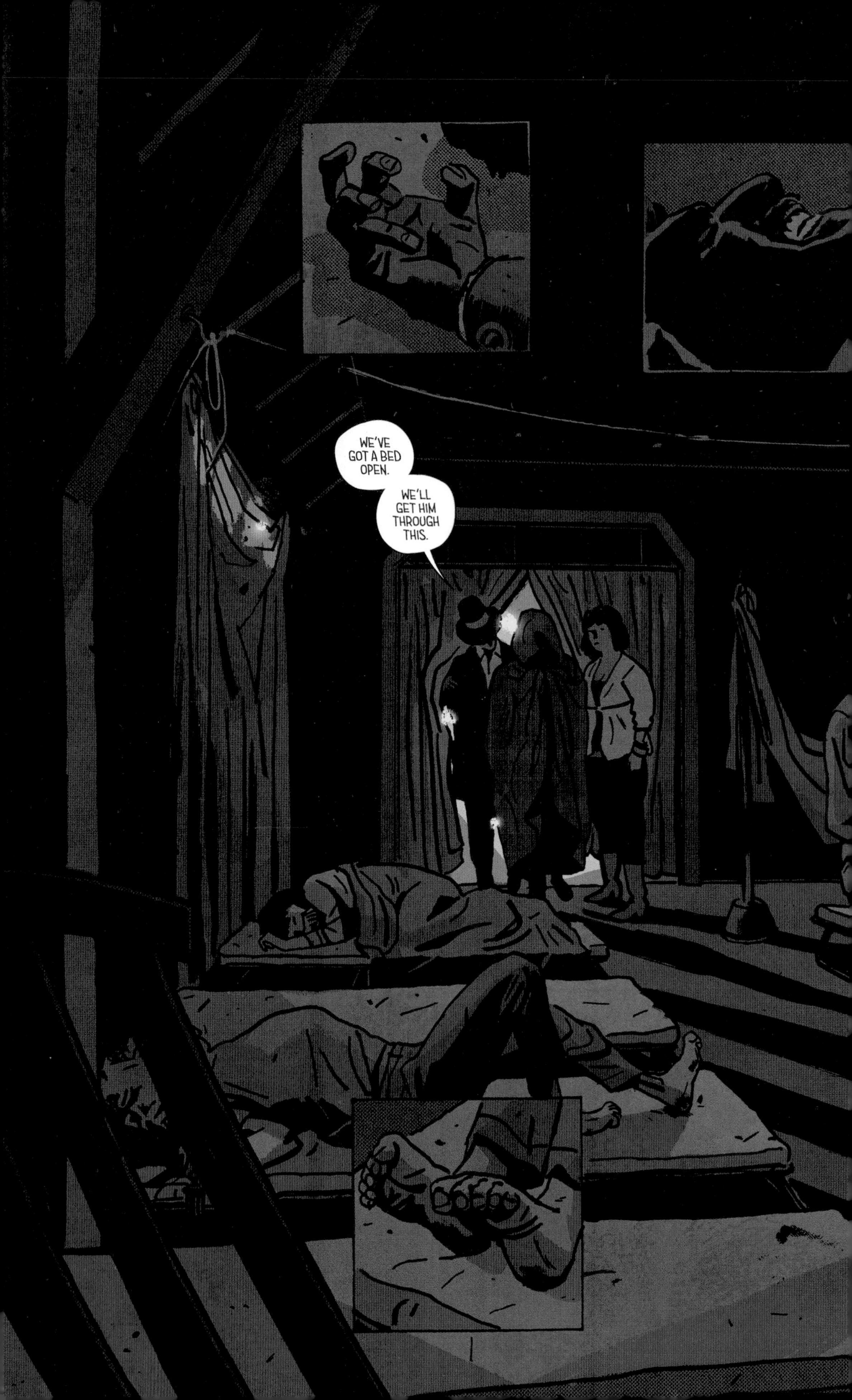
WE'VE GOT A BED OPEN.
WE'LL GET HIM THROUGH THIS.

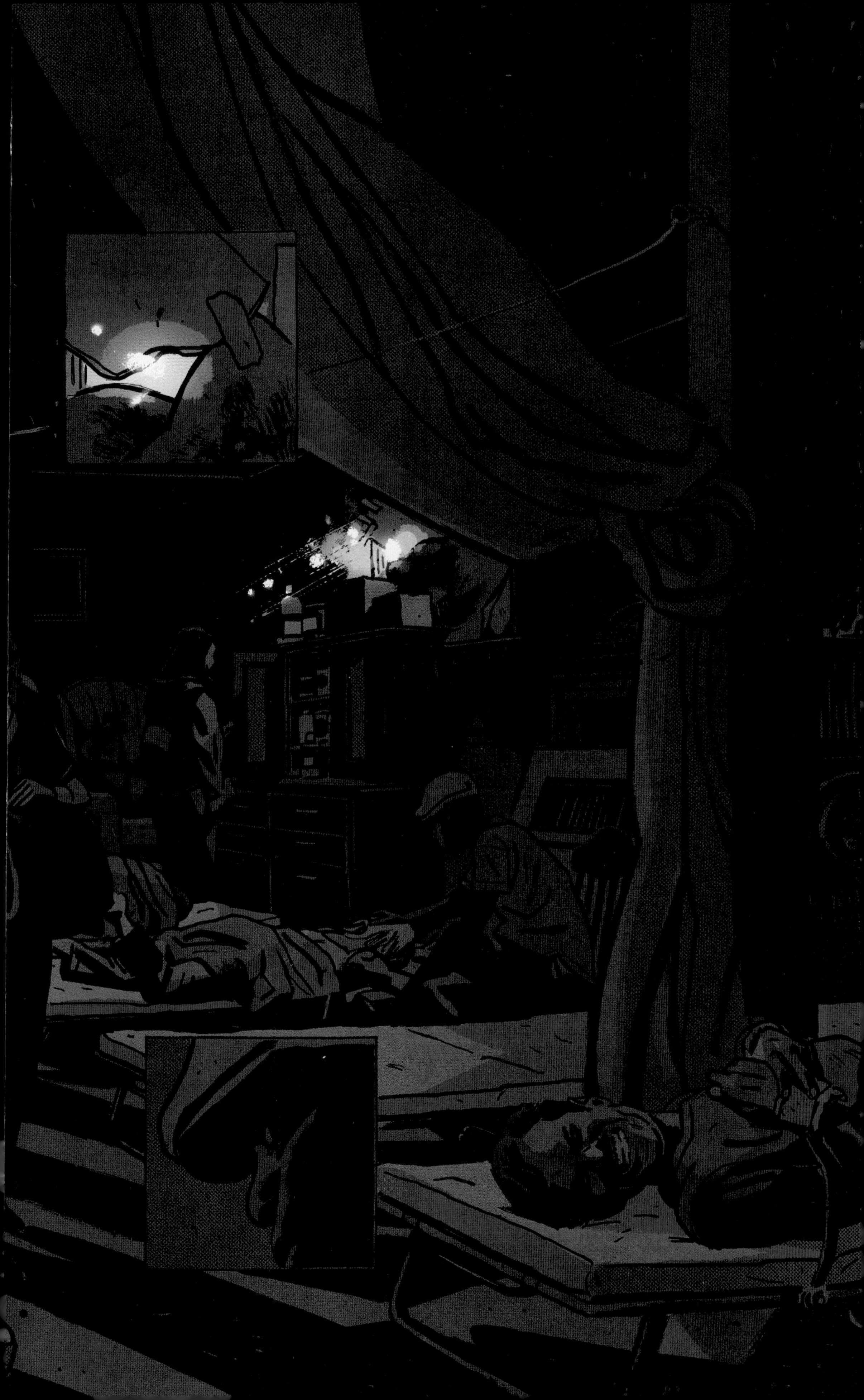

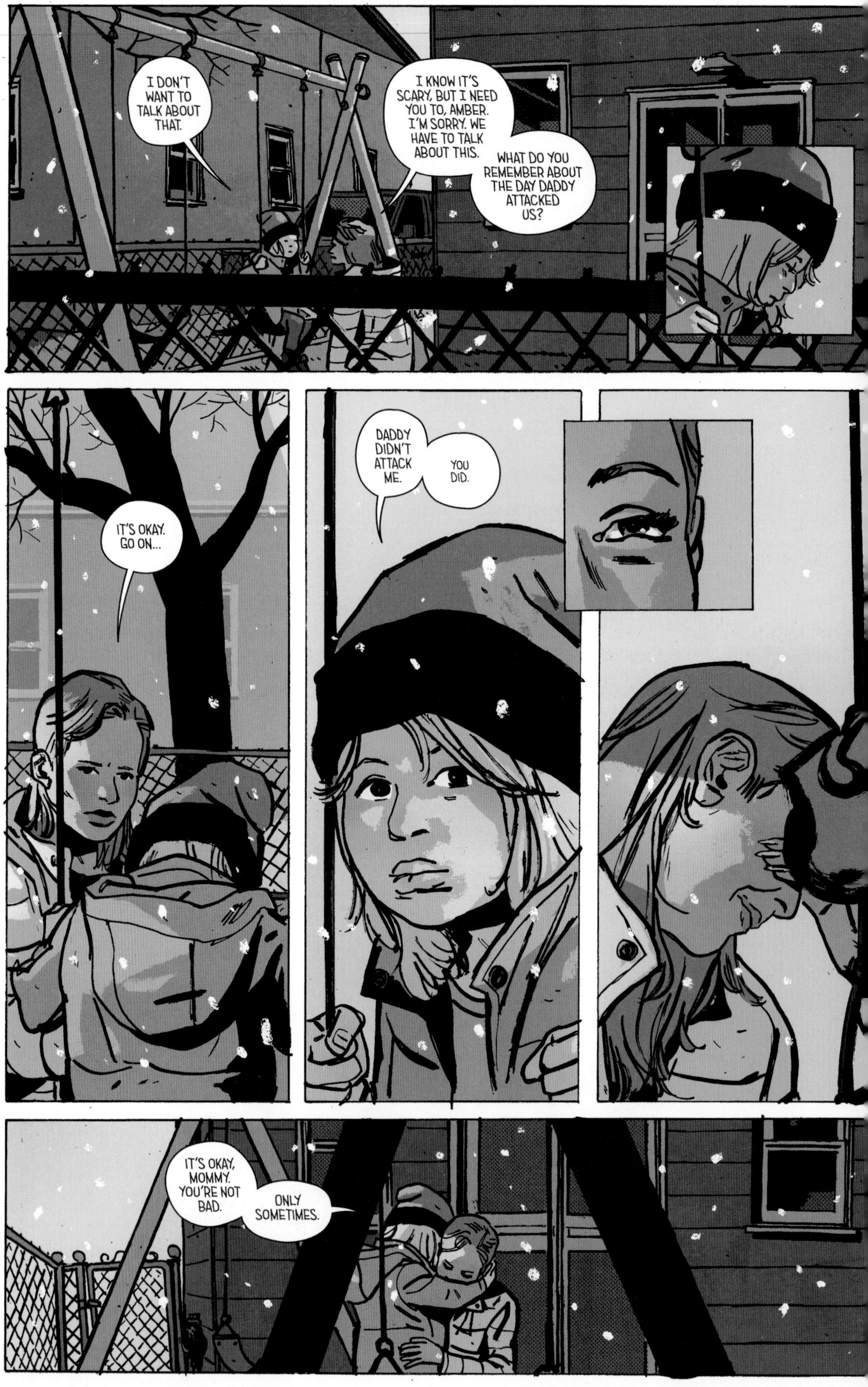

I DON'T WANT TO TALK ABOUT THAT.
I KNOW IT'S SCARY, BUT I NEED YOU TO, AMBER. I'M SORRY. WE HAVE TO TALK ABOUT THIS.
WHAT DO YOU REMEMBER ABOUT THE DAY DADDY ATTACKED US?
IT'S OKAY. GO ON...
DADDY DIDN'T ATTACK ME.
YOU DID.
IT'S OKAY, MOMMY. YOU'RE NOT BAD.
ONLY SOMETIMES.

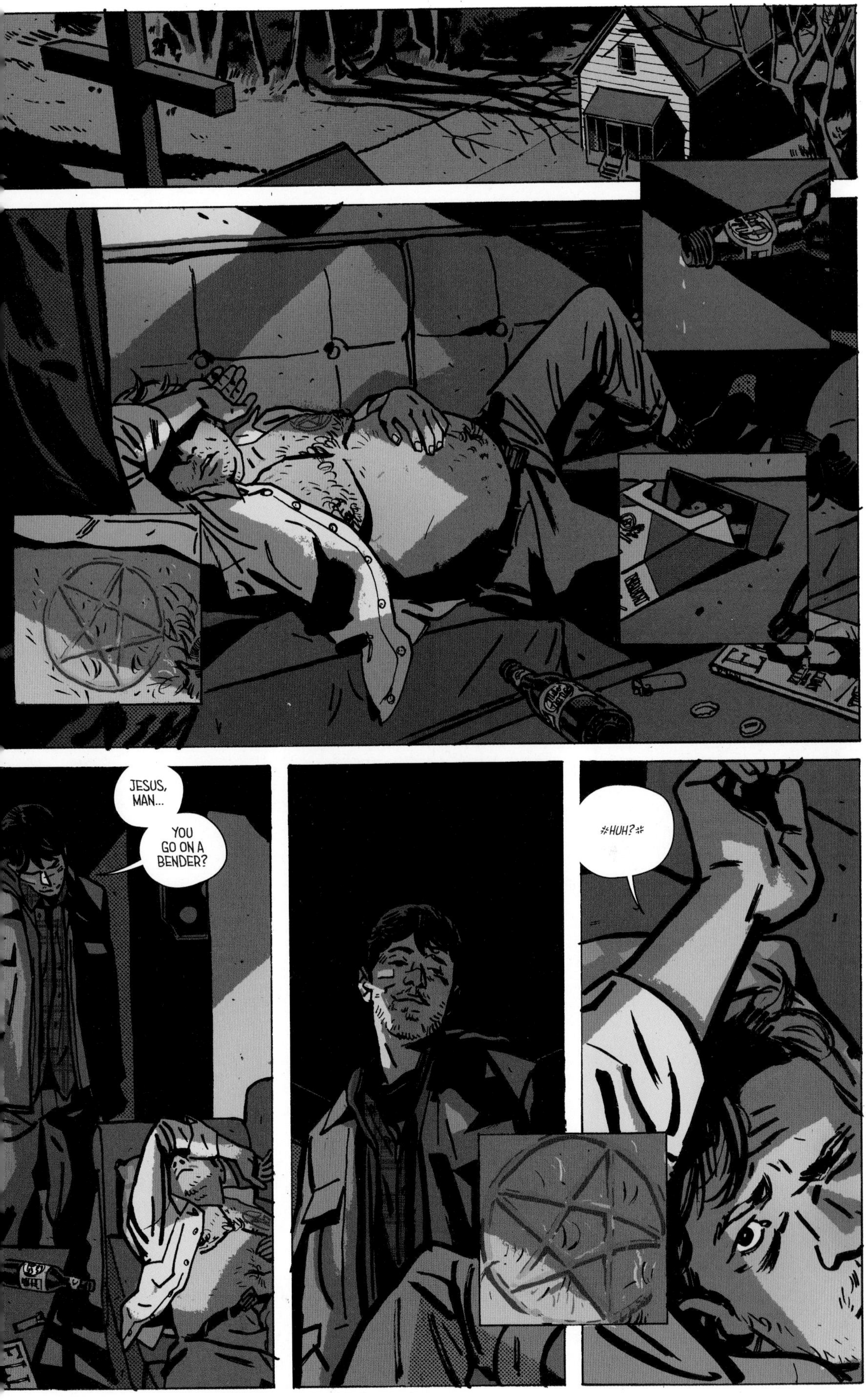
JESUS, MAN...
YOU GO ON A BENDER?
HUH?

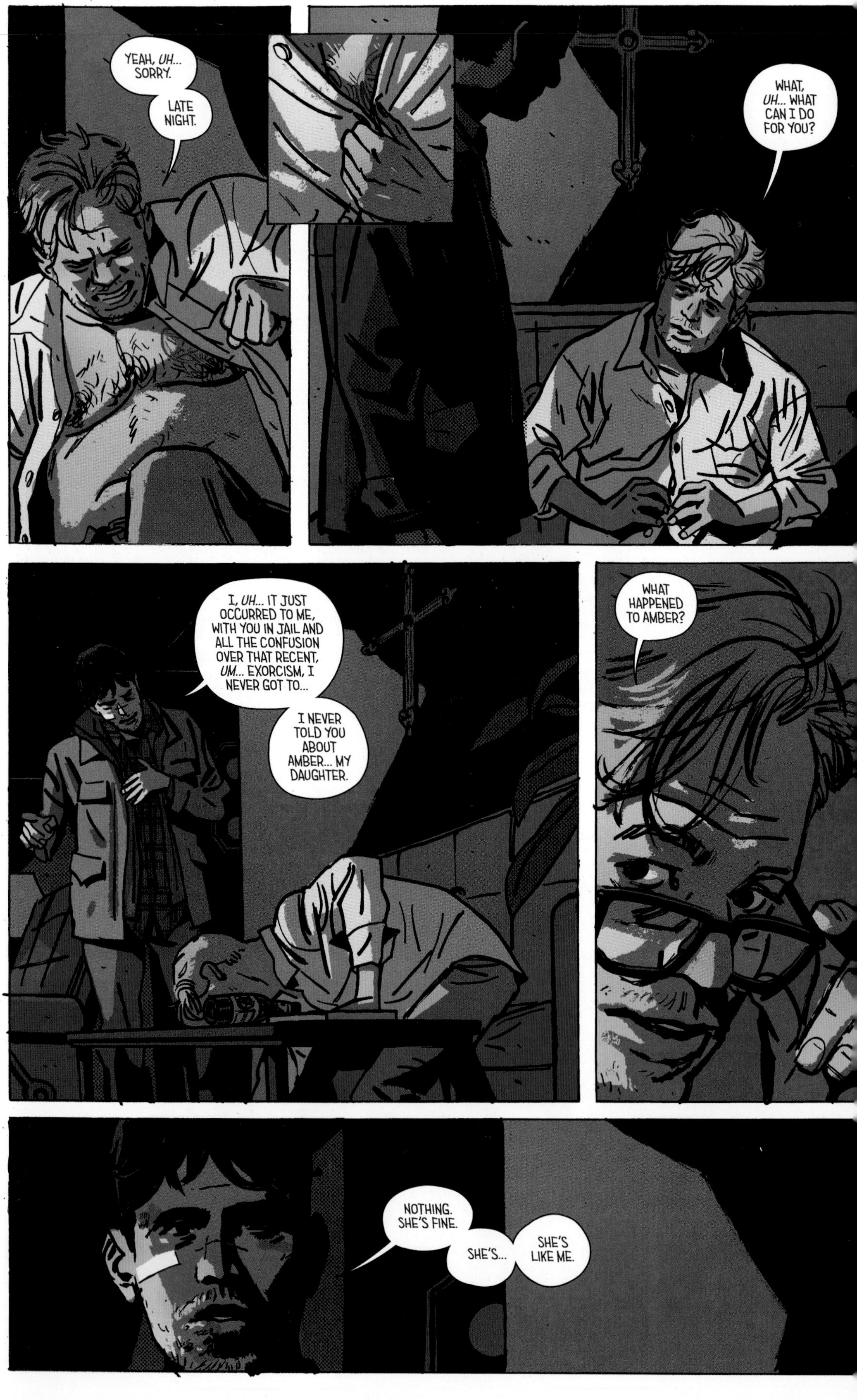
YEAH, UH... SORRY.
LATE NIGHT.
WHAT, UH... WHAT CAN I DO FOR YOU?
I, UM... IT JUST OCCURRED TO ME, WITH YOU IN JAIL AND ALL THE CONFUSION OVER THAT RECENT, UM... EXORCISM, I NEVER GOT TO...
I NEVER TOLD YOU ABOUT AMBER... MY DAUGHTER.
WHAT HAPPENED TO AMBER?
NOTHING. SHE'S FINE.
SHE'S...
SHE'S LIKE ME.

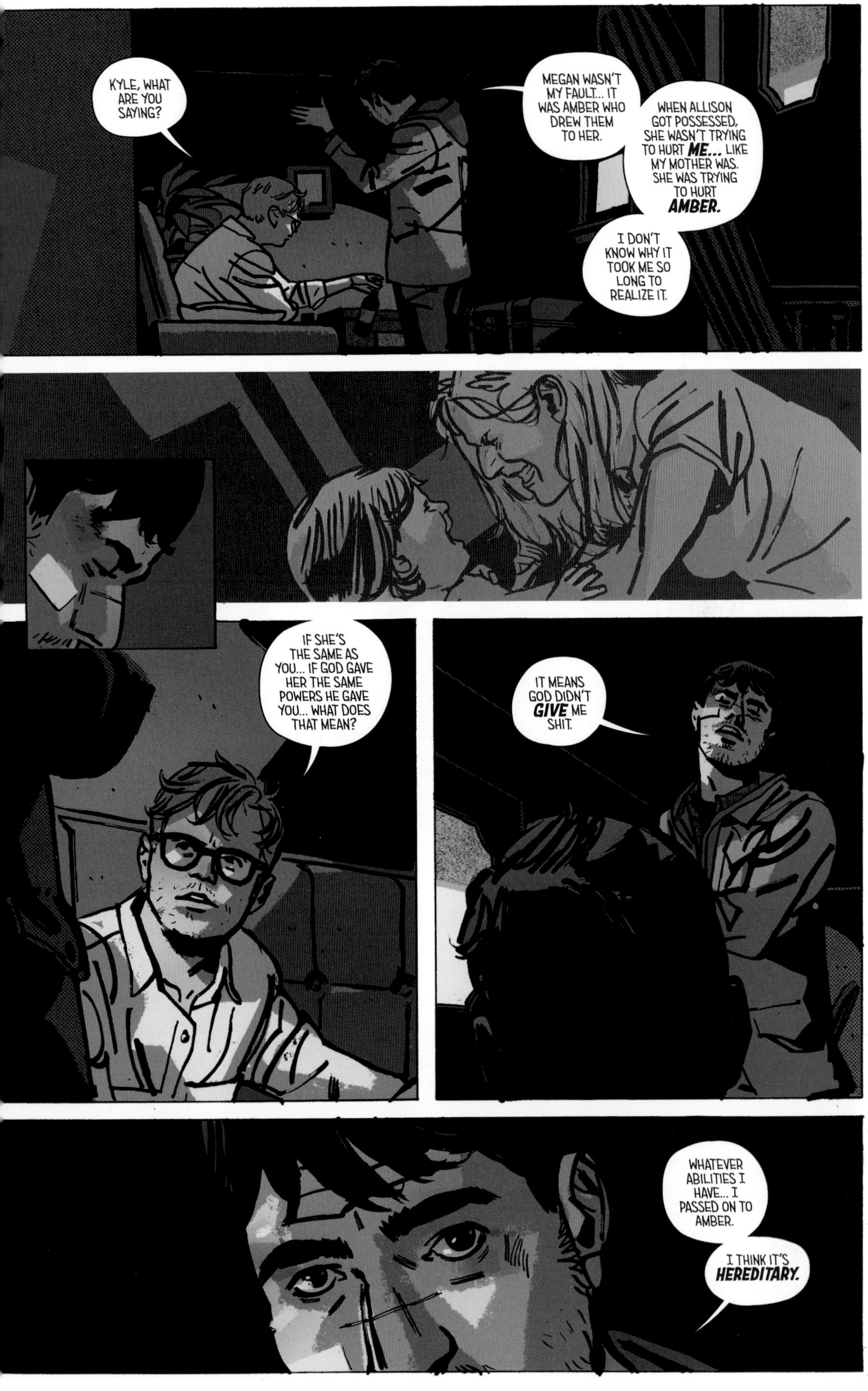
KYLE, WHAT ARE YOU SAYING?
MEGAN WASN'T MY FAULT... IT WAS AMBER WHO DREW THEM TO HER.
WHEN ALLISON GOT POSSESSED, SHE WASN'T TRYING TO HURT **ME...** LIKE MY MOTHER WAS. SHE WAS TRYING TO HURT **AMBER.**
I DON'T KNOW WHY IT TOOK ME SO LONG TO REALIZE IT.
IF SHE'S THE SAME AS YOU... IF GOD GAVE HER THE SAME POWERS HE GAVE YOU... WHAT DOES THAT MEAN?
IT MEANS GOD DIDN'T ***GIVE*** ME SHIT.
WHATEVER ABILITIES I HAVE... I PASSED ON TO AMBER.
I THINK IT'S ***HEREDITARY.***

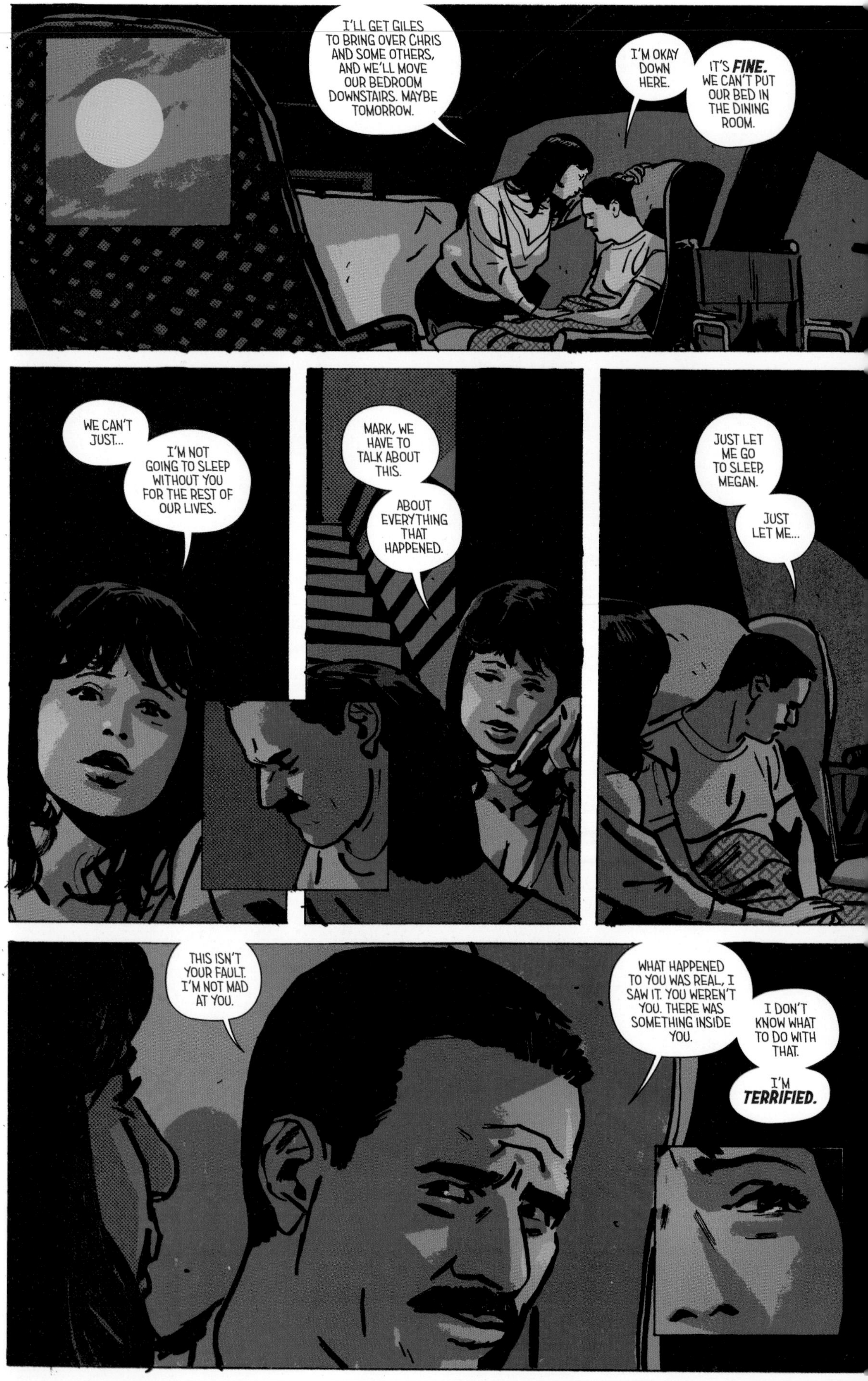
I'LL GET GILES TO BRING OVER CHRIS AND SOME OTHERS, AND WE'LL MOVE OUR BEDROOM DOWNSTAIRS. MAYBE TOMORROW.
I'M OKAY DOWN HERE.
IT'S **FINE.** WE CAN'T PUT OUR BED IN THE DINING ROOM.
WE CAN'T JUST...
I'M NOT GOING TO SLEEP WITHOUT YOU FOR THE REST OF OUR LIVES.
MARK, WE HAVE TO TALK ABOUT THIS.
ABOUT EVERYTHING THAT HAPPENED.
JUST LET ME GO TO SLEEP, MEGAN.
JUST LET ME...
THIS ISN'T YOUR FAULT. I'M NOT MAD AT YOU.
WHAT HAPPENED TO YOU WAS REAL, I SAW IT. YOU WEREN'T YOU. THERE WAS SOMETHING INSIDE YOU.
I DON'T KNOW WHAT TO DO WITH THAT.
I'M **TERRIFIED.**

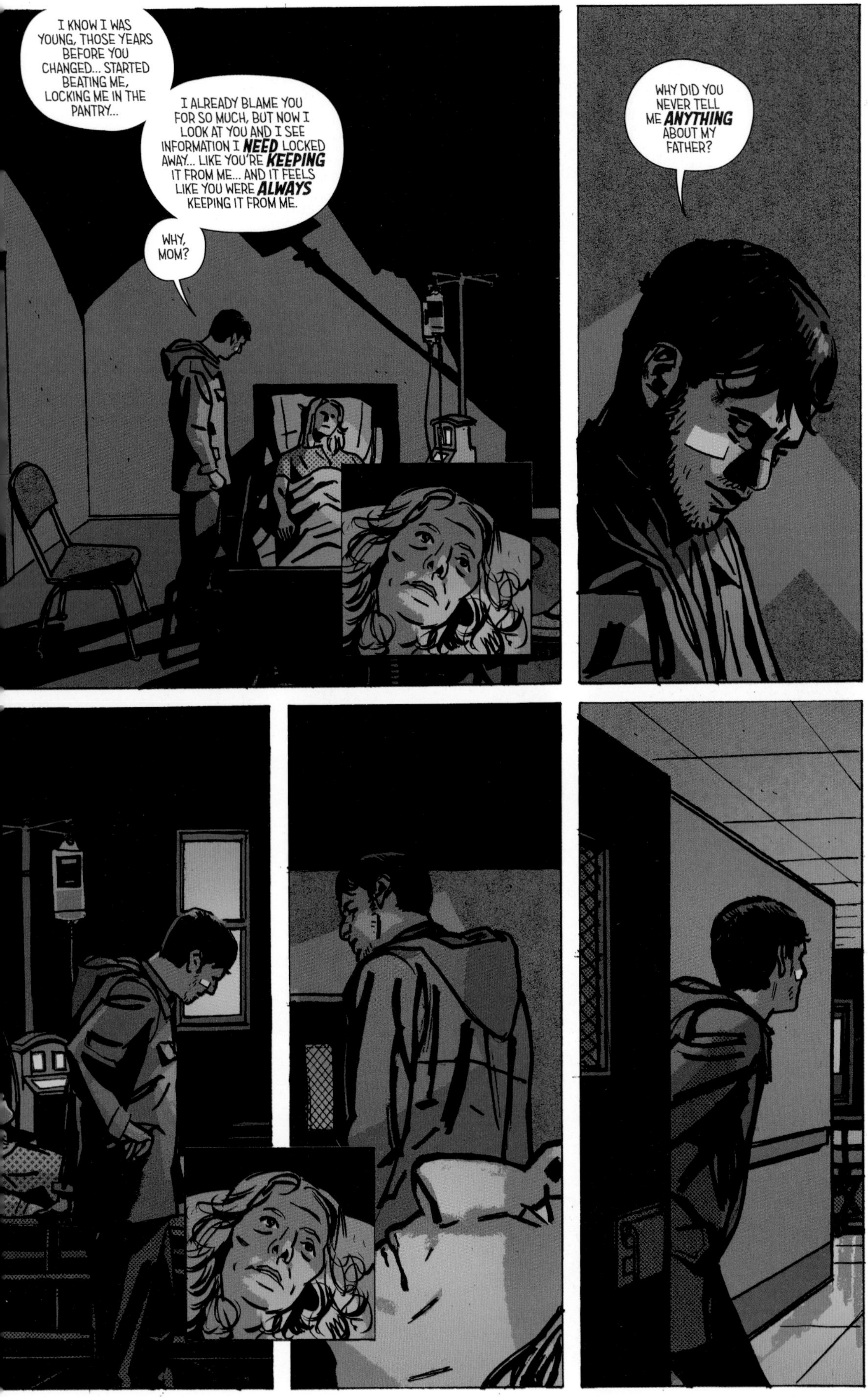
I KNOW I WAS YOUNG, THOSE YEARS BEFORE YOU CHANGED... STARTED BEATING ME, LOCKING ME IN THE PANTRY...
I ALREADY BLAME YOU FOR SO MUCH, BUT NOW I LOOK AT YOU AND I SEE INFORMATION I NEED LOCKED AWAY... LIKE YOU'RE KEEPING IT FROM ME... AND IT FEELS LIKE YOU WERE ALWAYS KEEPING IT FROM ME.
WHY, MOM?
WHY DID YOU NEVER TELL ME ANYTHING ABOUT MY FATHER?

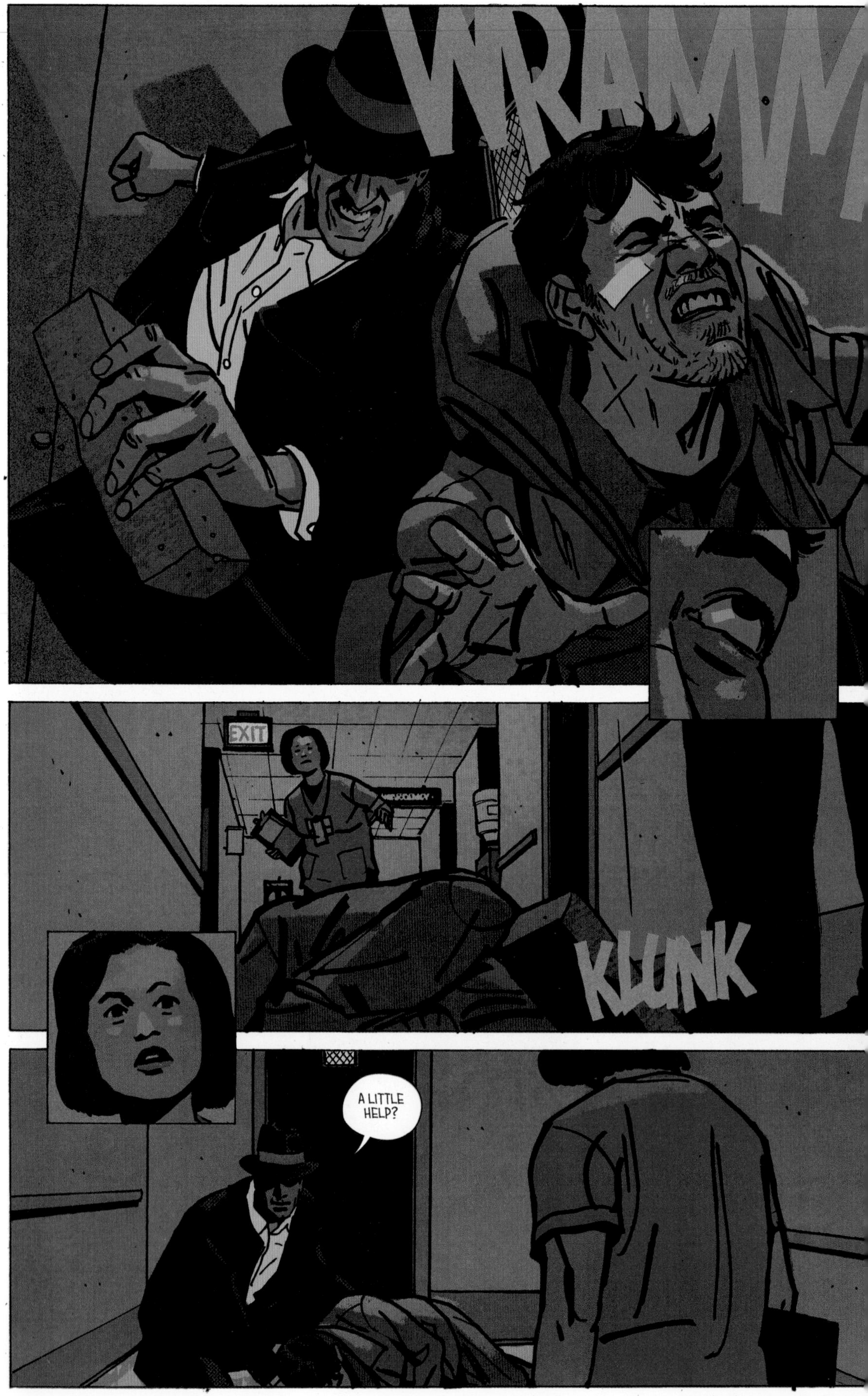
WRAMM
EXIT
KLUNK
A LITTLE HELP?

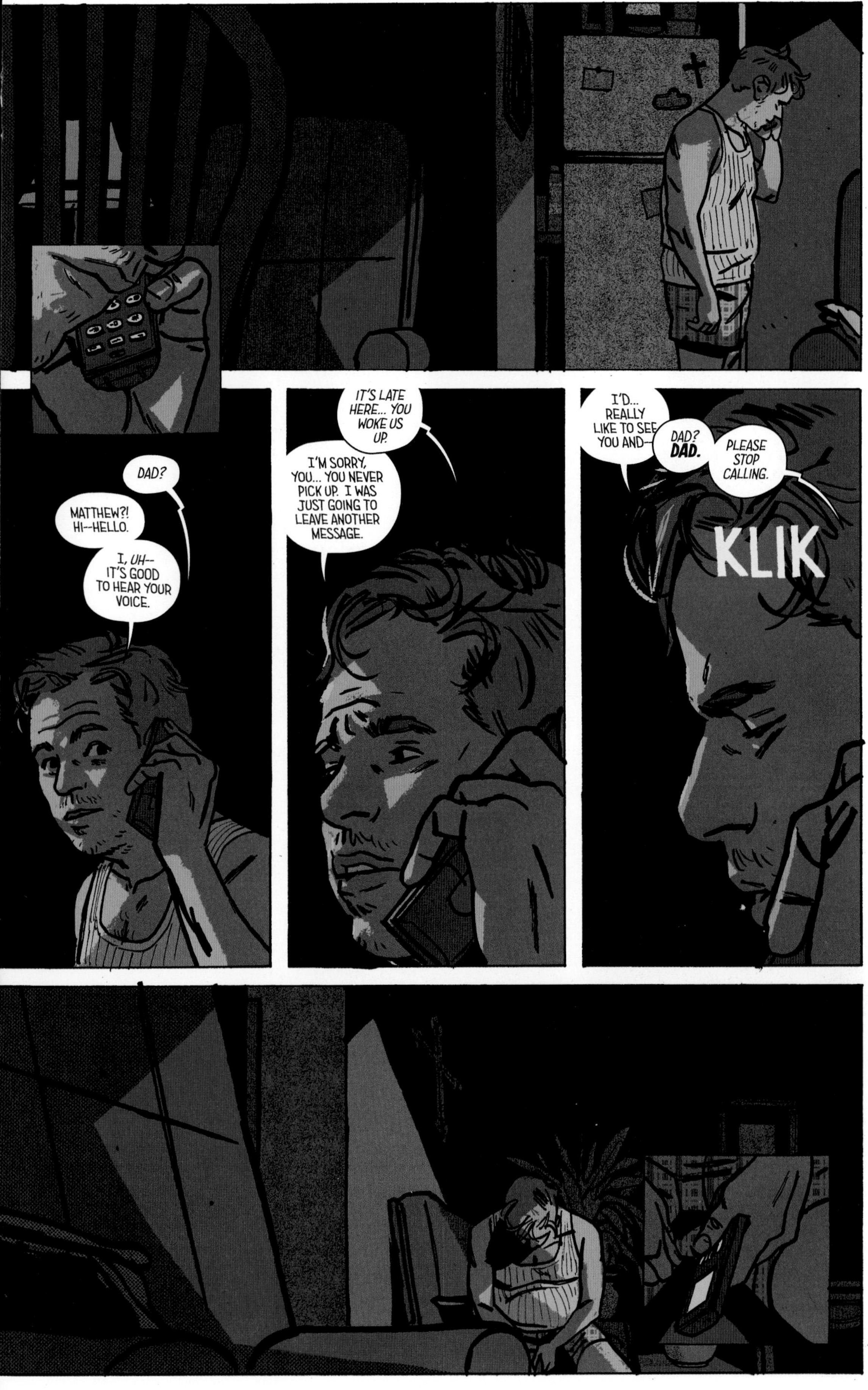
DAD?
MATTHEW?! HI--HELLO.
I, UH-- IT'S GOOD TO HEAR YOUR VOICE.
IT'S LATE HERE... YOU WOKE US UP.
I'M SORRY, YOU... YOU NEVER PICK UP. I WAS JUST GOING TO LEAVE ANOTHER MESSAGE.
I'D... REALLY LIKE TO SEE YOU AND--
DAD? DAD.
PLEASE STOP CALLING.
KLIK

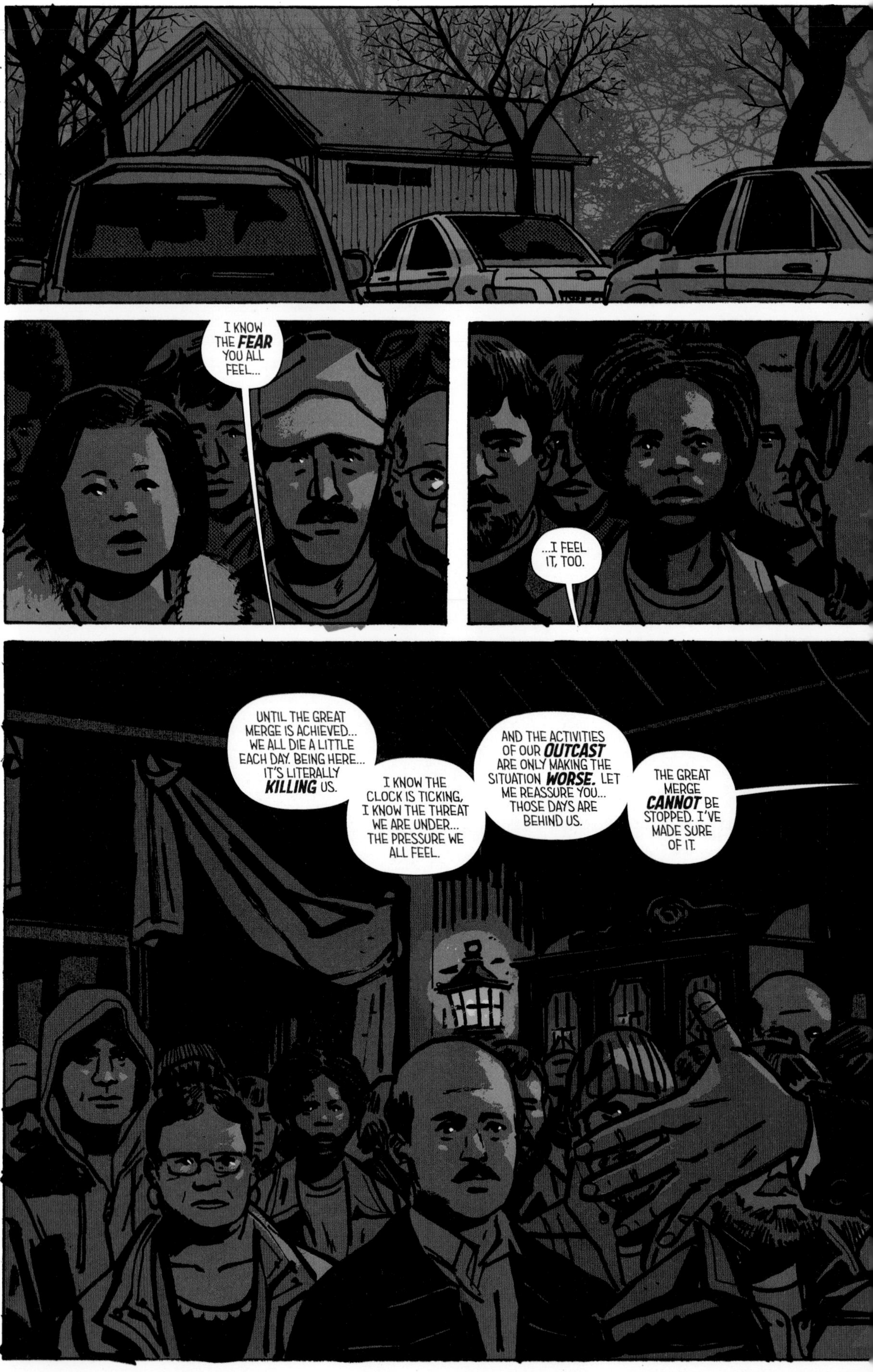

I KNOW THE FEAR YOU ALL FEEL...
...I FEEL IT, TOO.
UNTIL THE GREAT MERGE IS ACHIEVED... WE ALL DIE A LITTLE EACH DAY. BEING HERE... IT'S LITERALLY KILLING US.
I KNOW THE CLOCK IS TICKING, I KNOW THE THREAT WE ARE UNDER... THE PRESSURE WE ALL FEEL.
AND THE ACTIVITIES OF OUR OUTCAST ARE ONLY MAKING THE SITUATION WORSE. LET ME REASSURE YOU... THOSE DAYS ARE BEHIND US.
THE GREAT MERGE CANNOT BE STOPPED. I'VE MADE SURE OF IT.

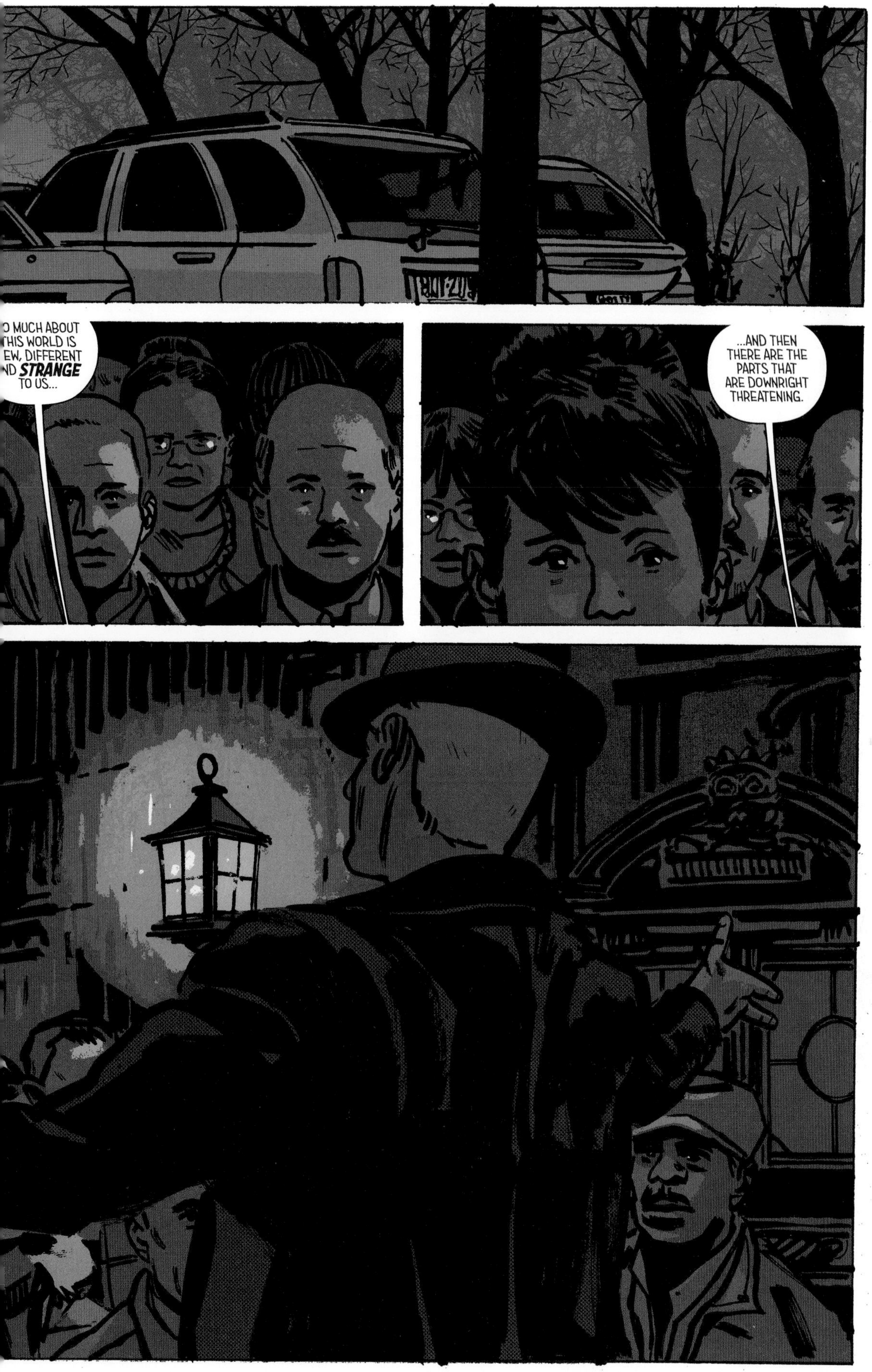
O MUCH ABOUT THIS WORLD IS EW, DIFFERENT ND STRANGE TO US...
...AND THEN THERE ARE THE PARTS THAT ARE DOWNRIGHT THREATENING.

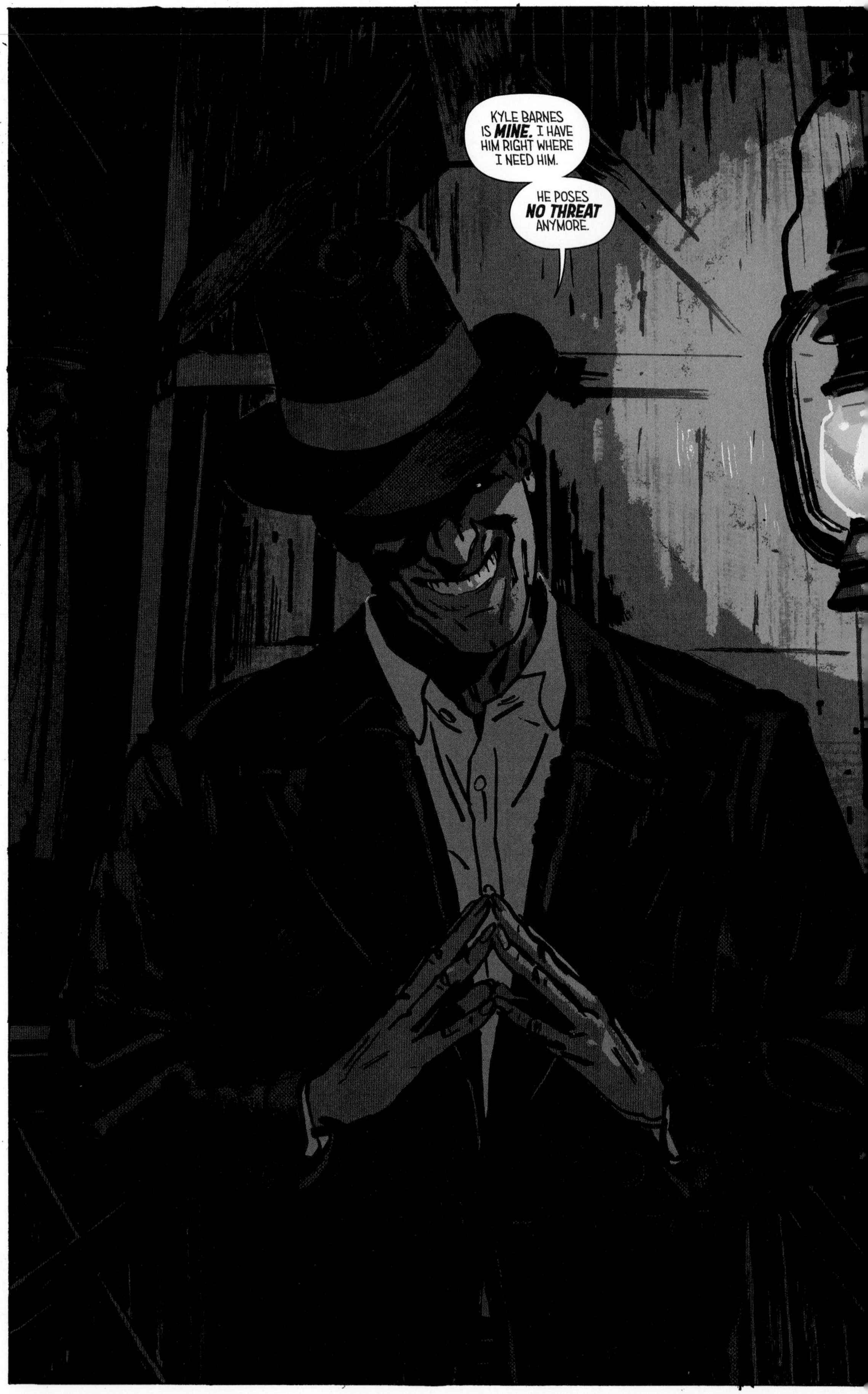
KYLE BARNES IS **MINE.** I HAVE HIM RIGHT WHERE I NEED HIM.
HE POSES **NO THREAT** ANYMORE.

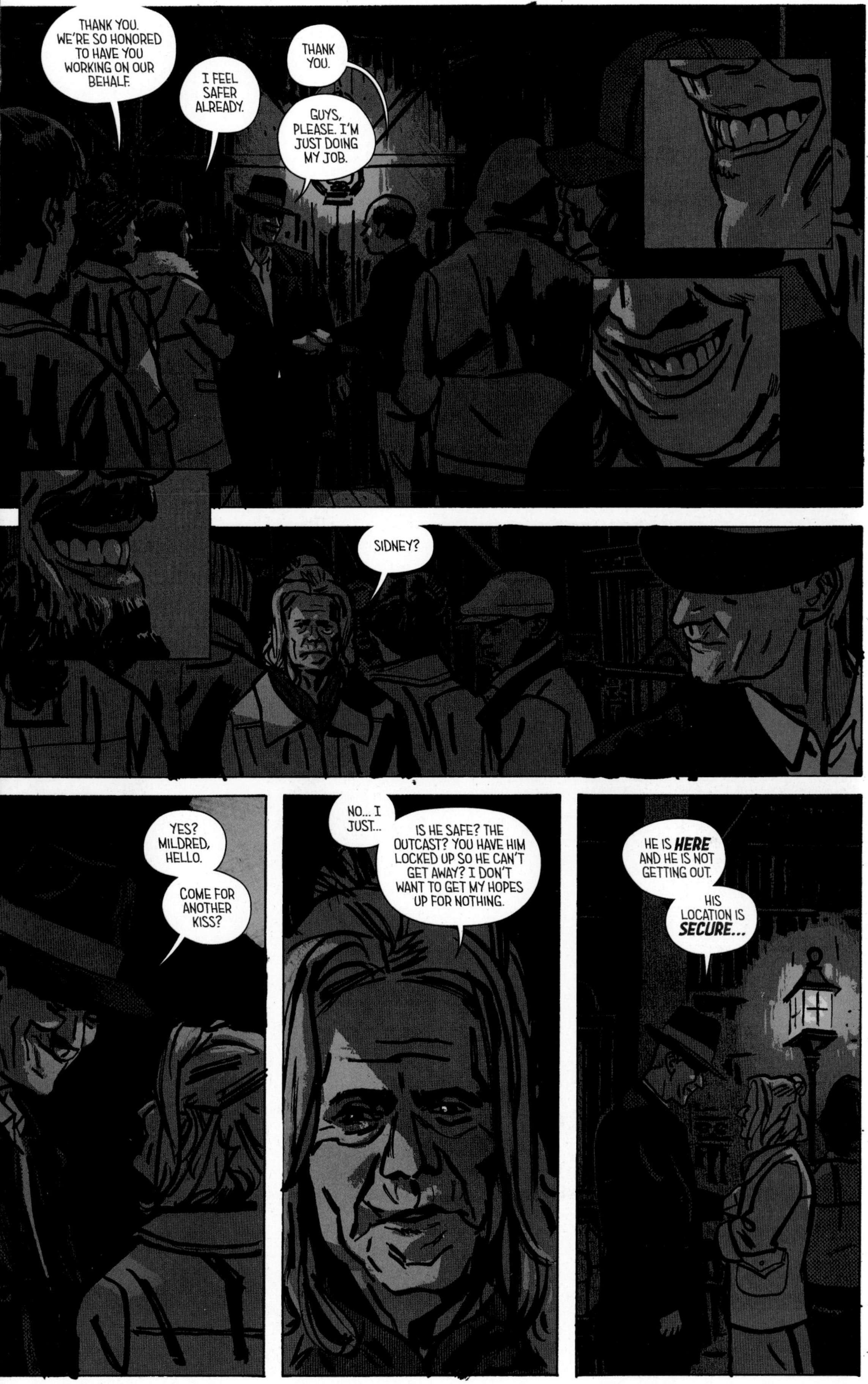

THANK YOU. WE'RE SO HONORED TO HAVE YOU WORKING ON OUR BEHALF.
I FEEL SAFER ALREADY.
THANK YOU.
GUYS, PLEASE. I'M JUST DOING MY JOB.
SIDNEY?
YES? MILDRED, HELLO.
COME FOR ANOTHER KISS?
NO... I JUST...
IS HE SAFE? THE OUTCAST? YOU HAVE HIM LOCKED UP SO HE CAN'T GET AWAY? I DON'T WANT TO GET MY HOPES UP FOR NOTHING.
HE IS **HERE** AND HE IS NOT GETTING OUT.
HIS LOCATION IS **SECURE...**

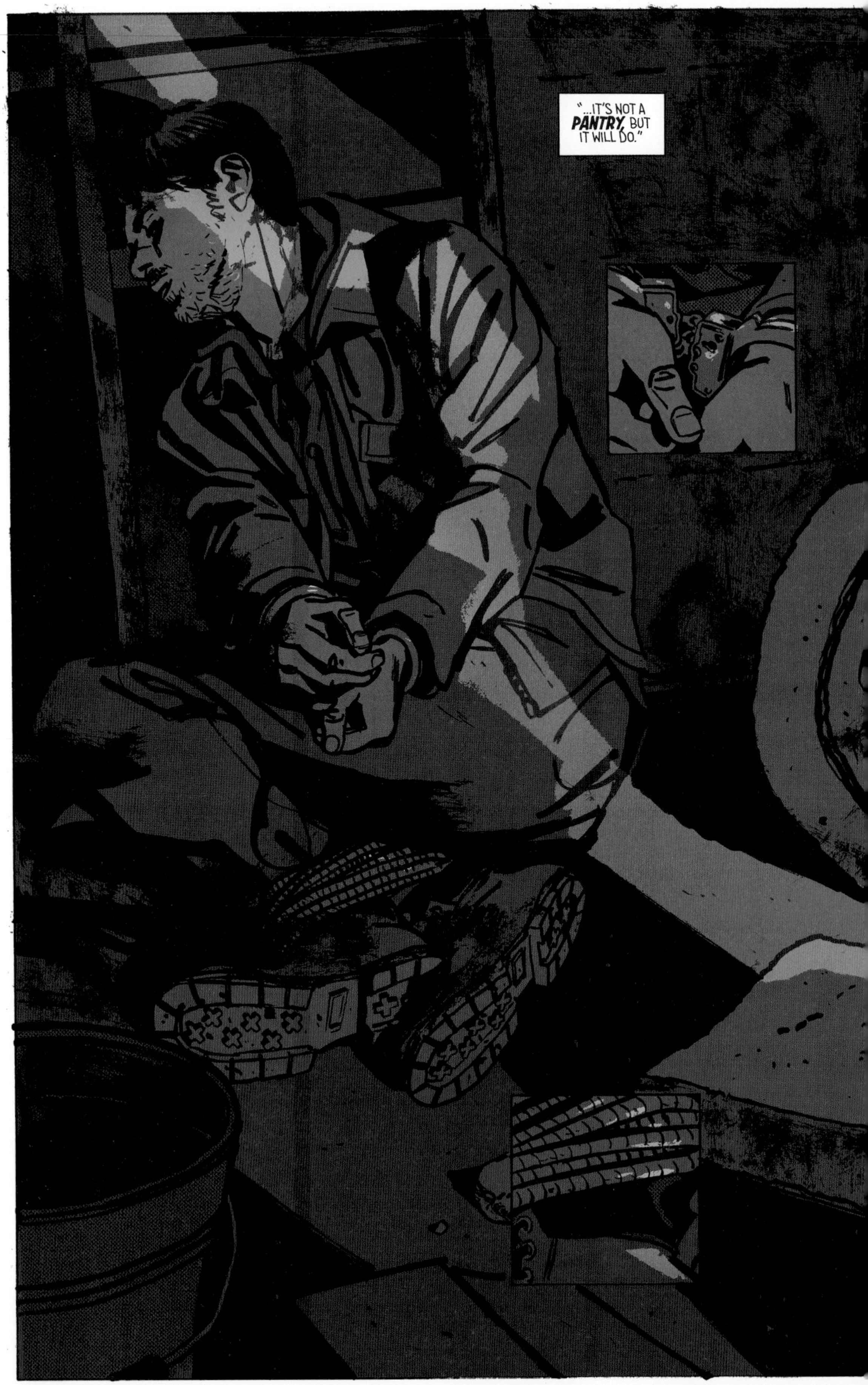
"...IT'S NOT A PANTRY, BUT IT WILL DO."